D1430109

The Dead Ringer
Sheila Kindellan-Sheehan

Library and Archives Canada Cataloguing in Publication

Sheehan, Sheila Kindellan,
    The dead ringer / Sheila Kindellan-Sheehan.

ISBN 978-1-897336-46-5

I. Title.
    PS8637.H44D42 2010   C813'.6   C2010-900353-5

Price-Patterson Ltd.
Montreal, Canada
www.pricepatterson.com

Price-Patterson Ltd. is supported by SODEC *(Société de développement des entreprises culturelles)* and thanks them for their support.

We acknowledge the financial support of the Government of Canada through the Book Publishing Industry Development Program (BPIDP) for our publishing activities.

In memory of

Denis Kindellan,
August, 1991
a loving husband, a father of eight,
a self-made man
a rich and textured legacy

And

Leslie Soden,
January, 2009
my friend, a seeker
whose final journey was a lesson
in grace and courage

LIST OF CHARACTERS

Caitlin Donovan: 34, a young, fiercely
   independent woman
Carmen DiMaggio: 32, her best friend and a daredevil
Mike Halloran: 31, Caitlin's fiancé, a brave hunk

The Old and Wealthy (OAW):
Lila Katz: at 88, a remarkable woman with a keen eye
Margaret Foley: Lila's best friend
Sophie: an 82-year-old hustler and dog lover
Muriel: a shy but wise woman
Abby Wiseman: OAW's legal advisor and friend
Jake Katz: Lila's son

Benito (Ponytail) Gomez: a scammer who makes a
   run at the big show
Daisy: a rat who knows when to run

Carlos Diaz: concierge at the Trump condominium,
   a handsome charmer with sticky fingers
Angel Hernandez: manager of the
   Trump condominium
James Tellett: second concierge at the Trump

Diego Gonzalez: young boss of the Cuban-
  American mafia
Felicia Alvarez: Diego's clever and beautiful sister
Jesús Alvarez: Felicia's husband who loves her money

Dr. Gabe Roth: doctor at St. Francis Hospital
  who makes one bad move
Sue Roth: Gabe's wife, who shares his secret

The Suits: Miami-Dade Detectives
Miguel Suarez: Metro-Dade Homicide, a good partner
Carly Smyth: Metro-Dade Homicide, no slouch either

The Bangers
Scar: 22, a corner man and a hustler for Diego
Bags: 17, Diego's drug slinger who sees too much

CHAPTER ONE

MIKE HALLORAN PULLED into the driveway of the Trump condominiums on Collins Avenue behind a fire-red Ferrari F430 Spyder. He leaned forward, curious to see its occupants. The sun from a crystal Miami sky stung his neck and beaded his shoulders with sweat even though the a/c was blasting against his chest. It was May. The sun was relentless.

The driver ahead of him didn't bother to wait for the valet. The ponytailed male was a few inches short of Mike's 6' 1" and a few years older, 35 maybe. In spite of the 90-degree heat, he wore a linen jacket. When he opened the passenger door, the sleeve rode up his wrist. Mike recognized the Patek Philippe, a $38,000 watch like his father wore. *Money.* The brunette he helped from the car wore white leather sandals and a white cotton dress, gathered at her hips by a gold cord. He could almost feel the bounce of her breasts as she got out of the sports car. The woman's dark hair, gathered in a French knot, revealed the delicate arch of her neck. *I can still look!*

Caitlin was arriving later that night. The showdown he had rehearsed, the one his father had set into motion, could wait another day. In his plan, there'd be no time for words. He followed the couple to the elevators because he had his suite number and entry codes provided by the company. He noticed a small raspberry birthmark behind her ankle. *No one's perfect.*

'Excuse me, sir!' Carlos, the concierge, stopped him. 'Yes?'

'May I inquire about the number of your suite?'

Mike watched the elevator door start to close. There was just a hint of a smile on the woman's face, and the man's as well for that matter. Not that he was looking, but the ring on her finger fit with the Patek Philippe. Mike winked at the woman and read his gold card. '#57.'

'Your elevator is right over there, sir,' Carlos said, pointing further down the hall. 'This elevator is reserved for permanent tenants.'

'What about this one?'

'The OAW elevator? 'Fraid not, sir. Those are very private tenants.'

'You're kidding, right? What am I, sand off the beach?'

'Company suites, sir.'

'What's OAW?'

'Old and Wealthy. I thought of the nickname and it stuck,' the concierge beamed. 'The old girls are the reason I don't usually work afternoons. I take them to synagogue, to the casino in Hollywood, to the dog track, to bingo, to Jai-Alai, to lunch, to the post office, and shopping. They're a great bunch.'

Only in Miami.

'I'm Carlos,' he said with a slight bow. 'Anything you want, I'm your guy. I deliver.'

'Good to know you.'

Carlos followed Mike into the elevator. 'I'll show you around. The facility is secure, with state-of-the-art surveillance. Nobody gets past us or the system. I shouldn't mention this, but Miami is the murder capital of the country, so we take every precaution.'

Mike almost said he worked for the security company that had installed the systems. He'd seen the cameras, motion alarms, lasers at the front desk and the jam blocks that weren't easy to compromise. He kept his mouth closed. Encouraging Carlos was a bad move.

'No need to feel obligated,' Carlos's monologue went on. 'It's my pleasure. I was here for the opening. Master of all trades, my old girls tell me. Can I show you the suite?'

Can you get lost? 'Thanks, I think I can find my way.'

'Good, sir,' Carlos said, staying on the elevator, dejected. Then he remembered that Lila wanted a large bottle of Metamucil from Walgreens. At the front door, he told Victor, the desk clerk, he'd be back in a flash.

🌱

'That's the Cuban we want for the work.' A man and a woman sat in a rented Jag, which looked like it belonged.

'Why here? Why risk all that surveillance *and* involve yet another person?' the passenger wanted to know.

'Fear factor, Daisy. You get inside a place like this, past security, into the suite itself, the mark is scared shitless. Knows you can do anything and gives it up.'

'I don't like it.'

'Relax. Ruiz did the IDs. The guy's a genius with a camera, paper and numbers. His work passes as legit anywhere. He was paid – he's also a parolee on his third strike. He won't be talking. I have to think about this Cuban. I'll know better when I meet him.'

'Still...'

'Scamming might be a two-billion-dollar business, but we haven't taken home much of that dough. I want one real job. Then we're out. What were the chances I'd be able to hack into Trump's clientele and come up with Felicia Alvarez, the old man's granddaughter? Doesn't matter that I couldn't hack past *her* firewalls and en-crypted files. Everybody knows the old bastard knew his ticket was punched and socked all his millions away with his family, even the ones who weren't part of the business, before he was sent to the farm. The *Herald* printed photos of their new houses and condos.'

The morning Daisy had rushed up to him with the *Herald*, stabbing a photo of Jesús with her finger seemed long in the past. 'He looks just like you!' The score had begun that simply. Jesús Alvarez was photographed with the "family," walking beside his wife, Felicia Alvarez, into court for the trial of her grandfather. On that day, "Ponytail" Gomez began his weeks of web searching. He read about the family enclave on Biscayne Bay. He followed the trial and the money trail. It was all there in the paper, protected by phrases like, *it was suggested that*, *it appeared that*… Nothing in his life had ever fallen into his hands. For weeks he plotted. He heard from a fellow scammer that Felicia Alvarez had left the family compound to live at one of the Trump condominiums in Sunny Isles. He cased the Trump, looked for a mark and found Carlos. Then he studied the Alvarez's routine. He spent over five grand of his own money on work for this grab. Cops, Ponytail knew, didn't work hard to help mafia members regain any lost money. This was his chance at a pot.

'If this isn't a clean job, we won't make it out of Miami. You can forget your dream.'

Ponytail continued as though he hadn't heard the note of caution. 'These last months of prep, the cell phones stolen from Wal-Mart, the computer at the internet café, all shit that can't be traced back to us, these risks, the money we've spent, it's all worth the ten million, and the end of nickel-and-dime scamming. If we make this score, we lay low in Toronto while I move the money around till the paper trail is lost. Then we retire out on the West Coast. We live straight, on a small vineyard in the Dry Creek Valley near Healdsburg. I found the information on the net. That's what I want, and a place in San Fran, an apartment on Ashbury Street. Right now, we're looking at the big tent. You make your luck in this world. You need an edge, and I have it. All winners have one.'

The wail of sirens triggered an uneasy alarm. The Jag pulled out of the visitors' parking and eased slowly into a traffic jam on Collins. Seconds later, two speeding cop cars with blaring sirens, sped down the south side of Collins, tailgating cars and angling their way through the traffic.

'No reason to take chances.'

🌴

When Mike reached his door, he lifted the brass knocker and tapped in the code he'd memorized. He also verified the code for the separate quarters. Inside, he was met with a panorama of oceanfront property. His luggage was stacked in the front entrance, a wall-to-wall glass patio door had been opened, and white curtains blew back into the room. Mike hardly noticed the plush furniture or the pink marble mantle or floors. Tossing off his shoes, he threw his jacket onto the nearest sofa, stripped off his shirt, revealing the sculpted chest of a gym bum, and walked out onto the balcony.

As he gripped the railing, wind began to curl his thick brown hair. Some of it fell in his face. He darted back into the suite and rummaged through his luggage until he found his trunks. Before he left for the ocean, he hung his suits in the walk-in. By-passing the blue-tented lawn chairs, the sprawling pools, the outdoor restaurant and bar, he sidestepped the loungers on the beach, anchored his towel near the water's edge with two handfuls of sand and ran hard into the cresting turquoise water. Like Caitlin, he was drawn to the wet depths of the ocean. He swam until the salt water began to sting his eyes.

He wanted to lie on the sand, but didn't have the time. *Two days off! This is the life!* Scooping up his flops and towel, Mike showered near the main pool. Stubborn sand clung to his feet. Mike reached down and ran his fingers through each of his toes and wiped his soles. Towelling off, he didn't notice the approving glances. Heading back to the building he saw a sign and walked over to it. 'Bathers' was neatly printed in red beside a yellow sailboat. *Good.* He pressed the button on the right and continued rubbing his chest. Mike stepped into the elevator without looking up. The collision was instant and charged. Mike and the woman he'd seen out front stepped back. His stomach muscles froze in rigid relief. 'I'm sorry. My fault.' Mike stumbled back to the edge of the elevator and nearly tripped awkwardly on his towel.

'Mine,' Felicia said, trying to rid her face of the obvious flush.

'Should have…' Both said simultaneously.

'Mike.'

'Felicia.'

Before either of them could utter another word, her husband appeared and stepped directly in front of Mike, grazing his arm. Their eyes locked as he took her hand.

'I am Jesús Alvarez and I am Felicia's husband.'

He might as well have been saying 'I am important and this is my Ferrari,' Mike thought.

Alvarez guided her to the pool as Mike stepped deeper into the elevator, out of the heat.

CHAPTER TWO

INSIDE THE CONDO, Mike left his flops at the front door, padded across the floor, grabbed two towels and stepped into the shower. The hell with a cold shower! He liked how he felt. Bone naked, he began to unpack, checking out the varied array of drinks in the bar each time he passed it. He saw the note leaning against a bottle of Scotch. *Enjoy everything but the 60-year-old single malt. It has a history!* He found beer in the fridge and grabbed one by the neck, shutting the fridge door with his knee. He chose tan Dockers and leather loafers, shaved again, applied Boss cologne and used his fingers on his hair. Then he reached for a light blue Charles Tyrwhitt with a white Winchester collar, found his watch and ring, took his wallet and keys and drove to the Outback for a steak. He called the airline and tracked Caitlin's flight. It was on time.

As he waited by the luggage carousels, he realized he'd forgotten to bring a blue rose. *Damn!* Mike looked up at the escalator and watched a horde of people step onto it like a battalion of ants. Would Caitlin search for him? He scanned their faces from where he stood. About ten minutes later, he saw her. Caitlin wasn't looking his way. Mike still felt a rush from Felicia. Up ahead, Caitlin seemed lost in thought, contained, confident as she rode down to the ground floor. Muscles in his stomach began to twitch as they had the first time he'd seen her two-and-a-half years ago. He wanted to run to her. *Dammit, let her come to me!* He balled his fists and waited.

He caught the glint of her hazel eyes. Caitlin held his gaze as she came towards him, as though she'd known exactly where he'd be. He strode over to meet her. He grabbed her shoulders and kissed her. 'Missed you.'

'Hey, you! I can taste salt water. You smell good. Let's pick up the bags and get out of here.'

'I have a pinot noir waiting in an ice bucket.'

'Won't need it.'

Mike forgot about Felicia.

Caitlin didn't bother to check out the condo. She pushed Mike onto the bed, and he didn't need a tour. He knew all the best places. As usual, oxygen was the only reason the action stopped. Her thick, curling blonde hair fell across her face. 'Amazing after all this time!'

'I have more amazement.'

'Forget any notion of foreplay.'

They held onto one another until their bodies began to feel the chill of the a/c.

'You hungry?' he asked.

'Not anymore.'

'I have two whole days, Caitlin. You don't have to begin work on your book yet, do you?'

'I can take a break. Is the other ensuite completely separate?'

Mike let go of Caitlin and steepled his fingers across his chest. 'No! And let's not go there.'

'What could I do?'

'You could have thought of us, alone, just one damn time!'

'She's my best friend.'

'You're not joined at the hip.' Mike headed for the bathroom. 'When?' he shouted back into the room.

'We have two nights, counting this one,' she called back.

The showdown was back on, just not tonight. Mike forced Caitlin to wait for five minutes. Times like these, he hated the pull she had on him, almost hated himself for loving her.

'Where are you going?'

Mike had thrown on a polo shirt and was stepping into jogging sweats. 'Running on the beach.'

'At this hour?'

'Why not?'

'I was wrong, alright? Don't go.'

He didn't slam the main door, but he was gone nonetheless.

In their first year, Caitlin would have run after him. Tonight, she lay on the bed rubbing her forehead. *What choice did I have? Carmen was so excited. She invited herself.*

When Mike reached the beach, he looked up at the balcony, figuring he'd wave back at her. No Caitlin. His eyes rode higher up. A lone female figure was looking down at the ocean, or down at him. *It can't be!* He thought about going back to the condo and declaring a *détente. She's wrong, dammit!* Mike took off with the fluid speed of a runner. His feet rarely sank into the sand.

🌴

On the Old and Wealthy floor, the corridors looked a lot like a smoggy L.A. sky, except for the smoke-free, spacious quarters of Lila Katz. Lila had lived every one of her 88 years with a fierce independence, a remarkable memory and a mind that could see humor in the blackest events. She was proud to sport salt-and-pepper hair that had never been dyed. Because Lila had long ago learned not to take herself seriously, humor hung around her like the scent of Florida oranges.

At this late hour, she was setting out her clothes for tomorrow's afternoon visit to the dog track. Her condo was not cluttered with a gluttonous display of family photos, or silly mementos that the other old biddies clung to or boasted about. Too many of the OAW women drank from noon on, often foregoing medication that would interfere with the liquor. The merry imbibers understood the serious consequences of mixing the two. Lila had never drunk, not even when she was young. She'd survived Harry and didn't depend on her two sons, who lived with their families on the West Coast. One photo of each of her men and two grandchildren was quite enough. She hated clutter and she wasn't going to leave any behind when the time came.

Lila knew she'd come to Miami to die. At least, that's what everybody said. This was it! At 5' 3", taller 20 years ago, only one thing threatened her independence. Her breasts were larger than huge pink grapefruit, and she was forced to ask her friend Margaret Foley to help her fasten her brassiere every morning.

'I turn mine around and fasten it in the front. Then I turn my bra back behind me and I'm done.'

'Won't work, Margaret. I can't see past these boulders.'

She was loath to admit a second weakness, but it was there. Lila had a crush on Carlos, not a silly high-school crush, but something that approached love because Lila knew his worth and his faults. Carlos was beautiful to look at, better to smell. Surrounded by mountains of wrinkled, aged flesh, decaying hopes and nightly rattles of fear, the OAW women were comforted by this beautiful young man who was trying to achieve his dream through them. Lila knew that besides the $50-plus fees he charged for the outings, the messages, the calls and his time, Carlos also sometimes took a cut from their track winnings and pilfered pocket change from their purchases. To Lila, these pittances meant nothing. Indeed they added some excitement to Carlos's obsequiousness, making him something more than a jellyfish.

Carlos was their lifeline, so Lila intended to have a private talk with him about the thefts. When Lila finally went to bed on her foam mattress, sleep eluded her – as it did most nights – so she planned a short speech and exactly where she'd give it. Around three, her thoughts morphed into her own life stories. Lila laughed out loud. *At 88, the whole body dries up and cracks!* She remembered too when she was eight and tapped her heart out on stage to 'I'm a Beautiful Poupée'… all of it.

🌴

The Jag was back on Harding Avenue and 69th Street, parked in a wooden garage out of sight. Inside the nondescript white bungalow, Ponytail was busy working on a make-shift wooden table in the kitchen. On a side wall, with neat manoeuvring, he pushed against a panel and slid it open, revealing maps and two hand-guns wrapped in work cloths. The hidden space he'd created also accommodated a filing cabinet, a desk and computer, a digital still camera with a telephoto lens, and tapes labelled and stacked against shelves above the computer. As long as the panel was open, there was decent space. Ponytail booted up the computer. He punched in his codes and a photo of Carlos Diaz popped up on the screen with a detailed account of his days at the Trump condo. Underneath was his home address, phone number in Hollywood and a photo of his wife holding their daughter.

Ponytail read Carlos's itinerary for tomorrow, paying close attention to the time he would spend at the track.

When she saw the screen, Daisy took a deep breath. 'We start tomorrow?'

'At the track, as planned. He'll be alone for five to ten minutes.'

Daisy nodded.

'I'll recheck the back of the garage, chair, tape and water. For tonight, a solid meal, no liquor, not even beer. We can't fail.' Ponytail removed the drive and hid it.

Then he paced the small room. 'We can't fail.'

Daisy watched him and took Ponytail in from head to toe. Just the hint of his thigh rippled through his pants, and she shivered. The ponytail did not bounce as he walked.

🌴

By the time Mike was back in the condo, running had taken the fight out of him. Caitlin lay on the bed, waiting for him. He tore off his shirt and threw it on a chair. 'You asleep?'

'Nope.'

He flopped onto the bed beside her. 'Never knew women could be so complicated.' He needed a few jabs.

'I'm not.'

'Sure. And Carmen?'

'Apology. I'm caught between the two of you.'

'You've put yourself there.'

Mike had learned something about himself on the beach. He was growing up and he hated it. He'd come to a point where he needed to see past tonight and to-morrow. Caitlin was still ahead of him. Was that where she wanted to be?

The hours passed quickly as Mike and Caitlin held onto what was firm and impenetrable. The bed shook; the headboard struck the wall behind it. The grunts and throaty moans were low and guttural until exhaustion, heavy and wet, descended on them. Then they were quiet. It wasn't a time for honesty or slights. It was a time to grab what was real.

🌴

Later, Mike lay quietly beside Caitlin. He could fashion a theory about his frustration or wallow in it alone. He chose a theory because he could make it fit.

At the core of her, Caitlin doesn't know what she wants. She won't or can't trust me completely. That's a choice she's made.
'You awake?'

'Barely.'

'Don't burn me again when it's our time alone. We're not a threesome. I don't blame Carmen. This is on you.' He got up on an elbow and brushed the hair from her cheek. 'How about another, "I'm sorry"?'

'That too.'

'Say it!'

'I am sorry. Why do you love me?'

'Goodnight!' He rolled over and thought of the lone figure on the balcony. A shiver of excitement passed through his stomach. Caitlin had broken up their time together. She'd opened a door for him in the process.

CHAPTER THREE

MIKE WOKE FIRST and lay beside Caitlin, watching her sleep. Shaggy blonde hair fell over her forehead. He couldn't hear her breathe, so he leaned closer until he felt the softest rush of air against his cheek. For the entire last year, he'd lost whoever he believed he was. Now, he'd wrong-footed himself. He didn't realize when it was that Caitlin woke and was looking back at him.

'It's not just Carmen, is it?'

Mike rolled off the bed and scrambled into his boxers.

Caitlin threw another pillow behind her and sat up, covering her breasts with the sheet.

Mike walked to the bed. The back wall seemed to shift. 'I want a date.'

'Is this coming from your visit to your parents?'

'You're skirting again.'

'I'm not. Is this your question or your father's? Doesn't matter. Either way, I'm becoming a disappointment to everybody.'

'*When*, Caitlin. That's all I want to know. Do you love me?'

'Yes.' Caitlin's green eyes were tearing.

Mike wanted to surrender. 'What is it then?'

Caitlin's sobs shook her shoulders. Mike sat beside her and held her. 'I had to find myself after Derek and Chris died. I like where I am, where we are. Marriage changes everything.'

Mike jumped from the bed. 'That's what you think marrying me will do, box you in or change us? You've become very self-absorbed. Damn!'

Caitlin stood up to face Mike, allowing the sheet to fall. Mike watched the play of tears as they fell on her chest. She whispered as though she were betraying the dead, 'I'm happier with you than I was with Derek.' She turned away from him and walked into the bathroom and locked the door. She slumped to the toilet seat.

What the hell do I do with this? Mike pounded on the door. 'You're crying because you love me or are you crying for yourself? Open the door or I swear I'll break it down.' The door was thick and solid and he remembered his football shoulder injury. *Dammit to hell!* 'Caitlin, come out, please…'

While he sat outside, leaning up against the door, he tried to figure out the damage love had done to him. Two years ago, he had girls for his every whim and he was free, not leaning against some bathroom door. He was a Harvard grad for God's sake, a Bostonian from Back Bay. Why had he fallen for Caitlin, who was making him feel more and more like his conventional father? He fell backwards when the door suddenly opened, and didn't get to entertain the thought that Caitlin might be a freer spirit than he was. He'd chased the small part of her that she kept from him, but that part now forced him to question himself. *Bottom line, she's rejecting me, no matter what other excuses she uses.*

She took him in her arms. 'I'm no picnic.'

Mike felt miserably happy and sad. He had to find his footing and that meant change.

Carlos's morning passed quickly, as it usually did on the dog track days. The OAW's spotless white van was parked beside one of the garages. Pencils and sheets with the list of names were stowed behind reception. At noon, not a minute later, the OAW elevator opened and the parade of gamblers, dressed to the nines in soft Florida hues, coiffed to excess, manicured like Florida lawns and toting Prada and Gucci purses, strutted, as much as their age permitted, across the lobby to Carlos.

'Good afternoon, ladies,' Carlos beamed and bowed. 'You are aware of the rain?'

'We've survived husbands, children, hurricanes and arthritis! We'll survive the rain. Lead on, Carlos.'

'Ladies, let me bring the van into the garage, at least.'

'Nonsense, lead on!'

'I don't know why Esther always feels she knows what we all want,' Margaret whispered to Lila.

'Herman bullied her for 59 years before he died right there on the fourteenth hole. Esther feels it's her turn.'

'You'd think that would have been enough for her,' Margaret laughed.

Huge hats protected their hair and makeup, so all in all, Esther had been right. Before the van left for the track, Carlos distributed the papers and pencils and collected the money from each of the nine women, except for Lila.

'Only playing with my winnings, Carlos.' Lila wanted to keep track of what she had today. She also wanted time to meet Carlos alone at one of the betting cages while the women were back in their seats. No one would be the wiser. Lila often took little walks 'to move the aches around.' Carlos looked puzzled, but he pocketed the cash, went to the front of the van and called back, 'Fasten those seatbelts!'

One block down Collins Avenue, the green Jag pulled in behind the van.

When the bettors walked across the lobby, past the booth promoting the retired greyhound adoption program, REGAP, the ladies' hair wilted in the humid air. Carlos steered his charges to a row of seats out of the rain. Then he ran back to buy the programs and handed them out. The ladies studied the dogs and bet straight trifectas. They cheered when the dogs came onto the track.

'Look at those cute little yellow raincoats!'

'The plastic hats are worth the rain! Look, Bessie, they're tied under their chins.'

Carlos went to bet.

Ponytail was waiting for him.

As soon as she was out of sight of the OAW women, Lila grabbed a wall for support. Another hip replacement, Dr. Faigan had told her. Inside her leg, travelling down to her knee, pain burned like fire. Doubling up on her flax and hemp protein hadn't helped. With a deep breath, Lila pushed on out to the betting area. Carlos had placed the bets and was turning from the cage. She walked towards him, but stopped when someone tapped him on the shoulder. The young man looked familiar. Lila decided to wait her turn, balancing on her cane.

'Good morning Mr. Alvarez!' Carlos said, hoping Alvarez hadn't seen him pocketing some of the bills. He bit his bottom lip when he saw it wasn't Alvarez, but someone else.

'I have a proposition for you, Carlos. Let's speak over here.'

That this unknown man knew his name startled him. 'I have to get back.'

'This will take only a few minutes, barely longer than it took you to steal from those old bags.'

The man was nothing like the Cuban hardhats or the Columbian day workers Carlos often saw. He was polished and full of menace. Carlos followed him to a side wall and heard him out. 'I'd lose my job if I let you onto that floor. Besides, security is state-of-the-art.'

Ponytail smiled. 'Security won't be a problem. Carlos, $1,500 for such a simple thing. If the old bags learn of your thefts, what then?'

Sweat crawled down Carlos's cheeks. He couldn't see

beyond the possibility of being fired.

Ponytail handed him a photo. Carlos was looking at his wife and baby daughter. His address was written at the bottom of the photo. Clenching his fists, he reduced the betting stubs to wet paper balls.

'Don't think of moving your wife and daughter. I'm not alone.'

Carlos gnawed the inside of his cheek. 'When?'

'Soon. I know where to find you.'

Lila had had enough. After all, Carlos was their chauffeur. She walked gingerly over to the men. Ponytail, intent on Carlos, almost collided with Lila as he turned to leave. 'Oh dear, I thought…' Lila was shocked.

His jaw tightened. He walked away quickly. *Fuck! A loose end.*

'Carlos, are you alright? You look terrible.'

'Lila, I…'

'Was it something that man said to you?'

'No, no. I just remembered that I haven't bet all the money. I thought I had. It means I have to run back to the cage.'

Carlos must know that I'm on to him. I won't have to say anything. But that man looked so much like…What are the odds…Carlos is terribly frightened. The poor man is shaking. Certainly not of me, but maybe of losing his job. Lila had to think. She needed time to digest what had just occurred. Something definitely had.

🌴

Ponytail had not left the track. He sat a safe distance from the women. For the moment, he was not concerned about Carlos. His gaze was intent on the woman in the blue cotton skirt, cradling a floppy hat. A few times, the woman looked over at Carlos, who'd gone silent. His face was tight as cement. The woman shook her head, obviously concerned. Then he drew another line in his scheme.

🌴

The women stayed for their four races; there were a few wins. Carlos collected them and dispersed the money without any skimming. Once he'd hoisted his charges back into the van, he stepped down and tapped his home number on his cell. As it rang, Carlos cowered as close to the van as possible, his eyes darting around, fearful he'd see Alvarez's double. 'Maria, is everything alright?'

'Carlos? Just a second, Perdita just managed to scoot out of the house.'

Carlos's heart was booming. 'Run and get her!'

'You're shouting. I can catch a 2-year-old.'

Carlos waited a full minute, his eyes stretched wide. 'Well?'

'Our little princess was halfway across the street.'

'Both of you stay inside until I get home.'

'But you're working tonight. It's too hot to be inside, Carlos. Besides, I have shopping to do.'

'Do as I say. Tell me what you need and I'll get the things tonight. Keep the doors locked.'

'What's wrong?' Maria's voice rose in alarm.

'Just do as I say!'

'Carlos?'

'Do as I say. For once don't question me!'

Lila saw Carlos's haunted eyes as he climbed into the driver's seat and drove back to Sunny Isles. This time, there were no jokes from the driver. Except for Lila, the group twittered together, oblivious of the brewing turmoil.

🌴

CHAPTER FOUR

MIKE AND CAITLIN had driven to 65th Street and Collins to an IHOP. Mike was devouring a tall stack of buckwheat pancakes while Caitlin was doing pretty well herself, adding syrup to her sausages. 'I only indulge myself like this once a year,' she laughed.

Mike came up for air, disarmed again by the glint in Caitlin's eyes and the soft, downy cheeks he reached over and touched. He'd let things go till she answered him.

Caitlin's cell vibrated on her hip. 'Better see who it is.'

'Leave it. We have only one day alone.'

A tiny stress crease threatened her right cheek as he took a peek at her cell. 'It's Carmen.'

Mike pushed his plate away. 'Take it!'

'Great news! I caught an earlier flight. I'll be there tonight.'

Damn! 'What time, Carm?'

'Around nine.'

'We just thought we'd have…'

'One more night together. Should have realized. Listen, I'll cab it from Lauderdale. I feel like shit.'

'I'll pick you up.'

Mike had grabbed the check and left.

Caitlin ran after him. He was already on Collins when she caught up to him. 'Why are you being like this? I thought we were the three amigos.'

'The worst thing is you don't even see what I'm talking about! How the hell would you like it if I dragged Hunter along everywhere we went?'

'He's not your best friend.'

'Actually, I've lost most of my friends since I met you.'

'I see.' Now it was Caitlin who stormed off.

'Hang on a minute!' Mike ran across the street after Caitlin and grabbed her by the shoulders. 'We're a couple. I don't always want to share you. Is that hard to get?'

Caitlin stopped. 'Look Mike, Carmen was there for the hard times.'

'I was there when Chris died. He was my best friend. I made the family sandwiches, kept out of your way and hung around long after Hunter had gone back to Boston. Are you forgetting that? Know what I thought? With me in your life, you'd see less of Carmen as I have of my friends. I often feel like the third wheel.'

'Well, you're not. You're the second.'

'You drive me nuts! Let's get back to the room. Forget the foreplay, we don't have time.'

Caitlin kissed him on the mouth, and he wanted to be inside her. He brushed his cheek against hers.

As they neared 70th Street, Caitlin saw an arts festival that seemed to begin on Collins and snaked around to the beach. 'Wow! Look at that! This whole area has been redone. There must be a couple hundred people here. Shoot, it ends Friday.'

'Go with your third wheel.' He looked over at Caitlin who blushed. 'You've already figured that out. Our quarters are off limits at night. Carmen has her own place.'

'Deal.'

🌴

Ponytail didn't tell Daisy about the old bag. She was skittish enough as it was. In his office, he began to proof the paperwork before he handed it off to Daisy, who had a good eye for detail. While she was busy at that, he rechecked everything at the back of the garage. He had done a good job with the plastic drop sheets and other

material that could be easily gotten rid of. Ponytail did
not intend to leave DNA behind. Their white plastic
suits lay on the chair. In one corner there was a com-
mode, water and thick, expensive duct tape. He laid the
tape on top of the body bag he'd made himself, beside
the syringes and vials of chloral hydrate. It still amazed
him what you could get on the internet. He'd brought
extra batteries for the camcorder. No way he was about
to allow any real communication between the couple.
Speed and disposal were absolutes. The bottle of Roed-
erer's Cristal was nicely wrapped for his encounter. Their
IDs were safely stored in the house. Ponytail was ready.
If Daisy balked anywhere along the way, he was prepared
for that too.

♣

Lila did not join her friends for dinner in Sophie's
room, even though fresh shark meat cooked to
perfection with a dill sauce was on the menu. Ramon,
the chef, had worked at Joe's Stone Crab on South Beach
before he was replaced with a younger chef. It was Esther
who'd discovered his sad lot and hired him for the
women, after a vote, of course. Ramon bought the sup-
plies and worked wonders for lunch and dinner six days
a week. Lila stayed behind with her door open, waiting
to see Carlos. Breaking a lifetime tradition, she took two
large sips of warm Scotch she kept in stock. Her cheeks
puckered at the taste, but her chest warmed.

The muscles in Carlos's jaw fought one another until
his whole face hurt. When he made his night check
down the warren of halls on the OAW floor, he hoped to
see no one. His face had become a clock, with each
second twitching under both eyes.

'Carlos?'

He walked on, pretending not to hear. Carlos had not

sworn, even to himself, on Trump's property, not even once. Fear dissolved those manners now. *Muthufucker!* 'Yes?'

'CARLOS! I have to see you.' Lila whispered too loudly, motioning him into her suite with bony fingers. When Carlos turned, Lila was startled by the change in him. The buoyant confidence that supported his fine Cuban features and his infectious flair had melted, like butter in the sun.

He bowed at the waist and reached for her hand to kiss it, but Lila waved that off. 'Sit down, Carlos. You don't look well.' Lila poured him a double Scotch.

'Not on the job, Mrs. Katz.' Nonetheless, he ached to swallow the alcohol in one gulp.

'Drink! No one will be the wiser.' Lila did not have to make that request a second time. 'Now, what happened at the track?'

A spike of panic brought the Scotch back up, and Carlos spat it through his fingers.

'Oh dear!' Lila went for a towel.

His eyes watered. 'Nothing happened, Mrs. Katz,' he replied unconvincingly.

'I know…'

Carlos jumped at the one thing that might save him. His confession spilled from his mouth much like the Scotch. 'I just took a little money. You ladies have so much. I have a wife and child. It will never happen again – I swear on my life! Have mercy, Mrs. Katz.'

Could Lila have been mistaken about the encounter at the track? Carlos was shaking. 'I didn't mean…'

'Nothing happened at the track,' he said desperately, speaking much too quickly.

Lila caught the slip. Carlos's cheeks were pinched. When she put her hand on his shoulder, Lila felt his shirt soaked with sweat. 'You'd better get back to work. We all need you. You can talk to me any time. Working out problems alone is overrated.'

Carlos shot out of the room. He felt his throat closing. He began to gasp.

Lila rummaged through her drawer until she found her old sketch pad. It had been decades. Did she still have her charcoal pencils? Then she saw her hands were shaking.

CHAPTER FIVE

FELICIA ALVAREZ, WHOSE striking dark beauty had caught the eye of Mike Halloran, sat sipping *café Cubano* as she followed the frenzied rush of her husband Jesús. The room she was in was a showcase of soft yellow carpet and light grey felt walls bordered in gold leaf. The end tables were solid crystal; the bar near the main patio was yellow marble. Lightness mingling with strength was the theme of the suite. 'Could you not have driven to the card game?' Her voice was low and melodious, edged with strength, like the room.

'The 'copter will get me to South Beach in ten minutes. Do you mind? Didn't we promise the best to one another?'

'You're going alone.' Felicia knew Jesús used the rooftop helipad to impress his friends.

Jesús paraded in front of Felicia in a light brown linen suit, a shirt to match and soft leather sandals. *He dresses like a wealthy Cuban, but he never speaks our language.* 'Am I handsome?'

Felicia smiled.

'Study the yachting books, Felicia. Our meeting is the day after tomorrow. Don't wait up.'

'You know it is not wise to chase losses.' *Jesús does not even consider the monumental loss we incurred after buying this condo.*

'I know poker.' His voice was as sharp as shale. Jesús caught the side of Felicia's cheek with a light kiss, then he was out the door.

Felicia dropped the books on the side table. Her brother's advice rang in her ears. *Money does not bring security. Family does that. Separating from us is not wise.* Felicia's pride would not permit her to admit her error of moving away. Yet, she would stand firm on this one issue. *There will be no yacht! Grandfather's money was given to me.* She changed and headed down to the beach.

🌴

Caitlin and Mike had showered and eaten. 'How about picking up Carmen without me, set up the rules while I take a night swim and a late jog on the beach?' *Perhaps he'd see Felicia.*

'Her flight's on time. I should get going. I'm still sorry.'

'Added point. Did you ever think that if you two didn't spend so much time together, you might be more willing to commit, and Carmen might actually find the guy she says she's looking for? I thought you wanted the time I was away at work to start on your book.'

Caitlin's shoulders tightened. She hated being wrong. 'Carmen has sales calls to make in Miami. I can still work.'

'Just think about it.'

'Love you.'

'Yeah, yeah.'

Caitlin planted a sloppy kiss on Mike's mouth.

She made good time to the airport, found parking close to an exit and waited at the bottom of the escalator that led to the baggage. Her shoulders slumped. *Mike's right. I had a bad feeling about this.*

'Caitlin!' Carmen was fast approaching. 'Great flight. Hello Florida!'

Caitlin waved and hugged Carmen as soon as she hopped off the escalator.

'I should have thought before I invited myself along. Sorry.'

Caitlin didn't comment. 'Let's get the bags. We'll all survive.'

The women watched luggage pass them by on the conveyor. Neither spoke till they were in the car and back on the road.

'Mike's rung the big *when* again.'

'So it's not all me, Caitlin.'

'Nope.'

'I date one shithead with different faces, and you can't commit to a great guy.'

'I don't want to get into it, Carm.'

'Then let's get out of here and see the Miami lights.'

🌴

Although it was close to nine, there was still faint light after Mike's half-hour run on the beach. Night swims were fast becoming his favorite. He saw joggers and walkers on the lip of the sand, but he was alone in the ocean when the riptide caught him and pulled him south along the beach. For every three strong strokes he took, the ocean pulled him back four. Lifeguards were long gone. Mike noticed when he didn't fight the tow, he wasn't yanked further back. He conserved his strength, looked down the shoreline and saw the pier. He went with the flow of the ocean. A hundred yards from the pier, he sucked in air and began his fight.

He dove underwater and stroked with vicious power. Fifty strokes and more. When he struck his temple on a wooden supporting pillar, he grabbed it in a bear hug. His lungs were bursting – air was escaping from his mouth. Clawing his way up the slimy pole, he surfaced, gagging and coughing up mucus. To get to the next pole, he'd have to swim a good thirty feet or be swept under and back out to deep water. On his first attempt to suck in more air, he choked. His grip was slipping. In desperation, he gulped air through his mouth and dove under a second time, using the pole for leverage to push away. Once he'd reached the second pole, he straddled it. He knew he could make it to shore. Mike tried to laugh, but choked. *Nothing flashed! The only thought I had was 'shit!'* He swam in a frenzied silence to the shore, stumbled forward and collapsed on the sand. The alarm faded. Mike had never thought of himself as inconsequential. He did now, gasping and wheezing.

Turning on his back, he reached for his temple, felt the wound and winced. His hand was bloody from the head wound when he found an outdoor shower and rinsed off. From the waist up, Mike was hyped; from the waist down, his legs wobbled, as though they were not his. He did not see Felicia.

She approached him. 'Your head is bleeding.' There was nothing else like *Are you hurt? Do you need help?*, just the simple words. She pressed her hand to his head. 'Come with me.'

Her hand was soft and comforting. She smelled of coconut and salty air. 'Mike.'

Neither one of them expected to see Caitlin.

Mike suddenly felt naked, guilty and almost disappointed when he spotted her. 'I got caught in a rip.'

Caitlin took in the woman with Mike and felt queasy.

Felicia smiled fully at Mike and left. There was no need for her to explain anything. There was a tinge of disappointment in her smile.

'Let's get you up to the room. Hope you won't need stitches on that beautiful forehead.' In fact he didn't. He lay on the couch, enjoying Caitlin's care. 'Can I tell Carmen what happened?'

'Get her in here.'

'Wow!' from Carmen added to the dangerous event.

'I have to work tomorrow!' Mike groaned.

'You're going to survive, Mike. It's mostly bruised. Keep the ice on it. Take it easy for the rest of the night.'

'Like I have a choice?'

'Precisely.'

'You don't have to be at work until ten. You should be okay.' Twenty minutes later, she helped Mike into bed. He was out cold in minutes. He didn't hear the phone ring. The Miami VP who was to begin training with Mike tomorrow had postponed the sessions until Monday. His father in Seattle had passed away, and he had flown out to be with his family. *Good for Mike! Sad for his boss.*

Caitlin grabbed a bottle of wine and tiptoed into Carmen's room. Before long, the two C's had forgotten about stumbling blocks in their friendship and were each cupping their mouths to keep their noise level down. Caitlin didn't mention the woman to Carmen. She didn't want to. It was enough that she had seen the look that passed between them. Caitlin couldn't admit why she was holding back from Mike. Something in her didn't want to move forward.

🌴

CHAPTER SIX

THE NEXT MORNING, Felicia saw no signs of fatigue on Jesús's face. *Quite a constitution!* He ate quickly and packed his gym bag.

'At the rates Tim charges, I have to be on time for my workout. Remember our meeting at two to see the yacht. I'll be back in plenty of time.'

There will be no yacht.

Jesús did not offer a quick kiss or a backward glance before he left the suite. Felicia did not especially care for her sister-in-law, Jen. Yet she had wondered if the young woman knew the life of loneliness ahead of her. Felicia knew her brother Diego rarely spent time alone with her. He was far too busy. She had tried to escape such a life when she married Jesús. The empty quiet in the suite was proof of her own failure. Her determination hardened. *There will be no yacht.* Pride kept her from confiding in her brother Diego. Admitting one had made a poor choice was never easy.

🌴

An hour later, freshly showered, Jesús left the gym in Turnberry carrying his bag. He headed to the clients' parking. He was startled when Ponytail caught up with him from behind. He wore dark shades, Ray-Bans, and had combed his hair straight back, minus the ponytail. He spoke in a low rasp. 'Santo has a job for you.'

When Jesús turned, his throat dried. His fist tightened around the bag as though he might use it as a weapon. Santo was Felicia's cousin, a captain in the family business. 'Felicia and I have a meeting this afternoon.' It was a weak feint and they both knew it.

Ponytail stepped up close, inches from Jesús's face.

He shrugged his shoulders towards the Jag, slid into the back seat and left the door open.

Jesús looked behind him. His armpits stuck. 'What about my car?'

Ponytail leaned across the seat. 'We'll drive you back to it.'

Jesús was not pushed into the Jag, but he felt shoved. The last thing he remembered was leaning over to pull the door closed. Ponytail's quick neck jab put him out.

🌴

When Jesús regained consciousness, he was tied to a chair and gagged. A noose around his neck pulled his head back and choked him when he tried to bring his head forward. From the sides of his eyes, he saw the man bend at the waist and lean in closer to him.

'You're awake. That's good. No harm will come to you if you do as I say. Nod if you understand.'

Jesús's face bulged as the noose caught him when he tried to nod. Blue veins roped in his neck.

'I'll loosen the rope. That's better. Now, read only what I've written; appear calm. That's all you have to do. It's simple really.'

Now that he was upright, Jesús saw he was surrounded by plastic. A woman to his right held a camcorder. A yellow stain appeared between his legs. His captors wore the white plastic suits cops used at crime scenes on TV. A film of sweat ran into Jesús's eyes. Its sting was muffled by the roar of blood surging up his neck.

'Look here, Jesús. Get a hold of yourself. We're wasting time. Read the first one, take five seconds and read the second. All you have to do then is wait. I'll take out the gag and loosen the rope. Take a few deep breaths, but don't be stupid and scream.' Ponytail spoke in whispers. He turned on the lights and handed Jesús the *Herald*.

'Hold that up, please. When I give you the signal, read the first message.'

The side of his neck began to spasm, and Jesús gasped as soon as the gag was out of his mouth.

'We haven't time for this. Be a man!'

A slow moan escaped his mouth. Jesús swallowed and tried to strangle sobs that rose in the back of his throat. 'Felicia, do as they say. My life is in your hands.'

'Count to five and read the second note.'

'I'm fine; I'll be home soon.' His eyes locked onto the lens, imploring Felicia to save his life. His light tan faded along with any thought of a yacht. His bowels loosened.

'Damn! At least we have the plastic.'

Ponytail walked behind Jesús. Before he could dodge Ponytail, he'd slapped tape across his mouth, then over his nose. For their plan, Jesús was ancillary stuff. Ponytail and Daisy stood with their backs to Jesús until the creaking of the chair had stopped. 'It's a wrap!' Ponytail laughed. He leaned over and took Jesús's watch, and then he and Daisy rolled Jesús in plastic, folded their package in two, taped it tightly and stuffed the body into the black body bag. They also rolled the plastic that had coated the room to catch body fluids and avoid trace evidence and stuffed that into the bag as well. 'What a stench!'

Daisy tried to walk away. 'Get over here! You're in this!'

'I just didn't think...'

'You thought I'd do all the dirty work? You want your share, you do the work.'

Daisy's elbows began to shake when she helped Ponytail hoist Jesús into the freezer.

'We didn't need the provisions after all.' Ponytail and Daisy took off their own protective gear, stored them in the trunk and headed into the house to prepare for their visit to the Trump. 'I have to look the part and count on our boy Carlos. It's on, baby.'

Daisy's face tightened.

'Get with it, babe. We said no collateral baggage. How can I become Alvarez if he's still alive?'

'I was focused on the money.'

'The body count goes with it, Daisy. Now, let's get to work. Change into those clothes you bought and take the bag with your own clothes with you. Cab it to the Turnberry and drive the car to Lauderdale, park in the long-term area at the airport. Use the second set of IDs. Change in the airport bathroom, dispose of the clothes away from the airport. Call a cab and get to the Trump.'

Ponytail pulled Daisy to him and kissed her mouth. 'This part is tough. It's uphill from here. It's ours to take if we stay tough. We'll be in San Fran before you know it. Did this asshole do anything to deserve this money? Forget him.'

🌴

Earlier, before he left for work, Carlos walked hurriedly around his block, searching for anyone spying on his family. School kids laughed and pushed one another off the sidewalk waiting for their bus. Dogs trotted listlessly. It was already hot. Small colored homes had begun to bake in the sun. The ants that could would fly in this heat. Every a/c droned. Carlos saw no one. He ran back to Maria and grabbed her shoulders. 'Take Perdita and go to your sister's, right now!'

'What have you done?'

'Nothing! There is no time for discussion; I can't be late. Get ready. I'll drive you both to the bus stop. Here.' Carlos grabbed some bills.

'Where does this money come from? It is not payday.'

'Maria, I provide. Get Perdita, pronto!'

Maria had never seen Carlos angry and frightened at the same time. She packed a few clothes and some food and carried their daughter without another word.

'Do not leave your sister's until I call. If something happens to me, you cannot go home.'

Maria began to cry; in short order, Perdita was wailing.

Carlos's eyes watered when he left the small duo, who continued to cry at the bus stop. He drove off and couldn't look back. On the drive down to Collins, he laid his cell on the seat beside him and willed the phone not to ring. Half an hour later, he stood by the front desk with his hand inside his pocket on his cell. How could he take the women out to lunch at Versailles, Miami's favorite Cuban restaurant?

On the OAW floor, the women were together in the social room with pens and paper. The four lap dogs were dressed with bows in their hair, yapping excitedly. Abby Wiseman, an estate planning attorney in her late fifties, was frequently invited to address the group on new developments in estate law. The women had made and changed their wills numerous times. They adored Ms. Wiseman and took copious notes from her talks. Sophie raised her hand for the third time that morning. 'I want to leave a million dollars in trust for my three little ones here and $300,000 to Max Schwartz from Snip and Clip. He's Little Caesar's and Mischa's and Israel's groomer. Beverley and Hershel have not bothered to call in over a week!' The women sighed. Sophie was into the booze again. Little Caesar was a Yorkshire terrier, Mischa a toy poodle, and Israel was a Pomeranian who wore a black rhinestone-studded collar. 'There is so much to consider and I'm not getting any younger. My babies must have the best.' Much to Sophie's chagrin, it was Mops, Margaret's miniature Littlefield sheepdog, who wore no jewellery, that was the girls' favorite.

'Well, Sophie, we can discuss this later.' Abby was Sophie's attorney, thinking she'd have to interview Max to assure herself he was not pressuring Sophie for the money, and arrange for a certificate of independent review from another attorney. She knew Sophie would change her mind if Max didn't match the right bow tie to Mischa's vest next week. After the meeting, she'd sit down with Sophie to set up the pooch trust.

Abby had a few clients and some friends here among the OAW. She knew better than most that a will, like life, was changeable. When Abby lost her husband to the legs of a 26-year-old who lived behind them, she went to law school and tackled real problems. The women made her laugh, but the waves of perfume, mingled with the smoke, had her gagging. En route to the meeting, Abby stopped by the OAW pooch room and dog-run. Inside she was met with color. One wall was flamingo pink, the one beside it lime green, and the final two Caribbean blue. The room was as plush as a suite with a small track; tiny, pastel-colored sofas; a wading pool; a toy and treat counter; a rainbow poop corner and music. *I wonder what's next!* Abby herself was a woman who firmly believed that a dog wasn't really a dog unless it could knock you over.

Today, Abby scanned the group. Something was amiss. 'Where's Lila?'

'I knocked on her door this morning,' Margaret told everyone. 'Lila said she was busy.'

'As long as she's fine,' Abby nodded. Lila and Margaret were her support when fun began to dialogue with the absurd. These two were clear-headed women who could control even the little four-footed treasured yappers who might chew off a toe if you weren't alert.

At the end of her talk, she met with Sophie in her suite. The focus of this meeting, the canines, yapped and attacked Abby's shoes. 'Regarding the 'pooch trust' as you call it, you have to be very careful when you choose Hannah, your niece, as the trustee of this money. A trust for animals is not binding in law.'

Sophie's brow furrowed. The dogs stopped yapping and stared up at Abby.

'You must be sure that Hannah loves animals.'

'Oh yes, that's a given with Hannah.' The dogs went back to yapping.

'Does Hannah love these little fellows? That's very important.'

Little Caesar, Israel and Mischa quieted down. They didn't want to miss this answer.

'Hannah adores them! She's promised to take them in if…' Sophie didn't want to mention a word that might frighten her and her little boys.

'That's wonderful. Since you know that she is trustworthy, I'll begin the paperwork. As an added precaution, I suggest a bequest of $25,000 to the SPCA Humane Society, which offers to care for your pets, find them good foster homes and check in on them a couple of times a year in the event of your death.'

Sophie agreed wholeheartedly. Everybody in the suite was happy.

Lila sat at her desk, smiling acidly at her right hand. For the last hour, she'd tried to sketch the face of the look-alike she'd seen at the track with Carlos, but her hand shook. The lines jumped haphazardly on the pad. Stiffly, she rose and went to her sizeable medicine cabinet and found what she wanted. Taping her wrist as well as she could, she held it with her left hand. When Lila tried again, the line she drew showed promise. Lila was no quitter. She worked on. Life might eventually quit on her, but not today, she determined. Her first result *rather* pleased her, but Lila wanted the adverb gone. She wanted *pleased*. With deeper earnestness, she began again. Lunch was an hour away. She and Carlos had not finished their talk. Was Carlos frightened of her, frightened she'd turn him in? Lila didn't believe that for a minute. If he needed her protection, he had it. In fact, she dressed, took her cane and left a note on the door to tell the girls she'd meet them downstairs. She had something she wanted Carlos to see.

CHAPTER SEVEN

PONYTAIL MOST ASSUREDLY looked like Jesús Alvarez. The resemblance was remarkable. He went over each of the papers, arranged them back in order and placed the pens and phone numbers he'd need on top of the file. When he felt sure that all was in order, he put them in the briefcase. He also carried a bottle of Cristal. This day was a celebration of sorts, even if the lovely Felicia did not join him in a drink. There was no reason to think Daisy would run into trouble. As for the all-important call to Carlos, he'd make that outside the Trump. Ponytail looked over at the freezer and his resolve hardened. The money for Carlos was in a side pocket. It was now a question of getting to the Trump and Carlos before he took the old bags out for the afternoon. Any miscue on timing was serious. There was no way Ponytail wanted the old woman from the track to see him inside the Trump.

Carlos's hand froze when he felt his cell vibrate inside his pocket. His wrist felt like sand as he reached in for it. 'Yes?'

'I'm there in ten. Small change. You'll have to let me inside the Alvarez suite as well.'

Air swelled in Carlos's chest. 'I can't.'

'Yes, you can. I'm adding $500 to the pot. I'll be there in ten minutes.'

'They might not even be home.'

'I'll wait. Be at the main door to meet me. I need you for camouflage.'

'But…' The line was dead. His legs felt watery. He thought wildly of calling 9-1-1. Carlos tried to seem casual as he walked unsteadily behind the front desk and sat at one of the computers, pretending to verify something. He looked around. The manager was down the hall. He could make out the gold band on his jacket. The code book was in his drawer in the main office behind him. The door was open. Carlos didn't know the password to get the information off the computer. He had to get into the office.

After he'd snuck in, his knees popped like one of the old girls' when he crouched behind the desk. All three concierges knew where to find the book. Tenants who'd lived there for over a year sometimes still forgot their combinations. For the OAW women, having the manager open the book was added attention. Carlos felt for the key taped under the desk, peeled it away and slid the drawer open. He held the book on his knees and ran his finger down the page. Alvarez was the 11th name. He memorized the number, put the book back, re-taped the key and closed the drawer. He was still on his knees when the manager appeared.

'What are you doing in here?' The voice was sharp.

Carlos groped frantically for the lucky coin he kept in his pocket. His knees popped again as he stood. 'I dropped my silver dollar and it rolled under your desk.' His scalp itched.

Angel Hernandez was 49. He was a tall, lean and stately Hispanic, serious and unforgiving. The only soft thing about Angel was his wavy silver hair. His name was deceptive. Angel had worked hard for the position he now had. He'd gone from one flea-bag motel to another, one step at a time, and finally to the Trump. At the moment, Angel stood ramrod straight, enjoying his authority and the young man's discomfort. 'This office is off limits. You know that, Carlos. I am responsible for the privacy of our tenants who pay us a great deal of money to protect just that. You have no permission to be in my office, not ever!'

'I apologize, sir.' Carlos bowed from the waist. 'It will never happen again. The silver dollar is my lucky piece.' Carlos heard the minutes ticking.

'Get back to your post. Mind what I have said. By the way, keep the ladies happy. They're very fond of you.'

'Thank you, sir.' Carlos fingered his lucky coin.

Ponytail sat back in the Jag and counted off the minutes. In a day, two at most, he'd go from minor scam artist to hyper-premium millionaire. His lower lip began to twitch. His new life of entitlement would begin in four minutes. *All the rich should be labelled globally imperilled.* He'd heard that phrase on TV applied to animals, and he'd liked it. 'Globally imperilled.' In San Fran, he'd run the words into a conversation. Make an impression. At the two-minute mark, sweat beaded his upper lip and he wiped it away. At the one-minute mark, he was spiked. *In and out, in and out!*

Daisy slipped into the passenger seat. She was chewing her nails. 'Are you sure this will work?'

'Get a grip! Get your finger out of your mouth. You want to jinx this for me? Take the wheel as soon as I leave. I can't start worrying about you.'

Daisy walked around to the driver's side when Ponytail got out.

He repeated his mantra as he walked up to the Trump. *In and out!*

🌴

Felicia had been to Saks for her hair and pedicure. Her nails had been done yesterday. Like many Hispanics, she was a natural beauty, and like elite French women, she wore little make-up. Today, she was dressed in soft blue cashmere and she was barefoot. She wore no jewellery except for her ring and one gold bracelet, a gift from her grandfather. Felicia stood on the balcony, lost in the argument of words she'd hear when she told Jesús she did not want a yacht. Scanning the beach, she wondered who the woman was who had taken care of Mike. Had he not been alone? Felicia had felt him tense when she touched him. Who was the woman? There was a time when Jesús, the sound of his name, would rouse her. It was not so long ago. Perhaps Jesús would see…

🌴

Carmen left quietly before eight for her meeting with the shop managers at the new mall in Aventura. Caitlin lay in bed awake with her arm lightly resting on Mike's shoulder. 'You awake?' She kissed the side of his ear.

Mike rolled into her.

'Whoa, my head is sore.'

'The bump is the size of an egg.' Caitlin ran her fingers over it and kissed it.

Mike took a whiff of himself. 'I stink. I'll shower first and go down and get Tylenol from the pharmacy. Then, I'll be good as new. Man of steel.'

'You know what happened to him. Be you.'

🌴

While Lila's elevator door opened first, Mike beat her across the lobby, coming from the other side. Ponytail had entered the Trump and now stood at the main desk, four feet behind a visibly jittery Carlos.

'Good morning, Jesús!' A tenant greeted Ponytail, taken in by the man he saw with the concierge.

Ponytail's eyes thinned, but he gave the older man a summary nod and turned away. Carlos shivered in the 87-degree weather, overwhelmed by a surge of fear.

Mike put on the brakes when he heard the name and gave Ponytail a good look. Felicia's husband had been rude to him after all. Mike was good with faces and names.

'Carlos! Carlos!' Lila called from half-way across the lobby, waving her cane above her shoulder. When she saw who was with Carlos, her suspicion heightened.

God dammit to hell! There were too many people to risk it now. Ponytail froze and rushed back out to the car. He passed within a few feet of Mike and looked right through him.

Ponytail hopped into the Jag and screamed, 'Take off! Don't say a freakin' word! What the hell was she doing there?'

'What can I do in this traffic?'

'*Madre de Dios*! Damn! Damn! Shit! Shut up!'

'I'm not saying anything.'

Ponytail punched in the number on his cell.

Carlos did not pick up. Ponytail slammed his fist into the dashboard and roared with pain. His words were a mixture of fury and panic. 'I have to refocus. That's it! Get the lines in order. First, I have to get to Felicia before she realizes Jesús is missing. Good. That's good. So? So what?'

'Get in touch with Carlos. Set it up.'

'See! When you calm down, you get us both on track. That's good. I mean, the package is not going anywhere, not yet anyway.'

🌴

Lila's hip was a cinder block by the time she reached Carlos. 'Didn't you hear me calling?'

Carlos looked outside and saw the dash to the Jag. He wanted this thing to be over. Now it wasn't. When his cell beeped, he couldn't take it, not with Lila in front of him.

'You don't look well at all, Carlos. Who was that man with you just now?'

'What?' Carlos barked. He could not have Lila knowing anything.

She fumbled with her cane. Lila knew not to plunge further into the identity of the man. Carlos was not himself. His face had glazed into a mask.

'Lila, it has been a busy morning. I have no time for conversation. That's all.' His cell beeped again. 'I have to take this. Will you excuse me?'

'I have something to show you.' The sketch was another matter. She was not about to throw that by the wayside.

'Not now, Lila, please.' Terror darted around his eyes.

'I'll keep this for lunch.' *Something happened at the track. I know that for certain now. If my eyes haven't failed me, that man was just here with Carlos.* Lila tucked the sketch into her purse and headed for a blue velvet chair to wait for the girls. Her chest began to heave. A terrible sense of foreboding slithered into the lobby and hung in the air like a dense fog. *If I were twenty years younger, I wouldn't be sitting on a chair like an old crone with a bad hip. I'd be up seeing to this! Carlos needs help.*

Carlos tensed when he felt his cell vibrating in his pocket. Reluctantly, he reached in for the phone and walked off. 'Yes?'

'Time change.'

'Excuse me?'

'I know you work tonight. I'll be there at seven. You hear me, Carlos?'

'I could be called to a floor. I can't just...'

'The door at seven. I want your cell phone. I have another one for you. Am I clear?'

'I don't think I can go...'

'Don't think. Be there at seven.'

The phone clicked off. Carlos stood holding it. What could he tell the police? He didn't even know the man's name. The man could tell the police that he saw him stealing from the women. Maria didn't have her green card. He should have married her, but he hadn't. In his heart, she was his wife. He wanted money in the bank, some security before marriage. Perdita had been an early surprise. It was funny, he thought, how someone so small could direct his life. Had he been alone, Carlos would have run and taken Maria with him. Now he was stuck. Seven hours from now, the whole mess would begin again. Now, too, he had Lila to deal with.

'Caitlin, it was the strangest thing. Felicia's husband walked right past me without the slightest hint of recognition. Some older guy said hello to him by name, but I swear there was something different about the guy. I don't forget a face.'

'True, but after that bump, you're not right in the head,' Caitlin called from bed.

'There's nothing wrong with my eyes. I know what I saw. The guy's an arrogant prick. He got in my face when I tried to open the door for his wife. Today he didn't know me and he seemed spooked when he rushed out of the Trump.'

Caitlin had no interest in Felicia or her husband. 'I guess I can't tempt you with a swim.'

'I have something else in mind,' he whispered as he came into the bedroom. 'I smell good.'

'Come a little closer. Let me be the judge.'

Mike couldn't let go. 'Thing is, it's out of character. I saw the guy the day he arrived. He likes making an impression. Doesn't jive – today he was trying not to be noticed.'

'Who cares?' Caitlin deliberately brushed off Mike's concerns because she saw they were leading to Felicia.

Was he going there as payback for her waffling or was there a growing attraction? She held Mike tighter, fearing the second possibility. It was easy to assign the blame to the two upheavals in her life. Harder to accept that selfishness was at the core.

🌴

CHAPTER EIGHT

CARLOS PICKED AT his lunch and drank his *café con leche*, immune to the chandeliers, murals and mirrors of Café Versailles on *Calle Ocho* and to the melodious sounds of his native tongue.

'I read that the name of this restaurant comes from a Hotel Versailles in Cuba. Don't you feel grand, Esther?'

'I must ask for the recipe for these black beans and rice. There's a secret here. I'll get it out of our waiter and share it with you, Sophie.'

Lila spent lunch breaking her fried whole fish and keeping an eye on Carlos, who had chosen not to sit beside her. Didn't he see that she might be of help?

🌴

Ponytail had come up with a better plan. 'I have it! Get me another phone.'

'It's in the cupboard.'

'You could help me out here.'

'You've stopped asking for my opinion. You get the phone.'

'Daisy, the glitch got to me.' He reached for the phone and outlined the plan.

Daisy was back in.

Ponytail called the Trump. 'Good afternoon, I have a message for Felicia Alvarez.'

'I'll put you through, sir.'

'No, I haven't time. Take the message for her. Her husband sprained his wrist at the club. I drove him to Mount Sinai for X-rays. He can't use his cell in the hospital. He'll be home as soon as he can, but he's in emergency and that could take hours. Have you got all that?'

'And you are?'

'Just a guy at the club who helped him out. I have to get back to work.'

'I'll pass that message along, sir.'

Ponytail tossed the phone onto the couch. 'We get rid of this cell, then we grab some lunch. Let me change out of these clothes. I have to look good tonight.'

Daisy smiled.

'We're back on, babe.'

'What about the package?'

'The lime, the hole, it's all there, but do we risk daylight? It's already past one. Jesús is okay where he is for now. Shit, I just thought of something. What if she has to call her adviser? It'll be too late for that.'

'With that kind of money, she'll have a private number,' Daisy assured him.

'See, Daisy, we are a team. All we have to do now is kill a few hours.'

♟

Carmen was pleased with her day that had ended up on I-95. At the moment, she was stuck in traffic on the bridge of 163rd Street on the causeway. Traffic began to move. The ocean enveloped each of her senses as she made her turn on Collins. Her body relaxed and Carmen dropped her head out the window and breathed deeply. *What a sight! I'm going to grab myself some sun. It's not too late.* Once she'd parked and gotten out of the elevator, Carmen opened her door as softly as she could, without success.

'You're back! Come on in. Guess where we're all going to dinner?'

Carmen felt awkward walking into their suite.

'I gave in,' Mike smiled over at her. 'Truth is I have to show up at the office after all, orientation or something tomorrow.'

'Tony's?' Carmen looked 21 when she smiled. Her dark eyes flashed.

'Tony Roma's it is.'

'Ribs, sauce, margaritas!'

'Mike's convinced someone here has a double. It's the bump on his head.'

'Do you have an appointment tomorrow, Carm?'

'Couldn't book one.'

'Good for us then. We can check out the arts festival on 70th Street.'

🌴

Carlos was on night duty. He'd called Maria. She was safe. 'Can Manuel take you both to your mother's for a few days?' Since the man would be here tonight, there was a chance Maria and Perdita would not be followed.

'Manuel starts work at six. He's tired. Why can't we stay here?'

'You would be safer in Little Havana. This is the only way. I must go back to work. Please, Maria, do not question me. Ask Manuel.'

'Will you come to be with us later?'

'I cannot talk to you now.'

Usually, Carlos liked night work. The lobby was quiet. When he had walked a couple to the front desk to retrieve jewellery from the main safe, he took out the sheet of paper Lila had given him with her tip. *She knows…* The sketch was not terribly well done, but it was clear that it was the man she had seen at the track, down to a small mole he had just under his chin. Lila had written, *I am not without resources. I may be of help, Carlos.* He was still cold. He checked the time. It was after six. He folded the sketch and put it in his back pocket. His stomach knotted as he waited. Carlos no longer thought of running. He thought only of seven o'clock.

🌴

Felicia thought of calling Mount Sinai, but didn't. Her determination about the yacht was set. Instead, she walked along the beach in the afternoon, in a yellow cotton dress that blew up her legs. Under a floppy hat, she smiled at the approving nods. Jesús might even stop off for a drink before he came home, so she was not about to wait anxiously for him. It was probably a sprain, nothing terribly serious. For dinner, she made a salad and poured herself a glass of Cabernet Sauvignon. She thought of calling her brother, but wasn't in the mood for a sermon. *Stay with your family…*

🌴

Ponytail and Daisy sat in the Jag across the street from the Trump and went over details. 'If I'm not back in an hour, move the Jag. I'll ring once if we're on track. Pull up in front of the Trump. Wait for us. Clear?'

'You have the camcorder?'

'I have everything. Stay alert.' Ponytail put on his shades and crossed the street. He rubbed the side of his nose when he entered the lobby and walked up behind Carlos. 'Let's do this.'

Carlos hurried to the elevator.

'Slow down!' Ponytail hissed.

When the doors slid open, they found the car empty and stepped inside. Ponytail put the briefcase on the floor and the Cristal beside it, near his leg. His movements were quick and practiced, intimidating. 'This is for you.' Ponytail handed Carlos the envelope. 'I want your phone too.' Ponytail handed him another cell phone, still wrapped. 'Take it out of the bag.' Ponytail dropped the bag into his pocket and slipped on latex gloves.

'I do not want the money or the phone.' Carlos shrank back against the wall of the elevator.

Ponytail said stonily, 'I insist.'

'Will you leave us alone?'

'Why would I hurt a partner?'

Carlos took the money and handed over his cell. The doors slid open, and the men crept down the hall. 'Punch in the combination and leave.'

Carlos hesitated at the Alvarez suite. 'This is not right,' he whimpered.

'Do it!'

Carlos couldn't move.

Ponytail levelled a sharp jab at the base of his back. 'Do it!'

The top of Carlos's hand glistened with sweat as he punched in the code.

'Get back downstairs. We know exactly where Maria and your kid are.'

Carlos ran for the stairs and collapsed against a wall. When he caught his breath, he ran down all 17 stories. He remembered the corridor cameras. He crumpled the envelope of cash in his pocket and tore up the sketch. *He has my cell, with Maria's number, all my numbers…*

🌴

CHAPTER NINE

FREEDOM IS SAVORED because it's temporary. When Felicia heard the door opening, she rushed in from the balcony to greet Jesús. The champagne was the first thing she spotted. Felicia was halfway across the room when her initial joy became a dull jab of dread. Her mouth was open, but nothing came out.

Ponytail had mastered the skill of speed. Don't allow the mark to catch up. Keep him off balance. 'Mrs. Alvarez, may I call you Felicia? Please sit. We can conduct our business so much better that way. No, don't scream. Please sit. Jesús needs you to listen.'

Felicia sat near the window before she felt that choice had been a mistake. She gripped the sides of the leather chair and held on.

'That's so much better. Thank you.'

Felicia was still checking this man to be sure Jesús was not playing a trick on her. When she saw that he wasn't Jesús, her back arched against the chair. She watched dumbly as the intruder put on a plastic hat over his hair.

Ponytail opened the briefcase and laid the papers on his knees. 'Jesús is safe. You can see him on this camcorder, but why waste time? The sooner we finish our business, the sooner he's back home.'

Felicia had not blinked.

'It's simple really – your money for your life. Actually, your life for ten million.'

Felicia heard ten million; nothing before it.

'All you have to do is transfer your accounts to my bank. Of course, you won't know where that is, but that's incidental. I have the releases right here for you to sign. Electronic transfer. Done in minutes.'

You will be a target, Felicia. Here, with family, there is protection. It might have been the plastic hat, something that small, that woke Felicia. Her eyes focused, she leaned forward and asked one question. 'Do you know who I am?'

Ponytail was prepared, but such nerve, especially from a seemingly delicate woman that he could toss over the balcony with one arm, brought back his tic.

Felicia noted it.

Ponytail stood and handed her the papers. 'Jesús's life is in your hands.'

Felicia did not know the brutality of her grandfather, but she knew that his whispers were like iron, hard and final. Even now in prison, he was proud and unrepentant. 'Signing these papers will not get you the money.' Her voice was soft and final.

'But it will.'

'I have to see my advisor. It's a protection my brother set up for me.'

'Don't take me for a fool!' Ponytail leaned over Felicia and whispered in her ear. 'Call him instead. For money like this, you know the number.'

'There is no place you can hide.'

The slap cut across Felicia's cheek and nose. Her head fell to the side, her long dark hair a rainbow arc that followed it. Warm blood flowed from both nostrils, down her neck and onto her dress. Felicia gasped.

'Sign the goddamn papers!' Ponytail balled his fist and stood bending over her. 'Then make the call.'

'I have to see him in person.' Felicia struggled to talk.

'Get your goddamn head back.' Ponytail put the heel of his hand under Felicia's chin and pushed it back. 'You want to live, you call.'

Felicia began choking. Her whole body shook. She was zoning out, or suffocating.

Ponytail grabbed her by the hair and pulled her head

forward. He pinched her nose. 'Spit.'

Her face had a bluish tinge. He slapped her hard on the back, and she spit up gobs of blood before she began to breathe haltingly. Ponytail shoved the papers in her face. 'Sign them!' The blood began to flow again. Grabbing Felicia by the arm, he hoisted her up, and pulled and carried her to the bathroom where she hung her head in the sink and watched her blood stain the ivory basin.

Ponytail emptied the medicine cabinet until he found a box of cotton balls. Hurriedly he twisted them into cones. 'Sit!'

Felicia sat, choking and spitting up blood.

Ponytail pulled her head back, not roughly, because he feared she might suffocate. Her death would destroy his future. 'Don't move! I'm trying to help you.' He plugged both nostrils with cotton, stuffing cotton as high as he could get it. 'Keep your head back as far as you can. Don't fight me.' Ponytail picked Felicia up and carried her to the bedroom. Propping up two pillows, he laid her in the bed with her head leaning back over the pillows. 'Don't move, don't force your breathing, or you *will* suffocate.'

Felicia obeyed. She had decided, even when she couldn't breathe, that she was not going to die at the hands of a home invader. Her head felt like cotton. As she ran her fingers over her cheek, she felt the welt on her cheekbone. Though she could taste her blood, she was able to breathe.

Ponytail stood sneering down at her. 'I don't get it. You'd rather die than give up your money! What about Jesús? He thought he'd be home by now. Because you live here, you think you stink less than I do? Where do you think this money came from? "The family," your family, committed murders so you could live like this.

Your grandfather's a convicted murderer. Even if I take what you have, you'll be given more. My old man works like a donkey and still has nothing, and he never will. He gave up on me a long time ago. If our deal fails today, no one's going to throw more money my way. I've had to do the dirty work for what I have. Who the hell do you think you are? You never even asked to hear your husband. What kind of wife are you?'

When he saw color in her face, he went for the papers and threw them on the bed. He grabbed her hand and forced a pen into it. 'Sign them!'

The cotton was a deep red, but there was no blood dripping from it. When Felicia tried to speak, her words were garbled. 'You can have the money.'

'Good! Sign.'

'Only in person.'

'You're still playing me!' he hissed.

'I'm not. Show me Jesús.'

'Why should I do anything for you?'

'Please…'

Maybe she'd sign the goddamn papers if she saw Jesús. He fetched the camcorder from the living room and set it up on the massive night table. 'Alright.'

Felicia began to choke on tears when the desperate face of Jesús appeared.

'That's enough. He'll be home as soon as you sign these. Do you think I'd be so stupid as to whack a member of your family? Come on, Felicia. Put your head back – you'll start bleeding again.'

Once she had come upon her father and her brother when they had not been aware of her presence. *Witnesses are like old injuries. They both come back to haunt you.* Felicia stopped gasping, but she made no attempt to stem the flow of tears. Jesús was dead – she knew that now. She had to worry about herself. 'I'll sign the papers in front of my advisor tomorrow.' Her words came out slowly, reluctantly.

Ponytail made his call. He grimaced as he punched in the number. His simple plan had gone to shit! *Dispose of Felicia and Carlos in the suite. Bury Jesús. Diego and the cops hunt him down for the murders, and we get the jump-start on them both.* Now he'd be spending the night in the suite and every minute was a risk for him. Dark veins in his neck bulged. He couldn't kill the bitch. He needed her tomorrow. The expensive tile seemed to fissure beneath his feet. Panic struck, but he rallied.

CHAPTER TEN

LILA WAS UPSET, but 88 years had not dulled her anten-
nae. The second sketch she drew was better than the
first. Her technique was improving. At the moment she
was on the phone with her son Jake, a San Diego
attorney.

He was signalling to his wife Carol, a familiar code.
Mom is off on some tangent! 'Mother, stop for a second. I
know who Carlos is. I met him a few months ago. Now
you're telling me he's a petty thief who's stolen from all
of you and *he* might need your help.'

'I've forgiven Carlos and I'm not certain he does need
help. He hasn't asked me for anything. I do know that
we would be lost without him. He's like another hand
for us.'

'There are wonderful places out here, Mother. Why
won't you consider a change? Aaron and I worry about
you.'

'If that were true, son, I'd see you a lot more often.'

'That's not fair, Mother. I have a busy practice.'

'My friends, the ones still breathing and a few of the
dead, are my ties, my community. I can't leave.'

'Your sons and grandchildren are here. We're family.'

'Jake, I didn't call to argue. You're all too busy out
there, and I understand that. I simply refuse to be an old
lady waiting for family obliged to visit me. I was hoping
you might help if Carlos *is* in trouble.'

When will Mother act her age? Miss Marple wasn't 88!
What frightened Jake most was that his mother did not
exaggerate, and her mind was as keen as a shark's tooth.
'Mother, stay away from Carlos. He might have stolen
from someone else or incurred a huge debt you know
nothing about. I want your word. Mother, I have to sleep

tonight. I need to know you're not putting yourself in harm's way. Does he have the combination to your suite?'

'I shouldn't have called.'

'That's not your word. It's no answer at all. Miami can be a crazy place. I shouldn't have to caution my mother about its dangers. I don't want you anywhere near Carlos. Just this once, please listen to me.'

'Even with my bad ear, I hear you. Good night, son.'

'Mother!'

Jake bristled at his mother's continuing ability to grab the last word. 'Why is she still driving me crazy? I'm almost 61. When does it stop?'

'She's Jewish. It doesn't.' Carol laughed but stopped as soon as she saw the concern. 'She's as tough as a 'gator.'

'I should have insisted she relocate. I'll call Abby. Mom likes her. Perhaps she'll listen to her. My hearing's tomorrow. I can't fly down to Miami right now.' Jake went hunting for the cigar he'd given up four days earlier. 'You get a kick out of my mother, but I don't have the time to watchdog her. When I try to reason with her, I hit a wall.'

'Lila's more than capable of taking care of herself. She puts us both to shame. Don't irritate your ulcer.'

'You conveniently forget her age.'

'Isn't she still line-dancing, Jake?'

'Give me a break. This is serious.'

'Call Abby or fly down.'

'I may do both.'

🌴

As the trio walked back from Tony's, Carmen felt she had to say something to Mike. 'Do you forgive me for making us a threesome? I promise I'll think next time.'

'Truth is I may have some late nights. You're good

company for Caitlin. There's a real character here, doesn't shut up. I'll introduce you.' When they were inside the Trump, Mike spotted him. 'Follow me. Carlos, I'd like you to meet the women in my life.'

Carlos was waxen. His face cracked as he turned. When he spoke, he was betrayed by a wave of nerves. 'Good evening.'

Mike took a better look at Carlos. 'Are you ill?'

'I am tired, sir.'

Mike recalled the dead-weight fatigue and fear he'd felt at Harvard before his finals. Carlos wasn't tired, he was frightened. He saw the terror in his eyes. It struck Mike then that the double had been very close to Carlos. 'Sleep well tonight then,' he said, backing off.

As they walked away, Mike said, 'Carlos is like a goodwill ambassador at the condo. I couldn't shut him up the day I met him. In fact, that husband or his twin passing for him was standing behind Carlos the day I saw him. I'm telling you both, there is something going on here. This bump hasn't fried my head.'

Caitlin and Carmen had cavalierly risked their lives the last time they were in Miami and lived to regret it. This time around, they wanted to survive Sun City.

'Don't go looking for trouble. If there is a problem, it doesn't concern us. This Carlos could be upset for any number of reasons. You've been through an ordeal, so take your own advice, Mike. Get a good night's sleep. Whatever time we have together, I want to make it good, for you and for me.' Caitlin was adamant.

🌴

Carlos felt he was breaking. He used the desk phone, wary of the new cell. 'José, give me a minute; I have to call Maria. Problems, you understand.' As soon as José reluctantly moved away, he called Maria.

'I have been so worried, Carlos.'

'We have no time for worry. I cannot explain what has happened. You and Perdita are not safe. The man who threatens us has my phone with all the numbers.'

Maria's wail wounded him.

'There is no time for tears. For your safety, you must leave again and stay with Isabel Montamores. Tell her it is a very serious emergency. Do not answer any phone calls tonight. None! You must leave as soon as you reach her. Do not tell your parents where you are going. They cannot know. Your lives now depend on secrecy. I love you, Maria. I do not know what will happen. My family is my life.'

'Carlos?'

But Carlos could not speak another word. He remembered then what Lila had said, something about resources. Certainly, she could offer money. Should he take what she'd give him and run to Maria? What if the backup men outside saw him? Yellow sweat seeped through his gold-beaded white jacket. Carlos did have the combination to the Alvarez suite…

🌴

Daisy was not married to Ponytail although that ruse had worked for some of their scams. In fact, Daisy was Elizabeth Hoyle. From sixteen on, she'd hated that name. She'd run away from Jefferson City because she had failed her final year. She wasn't about to hunker down and repeat it. Elizabeth came to Miami. She existed one level above the fringe dwellers who lived on the streets and she waitressed in fast-food joints, sharing rooms with other waitresses in cheap rooms that cost her as little as $40 a week. Better times began when Ponytail ordered two dogs with the works and a chocolate shake. He'd come on to her, and the rest was history. She told him she was just Daisy, like Madonna. She had no past or last name. He began calling her 'my little throwaway.'

For the next four years, they'd tag-teamed one scam or another, until the big score, until tonight. That wasn't really true either. For her, the score went sour when Jesús was snuffed. Talking about murder was okay by her. Doing Jesús was something else. Daisy knew that night she'd never forget the creaking chair in the garage or stuffing Jesús into the freezer. Complicit, that's what she was thinking about too as she sat in the car. She had a plan of her own. After Ponytail's call about the glitch at the Trump, Daisy started up the Jag and drove back to their place. Avoiding the freezer, she packed, lifted the carpet in the bathroom, removed a tile and took $4,100. For the next half-hour, she wiped every surface, threw cleanser into the tub and sinks, tweezed hair from the drains, threw the vacuum cleaner and all the dishes into a dumpster across the street, locked the doors and drove north to Tallahassee. Daisy changed the plates on her car. Ponytail had taught her well. The IDs would come in handy. Her heart was pounding in her chest when the cell rang. Daisy's front wheel caught the sandy shoulder of the road before she was able to right the Jag.

'Go home, babe, get some rest. How come I hear so much traffic?'

'Collins.'

'Be back tomorrow by nine.'

Daisy was approaching the highway when she began to think of what Ponytail would do to her if he tracked her down. She'd seen him take a hammer to a melon to prove a point. He knew all their aliases. What if he reported the Jag as stolen? What if he blew out her knees like he'd threatened to do if she ever left him? The package in the freezer drove her on. Ponytail had told Daisy that Florida was a death penalty state.

She began to count strip malls. At the tenth, she turned in, ditched the Jag at the far end of the mall under a eucalyptus tree and caught a cab to a Greyhound terminal. She looked over her shoulder as she stepped onto a bus. *I shouldn't have taken all the money.* For the next two hours, waves of nausea sent her running to the bathroom at the back of the bus. Her panic fired up. *What if Ponytail pulls it off and has ten million waiting for him? Do I have time to get back?*

🌴

Carlos was about to step into the OAW elevator when the new cell vibrated in his hand. He felt a cinch tighten around his neck. 'Yes?'

'What time do you finish?'

'Around eleven.'

Ponytail called Carlos on an ace he wasn't holding. 'We know you've moved Maria and the little one. I may need you tonight.'

'You said all I had…' The line went dead. He dared not think of what was happening in the Alvarez suite because he was part of it now. Carlos stepped away from the elevator. *He knows!* The lining of his mouth dried up. At the front door, the two private security cops were on their rounds. They wore guns. Carlos had to make a move. He eyed the OAW elevator.

🌴

CHAPTER ELEVEN

PONYTAIL WENT TO the bar for ice. Felicia had to look a hell of a lot better than she did now. His stomach twisted as he thought of blowback from the family and the needle from the state. *There's nowhere to hide.* That's what Felicia had warned. These thoughts evaporated when he found the ice. *Wow! This is what it means to be among the counted.* In one silver bucket, the ice was crushed; in the next, shaped like palm trees; in the last, small balls. *Probably Evian water.* He scooped the crushed ice into a towel and brought it to Felicia.

For her, the whole scene was still unreal. She watched the dark-complected Hispanic with jet-black hair. Lethargy had replaced her resolve. The cotton felt like boulders inside her nose – her cheek throbbed. Her throat was parched from breathing through her mouth. Her scalp was hot.

'This will help.' Ponytail handed Felicia the towel. 'Don't move. I'll take out the cotton. The blood has dried around your nose, so the bleeding's stopped.'

Her stomach turned as lumpy red cotton came out of her nose. She blinked back tears. Her lips thinned.

'I'll make us something to eat. I need a drink – one will do you good as well. It will be a long night.' Ponytail reached into his pants pocket and took out the vial of chloral hydrate. With his back turned, he poured it all into the crystal tumbler before he popped the champagne cork.

'I'm not thirsty. I need a warm facecloth to clean up.' What Felicia wanted was a hot shower, cleansing her, reviving her. She knew enough not to ask.

'Have a toast with me first that we both get out of this!' He put the glass in her hand and reached for his.

'Survival!'

'I doubt either one of us will survive.'

Ponytail blanched. 'Why are you so negative? You can make this work.'

'You remind me of Jesús.'

'Obviously.' The bitch should be more frightened.

'In other ways. Jesús is after my money too. He's taking it more slowly, that's all.'

'Do you want him back?'

'Should I?'

What the hell is wrong with this woman? 'Do you care at all about him?'

'The appointment today was for his million-dollar yacht.'

'You have the money.'

'Less than the ten you want. Jesús chose this condo. We paid two million for it a year ago. Now, all it's worth is one point four. In one year, he's spent close to another million. Jesús decided we needed to buy this condo in a market downturn. How much should I care about him? The only difference between the two of you is that you want it all at once.'

'I can persuade Jesús to leave. Toast your freedom, then! It will take the edge off for both of us.'

'Is he still alive? I see you're wearing his watch.'

Ponytail's arm tensed as he admired the timepiece. 'A small donation. Of course, he's still with us. I need him alive until...'

'Until the money is transferred?'

'I'm asking you again, have a drink with me.'

Felicia eyed the champagne.

'It won't kill you. If I wanted that, you'd be dead. Drink it all,' Ponytail said softly.

Felicia knew he needed her alive, so she drank the champagne. It mixed with the taste of blood.

Ponytail drank his. 'Why did you leave the family? You had protection, money, everything.'

Felicia smiled tentatively. Even with the welt on her cheek, she was quite beautiful. 'I wanted to get away from the life after my grandfather left. I thought I could live in peace.' Felicia had eaten little and the drug began to work. Her eyes opened and closed. Her head lolled to one side.

'Didn't you realize you would be a target?' Ponytail did not expect an answer.

'We are pro...' Felicia was fast asleep. She wasn't about to play her ace tonight.

Ponytail went for more sheets and rolled them into cords. When he re-entered the room, heat rose in his groin. He dropped the sheets. His breath was rapid and hoarse.

Felicia opened her eyes and mumbled a single word. 'Please...'

A rush of shame and horror swept over him. For all his failings, rape remained abhorrent to him. He bent down and grabbed the sheets and bound Felicia with them. He did not want to injure her further, at least not before the meeting at the bank. The first item on his agenda was collecting the phones. He found her Blackberry and cell in her purse. He also pocketed the bills. Next, he went looking in Jesús's walk-in closet. He chose carefully. Once he'd showered and shaved, he repacked his briefcase and sat in the chair across from Felicia. He'd allow himself only an hour or two of sleep. For a second, watching her repose, Ponytail wished that life had been different for him. Jesús was his first major. Felicia's presence filled the room. Ponytail watched her breasts rise and fall, rise and fall. His hand went down to his crotch.

Though it was well before eleven, Ponytail was tired. He'd fallen asleep for less than ten minutes when he woke shuddering. *What if the financial advisor has met Jesús?* Passing for Jesús from a short distance was one thing. *Will she know him? It's her money. Has the advisor looked that closely at Jesús?* Women took him in; they must have done the same for Jesús. Could he carry the *Herald*? Use it as a blind as he observed the transaction? Ponytail got up and went to look for rum. Just one stiff rum – he needed to be alert today. He drained the glass while standing over Felicia. He liked her; he even had the notion to let her live, but how could he?

That night, Mike took Caitlin and Carmen along the beach, recounting his bravery and narrow escape. The women listened, almost enthralled. 'I'm going on too much, right?'

'I should be taking notes.' Her words came out before she thought of them. They rang shallow in her ears and not funny at all.

Mike wrestled Caitlin to the sand. 'You could have lost me. Forget the wisecracks.'

'You were in pretty good hands when we found you that night,' Caitlin shot back, trying to break his hold. 'You're still here though and strong as a bull.'

'So that's it! You're jealous. I'm not going to feel guilty that a beautiful woman helped me.' Mike tried to make Caitlin laugh, without success. It was obvious she was ticked.

'You've made your point, Mike.'

'Let's head back to the suite.' Carmen felt an argument coming on.

'Carmen's right. Let's call it a night.' And they did. Felicia was becoming an irritant and a genuine worry for Caitlin.

CHAPTER TWELVE

JAKE DIALED HIS mother's line, unnerved by their conversation. 'Hello, Mother. I hope I didn't wake you.'

'You know I don't sleep well, so I'm generally up very late. When I was raising you and Aaron, I could never get enough sleep. Now that I have the whole night to myself, sleep is in retreat.'

'Something to look forward to.'

'Your father could sleep through a hurricane.'

'But he's not with the living anymore.'

'Do you recall the day you and I went shelling on the beach?' Lila didn't want to think of Carlos.

'I kept mine in a cup. When I reached in for one to show you, the shells moved. I'd collected snails.'

They both laughed.

'You know why I'm calling?'

'To scold me into submission.'

'I will come down in a day or two, depending on court.'

'I should scare you more often, Jake.'

'Be good till I arrive.'

'Someone's at the door.'

'Mom, check to see who it is before you open it!'

'It's Margaret come to tell me how Sophie cheated at poker tonight.'

'Mom, don't…'

'I'll see you soon.' Lila hung up the phone and opened the door, but it wasn't Margaret standing there. She tried to close it, but Carlos held it open.

'Mrs. Katz, you said I could talk to you.'

'It's late, Carlos.' Lila stepped forward, trying to push the door closed. Jake's words rang in her ears. Lila pushed harder. She simply would not be sandbagged by Carlos.

Carlos resisted by stepping inside. 'I need your help, Mrs. Katz.'

She wanted to help Carlos, but not while being physically pressured like this. Fear, lightly defined, began its tremble in her knees and shook its way to her stomach. She wished now that she had her cane with her as a weapon and support. 'Carlos, friends do not take advantage of one another. Please leave. We can speak tomorrow.' Lila extended her arm, pointing to the door. Her own safety was more important than the man she'd seen in the lobby with Carlos.

Carlos stepped deeper into the suite before he turned to her. 'My family is in great danger. I need money.' His cheeks flared red. 'You must help me! I can trust no one else.' He stepped towards Lila, invading her space. 'You have so much money.' His breathing raced as he spoke.

Lila wavered until the last sentence before her back grew rigid and hot.

Outside the sky darkened; the ocean was almost black. The lights of a cruise ship flickered. On the oceanfront, the hiss of traffic on Collins was silenced by the water.

'Leave the door open,' Lila ordered. She needed to sit down.

Carlos stepped aside as she passed him, but he advanced and stood in front of her after she was seated. Lila smelled cologne and sweat. Sitting had made her vulnerable. Her voice was urgent in its plea. 'You should call the police, Carlos. I forgave you for stealing from us. I don't feel that I should give you money until you tell me what has happened.' As soon as she had spoken, Lila regretted her words. She did not want to be pulled under with Carlos, especially if he had incurred debts as Jake had suggested.

'If I told you everything, you too would be in great danger.'

'Is it the man I sketched for you, the man in the lobby today? Is he frightening you? Can you tell me that?'

'I must tell you nothing.'

The instant shock contorting his face told Lila that the look-alike was terrorizing Carlos. The images back at the track and his demeanor in the lobby came into full focus. Carlos wasn't afraid of her. He was already shaking before she reached him.

'I need money Mrs. Katz, for my family, not for me.' He stepped inches closer to Lila.

'Lila! Tonight was the night. Esther caught Sophie red-handed!' Margaret stopped as soon as she saw Carlos at Lila's door. Mops had run to him and was jumping at his leg. 'Heavens, are you alright? If you needed help, Lila, you had only to call me. What's wrong?'

Mops too had sensed trouble and was growling as best he could.

'Leave Lila to me, Carlos. We'll see you tomorrow.'

His cell rang; he reached into his pocket, but didn't take it out. 'I must go.' He hurried from the room and took out his cell. 'Yes?'

'Make sure you're on duty tomorrow morning. I may need you. Remember, you opened the door to this suite. We're partners. Don't share what you know with anyone. Lives depend on you. Are you listening?'

'Yes.'

As soon as Carlos was out of earshot, Margaret inquired. 'Lila, what was Carlos doing here? He's a beautiful young man, but you're 88!'

'Margaret! I always believed you were sane.'

'You were both very intense when I walked in here. What *were* you both up to? But first, let me tell you about Sophie's downfall, even though you don't give a fiddle.'

Ponytail put the drink down and went for his flip pad. Before the morning, he'd have to come up with a revamp of his plan. If it had gone off today, he'd almost be in Toronto by now. He slouched in the chair – his optimism had taken a hit. He stared down at the pad; his mouth was open, set in a thinking pattern. *She has to call for an appointment. I gotta make sure the advisor comes out from behind the desk, away from the alarms. What if Felicia won't leave with me? Jesús is not working well. Gotta come up with something before the call. Damn!*

He dialed Daisy but got no answer. *I told her to lay off the sugar. She'd better not be snorting.* Ponytail rapped his temple with his fist. *She'd better fucking be here! What do I do with Carlos? Could get him up here, take back the cash, sort him out here and throw suspicion off myself.*

🌴

Carlos hovered behind the desk and watched the clock. What if Mrs. Katz called the police? He began to crack his knuckles. His bones popped like seaweed. He called Maria, using the desk phone, but there was no answer. For a second, he'd forgotten he told her not to answer calls from the Trump. Deep in his pocket, he began to finger the envelope of cash. Could he make it to Little Havana before the man discovered he was gone? What if he called the desk, checking up on him? Looking around the sumptuous lobby, Carlos felt his life here was over, one way or another. He had broken trust with Mrs. Katz. In time, if he survived tonight with Maria and Perdita, word would spread around the Trump from the OAW women. Could he risk calling Mrs. Katz, trying to explain, keeping her quiet? Did he have time after eleven? He knew her combination.

🌴

After Margaret had gone, Lila sat down, in the middle of her white sofa. Her heart raced. Jake may have been right. She should stay away from Carlos. She knew then that he was afraid for his life. To distract herself, she leaned forward, picked up the *Herald*, put the first sections aside and went directly to the Local News section. Another helicopter had gone down in one of the intra-coastal canals. The 7-year-old murder case of a child was to be reopened. Another home invasion…

Lila put the paper down. *Nothing but bad news.* She closed her eyes. The *Herald* triggered the idea. *Another home invasion…* The look-alike came to mind. If Carlos wasn't in debt as Jake had suggested, could it possibly be a home invasion at the Trump? Lila could almost hear her brain ticking, a brain good at solving problems. Carlos had access to the Trump – the look-alike could pass for Jesús Alvarez. Security cameras in the Trump wouldn't pick up anyone out of the ordinary if the look-alike invaded a condo with Carlos's help. Lila knew Carlos was not a willing participant. The man was visibly terrified. The tenants were discreet, but they all knew Felicia Alvarez and stories of her ill-gotten wealth. There must be money locked away in that suite. Lila began to take deep breaths.

Her hands trembled as she reached for her phone and tapped the memory number for security. *Jake told me not to get involved, but I cannot stand by and do nothing, even if I'm wrong.* Lila knew the staff got a small kick out of Sophie and Esther, but they were never taken seriously. *The two old crows on OAW.* She'd heard that one day, and Lila knew that once the young ones thought of you that way, you ceased to exist. *I don't want to be an old fool. But I won't be able to live with myself if I sit idly by and do nothing.* Folding the paper with the phone number, Lila had a better idea. *Tony and Franco will be here on their rounds. I'll speak directly to them and ask them to check on Jesús and Felicia. I'll even play the whole thing down. How can that hurt Carlos?*

Lila took her cane, though she hated the thought of using it, and walked in small measured steps to the OAW elevator. A bone on the top of her hand began to ache. The pain was sharp when she leaned on the cane. *Something new to add!* She transferred the cane to the other hand. A taupe sofa near the doors was very inviting, but Lila knew if she sat down, she'd need help getting back up. At night, every 88-year-old bone ached, a tenacious symphony of pain that pinched the crisscross lines in her face.

As best he could, Carlos eyed security and tracked them. When he saw Tony open his cell, Carlos froze. The quiet, safe, contained life he had here began to crack when he saw Tony and Franco walk briskly to the OAW elevator.

Both men liked Lila, liked even better the tips she often gave them. Smiling when they saw her, Tony asked, 'What's up, Mrs. Katz?'

'Tony, it's probably nothing, but I heard that there was some kind of commotion in the Alvarez suite. It may be a silly rumor that I have ninth-hand. I've grown fond of them both, Felicia mostly. Would you knock on their door and do one of your special routine checks? You could say that we've had another short power failure.'

'You're a sly one, Mrs. Katz.'

Lila handed Tony three twenties which he palmed like a dealer. 'You really shouldn't! We do quite well as it is, with our pension and all.'

'I won't be in your debt,' Lila smiled.

'Will do, right now, before eleven. I'll get back to you. How's that?'

'Appreciated.'

The men headed to the Alvarez floor. 'What do you think?'

'Always looking for that career bump, Tony; could be anywhere.'

At the Alvarez suite, Tony knocked twice, good and loud. These men were retired cops double-dipping with this security work.

Ponytail switched on the video intercom. *Fuck!* He ran to his briefcase for the blade. He stood at the foot of the bed. She hadn't moved. What if she was faking and screamed when he opened the door? At the side of the bed, he shoved Felicia's shoulders, nothing. Taping her mouth was risky. Her breathing was shallow from the drug. He ran to the door when he heard the second knock and wiped the sweat from his face before he opened it slightly. He kept his hand on the blade behind his back. Another show! 'What's the problem?'

Tony and Franco took in Ponytail before Tony answered. 'Annoying power failures. Are you and your wife alright?'

'As you can see, we have power. Felicia's in bed. It's late to be knocking.'

'Trying to help. I see you don't need it.' The men left without further inquiry.

'Thanks anyway.' Ponytail shut the door, jammed the blade into his pocket and fell into the nearest chair. *Carlos! Fuck!*

'What do you think?' Franco wanted to know.

'Nothing I could see. From where I stood, the suite was in order. Alvarez was never friendly. No change tonight.'

'I'll call Mrs. Katz and tell her all's well.'

🌴

On the way back to her suite, Lila heard Sophie

crying. Her door was open. There she sat on her Queen
Anne wing chair, dropping tears on Mischa, Israel and
Little Caesar, who sat reluctantly on her lap. When
Sophie saw Lila, she looked up with black mascara
pooling under her eyes and running down her cheeks. 'I
suppose you've heard.'

'If you're crying because Esther caught you cheating,
don't! We all know you cheat – you've been doing it for
a year.' Sophie tried to mount a weak protest, but Lila
waved that off. 'Leave that extra deck at home on poker
night.'

'I like to win,' Sophie mumbled unabashedly.

'Don't we all! You'll have to behave if you want to get
back in with the *yentas*. You might even win fairly.
Wouldn't that be a treat, something to shoot for? Stop
crying and get to bed. Just a second, that's my phone. I
have to go.'

Back in her living room, Lila leaned close to the
phone to read the ID and saw that Carlos was calling.
'Did you send security to the Alvarez suite, Mrs. Katz?'
he asked abruptly, his voice rising with disbelief.

Lila was flustered for a few seconds but she regained
her composure. 'I didn't mention you. Your family is safe.
Carlos. Anyway, security found no disturbance.'

He felt a small relief, but the hairs on the length of his
arms bristled. *Why did you do that? How could you know?*
There was an anxious silence before he spoke. Because
he was desperate, he couldn't berate her. 'I apologize for
the intrusion tonight. I need help. I thought of you.' His
words were chopped and clipped with fright.

'You mean a great deal to me, Carlos, but if you have
gotten yourself into trouble with money…'

Carlos was about to say *I have done nothing wrong*, but
that wasn't true. He hung up the desk phone.

'Carlos? Carlos?' Lila reached for the side of the

couch and eased herself onto the cushion. Her head drooped. Carlos's world had intruded into hers and that frightened her. Jake had unsettled her as well. It was so much easier to like people, be very fond of them really, as long as they remained preconceived images. Perhaps, Lila thought, perhaps that was the reason she had not relocated to the West Coast. She might not like her family if she got to know them and they her. Lila laughed ruefully. *I've appreciated some of my friends better after they died.*

She called the desk again, but Carlos was not there. Tears filled her eyes, as much for Carlos as for herself. She was letting him down, and that was not a good feeling. Lila regained her composure, called the desk again and said she must see Carlos before he left for the night. It was an emergency of sorts. With some pain, Lila got up and walked slowly to her grill in the kitchen. It was something she never used because it was a bank. From it, she took all $5,000 she kept in reserve, hundreds and fifties. Standing was hard at this time of night. A small spasm was knifing its way up the left side of her back.

Another thought came to mind, quite apart from Carlos. Was she letting her sons down as well? Had she become a disappointment to her boys because she was living too long? Was she a bother, even so far away? Self-pity was not a dialogue Lila enjoyed – she ended it with a truth. *Well, boys, the revenge of Jewish mothers is longevity. I'm still in the tunnel of life. The light at the end is dimmed by the years, that's all.*

Perhaps Carlos wouldn't come. She didn't dare get ready for bed, so she waited for him.

Inside the stairwell, Carlos had his hand on the railing. He had a decision to make, and three minutes to make it. In his own clothes and a Dolphins' cap, he began to run up the stairs, trying to dodge the cameras, using his hat as protection. Being spotted here after his shift would be disastrous. On the 11th floor he heard his beeper. Panting and cramping in his thigh muscles, he stopped, sat on the stairs and tried to rub out the cramps before he called the office. 'What is it? I'm off duty in two minutes.'

'Katz wants to see you, small emergency. Get up there, golden boy.' James Tellett, the lone anglo on desk staff, knew about the perks Carlos pulled in every day with his messenger service and outings. *Fuck him with being off the clock! What kind of an asshole works from seven to eleven five days a week?*

His plan of surprising the man in the Alvarez suite fell apart. Carlos was relieved. What if Katz had security with her? He called the desk. 'Jamie, doesn't she want security?'

'Let me check with them. Stay on the line.'

Carlos could hear Jamie.

'They're on 19. You're out of luck. Snap to it, Carlos!'

She's alone. When he reached Katz's door, he knocked gently and backed up three steps. He knocked again more loudly and hopped back as Lila opened the door. She held out an envelope with a wad of bills that he could see because the package wasn't sealed. 'Take this.' His eyes had been reduced to dark marbles; his face seemed gaunt. Lila detected a look of resignation, helplessness. 'I don't want to know more, but I'm keeping the sketch I made for myself.'

'Thank you, Mrs. Katz.' Carlos bowed with the money in his hand.

Lila closed her door. Something had changed in the way Lila saw Carlos.

CHAPTER THIRTEEN

THE TWO HOURS of sleep Ponytail had counted on getting didn't happen. After security's visit, waves of panic kept him stiff and sweating. Around five, he stood over Felicia and gave her another shove. *She might as well be dead.* He hadn't walked two steps from the bed when he scurried back. *What if she is?* He got onto the bed and laid his palm an inch from her nose. Her breath was thin, almost imperceptible. *This can't be for nothing!*

He slapped her on both cheeks once, then again, which drew a slight moan. Ponytail rolled his arm under Felicia and lifted her off the bed. Throwing one limp arm over his shoulder, he grabbed her side with the other. He dragged her like a corpse across the floor. 'Wake up, Felicia! Wake up!' In a few minutes, he let her flop on the nearest couch. In the kitchen, he hastily made strong coffee. He looked under the sink for something with ammonia, tossing out the cleansers as he searched. *Fuck!* On the dining room table he found long wooden matches. He quickly lit all of them and blew them out beside Felicia. He put the black tips under her nose while the grey mist was still rising. Her head fell back and she began to choke.

He got her back up and dragged her along. 'Wake up or you'll die.' One of her eyes opened. Her head was on his shoulder. Her eye was confused and she tried to close it. 'No you don't! Stay with me Felicia.' Dragging her into the spacious bathroom, he ran a cold shower and lifted her into it. Shocked, she began to flail with both her arms and legs. Ponytail bear-hugged her and kept her under the spray until they were both shivering. 'Enough!' He could tell by the sheer hatred in her eyes that she was awake. 'What you need is coffee and food.

I'll take care of both.' He tore the duvet from the bed, wound it around her and sat her in a chair where she continued to shiver, approaching shock. He went back to her and shook her. 'Get control of yourself. You'll stop shaking with food. Relax.'

He had hot coffee and toast with honey ready in no time. Dripping wet, he too began to shiver and poured himself a cup. While Felicia tried to eat, he towelled off and went looking for more clothes, dragging her into the room with him. He saw her eyes close. 'You can't fall asleep again. He shook her once more. Felicia's head bobbed from one side to another. He got her up walking. The corners of her mouth were turned down. When he sat her back on a chair, he knelt in front of her and slapped both cheeks till she moaned angrily. 'Don't fall asleep,' he shouted in her face. Ponytail forced pieces of toast into her mouth. She ate it mechanically. 'Keep at it!'

As she chewed, he noticed the muscles in her cheeks begin to work normally, but there remained a pale cast to her face. His own hand shook as he shaved and he cut himself twice on the side of his neck. What if she died? He heard his own breath, fast and desperate. It was almost six. In the next three hours, Felicia Alvarez had to sober up and speak clearly when they got to the bank. It was then he noticed she hadn't said a word.

Although Felicia felt there was cotton behind her eyes and stuffed in her head, she was thinking clearly. Outside her brain, her body felt like sand. The piece of toast in her hand felt like a block of cement. When she tried to raise her leg, it was sluggish and heavy. Panic darted to the corners of her brain. Felicia knew she'd die if she couldn't stand – he'd smother her here. The toast cut into her gums and the roof of her mouth. The coffee stung her tongue and throat. When she tasted blood in her mouth, she shook her head to get rid of the drug haze. To survive, Felicia knew she had to get outside the suite.

Ponytail swore when he saw the blood on her lip. 'Don't screw with me! Can't you even eat toast? Finish that and drink up. Then I'll help you clean yourself up.'

'I'mmm trinnn.'

The muscles in his jaw bulged as he came to her side. Grabbing her middle finger, he pushed it back until she screamed. 'Nothing like pain to clear a head! I should know. My father often got my attention that way.'

Felicia's face locked into a seething resentment as she rubbed her finger. Inside, she swelled with a fierce will to live. Outside the suite, she'd manoeuvre into a position where she could cry out, perhaps even run from him. That was the private goal she set. To achieve it, she'd pretend to be weaker than she was. When his attention was elsewhere, Felicia moved her legs up and down and rubbed circulation back into them.

From the patio, Ponytail saw that the early morning clouds had begun to pull apart. Mist was rising on the water. 'It's going to be a good day! Repeat that. Speaking will clear your head. Finish the coffee; I want another cup in you. Don't forget the toast.'

'Ithss gointho be a goo da.'

'Not bad. Try again, louder.'

The lessons, as Ponytail walked her back and forth, went on until he could understand her. Her throat was no longer dry. In her head, a plan formed. By eight-thirty, she was dressed and had done good work with her make-up. Her cheek was swollen, but her long hair covered much of it. Her eyes were yellow and glassy. Visine helped.

It was Ponytail who felt the squeeze of alarm when he called Daisy. 'Where the hell is she?' He spoke into his closed fist to keep Felicia in the dark. *Is she in traffic? She's the only bitch I know who won't pick up her cell in traffic.* He'd try again at nine. That was the set time to be out front.

'I want the name of your bank. I'll make the call. Your voice is still slurred. By the time we have our sit-down at the bank, you should be okay.' Without sleep, he was buzzed and jumpy as he went through a mental review of his plan in linear fashion. *That bitch better be there!*

For the next little while, they watched and took measure of one another. 'Once the transfer is made and you're free, remember that I didn't take advantage of you last night. If you follow my instructions, I won't kill you. Your family is the reason for that. This is a simple heist. No one needs to die. When the transfer is made, leave the bank with me. Jesús will be close by. He can even have the Ferrari. We'll be long gone.'

Felicia listened to his lies and nodded meekly.

🌴

Earlier that night, Carlos did not go near the Alvarez suite to confront the man after he'd received the $5,000 from Lila. Driving to Little Havana was out of the question. He might be followed; it had to appear he was going home. The small wooden house was dark when he got there, but he saw nothing suspicious on the street. Once his door was locked, he was about to call Manuel's neighbor when he'd found their number, but he saw it was almost midnight. Carlos ripped the number to shreds and fell on their hide-a-bed. In his pocket, he grabbed the money and held on to it. He was certain the man was not acting alone. They knew the family had moved. If he went to them, they might all die. After all, what did his family matter to anyone? Carlos went to the bathroom, showered and shaved, found adhesive and taped the money to the inside of his thighs.

Was this the punishment for his thefts? Places like the Trump would not come his way again with the problems that multimillion-dollar condos were facing. Their money woes were often on the news. As soon as he set the alarm, Carlos fell asleep.

In a few hours, he would see the man. He'd ordered Carlos to be on duty, and Carlos was too weary for a plan.

CHAPTER FOURTEEN

MIKE WOKE EARLY, thinking about the impression he wanted to make in Miami. Caitlin was curled up beside him with her hand under her chin. He ran his fingers softly through her hair, and she nudged in closer. Without a headache, he felt better, more alert. Scooping his arm under her, he lifted Caitlin on top of him. When she opened her eyes, he saw again how startling her hazel eyes were with small slashes of green and blue in a sea of dazzling white. Mike could never recall their color because they changed with what she wore. Her head snuggled into the side of his neck. For all the passionate times, he loved this early, quiet warmth of Caitlin close to him best.

Of course, it was followed by an urgent need.

'How come your breasts are so perfect?' He was holding each in his hand and supporting her weight with his forearms before he let her fall on him and he took one in his mouth. In a familiar rhythm, they began to rock together, first gently, then with a fierceness that had begun with their first coupling. 'Well,' Caitlin whispered, 'you've recovered. You nervous about today? You can admit it,' she coaxed.

'They already like me.'

'Really like you, you mean?'

'Cut it out!'

'Alright, survivor. I'm going to stay in bed a while longer.'

'It's 9:30, Caitlin.'

'You jest!'

'I don't and I have to shower first.'

'That's okay. I'll go in and roust Carmen. We want to get to the festival before noon.'

🌴

There were days that Lila wanted to stay in bed to delay the stiff joint pain of osteoarthritis that worsened as the day went on. There were two items her age did not allow her, the first was long-term bonds, the second, sleep-ins. There were not enough days left for either of them. Much earlier, she'd made a decision. Once she was dressed and had eaten breakfast, Lila was going downstairs to see Carlos. After all, someone had to do something. Sophie, who was only 82, had called in Ramon, who was busy in her spacious kitchen making sweet rolls. She felt she'd have to buy her way back into the *yenta* group with sugar. The trio, Mischa, Little Caesar and Israel, were gnawing tiny bits of dough that would upset their stomachs. *You only live once*, Lila thought to herself. Margaret was busy brushing Mops. The early smokers were puffing away.

🌴

Daisy couldn't sleep. Her body was sticky and grimy – she hadn't taken a shower. Every suspicious noise had sent her running to the bathroom, cowering behind the door. Apart from thinking of Ponytail, another thought tore at her all night. What if she had just walked away from $10 million? She huddled on a soiled comforter that didn't live up to its name. The chips and soda were unopened. What she did know was that she was on her own now and back to humping trays in fast food joints.

🌴

Jake was able to reach Abby Wiseman before she left for the office in Aventura. 'Jake! Good to hear from you.'
'I need a favor.'
'Shoot!'

Jake recounted his mother's story. 'Mother can raise my blood pressure at the best of times, but I don't want anything to happen to her either. I've surrendered to the fact that Mother will never act her age.'

'Jake, you know that's not true. Lila is one of the sanest people I've ever met, young or old.'

'You know what I mean, Abby.'

On a daily basis, Abby spoke with family members who wanted their elderly parents quiet and out of their lives, even though they loved them. Abby was clearly on Lila's side. 'I'll run over there this morning and spend an hour with her. If she has discovered something important, I'll help her with that. You know she has a soft spot for Carlos.'

'He stole from them!'

'Jake, you're not around. Whatever he took I'm not condoning, but Carlos is a servant, friend, go-boy, flatterer when needed, and a shoulder. He's brought them into Little Havana, to the races, to good restaurants, all things the women couldn't do on their own. Most of all, he fills in for family.'

'Mother told me his life is in trouble. I don't want her involved. Is that unreasonable?'

'I'll drive over today as soon as I can re-arrange some appointments.'

'I wanted Mother out here with us. She didn't want to come.'

'Jake, I'll see her this morning.'

'I'll fly down today or tomorrow. Thanks for today, Abby.'

'Lila's a friend.'

🌴

Ponytail called Daisy at precisely nine o'clock.

Bleary-eyed, she watched the cell vibrate across the

night table. The tune it was playing was 'California Dreaming'. Grabbing the comforter around herself, she paced back and forth across the small motel room. When she heard the message, she fell on the bed. 'You'll pay for this. I'll hunt you down, bitch.' When the phone rang twice more, Daisy smashed it against the nearest wall and bruised her hand. On the bed, she rocked back and forth.

🌴

Before he made that call, Ponytail led Felicia into her bedroom. His heart was booming. No damn way he'd be a custody today, cop-talk for an arrest. No way was he about to tank either. He was on his own, without a car. With racked nerves, he made the adjustment. 'Felicia, I need the number of your bank and the manager of your portfolio.'

Felicia walked unsteadily into the sitting room, pressed a side panel on a protruding column, and it opened, revealing a safe. She ran the combination and opened it. When Ponytail saw the cash, he reached over her shoulder and took it. 'Must be what, five grand?'

She nodded and handed him a black leather binder. 'It's on the top. Richard Watts. He's in at ten.'

'Banking hours. There are a few changes. We'll need your car. Jesús had stomach problems. My partners are cleaning him up. You're edgy on your feet, so practice for a while.' No goddamn compromise; he was going through with the score. He had to think positive thoughts. A couple of things strengthened his determination. For all his scamming, he'd never been arrested. There was no record of him in the DMV or NCIC, the National Crime Index Computer. That was an accomplishment. Twice he'd been hauled in with a few hundred others on large company scams, but the cops had nailed and printed the owners, and released those they felt didn't understand they were scamming with warnings. Both times, he'd made certain he'd kept to the back of the long line. They ran his name, but nothing came of it.

Jesús was a different story. Neighbors knew him there. Packages had to be buried. He'd first planned to meet up with Carlos the day after the job. Now, that wasn't possible. Carlos was a witness. He watched Felicia walking her beat, checked his watch. Forty minutes till he made the bank call.

When he went looking for a robe, taking Felicia by the arm, Ponytail permitted himself to long for the ease of the plan that was now lost. The transfer would have been made from the room, Felicia done, packaged and stored in the bathroom, Carlos beside her and the a/c as cold as it could go to preserve the bodies and delay the death stench. Now he had to be alert to any contingency when he got Carlos to the room and he had to do him before ten.

'How many clothes does this man need, seven robes?'

'Jesús likes mirrors.'

'Your voice is much better.' Ponytail took a blue robe of the softest terrycloth he'd ever felt. *Good absorption.* 'I'm clumsy with food, especially fruit that you guys have plenty of. Don't want to spot my suit.' He brought the sides of the robe across his chest and tied the belt tightly. 'I have to put you in the bathroom. Private business. The less you hear, the better.' In the spacious room, he sat her down on the yellow cloth bench across the jacuzzi. Early on, he'd noted that all the doors had locks, like small safe rooms. *Some protection!* Both the intercom and the hand-held phone were disconnected. 'Stay here. I'll be back soon. Don't look for a makeshift weapon. I've cleared those out while you slept. Be patient.'

When the door was locked, he called Carlos.

CHAPTER FIFTEEN

'LILA?'

'Yes.'

'Abby. Happy I caught you. I'm close by. Can we visit a little?'

'Jake called you.'

'You're good!'

'I was just on my way to the lobby.'

'Wait for me, we'll go together.'

'I want to speak to Carlos.'

'Make me happy and wait till I get there.'

'You're more difficult than Jake.'

'Years of practice.'

Carlos occupied himself with desk work, allowing James to look after the door and elevators. He knew the call was coming and he wanted James back at the desk when he had to leave. That way, the manager wouldn't notice he was off his post. With no news of Maria and Perdita, he fidgeted and cleaned his nails with a plastic card. If only he hadn't stolen from the women... Mrs. Katz had forgiven him. Had he known she would, he... Carlos felt like the condemned. The noose was around his neck, and he was standing on the trapdoor. When the cell rang, he bowed his head and took the call.

'I need you up here.'

He shut his eyes. Carlos would not hurt Felicia or Jesús. He drew that line.

'You there?'

'Yes.'

'Finish off – one minute.'

'This is the end?' Carlos said, with the best imposing

tone he could muster.

'Once this is done, you're out.'

'I will come.' He would take no further risk with the lives of his family.

When Abby walked into the Trump, the elevator door to the Alvarez suite had closed seconds before.

Carlos didn't think of the cameras. He was busy praying, steeling himself. At the door, he blew into his fist before he knocked.

Ponytail opened it quickly, smiled and motioned Carlos to follow him into the second bedroom at the end, far from the main bathroom where he'd left Felicia. Carlos followed, balling his fists, waiting for the man to turn around. Both men had stepped inside the room when Ponytail turned and caught Carlos with an elbow to the jugular, the move he'd used with Jesús. Lunging for him before he fell, Ponytail dragged him to the ensuite bathroom. He knelt beside Carlos and withdrew the three-inch serrated knife from the pocket of the robe. He grabbed a towel from the rack, held it against Carlos's neck to absorb the spray, yanked his head back and slit the side of his throat. Jamming the towel against the wound, Ponytail crept backwards and hauled the comforter off the bed and rolled Carlos in it. When he saw the unnatural bulge inside both pant legs, he used the bloody knife to slit them. *What do you know – a freebie!* Bills that stuck to the tape, he left. Hoisting Carlos into the bath, he stuffed more towels around his neck because the blood stank. He turned the a/c on high. He washed his hands, locked the door, and left the robe behind. The one item he took was the knife, after he cleaned it in the sink.

He felt no after-burn – Ponytail was on cruise control. The only sign of panic was the last-second dash back to the bathroom and emptying out. It wasn't so much that he had no feeling; he was on borrowed time himself. If Felicia's brother caught up with him, he wouldn't go as quickly as these two morons. *I don't feel much different after doing Jesús and Carlos.* But he did. The tic under his eye was twitching. *Shit!* He clenched his teeth, cracked a molar and pushed the piece out with his tongue. *Shit!* His tongue caught on the broken tooth and it drew blood. *I need this!* How could he give a shit about some petty thief when he'd witnessed up close how easily these guys died? *No one counts – not even the rich.* Now he had his fucking tooth to worry about.

Ponytail was too far away, tight in his own plot, to hear Carlos moan. One had to be very close to catch it.

CHAPTER SIXTEEN

FELICIA HAD SCOURED the bathroom for something she might use to defend herself, but all she came up with was a toothbrush. The man had emptied most of the cosmetics and solvents, so she waited. Getting outside the suite was her only chance.

'Alright, let's make the call and tell the manager that we're on our way over. Ask him to sit with us and not behind his desk. I don't want him pressing any alarms. Are you listening?'

'Richard always sits with us.'

'Good.'

'Don't sabotage this! I have nothing to lose. If I have to run without the money, I'll kill you right there. Either way, your brother and his goons are coming after me. I know that. The small leeway I have is leaving you alive and getting you back with Jesús. And that's up to you.' He punched in the number. 'Richard Watts, please?'

'Good morning, Watts here.'

'Good morning. This is Jesús Alvarez. Felicia and I would like to see you briefly this morning. A wonderful opportunity has just come up for us.'

'I have a meeting in fifteen minutes.'

'Would you delay it for an hour? This is rather important. We apologize for the inconvenience.'

'I'm always available for preferred clients. I'll see you soon.'

'We both appreciate this…'

He hung up. 'We're on! Felicia, stay very close to me. Give me your car keys. Don't think of tossing them. Remember, I can kill you before you have any chance of escape. I didn't rape you and I don't want to kill you. Let's go.'

🌴

'You look good enough to eat. Carmen, come see this handsome guy.'

Carmen played along, oohing and aahing.

'Try to control yourselves!' Mike laughed.

'Good luck and stay away from water! Don't be nervous either.'

'You're talking to the king of cool.'

'Go, do good!'

'Such grammar! See you tonight.' Mike had one thing to check before he drove to the meeting in downtown Miami.

'Let's get dressed and hit the road ourselves, Carm. It's been three years. We loved Miami before we got stupid – we can love it again as tourists.'

🌴

Lila was at the elevator door on her floor when Abby got off. 'Humor me please, Abby. Come back down to the lobby. I must see Carlos. He said he had to work this morning.'

Abby could see that Lila tried to put up a good front by working on a smile that didn't succeed.

'I'm not an unbalanced old fossil.'

'Far from it. You're wily, determined and alert.'

'Guilty. Here we are.' Lila had her cane and the women walked slowly to the desk. 'James, good morning! I must speak with Carlos.'

'Last I saw, Mrs. Katz, he was getting into the 'L', the luxury elevator. I needed him down here twice. I've called him four times, but he didn't answer.'

'I *know* there is something wrong! I know it in my arthritic bones.' Lila gave her cane a good whack. 'Get security up to the Alvarez suite! There's no time to explain.'

'I can't just disturb them,' James replied, bristling at the order. 'We have strict rules.'

'Abby?'

'Wait a minute. Let me at least call the suite.' James glared at Abby. He waited for four rings. 'No one's there.'

'Please call security! You won't want to be responsible for any mishap, particularly when we're alerting you to it,' Abby advised.

'I don't know. The manager's in a meeting.'

'James,' Lila ordered, 'call security and go up with them. I will take full responsibility.'

James lost the staring match with Lila. It was his job after all. 'Alright, Mrs. Katz.' He buzzed the team, looked up the code in the manager's office in case there was trouble and gave it to Manuel and Greg. 'Guys, knock loudly twice; then go in to check. I'll get Tom to relieve me here and I'll go up myself. Don't hesitate – go in without me. Understood?'

'Roger.'

'How's that, Mrs. Katz?' Although he hated it, James knew the weight these old bags could throw around, and he wasn't their golden boy, although he had tried. 'Tom, I need you on the desk asap! In less! Possible emergency.' James was getting into it. He stood beside Abby Wiseman, waiting to join the others. When he saw Tom at the far end of the lobby, he motioned to him to the desk and made a beeline for the 'L.'

'Now, we wait,' Lila said.

🕯

CHAPTER SEVENTEEN

MIKE WENT HUNTING for the red Ferrari. He had a good idea of the parking level. It coincided with the condo floors, three to a level. He also figured wealth meant lobby level, first class. When he heard the garage elevator open, he didn't turn, but kept looking.

Felicia felt a dull pain in her side. She had hoped the elevator would stop for other passengers, but it hadn't. While Ponytail's tongue explored his broken tooth, he held her close as she led him to her Mercedes beside the empty space for Jesús's car. They were not behind Mike as much as they were approaching him sideways.

'Keep any exchange short, Felicia.' Ponytail saw Mike before she did. Felicia was still sluggish.

When she recognized Mike, her body tensed. She was ready to throw herself at him.

'Don't!' Ponytail pinched her arm so hard it would leave a bruise.

Mike was only a few feet away from the couple when he saw them. 'Well, there you are! Where's the Ferrari?' He would never have admitted he was concerned. Mike hadn't looked at Ponytail. His eyes were on Felicia. Nerves in the back of his neck grew warm when he saw Ponytail, but it was too late.

He stepped into Mike and drove his blade high into his chest. Mike hadn't seen the knife, but instinctively, he backed away as he was stabbed. Breath burst from his mouth. Surprise and shock forced him to fall slowly to his side, clutching his chest. He looked at his hand and saw blood and brought it back quickly to the wound. He began gasping on the cement floor.

'Forget about him. Get in the goddamn car. No, in the driver's seat. I'll have the knife against your ribs till

we get to the bank. Don't fucking try anything! Damn!'
His tongue had been cut on the tooth again.

Mike watched them leave, but they seemed to be far
away. Breath was all he could think of – then all he wanted to do was breathe. He sucked air in and pushed it out.
His head felt light, then dizzy. He looked longingly at
the door leading into the lobby. His shoulders felt light
– he needed to lie down and rest before he tried to make
it to the door. When he saw blood seeping through his
fingers, he began to crawl to the door. Every movement
caused blood to gush from the wound. *Where is everybody?*

🌴

Carmen and Caitlin wore their new *Life is Good* t-
shirts, sky blue and bubble gum pink, with matching
biking shorts and open-toed sandals. 'I wish I had some
color!' Carmen whined.

'You're Italian, you always have color.'

'You know what I mean.'

'Your 'bahama mama' look is too dark. Bring sun
block today.'

'You kidding? Not on my first day. I want the rays.'

The C's saw no commotion in the lobby when they
passed through and out the front door. Caitlin looked
north along Collins and saw a bus. As soon as they could,
they ran across busy Collins Avenue to the bus stop a few
hundred feet to their left. 'We'll make it!'

'Carm, do you have change?' Caitlin shouted behind
her as they ran for the bus.

'For both of us.'

'Thanks.' They found seats on the ocean side. Within
the first two blocks, they saw the massive changes since
their last visit. 'Where has everything gone?' To their
left, ten or eleven cement trucks were idling haphazardly

on the street or the sidewalks or the sites. Day workers with red flags halted traffic, motioning the trucks onto or out of the many condominiums under construction.

'It's gone!' Carmen looked at her friend in shock. Club I, the site of all their adventures, grand and horrid, was a sandlot boarded by a wooden fence. The developer's name and the condo's were plastered on the side. 'Construction 2008, *A Step Above.*' It was a sudden collapse of memories for both women. The friends turned in on themselves, but not for long because Haulover Beach came into view.

'Caitlin, look! It hasn't been touched. What a time we had there!'

'No more sleuthing. Peace is our goal.'

Riding across Haulover Bridge, the C's grabbed hands and held on tightly, remembering their panicked run across it. The construction ball had not spared Bal Harbour from the onslaught of foreign investors and their money dreams. 'They've demolished the Sheraton!'

The bus rolled along Harding, passing 78th Street, past a rented house where Jesús was doing his time in a freezer. At 70th Street, the C's got off the bus and walked down to Collins where they were met with a burst of music and color and dancers and flags. 'Isn't this great, Carm?' Walking down to the ocean, they stopped at kiosks of watercolors, oils, crafts, and sculptures, mostly of Cuban origin. The oceanfront was a sea of art, bursting with reds, blues, greens and yellows. Some of the oils were four feet or five feet tall. At the far end of the street, the sides were banked with a myriad of burning grills and cooking food. Their aromas mingled.

'Don't even think of eating, Carm. We've only been here twenty minutes and it's early.'

'So? Gosh, look at those cute little flamingos. The pinks and yellows and whites are perfect for the light-

house on my bookshelf. I have to have the watercolor.'
Carmen dug into her purse.

🌴

Manuel and Greg almost knocked the Alvarez door
down with their banging. 'Punch in the code. Let's check
this out.' Greg was buzzed. They were drawn to the
aquarium that took up half a wall. 'Wonder if they own
endangered species?' Greg whispered. 'Mr. Alvarez or
Mrs. Alvarez, security! Are you alright? Why is it so
freakin' cold in here? Start with the large rooms, Manny.
Don't pocket anything. I'm not losing this job.'

'You be careful too!'

Greg walked into the room at the end of the suite. He
was about to leave when he saw that the door was closed.
Hesitantly, he pushed it open. 'Anybody in here?' Poking
his head inside, he saw the blood smear on the shower
door. 'Manny, get in here!' He kept as far away from the
door as he could while he slid it open. 'Manny! What
the...? Get in here!'

Holding his hand over his mouth to keep from hurl-
ing, he leaned into the bath. Greg did not immediately
recognize the bloodied face of Carlos because he was not
in uniform. His face was sickly white behind the blood.
'Manny!'

'I'm here,' Manny croaked.

'Call 9-1-1 and the desk!'

Manny did both. 'I don't know if he's alive... he has a
hand on a bloody towel against his neck! I don't know!
I'm not a doctor. I'm just security. We need help right
now! I'm trying to calm down, but you haven't seen him.'

'It's Carlos!'

'Shit! Not you. He's one of ours, a concierge. What?
Greg, keep pressure on his neck and don't move the
towel. What? Is he cold, Greg?'

'It's freezing in the suite, but he's not ice cold.'

'Can you get a pulse?'

'Too much blood. My hand's shaking.'

'Yeah. Don't move him, Greg, got that?'

'Yeah.'

'What? What are you talking about? We're on 17, not the lobby. Another victim? Come here first – he's one of ours!'

CHAPTER EIGHTEEN

A FEW FEET from the door, Mike realized he might not make it. He lay on his good side and held his chest with both hands. *These floors are really clean. I don't want to die on a floor. Where's Caitlin?* He looked at his shoulder. Adrenalin got him to his knees, but no further.

Then the door opened.

'Oh dear God! Roselyn, stay where you are!'

'Be careful, Sydney!'

'Roselyn, go to the lobby and get help!'

Sydney knelt on one knee beside Mike. 'Sir, you'll be alright. I've sent for help.'

'Get me into the lobby, please.' Blood trickled out the side of Mike's mouth.

The door flew open, and James and Angel Hernandez came running. 'We've called 9-1-1.'

'Inside,' Mike pleaded.

James and Angel lifted Mike as gently as they could. Blood oozed through Mike's fingers. 'You shouldn't have moved him. Put him down,' Sydney ordered. They laid Mike on the floor inside the lobby's side door. 'I'm a retired dentist. Young man, don't talk, don't try to move. As soon as the EMS arrives, the paramedics will try to stem the flow of blood. Try to relax.'

The advice didn't have much effect on Mike. As soon as he saw the light of the lobby, he let go and passed out.

'Get some blankets and keep him warm, but don't move him.'

Angel was close to a stroke when he heard the wail of sirens and knew they were coming to the Trump. *Very bad publicity! Very bad! Two victims!* 'James, do you know this man?'

'No, sir, but he was in the garage. He must be a transient renter. Carlos knows every...' He stopped when he realized that Carlos was the other victim.

'James, keep everyone away from this area.' Angel made a call and got the immediate okay. 'When help arrives, we can airlift the men from the helipad. The 'copter is waiting.'

🎋

Lila and Abby had taken a seat, waiting for news, fully aware that something terrible had occurred. When they saw Mike carried into the lobby and laid on the floor, Lila asked Abby to get James Tellett. 'Lila, you were right. I never doubted your instincts, but James is obviously occupied.'

'I've lived my life not making demands. It's time I started! I sounded the alarm. It's my right to know what's happened. Please, fetch James. Tell him I won't keep him.' As Abby walked across the lobby, the paramedic teams arrived. Seeing stethoscopes on two of the men, she was relieved that a doctor-request had been made at the call center. Behind them, two gold-badged officers followed closely, removing shades. *Robbery-Homicide from the Violent Crime Unit*, thought Abby. 'James? One minute, please.'

James looked pleadingly at Angel. 'It was Mrs. Katz who sent us up to the Alvarez suite.'

'We don't want any of this in next week's tabloids. I'll see her myself.' He reached Lila before he was called back to the police. 'Mrs. Katz, you may have saved Carlos's life. He was badly wounded.'

'In the Alvarez suite?'

Angel did not want to offer more, but he knew the power of money. 'Yes.'

Lila's arthritis flared. 'Tell the officers to see me. I have information. Now, I must go back to my suite. Is the other young man alive?'

Angel was about to say, 'For now,' but instead he nodded and left.

Additional cruisers began to arrive, along with the inevitable: press and TV vans, one with a satellite on its roof. The case belonged to Detectives Miguel Suarez and Carly Smyth, a tag-team that worked.

'Smyth, keep the vermin outside, set officers up around the entrances, assign another to keep the hordes behind the tape, once it's up.'

'Pulling gender?' she asked.

'Grey hair,' Suarez replied.

'I color mine.'

'Doesn't count.'

Smyth had partnered with Suarez for the past four years. Between them they had worked 46 homicides. Both were slim and tall, gym freaks, and meticulous. In the looks department, they scored a seven; good days, eight. The two had been intimate only once, after a long and trying case. Smyth made sure it never happened again. Now they were solo and preferred it – just neater. Suarez liked to be in control of the flow of action and information. Smyth called him on every point.

Initially, Suarez had taken a ribbing about partnering with a female. He fought the pairing at first. But by working with a visible minority, he soon figured he could manage cases so they'd stand out. Four years later, they were high profile. Smyth smelled good, he liked that. He liked her because she had balls and she knew baseball stats. His last partner, Chew (so called because he chewed away at the skin around his fingers till they bled) had Suarez cursing like a cheap drunk. Chew fell down four stairs, fractured his hip, and now shuffled papers behind a desk. Suarez stopped swearing.

Outside the job, Smyth had fallen into Suarez's

pattern of 'selective hook-ups.' 'You nailed it, Suarez. No promises, clean breaks.' She dealt with the empty void that haunted her at four in the morning. 'The job's the buzz, takes up a life and doesn't leave much time after the gym for anything else.' Smyth voiced her own opinions with a brash confidence. 'Cops make ravages of marriages, starters and seconds. I don't intend to be one of them. Civilians don't get my war stories and they often bore me.' She liked being treated as an equal and fast-tracked by Lieutenant Ryder. On the job, Suarez's presumption bothered her, but Smyth had a mouth and gave as good as she got. 'I trust you with my life, Suarez. How many people can say that of anyone?'

'You finished?' he'd teased.

'For now.' She was always easier with men than women, less fuss. Men could bounce.

When Smyth walked out to the front of the Trump, she didn't mince her thoughts about the media. *Another circus. That's all we need, to lose big-buck people who actually live here,* Smyth groaned. She had things outside in place in record time and rushed back with Suarez. To the "vermin" she quoted the cops' bible, 'We'll address press and media as soon as we have information.'

Angel's armpits were sweating. He cursed silently when he had to defer to James.

Smyth left Suarez with James and went back to the desk to interview Sydney. 'Detective Smyth, sir. Did you see anyone else in the garage?'

'No. Our full attention was on the young man. Roselyn, did you see anyone that I might have missed?'

'I think I heard one of the garage doors closing – I can't be certain. My hearing is not what it used to be.'

'Did you find the victim near the door?'

'Yes.'

'Did the victim say anything?'

'He begged us for help to get him into the lobby.'

'About the attack?'

'Nothing about that. He only said a word or two. He was badly injured.'

Smyth took his number and went back to her partner.

The EMS doctor had blood-typed Mike, and he was already on a gurney receiving a bag and fluids. He was still out. The suits retrieved Mike's ID and contacts, found his suite number at the desk and followed the gurney. It was wheeled to an elevator that would take it to the helipad on the roof.

Suarez spoke to James. 'Detective Suarez, sir. Do you know this Mike Halloran?'

'No, sir. I checked. He's a recent rental in the business suites.'

'Do you have any idea what the concierge was doing in the Alvarez suite?'

'He might have been called up.'

'Have you ever been summoned there?'

'No, sir.'

'Did you ever see the victims together?'

'No, sir, but I don't see everything.'

'Why did you send security?' Smyth asked.

James's face fell into a peevish grump. 'Mrs. Lila Katz did, OAW, 21000.' He explained.

'Old and Wealthy? How old, James?'

'88.'

'Functioning?'

'Better than most, Detective Suarez.'

'Do you want me to question her?' Smyth asked.

'No, get up to the Alvarez suite. Note everything you can before the airlift. Call for back-up and seal off the room. I'll join you as soon as I can.'

'James, did security see the Alvarez couple in the suite?' Suarez continued.

'All they found was Carlos.'

'We'll talk to you later if need be.' James felt the brush of dismissal. His cheeks brightened and he turned back to the suits. 'We have security cameras on the floors and elevators. Maybe you'll be able to see if someone opened the Alvarez suite!' James bounced on his toes.

'Thanks. Smyth, get the video recording for the last couple of days. Place like this should have a video run-time of forty-eight hours. We need everything we can get. We'll run them all through the DMV.'

'Don't preach. We don't have time for another argument.'

'Shoring up for my OAW witness. Before you go, do you see a connection here? Do your good stuff, kid.'

'Take one! The attempt on Diaz came first – the perp or perps left through the garage and ran into Halloran, bystander.'

'Why try to take him out?'

'He knew them, him, whomever? Was suspicious?'

'Halloran just got here, Smyth. Who could he know?'

'The Alvarez couple – or this attack is totally unrelated, a car-jacking.'

'Before I tackle the old lady, I'll check to see if all three vehicles are here. Halloran must have had one. If his car's there, it's not a jack.' His cell rang. 'We better get up to the suite. They're ready to airlift Diaz and Halloran to Jackson Memorial.'

†

CHAPTER NINETEEN

PONYTAIL'S RUSH FROM cancelling Carlos and the shit in the garage faded when he saw the rust-colored splatter on his sleeve. 'Shit! I got blood on my pants too. How far are we going?'

Felicia's teeth chattered uncontrollably.

'Stop with the teeth! It's driving me nuts!' He spoke too quickly and cut the side of his tongue again on the sharp edge of the broken tooth. 'Where's your bank?'

'178th Street.'

'Then we're almost there. What do you have to clean this stuff off?' Ponytail couldn't work on the blood because he had the blade against Felicia's ribs.

'Kleenex.'

'Shit! Nothing in the trunk?'

'Golf clubs.'

'Figures.'

The Mercedes pulled into the small parking space of Bank of North America that was a stone's throw away from the City Hall. Ponytail was about to direct Felicia to that parking lot when a car pulled out. 'Take that space.'

Felicia's ace in the hole had faded too. If she revealed it, she'd increase the threat to her life. From the surprised look on Mike's face, she knew how quickly this man could act to snuff out her life.

'Don't move while I try to wipe off this shit.' The Kleenex kept tearing and Ponytail kept swearing. He tore his tongue again. 'Fuck!' He turned and pulled down the mirror on the visor, stuck his tongue out and checked the damage. He daubed it. 'You have any gum? I could use it to cover the spear inside my mouth.'

'No.'

'Shit! All the money in the world, and you buy regular Kleenex and you have no gum. I'd keep myself well stocked with the best stuff.' Ponytail decided to take off the jacket. The shirt alone was fine. He'd carry the jacket and hide the stains on his pants.

Felicia had stuck her own tongue between her teeth to keep them from chattering.

'Hey you! Get with things.' Ponytail gave Felicia a tough nudge. 'This can still be easy. Keep it simple; get him to sit with us, away from his desk. Don't be stupid. Don't lose your life over money. When the transfer is made, walk back with me out of the bank. I'll take you to Jesús. You have my word. Take a minute to compose yourself.'

Felicia had planned to make a run for it as soon as they got inside the bank. The knife prevented that possibility. Her body still felt heavy. The coffee hadn't changed that. There was no way she'd walk back outside the bank with him.

Ponytail raced around the car to get Felicia out of it. He himself was squirrelly. The original plan had given him a leeway of three days. He'd have had the time to get rid of Jesús. Carlos and Felicia would have been stored in the Alvarez suite. If the transfer by phone had been as successful as he'd planned it, he wouldn't be walking into the bank right now. The tooth knifed his tongue again that was now raw and ragged.

While Jesús was on ice and Carlos was chilling, the guy in the garage was worse than his tooth. The cops would already be swarming the Trump. 'Move it!' He took Felicia's arm and pulled her close before they walked up the sidewalk into the bank. What if he forgot about the transfer and demanded a certified check? A check that size would trigger suspicion. Back to plan A. 'How much real cash am I looking at?'

'Five.'
'Your heart is four inches from my blade.'

CHAPTER TWENTY

SMYTH WAS STRUCK by the neatness surrounding the attempted murder. There were no signs of a struggle. That was odd. The only place she found blood was the bathroom where the victim had been found. Carlos Diaz was in bad shape. The doctor had told her his condition was grim. *Not good for the investigation,* Smyth thought. He was tightly wrapped on the gurney in a 'C' collar and bagged when she came into the suite.

'We'll red-line him to the OR as soon as we reach Jackson Memorial – no bets that he doesn't crash en route. I haven't been able to completely stop the main bleeder. OR might have a better chance if we get him there in time. Here, we found his cell. Sorry, we have to go!' He turned his attention back to Carlos and tapped his forehead. 'Stay with me!' He tapped harder as he followed the gurney to the elevator. 'Stay with me!'

Smyth remained in the suite and waited for the crime crew. In the massive bedroom that was almost larger than her apartment, she found a photo of the couple. '*Handsome!* Something about the woman's face rang a distant bell. Under a lamp, she took a better look. *I've seen this face somewhere.* She opened her phone and made a call. 'Have you run Felicia Alvarez and Jesús Alvarez through DMV yet?'

'Just about to get back to you, Detective. Ready for a surprise?'

'Hit me!'

'Alvarez is her married name. Her maiden name is Gonzalez.'

'Of the Ernesto Gonzalez family?'

'Same, sister of Diego Gonzalez, the newly appointed head of the family.'

'That's just great! The mob's working this case now, and they don't follow rules. We don't even know if she's a perp or a victim. She and her husband are both missing.'

'Your work's cut out for you.'

'Suarez will love sharing information with a crime family. Thanks.'

🌴

Carmen reluctantly agreed to put aside the idea of eating at the arts festival as soon as she and Caitlin got there. 'What about a strawberry margarita before we eat?' Carm laughed. 'There were all sorts of new places just around the corner on Collins.'

In this area, gentrification had worked. Two blocks of small bistros, bars and decorative boutiques lined the street. The C's stopped at each one. Carmen bought herself a palm tree key chain. She'd blown her budget on the watercolor.

'Look, there's a bar up ahead!'

Ten feet from it, the C's both stopped dead in their tracks. 'Money Bags?'

The name and logo of the bar were two yellow money bags. The C's turned to one another.

Caitlin's face morphed into a question mark.

'Let's not be ridiculous. It's a good name for a bar and yellow's a popular Florida color. I want my margarita.'

'I'm being paranoid. Lead on, Carm!'

Inside, everything was upscale, much like the A-clubs in South Beach. The bar was buzzing. The drinks were flashy and came in frosted pink and yellow glasses. Their paranoia dissolved as they got into the rhythm of the Beach Boys, playing in the background. When a waiter appeared in grey tails, the C's first saw the suit and smiled. They'd chosen well. 'What will you beauties have?'

Carmen looked up first and ordered for both of them. 'Two large strawberry margaritas, please. Larry? Oh my God, is that you?'

Larry's face turned grey, like his pants.

'Carmen and Caitlin, you remember us from Club I?'

'Wow! Long time.'

'Everybody was so worried when you disappeared. What a great job! A long way from the cabana. I'm proud of you.'

The C's stood and hugged Larry, and he relaxed.

An eerie silence registered. Caitlin pushed her chair away from the table. Larry was grey again.

'We have to get back.' Caitlin got up. Carmen followed her. 'We're actually late.'

Larry watched them leave. Then he went to the door and followed their route up Collins before he drained the two glasses.

'You don't think Larry...? I mean the name of the place and all.'

'Carm, we were lucky. That part of my life is over. Now let's get out of here!' Caitlin's cell vibrated.

'Thought you said no phones.'

'Shut up for a sec!'

'What?'

Caitlin turned her back on her friend and listened intently on her cell. 'Jackson Memorial, thank you.'

Carmen's shoulders were stiff as boards.

Caitlin turned back to her, 'Mike's been badly injured at the Trump. We have to get to the hospital. He's in surgery.' She ran into the street. Cars screeched to a halt. Drivers gave her the horn.

'Do you want to get yourself killed?' Carmen shouted from the sidewalk. Running out herself, she grabbed Caitlin and pulled her off the street. 'Let me try.' Within three minutes, they were huddled together inside a cab. 'Wait till we get there – try to calm down.'

'We need to be at Jackson Memorial asap,' Caitlin shouted at the cabbie.

'Sit back, then.'

'Who called to tell you?'

'Some detective; didn't register his name after I heard about Mike.'

CHAPTER TWENTY-ONE

JAMES DIRECTED DETECTIVE Suarez to the OAW elevator and watched the doors close.

Suarez checked his watch. He would rather be redlighting it to the hospital, but he knew the value of immediate interviews. *How with it can this woman be? She's more than double my age, probably doesn't see well. Then again, she did send security to the Alvarez suite.* Nonetheless, he adjusted his tie and ran his hand over his hair when he checked himself out in the mirror. Age could be intimidating. Frankness was one of its perks.

As soon as he walked on the floor, he began to cough. *They're still smoking! At their age – gutsy!* He gave the door a good rap and was startled when a much younger woman opened it. *This can't be Katz?*

'Abby Wiseman, Detective. Come in. I'm a friend.'

'I'm looking for Mrs. Katz.'

'You've come to the right place,' Lila answered. She was sitting on a soft tan leather sofa.

'Detective Suarez, Mrs. Katz.' The woman was impeccably dressed in a tailored suit and matching shoes. Through the natural creases that crisscrossed her cheeks, there was also tension Suarez recognized. His own knees ached today with arthritis, a leftover from varsity basketball.

'Lila, please.'

He wanted the interview to go smoothly. 'How well do you know Carlos Diaz? You may have saved his life.'

In a simple, fluid, precise answer, Lila told Suarez first about Carlos: what he meant to the women despite his petty thefts, the threat to his life and family, his visit to her, the $5,000 she gave him, everything she knew. Suarez knew not to interrupt her. He took notes.

Better than most! Suarez fought to hide a smile. *She's the best!* He asked her a second question. 'What prompted you to have security sent to the Alvarez suite?'

Lila took a folded sheet from the sofa and proffered it. As Suarez took the sketch, Lila began. 'I think this man is impersonating Jesús Alvarez.' Lila handed Suarez the paper with the story of the home invasion, circled in red. Just as concisely, Lila then explained what she had seen at the dog track and in the lobby and what had prompted her to send security to the Alvarez suite.

'Have you ever thought of police work, Lila?' Suarez couldn't resist.

Lila accepted the detective's recognition with a nod. She knew how Jake would rant, but Lila's heart was pumping with the joy of walking back into the chaos of life, of standing on the front line. Being driven here, and served there, and settling Sophie's problems with the *yentas*, were tedious tasks that gnawed at Lila's sense of herself. Gentle 'good nights' were not for her! The sketch prompted Suarez to ask another question.

'This information is of great help.'

Lila broke out in a warm smile.

'You saw this man close up?'

'Yes, at the dog track. It wasn't Jesús, and he wasn't trying to look like him then. I was close enough to see he was threatening Carlos. Before you ask, yes, I would recognize him again. The sketch should be proof enough of that. As far as the lobby is concerned, I have to admit I wasn't very close to him. He was dressed like Jesús, but I couldn't swear it was the same man I saw at the track.'

'Is there a chance it was Mr. Alvarez you saw in the lobby?'

'Carlos was obviously as frightened by the man with him as he had been at the track. That's the reason I feel it was the same man, but Mr. Alvarez and the other man could be identical twins.'

'You have a cop's eye, Lila. Here's my card. Call me immediately, day or night, if you remember anything else. You look very concerned.'

'My son is arriving tomorrow. He'll be put out.'

'He should be proud of you.'

'Detective, don't patronize me. Jake's an attorney.'

He gave Lila a sympathetic nod.

Suarez left Lila's suite with a renewed respect for age. *Lila is every prosecutor's dream and a cop's best witness.* He began to review what he had so far. *The couple is missing. The double looks good for the stabbing. I need to see that video recording and interview Halloran. He might have seen the double in the garage.* Opening his phone, he called Smyth. 'Put an officer on both men after surgery. I'm coming down to the hospital as soon as I pick up the recording for the condo and the garage. How about a video night at my place?'

'Fun.'

'What do you have on the next of kin?'

'I have Diaz's cell with the last numbers he called. No answer at the family home.'

'Roll the cell numbers.'

'In progress. Stop dictating. I reached Halloran's friends. What about the OAW witness?'

'Solid stuff. I'll save it till I see you.'

'The Alvarez couple?'

'Alvarez is her married name. Her maiden name is Gonzalez. Ring a bell? She's the old man's grand-daughter.' Smyth was satisfied with her discoveries.

'Who's Diego Gonzalez to her?'

'Brother and new head of the family. You know him, Suarez?'

'Unfortunately, before we teamed up. Diego will jump all over the case. He'll snag better leads. He's got cops on his payroll. Gonzalez is dangerous, cocky and smart.'

'Like you. We have to work faster.'

'Post two good men on the victims' doors if they're brought to the ICU before I get there. No telling what Diego would do to either one of them to get information on his sister.'

'I won't contact him till you get here.'

'Hernandez, the manager, might have beaten me to it.'

'Then don't waste time getting here.'

CHAPTER TWENTY-TWO

FELICIA ZEROED IN on the guard's taser and gun as she and Ponytail walked up the entrance to the bank. Still off-balance and unnerved by the stabbing in the garage, she saw that Ponytail had positioned himself between the guard and her. The stabbing alone was unsettling, but the quick, cat-like pounce of Ponytail really rattled her. *Four inches from your heart.* If she threw herself at the guard, Ponytail could easily stab her. What happened to him wouldn't matter to her. Aborting the attempt was the guard himself who was on his cell and not paying them any heed.

When that chance evaporated, Felicia walked dully beside Ponytail into the bank to the business counter at the far right of the tellers. Accustomed to the well-heeled and the service that kept their money with the bank, a young woman rose immediately to meet them when they reached the counter. 'Good morning! How may I help you today?' Her voice was pleasant, but formal.

'I'm Felicia Alvarez. We have a meeting with Richard Watts.'

'Mr. Watts is expecting you. He is just finishing up and will be pleased to see you in about five minutes. Please follow me.' She took them to an empty office where Felicia could see that Watts's office door was closed. 'May I get you some coffee or water, Evian, while you wait?'

'Felicia?'

'Evian.'

'For two then.'

'I'll close the door a little to leave you some privacy and be right back.'

As soon as the receptionist left, Ponytail read Felicia's

thoughts. 'If you try anything in Watts's office or here, for that matter, I'll kill you. No one can get to you faster than I can. I have nothing to lose if you force my hand. Long term, it's in my best interest not to kill you. If that weren't the case, last night would have been different.' Ponytail stopped talking and smiled as he saw the young woman at the door. He stood and took the tray. 'Thank you.'

'It won't be long.'

'Good.'

It doesn't matter whether you raped me last night or you kill me today, you lost your life the second you walked into my suite. My brother will find you. Diego had installed the cameras in her suite. She had activated them when Ponytail went for the drinks. *Your face and everything you did inside my suite, Diego will see and avenge.*

'I'll make certain the door to Watts's office is closed. Stay beside me and don't play games. All the paperwork is done. I'll do most of the talking. Do you understand?'

'Yes.'

'That's what I want to hear. When we leave the bank, I promise to take you to Jesús. Then you're free. Let me check to see if all is ready.' Ponytail pretended to make a call. 'That's fine. We should be there in two hours or less. Is he eating? Alright.' He closed his phone. 'Your husband has quite a temper. He spits out the food we offer.'

Was it possible Jesús was still alive? Was it possible she might survive?

Ponytail saw hope rise uncertainly behind Felicia's beautiful eyes. He felt it himself and wanted to believe his lie.

'Excuse me. Mr. Watts will see you now.'

'Come Felicia.' Ponytail was impressed with Watts's office. Spacious and modern, he could smell the money that passed through his hands. He could almost touch it.

'Mr. and Mrs. Alvarez! Come in and excuse the delay. It was unavoidable. Please, sit,' he said, pointing to plush leather chairs behind his desk.

'Let's sit together over there. We can more easily show you the work.'

Watts frowned. He was not about to relinquish his position of authority and sit with clients. It was hard enough to see wealth up close every day, to know that he would never achieve it, so he didn't want to give up the one perk, his seat! 'It might be easier for any paperwork if I sit at my desk.'

'Please, I insist,' Ponytail said, still standing.

Richard Watts was a traditional man. He rarely varied from banker's apparel, a navy suit and a red tie. Thin hair on the sides of his head was combed back neatly. His bald pate sported a golf tan. He had a pear face, a slack jaw and lumpy jowls that ran down his neck. In fact, when he reluctantly left his desk and walked his solid belly over to the green couch, his neck bounced.

'This will be so much better. Our business today is simple, but most exciting for us. Felicia and I decided against the yacht because I have found the perfect surprise for my beautiful wife. To accomplish that, we need you to transfer this amount.' Ponytail opened his case with one hand, keeping the other on Felicia, and gave the figure and the transfer sheets to Watts.

Directed to sit beside Ponytail, Watts couldn't see Felicia directly.

It was not his affair what these people did with their money. His business was the five million less he would be managing. 'Well,' he said, 'this is…'

'A large amount, we know, but the opportunity is wonderful.'

Watts leaned forward, but Ponytail cut him off. 'Felicia, tell Mr. Watts that we are in this together. I wouldn't want him to think I'm pressuring you.' He took Felicia's arm and squeezed it.

'I have agreed, Mr. Watts.'

Something was off. Watts felt that as soon as he left his desk. He wasn't law enforcement; he was a banker, not a man to take a risk. But Mrs. Alvarez appeared to be in agreement – his hands were tied. They were following the protocol they'd set up themselves, being present for large transactions. 'Well,' he said, 'I see you'll be re-locating …'

'Please don't spoil the surprise.'

'I'll need a signature.'

'Felicia?' Ponytail handed her the sheet.

'Will the transfer be made in Mrs. Alvarez's name?' Watts was curious and suspicious.

'In my name, if you will.'

'Mrs. Alvarez, please make a note of that beside your signature.'

Ponytail watched Felicia write. 'There, things are in order.'

Watts held the papers, took a few steps and tried to stand directly in front of Felicia. Ponytail stood and took Felicia up with him. 'If this opportunity doesn't work out as we wish, I have your card.'

Watts extended his hand to the couple. Felicia's hand was cold. He ran his fingers across his forehead. There was nothing Watts could pin down. The rich were different – he saw that every week. At his desk, he tapped in the transfer, but did not send it. He checked his papers again and found a private number in the Alvarez file. He'd call Mrs. Alvarez in an hour and confirm this privately. Then he'd send the transfer.

'How long will the transfer take?'

'A few hours.'

'Thank you for your good service. I'll check with the

bank this afternoon. They are expecting the transfer.'

The money didn't matter to Felicia. She was picturing the private washroom. Could she pull away and run to it? Watts would never know she had saved his life with her compliance in his office, and her own, of course, for the moment.

A wuss-bag! Ponytail smirked. As soon as they got to the door, he laughed. 'Let's celebrate!' He kissed her cheek.

The bathroom was out, but her head was clearing. When they reached the door, Felicia tensed, planning to push Ponytail into the guard and run.

'Don't!' he whispered in her ear and pulled her so close they bumped one another. The guard was of no use. He was busy talking on his phone, oblivious to customers.

He forgot to ask me for the car keys! I have to distract him so he doesn't remember that I have them. 'Jesús is difficult about food.'

Ponytail was buzzed. For the first time all day, he had hope. Felicia's comment took him by surprise and he didn't suspect it. 'I had to work out and starve myself for a month before I could make a move.'

'You have what you want.' Felicia was careful not to set up alarms with easy banter when silence had been her way since the home invasion.

'You and Jesús can ride away in that Spyder. I've left you both that.'

They were 20 feet from the Mercedes.

If I get into the car first like I did the last time...' She purposely hadn't locked the car. As they drew nearer, she saw the red flashing light of the alarm at the top of the door. The Mercedes had locked itself automatically.

'Stop tensing! You're almost out of this.'

CHAPTER TWENTY-THREE

DETECTIVE SUAREZ FLASHED his badge up to the OR and found his partner on the phone outside the doors of one of the many operating theatres. Still talking, she waved him over. 'Here's the address. Get a car over there and try to locate family. Life and death for Diaz. Get back to me.' Smyth pointed to Caitlin and Carmen who were huddling against a wall. 'Halloran's friends.'

'Any news on Diaz?'

'The field doctor held out hope because Diaz was still alive when they got here. He also said that he might still bleed out. Nothing since.'

'Halloran?'

'Still in surgery – no news there.'

'Sent a car to an address at one of the numbers not answering. Can't locate the wife.'

'Good move. Carlos told Mrs. Katz, OAW, his family was at risk.' Suarez filled her in.

'A double?'

'Looks like it. Katz felt she also saw him in the Trump lobby. She's a very solid witness, besides giving us the sketch.'

'So we're looking at an abduction, Suarez? Of the sister and now maybe her husband?'

'Don't know yet, but Katz was very credible. The Trump manager did call the emergency number for Alvarez. We can expect Diego Gonzalez any minute, focused as a laser. Stay here – signal if the slimeball shows up and I miss him while I'm interviewing those friends.'

'I'll take them, Suarez – you watch for Diego.'

'Go.'

Smyth saw the friends were teary. 'I'm Detective

Smyth. I'd like to get your names and numbers first and ask you a few questions about your friend, Mike Halloran.'

'Caitlin Donovan. I'm Mike's fiancée. This is Carmen DiMaggio. What happened? We don't know anything except that Mike's in surgery.'

'First off, are you residents?'

'Mike's from Boston, on a job-training program that was supposed to start today.' Tears streamed down Caitlin's cheeks. 'What happened?'

'Your friend was assaulted in the Trump garage. We think it's connected to an event at the Alvarez condo.'

'Assaulted?'

Carmen took Caitlin's arm.

'He was stabbed by an assailant.'

Color drained from Caitlin's face. Carmen dropped her head. 'How badly is Mike hurt?'

'We won't know that until he's out of surgery.'

'Oh God! I can't believe this! I can't believe I didn't take him seriously. Oh my God!'

'How could we know, Caitlin?'

'Please explain.'

Caitlin, visibly shaken, tried to make sense of what little she knew. 'Mike felt that Felicia Alvarez might be in trouble. He'd met the couple briefly the day he arrived. A couple of nights ago, Mike got caught in a riptide. Felicia found him on the beach and helped him back. He said her husband was jealous. I thought he might have fallen for her. I told him to worry about the lump on his head, and I deflected all other talk. Oh God!'

'What exactly did he say?'

Caitlin slumped against the wall and went quiet.

Carmen helped Caitlin out. 'The next day in the lobby, he thought he saw the husband's twin, but the man was pretending to be her husband.'

'I didn't give that much weight either. Mike had a concussion after all,' Caitlin said worriedly. 'He might have been mistaken.'

'Thank you.' Smyth walked back to Suarez. 'Something's up with the sister. Halloran sensed it.'

'Great. Why can't we get any news in this place? We're cops! I hate this waiting and we still have to go through the video recording.'

'While we're stuck here, I'll put out an APB on Felicia Alvarez and her car.'

'Do the husband as well. Both cars were missing.'

At that moment, with muscle on either side of him, Diego Gonzalez, in a cream suit with ultra thin white stripes, marched up to the cops. He waved his bodyguards off. His eyes were black coals. His hair was as lush as his sister's – the cut of his suit was Calvin Klein, down to the oxblood loafers. He was quite beautiful, chiselled, like inmates who work out all day. The only difference was that Diego had never been to prison.

He stood rigid, eye-balling both cops. He loved his sister. She was blood. From the time they were kids, he had protected Felicia, even been in awe of her. When she struck out on her own with Jesús and moved off the Bay when they married, he was angry and felt betrayed. He stepped closer to the cops.

Both detectives turned away, ignoring him. A surgeon had just come from the OR.

🕯

Caitlin and Carmen huddled together. 'Do you have their number?' Carmen asked.

'Since Chris died, I keep all family numbers.' Chris was Caitlin's only brother who had been killed in a hit-and-run a few years back.

'Shouldn't you wait for news before you call?'

Caitlin wiped her eyes on the back of her hand. 'I can't take a chance.' Cupping her forehead, she tapped in the Hallorans' Boston number. 'It's Caitlin, Lynn. I'm so sorry to have to tell you this, but Mike's been injured. He's alive and in surgery. I'm outside the OR, waiting for news.'

'How did this happen?'

'I don't know, Lynn. He was attacked in the garage of the Trump on his way to his new job this morning. I'd better call his company too.'

'Was he alone when he was attacked?'

'He was going to work, Lynn. Would you like me to see if there is a suite available for you at the Trump?'

'What hospital is Mike at?'

'Jackson Memorial.'

'We'll stay in Miami. We'll fly down tonight. Please call me with any news.'

'I will.' Caitlin hung up. 'She was very cold, Carm, as if I were somehow to blame because Mike was alone when he was hurt.'

'Caitlin, she's worried, that's all.'

'They're both angry at me for my waffling on the marriage thing.'

'So stop.'

Caitlin broke down again. 'First, my husband, then my brother, now Mike. Mike's mom is probably thinking the same thing.'

'Mike's not dead. I'm still here. The closest I've come to death in the last few years is wanting to murder you.'

Caitlin stood in a daze.

'Mike will pull through. Have some faith. I wish there were some chairs around.'

'Do you have an appointment tomorrow?'

'I'll reschedule. Better do it now.'

'Thanks. I don't want to be alone.'

'I know.'

🌴

When the phone rang, Abby took the call. 'Lila, Jake can't get here till late tonight.'

'Good, a reprieve. You don't have to stay. I wish I'd asked the detective to give me news of Carlos.'

'I'm staying. You may need some defence with Jake. You deserve kudos for the way you conducted yourself. Carlos is fortunate to have you as a friend; so am I. I'll call the hospital a little later for you.'

'I have the detective's private number.'

'We can try that as well, Lila. There's the door. I'll get it.'

'If it's Sophie and her canines, don't open it. I'm not up for a chorus or a fashion show.'

'It's the chorus. We'll have to whisper. We don't want her to hear us and then be hurt.'

'She couldn't hear us through a sheet.'

'You're terrible.'

'On occasion.'

🌴

Maria watched the flashing lights of the police from behind the curtain in a basement apartment on 11th Street in Little Havana. She froze. Perdita was napping. José went to the door, looking back at Maria. 'Yes?'

'I'm Detective Suarez. Is Maria Diaz here?'

'Why are you looking for her?'

'Is she here?'

Maria had stepped out into view. 'I am Maria.'

'Maria Diaz?'

'Yes.'

'I have been instructed to take you to the hospital. Your husband has been injured.'

Now moving behind José, Maria dropped her head on his shoulder and began to sob and shake.

'We have to leave immediately.'

José rushed to the kitchen and told his wife, who was washing dinner dishes, that he would accompany Maria. Isabel understood. The police would not have come if the matter was not serious. For the entire car ride, Maria wept. Suarez knew nothing he could tell her.

CHAPTER TWENTY-FOUR

AS A DECENT scammer, Ponytail knew the code of his trade – never take your eyes off the dupe. When he'd used a phone, he'd controlled the conversation. Still elated as he and Felicia left the bank, he kept his eyes on Felicia's closed fist as they reached the car. 'When you unlock the Mercedes, hand me the keys.'

Felicia brought her hand up to toss the keys into the bushes behind the car. Ponytail dropped his briefcase. His arm flipped around Felicia and caught her wrist, pulling it back behind her. 'You are so close to the end. Why be stupid now?' He gave her wrist a vicious twist. The keys fell to the ground.

Felicia's face was white as she was forced to wheel around. Her wrist quickly began to swell. Ponytail pulled her to the ground with him to scoop up the keys. They bent awkwardly, heads meeting. Felicia was moaning when a couple approached them. Ponytail grabbed Felicia's elbow and dragged her up.

The woman looked suspiciously at Ponytail; the man beside her kept his eyes off them.

'First year fights!' Ponytail laughed. 'What can you do with such a beautiful woman?'

The knife at Felicia's ribs broke the skin. Her mouth clenched.

The woman looked back at them but walked on. This was Miami. She didn't want to risk injury for someone else's problem. She had her own.

Recalling the simplicity of the original plan, Ponytail felt bile rise in his throat. Whatever fleeting kindness he'd felt for Felicia vanished. Like Jesús, she was now waste to be disposed of. A nagging thought scurried around his ears. What if the transfer did not go through?

Grabbing his case, he hurried her into the Mercedes, back into the driver's seat. He threw his case on her knees and ran around to the other side of the car and jumped inside.

Both jerked back when a cell vibrated inside the case. 'Don't move!' Pulling it over to his knees, he flipped the case open and saw that it was her cell. He opened the phone and swore when he saw that it was Watts. 'Take the damn call. I can kill you here. Watch every word you say. Confirm the transfer!' He felt as though he were lying on glass. His code broke – he wouldn't know what Watts was saying. It was the fourth ring. 'Take it!'

Her voice was pinched with pain when she spoke. 'Yes?'

'Richard Watts. Just reconfirming the transfer, Mrs. Alvarez.'

She looked at Ponytail. 'Has it been sent?'

'Not yet, I wanted a final confirmation. I'm a stickler.'

'That's good to hear.'

'You don't want the transfer?'

'That's right.'

Ponytail was running his index finger across his neck, a signal for her to end the call.

'Good day.'

Watts began to perspire. Things like this made him nervous, but now, he was a hero of sorts. With that thought, he called the police.

'Good work, Felicia. Get back on Collins and drive south. It's almost over. I really don't want to use my knife. You've made me a rich man. I'd drop you here, but I need at least an hour's head start.'

As soon as they hit Collins, they were snarled in traffic, but they were crawling at least. Ponytail thought of going up 163rd Street, but the traffic was probably bad there as well. It was also five miles out of their way.

It took almost ten minutes to reach Haulover Bridge. He began to shake his knees, kicking around his plan for Felicia and 'ice cube Jesús.' When they passed Bal Harbour, he smiled for the first time. 'I can afford this kind of shit. This is some day! You'll come into more money, Felicia. I've never had a red carpet, never driven a Mercedes, never wore a five-grand suit like this…'

When they got to 79th Street at Harding Avenue, Ponytail was tapping his feet. In less than half an hour, Felicia wouldn't be a problem. He shook off excited jitters and stopped shaking. He was ready. Suddenly, traffic up ahead was stopped. 'What the fuck!'

Felicia gunned the Mercedes toward the stopped cars. 'Stop, bitch!'

At the last second, she veered sharply to the left and hit both cars ahead on the passenger side. The airbags popped and struck Ponytail in the ribs and face. Felicia had pulled back to avoid the hard punch of the front and side bags. She got her door open. Ponytail moaned as the bags deflated and he stabbed wildly at her with his knife, catching her in the back.

♟

Carlos lost the fierce battle to save his life.

'Call it!'

'One forty-seven.'

Dr. Greg Watson, the attending physician, wiped the sweat from his face with his blue mask. 'Clean him up for the family. I presume they've been located.' He headed out to the corridor with the chart and found Suarez and Smyth. He knew the homicide team all too well.

Smyth saw him first and nudged Suarez. 'Not good, right?'

'Law of averages, he shouldn't have made it here. Moderate hypothermia got him this far. He bled out.

Did what we could for almost an hour. Young guy.'

'We need a name. There are two victims.'

'Didn't know. Like you guys, we're not always aware of what's going on in the next room. Carlos Diaz.'

'Is there any way you can find out the status of Mike Halloran? They were airlifted together.'

'I was called out from another surgery. Didn't know about the airlift. I'll try to get what I can for you.'

Mrs. Katz might be their sole eyewitness. Suarez hoped there was a good chance Halloran had seen the perp as well.

🌴

Diego Gonzalez had had enough. 'You in charge of this dog show?' Unschooled in any form of restraint, he barged into Suarez's private space.

'Actually…'

'Why wasn't I called? We're talking about my sister. My sister! We pay taxes. You should know that.'

The cops did know that. Legit all the way. The family now employed tax attorneys. To move their money in large blocks, they had bought up a ton of real estate in North Miami, filtered other blocks to off-shore Baham-ian and Swiss banks, and layered shells. Much of the family fit right in with the greedy, ugly rich. The cops also knew what a hit they had taken on the mortgage crunch. Behind the scenes, the mobsters still worked the clubs, streets and trucking.

'We have police out looking for your sister and her husband.'

'Was I talking to you?'

'We're the team.' Smyth moved up close and per-sonal, inches from his sexist, chiselled face. '*Por qué no te callas?*'

'Nobody tells me to shut up! So, you guys have no

idea where my sister is?' Gonzalez stomped away and hung his head. When he walked back, his eyes were reddening. 'This is my sister. She had nothing to do with any family business. Help me out here!'

She paid for the Trump suite with hard-earned money? Smyth wanted to shout in his face.

'The manager told me the concierge was in her room; that he got cut there! What was he doing in her suite? Was my sister hurt? Was she there with Jesús? Did he do this? Do you know anything?'

'I will keep you informed.'

'What about the concierge?'

'He didn't make it.'

'That's it?'

'You know we can't discuss a case with civilians.' Suarez did feel a twinge for Gonzalez. His stress was real.

'I want to get into the suite.'

'It's a crime scene.'

'*Yo tengo mis conectos. Puedo ayudarte.*'

'The day I need your help…'

'I have something you need. *Tu me ayudas y yo te ayudo.*'

'There won't be a swap of information. You've heard of subpoenas?'

'*Dime lo que tienes y yo te digo lo mío.*'

A look passed between Smyth and Suarez. Gonzalez had something. 'Let's see what you have and we'll see.' Smyth conceded to get what they wanted. Neither she nor Suarez ever intended to give anything to Gonzalez in return.

'The suite is equipped with concealed cameras in every room. They are activated when the suite is empty. When Felicia is alone, I've told her to use them. You have video recording of what went on there. *Quiero verle la cara.*'

The detectives had no intention of allowing Gonzalez to see the face of their perp.

CHAPTER 25

SMYTH WAS ABOUT to fill him in on procedure when Suarez tapped her arm.

'I think the wife just walked in.'

The woman between the two cops was small and young, 25 at most. Her face was swollen from crying. *When you're young, the pail of tears is full*, thought Suarez. 'See if you can get somebody over here.' Smyth pushed through the OR entrance and was quickly ushered out by a nurse. When she understood the situation, she called Dr. Greg Watson, who appeared in minutes.

'Mrs. Diaz, I'm Detective Suarez and this is Detective Smyth.'

'I want to see Carlos,' Maria sobbed.

'I understand that. Just a second, that's his doctor coming.'

Diego was marching up and down. *Forget about this guy. It's over for him. I want to see the asshole's face who hurt my sister!*

'Maria, this is Carlos's doctor.'

Maria was weaving back and forth, waiting to receive the blow.

'I'm sorry, Mrs. Diaz, your husband did not survive. I tried very hard…'

A piercing wail blocked everything out. Diego hiked his shoulders. 'I want to see Carlos.' That became her mantra. Dr. Watson led Maria into the OR, to the Quiet Room where Carlos had been taken.

'Are you up to talking to her?' Before she could answer him, Suarez was back on the phone, stepping out of earshot. 'No one gets into that suite. Get another man up with you on the door.'

'Techs and crime are in there,' an officer told him.

'No civilians,' Suarez ordered.

'Got it.'

'Smyth and I will get there as soon as we can.'

Suarez waved Diego off again as another OR doctor appeared.

Anger flared behind his dark eyes as he glared at Suarez. 'You guys play as dirty as we do. You hide behind badges is all. We put ourselves out there.'

'Back off!'

Suarez turned to the doctor. Caitlin and Carmen approached together.

'Family?'

'Fiancé and friend. Mike's parents will be here tonight.'

'And?' He saw the badges. 'Well, he will pull through.'

'Thank God!' Caitlin said, smiling through tears and hugging Carmen.

'The single wound cut through the sternum and tore muscle. There was considerable bleeding in the muscle tissue and a collapsed lung. We've suctioned most of it. The drains will do the rest. He's sedated now and resting.'

'Can we see him?'

'For a few minutes.'

'How soon before we can talk to him?' Suarez asked.

'Could be a few hours or less. He needs the rest.'

Caitlin and Carmen disappeared inside the OR. Suarez broke up the team. 'I want to get those cameras. No telling what he'll do,' he said, canting his head at Diego. 'Can you take the wife and Halloran?'

'No problem, but we should have somebody up here with *him*.'

Suarez made the call for additional backup.

Diego shouted over to them, 'The cameras are well

hidden. You'll waste time trying to locate them. I can help you. They're very small. I want to see his face. Is it Jesús? Anything, you fuckers?' Diego stood seething. 'I won't forget this!'

Suarez got back on the phone. 'Do an electronic sweep. There are surveillance units in each room. Collect them.'

'When will you be here?' the field CSI wanted to know.

'A little over an hour.'

'You want the cameras here or sent to the lab?'

'Keep them at the suite.'

'Your call.'

Suarez had had enough of Diego. 'You've seen enough cops to know how we operate. We are looking for your sister. You will be kept informed, but don't make the mistake of thinking you're working with us. Understood?'

Diego gave Suarez the finger and stormed off to the other side of the corridor.

Suarez went after him. 'Don't get any ideas with my partner.'

Diego turned his back on Suarez and got on his cell.

On the elevator, Suarez called Smyth. 'Diego's still there. Keep him away from Halloran. Keep the backup on him.'

'Stop with your directions. Last time I looked I was a D2. I know what to do.'

🌴

The hood of the Mercedes had popped and dull grey smoke rose from the car. Engine oil leaked onto the street. The side wheel had been pushed up against the engine. The passenger door was dented. Cars honked, but a ring of people who suddenly appeared were oddly quiet. An older driver whose car had been struck was holding his head and leaning unsteadily against his car. The other driver had been stunned by the airbag and was cradling her nose. Wailing sirens closed in on the scene of the accident.

Ahead, a water main had broken, and traffic was single-lane, stopped for the most part.

Felicia had gotten out of the car before anyone knew what had happened. Ponytail's briefcase had hit the dash under the airbag and burst open. He could see her outside the car. Scrambling across the driver's seat, he crawled out and attempted to go after her.

'You can't go anywhere!' someone shouted. 'You can't leave till the police come.'

Felicia couldn't run, so she stumbled forward along Harding beside small stucco homes with cement driveways. The knife had caught her above the hip, but well below her kidney.

Three men stood in Ponytail's way. 'My wife's been hurt! The papers are in the car, insurance and all the stuff the police will need. I'm not running! I have to see how my wife is. She's disoriented. I have to help her. If she's okay, we'll be back.'

The men and women didn't move. The crowd grew.

Ponytail raised both arms and barrelled through the bystanders. 'You're all fucking nuts! My wife is hurt!' He took off after Felicia. One man ran after him a short distance before giving up the chase.

Felicia wasn't that far ahead of him, when Ponytail sputtered to a stop. His kneecaps blew out. *My papers are back in the car! The signed bank transfer!* He looked back at the Mercedes. Flashing lights told him the cops had arrived. His throat dried, his hope collected in pain behind his knees. He felt for his wallet. He had that. A roaring laugh came out of his mouth. 'I have duplicates at home, but not signed. But I have the numbers.' He began to run the last ten blocks, down a lane he often took between Harding and Collins. He didn't have time for Felicia. Two blocks from home, his world crashed. *The Alvarez ID was in the briefcase. I can't leave until I see Ruiz again. That little rat has to set me up with new papers. I did so much goddamn planning for this!* Ponytail threw his shoulder into a mailbox and knocked it over.

♣

Watts had called 9-1-1 to report the possible extortion of Felicia Alvarez that had taken place at the Bank of North America on 178th Street. Since there was an APB out on Alvarez, the computer caught it. So did Suarez on his way back to the Trump. He contacted Watts immediately.

'This is Detective Suarez. What can you tell me about your report?'

Watts was flattered, frightened and precise.

'Was her husband with her?'

'Yes.'

'Would you know Alvarez by sight?'

'I met them when they opened the accounts. Maybe once after that.'

'Can you positively say it was Jesús Alvarez?'

'I honestly can't, Detective. He wouldn't allow Mrs. Alvarez to talk today. He blocked me from any direct contact with her during the transaction.'

'What transaction?'

'A five-million-dollar transfer to Toronto, Ontario.'

'What time did this occur?'

'That's the thing, Detective. It didn't.'

'What do you mean?' Suarez gained a new respect for Felicia. He also now knew where the perp was headed. He didn't know that there was no money train waiting for him in Toronto. In short order, he faxed Lila's sketch to the precinct and had it sent to both airports. Then he assigned backup at Lauderdale and Miami. As soon as he had the video recording, he'd send the photo to the *Herald* and TV stations. The perp's ignorance worked to their advantage.

Leap-frogging along Collins, he parked at the curb near the Trump. A crush of press was already there. Suarez took the call in his car. 'Hello, Lila.'

'Do you have any news?'

'Carlos didn't make it. The doctors worked very hard.'

'Poor Carlos. Has Maria been told?'

'She's with him now.'

'Poor us too.'

'Mrs. Katz, how closely did the double resemble Mr. Alvarez? Are you there?'

'Carlos was a decent fellow. What was the question?'

Suarez repeated it.

'I didn't know it wasn't Jesús, until he spoke, and I was two feet from him.'

'I have to go.'

'Thank you.' Lila looked at Abby and shook her head. Lila hadn't cried in a long time. 'I'd grown quite fond of Carlos, even after I discovered he'd stolen from us. The *yentas* will miss him too.'

'Do you want me to make you a cup of tea?'

'No.'

Lila had given Suarez another idea. There was a photo of Jesús in the suite. He'd use that until he saw the quality of the recording. He'd call Brianna Melanson at the *Herald*. They had an understanding. She was more trustworthy than the other news hounds. The perp's face would be in the morning paper. He called the precinct again. 'Send the sketch to all auto rentals.'

'Now?'

'Yesterday!' Lila Katz was the only living witness who knew that the double was not Jesús Alvarez. Halloran was the only other possible witness.

CHAPTER TWENTY-SIX

CAITLIN AND CARMEN stood at the side of Mike's bed in the ICU. He seemed to know they were there. Caitlin took his hand. He squeezed it. When she leaned over the bed and kissed him gently, he opened his eyes. 'Hey!' he smiled weakly.

'Thank God, you'll be okay.'

'What happened?' His voice was hoarse and dry.

'You don't remember?'

'Caitlin, give Mike a chance to think. It's probably the anaesthetic.'

'I'm sorry I blew off your concern about Felicia.'

'The garage...'

'Don't try to sit up. Just rest.'

'Can you raise the bed, Caitlin?' he asked.

'Just rest. We only have a few minutes. Can you recall anything?'

'I went to see if the Spyder was in the garage.'

'Why didn't you just go to work?'

Carmen gave Caitlin an elbow in the ribs.

Mike managed another smile. 'When have you two ever left anything alone?'

'Okay, what happened then?'

'I was about to leave when I saw Felicia with her husband.' Mike's eyes closed.

'Let's leave him alone, Caitlin. We can come back.'

'I'm tired. Can you get me some ice chips? My lips are cracking.'

Carmen went looking for them.

'Mike?'

He focused again.

'Did her husband stab you?'

'Didn't really see him. I was looking at her. She was

scared. He sprang at me and I went down.'

'Her husband tried to kill you?'

'Yes.'

'Rest. You'll be okay. That's the important thing. I'm sorry for everything. I called your work. I love you, Mike Halloran.'

He smiled again.

Caitlin kissed him and waited for Carmen. They left the ice chips near his hand on the bed when a nurse signalled that time was up.

'You can go in for two minutes an hour from now.'

'We'll be here.' As soon as they walked through the swinging doors, Smyth caught up with them. Diego hovered.

'Get over there, please. Officer, escort Mr. Gonzalez away from here.'

He backed off two steps, but no further. Diego threw his arms up. 'Get your hands off me. This is a public place.'

'Caitlin, was Mike able to talk?' Smyth asked. She spoke with her back to Diego.

'Yes, but he's asleep now.'

'Does he know who assaulted him?'

Diego stepped closer.

'If he doesn't back off, cuff him!' That worked.

'He thought it was her husband, but he wasn't certain. Is Mike still in danger? I saw an officer inside the door.'

'Precautions. When I speak to him, I might be able to get a little more information. You're both staying at the hospital?'

'Of course.'

'Don't speak to that man over there. That's a police order.'

'We understand.' A nervous shiver passed through both women.

Smyth called Suarez. 'The second assault is connected. I won't leave till I see Halloran. What's up on your end?'

'Special Crimes lasered the suite and sent the prints to Latents. I'll use the TV here to go through the video recording, so I'm staying. CS Cleanup is already at work. See Halloran, get what you can and post an officer in the corridor and inside the OR doors. When Gonzalez sees you leave, my gut tells me he will too. Get down here after Halloran – I'll order something for both of us.'

'Not Chinese; I get indigestion from that crap. Summarize what we have. You're the 'Grand Poobah' of repeats, Suarez.'

'Gut again. Identification fraud elevated to a new high. Knock off the victims, transfer their holdings, walk into their lives in another state or country. Jesús is probably dead meat somewhere if the double has the wife. Katz is a viable witness; Halloran, a maybe. If Jesús is dead, we have ourselves a double bagger if we nab the fucker.'

'Good take,' Smyth added.

'I have more. The bank manager, a Richard Watts, reported the extortion. Here's the gold star. He got through to Alvarez on the phone after their meeting and she played the fucker. The money wasn't sent. He doesn't know that yet, I assume. I'll flood the airwaves, airports and bus terminals with photos of Jesús. If the double's that good, we'll be fishing for the two of them at the same time. Someone's seen him.'

'What about hers?'

'I don't want to give the perp an added reason to do her.'

'So far, she's holding her own with him,' Smyth pointed out.

'She has balls. I'll wait here at the Trump for you.'

Suarez walked out onto the balcony and realized how cold the suite was. Moderate hypothermia he now understood. Nothing would melt in there. It was before dusk, but the distant sky was a water-colored mass of layered pastels. Heat brushed up against him. His shoulders relaxed. The ocean was quiet. Small waves lapped the shoreline, wetting a lazy line of dark seaweed that snaked along the water's edge.

Somewhere behind this quiet, a young woman had felt the seconds slip from her life and was managing to hold on. He began to root for Felicia. Suarez went back inside, turned off the air. He'd start the recording without Smyth.

CHAPTER TWENTY-SEVEN

FELICIA HAD FELT a punch as she scrambled out of the Mercedes, but adrenalin, pumping with the thought that she'd survive, kept her focus off the injury. The searing pain she could feel was coming from her wrist. Her eyes narrowed with it. Stumbling on, she didn't look back. Felicia did not know that Ponytail had turned down the lane. The pastel homes she scrambled past had iron-grated windows and doors. Everything was locked up.

A tearing throb in her back began to slow her down to an awkward walk. Ahead, a jogger approached. Felicia stopped and grabbed a white iron-spiked fence and held on. Her back was facing the road.

Jessica Wessman had been running 70 blocks three times a week for the past few months since her real estate sales dried up. She had enough put aside for the down-turn. The woman leaning against the fence reminded her of when she'd done the same thing. Joggers hung on fences when they'd pushed too hard. When she got closer, Jessica saw the woman wasn't jogging. She was in some kind of trouble. 'Are you alright?' Jessica asked tentatively when she saw blood on the back of her cotton skirt. 'I'll call for help,' she said, pulling her cell from her waistband.

'Please, I have a number,' Felicia pleaded, turning to face Jessica.

'Sit down. Your hip is soaked with blood.'

'Please, I have someone to call.'

Jessica wanted to call 9-1-1. The woman was about to faint. 'Give me the number, I'll make the call for you and hand you the phone.'

Smyth was giving last instructions to the officer posted out in the corridor when Diego's phone rang.

He brought the cell to his ear and covered the phone with the palm of his hand. He raced back and forth. 'You have somebody with you? Put her on. Can you stay with my sister?'

'I guess, but she needs medical help. I was just out jogging.'

'She'll have it. Where are you?'

'Allison Park, near 77th Street.'

'Call a cab. Take my sister to St. Francis Hospital on 63rd Street. I'll reimburse you and add $500 for your time. Ask for Dr. Gabriel Roth. He is a family friend. I'll call him now to advise him that you will be at the hospital.'

'Dr. Roth?'

'That's correct. I will see you soon.'

'You can pay for the cab, but no money to help someone out.' Jessica did not want to be this involved, but the woman needed help.

'I love my sister more than life. I will be at the hospital in 30 minutes. Your generosity will not be forgotten. May I speak to my sister again?'

'Felicia, do you have ID?'

'No. Diego, do not worry. The injury is not serious.'

'Good, use your middle name and Gonzalez, not Alvarez. I'm on my way. *Te amo!* I'll take care of you.' Diego ran out of the corridor. He shouted back at Smyth. 'I don't need cops!' He wanted Roth caring for his sister. He suspected the attack on Felicia might have something to do with inter-gang war and he did not want to make his sister more vulnerable by sending her to one of the larger hospitals.

She took off after him, scrambling to call Suarez as she ran. 'Diego's found something. He just tore out of here!'

'See if you can catch his tag at least'. He has six or seven vehicles; I'll get those tags for you.'

Smyth flew down eight flights of stairs. The elevator was too slow. Diego was gone! 'He's in the wind,' she rasped into the phone.

'He's on to someone – we have to find out who that is!'

'Fuck!'

'Swearing won't get us anywhere. Get back up to the OR. I'll issue another APB for him and all his cars. I just saw the recording of Carlos's murder. This is one cold-blooded bastard. Just sliced him and threw him in the bath. Cleaned up and went back to the sister who never knew what happened. Without Katz, I would have sworn it was Jesús. I'll pack up and haul all this to the precinct.'

'What about the paperwork?' she asked.

'Later for the Prelim Report. I'll leave the Chron-ology work to you. Right now, we have to find Diego.'

'What about hospitals?'

'I'll cover that. If there is nothing with Carlos's wife, get to the station.' The Beach Police Department was located behind Sunny Isles City Hall in North Miami Beach, close to the Trump. Miami-Dade Police handled homicide. Suarez and Smyth worked at that precinct on Biscayne Boulevard.

On the OAW floor, the *yentas* held their weekly association meeting. The first point on the agenda was Carlos Diaz and the fruit basket and money for his wife Maria. The fourth point of order was Sophie and her repeated misdemeanors. Margaret Foley had absented herself from the meeting. Since word had spread from James about the terrible fate of Carlos, she knew that

Lila might need her, and she called her and told her as much.

'Abby's here with me. Would you like to join us?'

'I'd like that very much. I'm feeling low myself.'

Abby poured hand-squeezed cherry lemonade for the three women, but for the most part, they sat in silence. What they shared was a human presence and a loving silence that was broken half an hour later when Sophie's wails burst ahead of her down the hall. 'Let me see what's happened.'

Sophie's cheeks were blotched with mascara and tears fell from her chin.

'What's happened, Sophie?'

'I've been suspended for three games! They don't want me.'

'Slow down. You don't want to fall!'

Sophie blubbered past Lila into her suite, tripped over Little Caesar and fell hard on the marble entrance.

'Help! Help!'

All three women went to her and found Sophie splayed across the Italian marble. Little Caesar whimpered beside her. 'Don't move, Sophie,' Lila ordered. 'You may have broken a hip!' Margaret called down to the office. James was only too pleased to get security and take them up. A whole new revenue path was opening up for him if he played nice and comforting to the old crows.

The OAW women lined the corridor as Sophie was wheeled out on a gurney, hollering and moaning. 'I tripped right over poor Little Caesar!'

'I'll take care of the pets, Sophie.' Margaret called after her.

When Sophie saw Abby, she stopped hollering and pulled Abby to the gurney. 'Who can I sue for this?'

Abby suppressed the belly laugh that threatened her

friendship and work with Sophie. 'Unfortunately, you can't sue anyone.'

Sophie's cheeks fell into her chin and she went back to hollering.

Behind her, in a wild chorus, Mischa, Israel and Little Caesar pierced a few eardrums with their high-pitched howling. Little Caesar wasn't at full strength. He was limping.

Muriel was a quiet woman who loved being part of the OAW club. When she spoke up, all the women were taken aback. 'Even if Sophie hasn't broken her hip, we should grant her a full pardon. Invite her to our next poker night. She's done enough penance with this fall. We all have faults!'

There was consensus on the second vote. Muriel's comment commanded a new respect.

Smyth ran back up the stairs and located Maria Diaz in the Quiet Room. 'Mrs. Diaz, I'm Detective Smyth. I have a few questions that I must ask. We want the person responsible for this.'

Maria slumped on the chair and kept her eyes on Carlos while she held his hand.

'Was Mr. Diaz frightened before he was attacked?'

Maria's shoulders began to shake. 'He said we must leave our house. Twice, he ordered me to go to another house.'

'Did he say who was threatening you?'

'He gave me no chance to talk. He said someone was watching the house.'

'Did he say who?'

'Carlos did not tell me.'

Smyth couldn't wait around. She found Mike Halloran with his friends. She began her questioning. There was no time to waste. 'Mr. Halloran, Detective Smyth. Did you get a good look at the man who stabbed you?'

Mike's memory had begun to clear. 'I saw Felicia first. Her husband was pulling her along. She looked scared.'

'What about him?'

'When he sprang at me, I saw him.'

'Her husband attacked you then?'

'I don't know. The other day I saw what looked liked his twin or a relative in the Trump, pretending to be him. There was something out of sync with the guy I'd first seen. I told Caitlin, but she thought I was nuts.'

'You saw the husband a few days ago, according to Caitlin. Was there anything different about your attacker that you might remember?'

'It happened so fast. I never saw the knife.'

'You still might recall something. Give it time. When you're released, I assume I can find you at the Trump.'

'Yes. Just a sec. The guy who knifed me was taller than the husband, I think. I can't be sure. It was so fast.'

'Give it time and get well.'

'I feel better already.' There were dark circles under Mike's eyes. He didn't look much better.

Speeding along I-95, Smyth used her lights and siren, even when she exited on NE-95th Street down to Biscayne Boulevard. *Except for Lila Katz, we have no stand-up proof of a double. Halloran was too busy hitting on Felicia to ever get a good look at the perp. The video record might be our only evidence. The problem is the perp's a dead ringer…* Her stomach honked. Smyth gave it a few whacks. She reached into the glove compartment for the half Hershey bar she'd saved. *Damn!* She called Suarez en route. 'Did you finish off my Hershey?'

'You said you were dieting. I've started eating without you.'

'Double damn! Is there anything you ever let me get

to first?'

'Is it that time of the month already? I have club sandwiches.'

'Don't even breathe on mine. Halloran's still a possible. He saw the double before the assault at the Trump. His head'll clear.'

'Sec, I have another call.'

Smyth waited.

He slapped the cell shut. 'Felicia Alvarez's Mercedes back-ended two vehicles on Harding Avenue almost an hour ago. She ran from the scene. According to witnesses, a male passenger went after her. Fuck! We know who called Diego.'

CHAPTER TWENTY-EIGHT

A FEW BLOCKS from his house and its freezer, Ponytail ripped off the gold clasp in his hair. For the time being, he wanted to look like the man his neighbors knew. The heat was nearing 90 degrees. Ponytail's shirt stuck to his chest and back. He took off the watch. Neighborhood kids were crooks who travelled in packs. The last thing he needed was an ambush. Pocketing the watch, he threw the jacket into one of the trash cans that lined the lane, passed the fenced house where the owner had three orange trees, and began to run.

His rented place was one block past the smallest house he'd ever seen. This was wood, flecked with peeling white paint, and a sinking roof. It looked like a boxcar but wasn't, had one-foot windows and one hand-made wooden door at each end, both locked with a padlock that a kid could pull open. What always got Ponytail was the satellite dish on the roof. He could reach it and so could anyone else, yet no one had stolen it. It had also survived the hurricane a few years back.

Ah shit!

The landlord was out sweeping, a widow who had nothing to do but sweep and talk. 'Where's Daisy? I thought you two might have skipped out on the rent.' Shirley was as thin as her broom and as old. Her heels were cracked with dirt, and her ankles were swollen. Soap and water weren't her favorite accessories. Her life savings was the house she rented to Ponytail.

Later on that one. 'Daisy's mother's sick. She took a train back home. I have to go, Shirley, I'm in a bit of a rush.'

'Where's the Jag?'

'Garage.'

'The Brits never made a good car. That's what Fred used to say.'

'Americans produce it now. Shirley, have to go.'

'Well!'

As soon as he locked the door, Ponytail ran to the freezer. Jesús was there. He tried to lift him, but he was as heavy as an ice truck. 'Fuck you. Good riddance!' He called Ruiz. 'I need more papers for Jesús Alvarez.' He was on his own now.

'Didn't keep the dupes.'

'Cost?'

'Same as the first time.'

'You're screwing me.'

'Didn't lose the stuff – you did.'

'I'll be there before seven.'

'Cash.'

Ponytail tossed the receiver onto the bed. In the shower, he slipped and banged his shoulder and knee before he caught himself. When all the balls you're juggling at once fall, you can't catch each of them before they hit the ground. *She took the car!* Ponytail stepped dripping out of the shower and ran to see if Daisy had taken their stash. He fell on his knees and punched the floor. *Bitch!*

He had to get the IDs and get out of Miami tonight with the money he'd taken off Carlos. He might still make it. His muscles loosened, like they were falling too. Her brother knew about him… What if they reversed the transfer? What if her brother just came after him? There was a stash of pot in the toilet tank. He couldn't take a chance. He had to be alert. For a second, he felt like a fuckup. Then he was a rabbit and he began to run.

🔎

Dr. Roth was with a patient when his personal cell

vibrated in the pocket of his white hospital coat. He saw the caller ID and wished he were on the greens at Sawgrass in Ponte Vedra Beach, hitting balls. Two years ago, he had invested heavily with a persuasive advisor who, it turned out, operated out of a windowless store room. Gabe figured he'd lost a million and a half in the scam. Apart from his wife, family and friends didn't know. In a moment of despair, Sue had confided in Jennifer Gonzalez, who golfed with her, without ever telling him.

Although Jennifer and Diego Gonzalez kept to themselves on Biscayne Bay, neighbors knew who they were and gave them a wide berth. Many of the good folks secretly envied the new 'godfather' who simply took what he wanted and spent lavishly. His mega yacht was in its own league.

Gabe worked overtime attempting to recoup. He hadn't told Sue the debt was actually a million and a half. Four months later, he was wary when he opened the door to Diego Gonzalez. 'Here Gabe, Jen told me you lost something that I thought you might need. Just came across it – wanted to be a good neighbor.' When Gabe took the envelope, he felt he had to open it in front of Diego. A certified check for a million dollars was made out to him. Relief, gratitude and fear spiked around his heart. Gabe owned DVDs of *Goodfellas*, all three *Godfathers*, *The Sopranos* and *TheBrotherhood*. It might only have been only fiction, but Gabe's debt came with this check.

'Diego, I can't take this.'

'No one was hurt. It was just a question of moving money from him to you.'

'I can't be involved in…'

'You're not. He thought he was donating this money to the family. No link to you, no harm to him.'

Someday, Godfather will need a favor… Gabe heard the words the consigliere had said to the undertaker in *Godfather I*. Danger buzzed up Gabe's back – his eyes locked with Diego's. It was a high. He licked his bottom lip. Gabe wanted his money. He thought of the extra half million he'd lost.

Diego saw Gabe's hesitation, the weakness, and he stepped on it. A clean contact had great value. 'Take it! It was always yours. However, if you want a reason for my largesse, I'll tell you. Your wife is the only person who befriended Jennifer at the club. Family and friends count highly in my life. You are good neighbors. Money is only money.' Diego thrust the check into Gabe's hand and left before Gabe could respond. *Done!*

For the next month, Gabe's pressure spiked. Nothing happened. He stopped screening his calls and began to relax. When he heard the phone, he grabbed the receiver without a tweak of dread. 'Yes?'

'Diego Gonzalez.'

'Hello, Diego.'

'I need your help.'

There it was – the debt.

'My sister's life is in jeopardy; she's been injured and taken to your hospital by a woman who found her. Felicia has done nothing wrong. Would you meet her in the ER? She's wounded and bleeding. You have seen Felicia in the past, so you know her. I don't want the admittance recorded anywhere, or the police involved. They tried to find her and couldn't. I want to take my sister home with me as soon as possible.'

'Diego, there are laws.'

'I'm on my way and should be there minutes after she arrives.'

Gabe didn't answer.

'Are you still there?'

I could lose my licence. 'I'll go down to the ER.'

'I will see you soon. This will not be forgotten.' Diego knew enough about cops to know they were out looking for him. He parked his car and cabbed it to the hospital.

The buzz Gabe had felt four months ago was gone. He rushed down to the ER to wait outside.

'Dr. Roth? Slumming?' Mandy called out to Gabe from the nurse's station. 'Have you heard the news?'

He stopped.

'Felicia Alvarez has been injured, and the police sent us photos to be on the look-out! You know who she is, right?'

Gabe nodded, pinching his cheeks.

'I guess everybody does. The bulletin says she might come to smaller hospitals. Are you off shift, by the way?'

'No, I just need a little air. Indigestion.' Gabe knew he'd lose a lot more than a million if he lost his licence. Sweat ponds began to form in his shoes. Outside, the heat was like walking into woolly insulation. Gabe took out his cell and memorized the number he saw there and dialed. 'Diego?'

'I'm almost there.'

'There's a police bulletin with a photo of your sister all over the ER and the entire hospital. I can't get your sister in without her being recognized.'

'Where are you?'

'Outside the ER entrance.'

'Get a medical bag, catch her outside the hospital, take her to your home and treat Felicia there. That is, if her life is not in danger.'

'I can't do...'

'Yes, you can.'

'I think I see her. Wait a minute.' Gabe ran up to the cab.

The jogger got out quickly. 'This woman needs help.

I thought you'd have a gurney or something. I found her. I don't have the fare for the cab.' Jessica chose not to stay around.

Gabe gave the cabbie two twenties and climbed into the back seat with Felicia. When he saw the blood, he called the ER and Diego. 'Your sister requires treatment now. I'm taking her to the ER.'

'I want you working on her.'

'Is that a threat?'

'Why would I threaten someone who's into me for a million?'

CHAPTER TWENTY-NINE

SMYTH AND SUAREZ had demolished the club sand-wiches. 'Look at this photo. Now, look at the blowup. Can you see any difference between the two?' He held it up under a light.

'Not really. It can't be the husband. He wouldn't have needed Carlos. The double needed Carlos to get into the room. Why create an extra mess when you don't have to? Any luck with Diego or Felicia?'

'Nothing yet.'

'I've had photos sent to the hospitals. She's injured – she has to go somewhere.'

'Look at this.' Suarez cued up the second video. 'What do you make of the fact that he doesn't rape her?'

'He's not stupid. He knows who she is.'

'What I figured. Just a sec!' Suarez took the phone. 'That's it? Shit.' He closed the phone. 'They found Diego's car, one of them, anyway.'

'Is it close to a hospital?'

'Get the map.'

🌴

Snip and Clip was popular because it also had an in-house vet, Max, who was called to the Trump when Margaret discovered Little Caesar couldn't walk after his first few limping steps. It took Max little time to see that the terrier had broken his right hind leg. 'He'll need a splint or a cast, Margaret. I have to take him in for X-rays. How's Sophie doing?'

'We haven't heard.'

'Sophie wouldn't want him spending the night. Is there any chance you could have him back tonight?'

'I'll get on it. Do my best, but no promises.'

'Your best is good enough.'

'Take off his vest and diamond-studded collar. That stuff is tempting to the younger guys on staff.'

Little Caesar began to cry when Margaret took off his collar. His name belied a courage he didn't possess. Margaret's Mops took in the whole scene and was relieved to be rid of one of Sophie's intruders on his territory. Max left with Little Caesar who was carefully wrapped in blue terrycloth. Mischa and Israel looked over at Mops and backed into Margaret's legs. They knew their presence was not appreciated.

🌴

Diego got to St. Francis before Felicia was wheeled up to the OR. At least Gabe Roth had stayed with her. It was Dr. Roth he spotted first and he ran past nurses and gurneys and waiting patients until he found Felicia. The initial thrill of knowing she was still alive vanished when he saw her. Her face was gray, the bruise on her cheek had swelled and her eyes were hollow. 'Sis!' He kissed her good cheek, and she grabbed his hand. 'What happened to your wrist?' It was clearly swollen. Diego balled his fist and bit his finger. *The fuck who did this will pay!* 'Can you talk?'

'I gave her a mild sedative,' Gabe said.

'Did Jesús do this to you?'

'No,' Felicia whispered weakly. 'How is Mike?'

'Who's Mike?'

'He tried to help me, but the man stabbed him.' A peace settled in her eyes.

'I have to take her now. She suffered a knife wound in her back.'

Diego pounded a fist into his hand. 'Felicia, you'll be okay. I'll call *los viejos*. *Mamá* and *Papá* should know what has happened.

Felicia was letting go. Her eyes closed. 'How long will she be in surgery?'

'At least a few hours. Diego, they know who she is.'

Diego turned and saw he was under the scrutiny of many curious eyes. 'Gabe, work miracles and call me as soon as Felicia's out of surgery. She was abducted. Your only worry is the surgery. Call me! I don't want to be here when the suits arrive.' *Mike knows who did this!* Diego cursed for not having a car. Instead, he took a cab back to Jackson Memorial. On the way, he made a call demanding one of his soldiers find hospital whites. *Fuck it!* He flipped open his phone. 'Forget the whites. I need Pedro.' *This is a free country – I can talk to whomever I want.* He snapped the phone closed.

'Do you mind if I put on some music?' the female cabbie asked. She'd flipped on her station before Diego could answer. Fergie was singing "Big Girls Don't Cry."

Diego was about to tell her to *turn that chick shit off* when he heard a few of the words. In spite of the anger that worked its way through him like the heat outside the cab, his nose began to run. To Diego, Felicia would always be fragile and soft, a beautiful diver, a sister he had to protect, someone better than he was. Jennifer was his wife – Felicia was blood. He missed her when she left the Bay. His devotion remained as dependable as a Miami sunrise. And yet she'd survived where the concierge had not, and without him. She'd also thought about this Mike before herself. He wrapped his hand against his heart. Now he was proud of his sister. 'Music's okay.'

🌴

Torn pieces of white toast were scattered on two Styrofoam plates and empty Coke cans when the call came in. Smyth grabbed it. 'St. Francis! Got it!'

'Felicia got away from the double. She's in surgery at St. Francis. Diego was there.'

'The race is on to see who gets to the perp. Diego will pull out all the stops. He can't know about Lila. Flip on the TV.'

'Now?' Suarez asked.

'Jesús's face should be looking back at us from Channel Seven News and the others as well. His photo was the clearest and the perp's a double. We hunt Jesús and the perp. Good call on my part.'

They didn't have long to wait. The early anchor announced that Miami-Dade police were looking for the man featured in the photo. He was armed and dangerous. If he was spotted, citizens were advised to call the police and not attempt any confrontation. 'Good!' Suarez said. 'He can't fly out. His mug's on every terminal, domestic and foreign. Greyhound has been sent their individual photos. The roach will scurry into corners. Let's get down to St. Francis.'

Another call came in. Smyth was faster again. 'Diego's left the hospital.'

'She's told him something. We can't afford to be behind.'

🌴

CHAPTER THIRTY

IT WASN'T QUITE 5:30 when Shirley, Ponytail's landlady took out her boxed wine and poured herself a tumbler. On the stove water was boiling, and she emptied her Kraft dinner into the pot. Small diced blocks of American cheddar and cherry tomatoes lay on the side of the sink. With a fresh, seeded rye, Shirley was set. After she angled the TV fold-up table, she went to the stove and stirred the pasta. Once the macaroni was drained, slithering in a yellow bowl, she added the cheese and tomatoes and waited for the cheese to melt before she added pepper.

Shirley always watched the early news as she ate. At six, she flipped to reruns of *I Love Lucy* or *All in the Family.* Before she began to eat, she was on her second glass of white wine.

Ponytail was counting the money that he had spread across the bed. *Not even seven grand!* Back in his makeshift office, he took out his hard drive, tore up any paper that could incriminate him and bagged it, cut up the other cards, packed the stuff he'd take with him to San Fran and thought about a car. A rental meant exposure and risking phoney ID and money he needed. He remembered the landlady's junky Taurus.

Shirley had a mouthful of wine when the photo of Jesús came up on the screen. For a second, she didn't swallow. Her eyes were riveted to the 27-inch screen. *Is that Ponytail? Is there a reward?*

He knocked twice. Shirley was riveted to the screen. He let himself in and called out. 'Shirley? I need a favor.'

Shirley slipped down into her rattan chair.

'There you are!' In the living room, he saw a TV, three old chairs and one end table. The walls were plastered with old photos in dollar-store frames. 'Didn't you hear me?'

'What are you doing in my house?' Her words were slightly slurred.

'I need your car. I'll give you 20 bucks and pump another ten of gas when I get it back.'

'I don't lend my car.' Shirley had grabbed her fork.

'What's wrong with you?'

He saw when the photo popped back up on the screen.

'Shirley, you think that's me? Wow!'

Shirley grabbed her glass.

'The guy looks like me and how many other Cubans? Come on, Shirley.'

'I need my car. That guy on TV could be any Cuban. You're right.' Her eyes twitched. She knew she'd given herself away. Shirley tried to get up quickly. The bowl fell on the floor and broke. Macaroni slid all around her.

'What a mess!' Ponytail looked behind him. He had closed the door. 'Here's a 20. Give me an hour.'

'Please get out.' Shirley moved away, stepped onto the macaroni and slid awkwardly to the floor.

'Shit, let me help you up!'

Shirley wanted to scream, she heard the scream in her head, but it never came out. Her neck broke like a dry twig. Ponytail dragged her through the macaroni, across the floor to a cleaning closet. The last thing Shirley saw was her favorite dinner on the floor. He grabbed her underarms and threw Shirley inside the closet.

The photo on TV meant he had to get to Ruiz before he made the connection or he was fucked. At least he had a car and an extra $20. He found Shirley's purse and took what she had, $42. A miser all the way. Scrambling through the house, he finally found the keys under her pillow, checked the lane before he let himself out and hurried back into his own place. Once he had the IDs, he'd take off. He cursed Daisy. This was a two-man job – he'd needed her, and the bitch had cleaned him out.

Ponytail saw his reflection in the bathroom mirror when he threw water on his face. He tried to see a murderer, but he didn't. His eyelids were crusty from lack of sleep, and dark lines ran under his eyes. His face had taken a beating, but the only striking change was a constant sweat that he wiped away. In seconds, the sweat was back. He concentrated on the sun lines that began at the side of his nose and travelled to his mouth.

Why did Daisy skip town after Jesús? People murdered each other all the time. Killers walked the streets every day: drunks destroyed whole families, soldiers gunned down civilians, cops used guns and tasers, students turned on each other and old farts drove half blind and mowed down pedestrians. They were still human, and many of them bullshitted their way back into society. He took his run at thieves. When he was casing marks, he had seen their Infinity pools and the yachts. Once he had cased a home that looked like a French palace. Why should a handful have all the power and money? Felicia had never earned a cent of her millions. In a way, Ponytail thought, he was like the TV character *Dexter*. He'd gone after the bad guys.

He looked out the window, wishing for dusk. His theories and bravado began to evaporate. The only part of his plan that was still viable was flying out to San Fran. He missed Daisy. He was alone with his secrets and had no one to back him up. The sun was too bright, sweeping through shadows and hideouts, making things too clear. Ponytail had to get to Ruiz. His stuff was against the front wall and he was at the door when a thought cut into his plan. He had a car, but could he come back here with Shirley in her closet and Jesús in the freezer?

Caitlin and Carmen had just left Mike, looking for a vending machine. They were halfway to the elevator when Diego stepped out. The officer was posted back at the entrance to ICU. The police hadn't told them anything about Diego. 'What do we do?' Carmen whispered with her head down, loud enough for Caitlin to hear.

'Keep walking – what can we do?' Caitlin shot back, getting the words out between her teeth.

'Stop, please.' Diego saw Caitlin first. A runway face – eyes the color of the ocean and a thick mass of blonde curls. In Carmen, he saw Felicia, silky hair and dark eyes, vulnerable but strong, as he now knew.

'We were told not…' Both women were drawn to the aura of power and sex that Diego gave off.

'I'm not the bad guy. Cops have it in for me. I'm Felicia's brother.'

'We heard.'

'I *was* shouting, I know. I found my sister.'

The C's stood listening.

'She got away; she's in surgery.'

'Good for her!' Carmen said.

'She's not in great shape. Look, here's what I wanted to say. The first words Felicia uttered were, "How is Mike? He tried to help me." He's your friend, right?'

Caitlin's stomach moved nervously.

'Mike's a good one.' Carmen knew what Caitlin was thinking and shielded her.

'I'm in his debt. Is there anything he needs? Any help I can offer?'

'We're okay,' Caitlin assured Diego.

'I asked my sister if her husband had assaulted her. She said no.'

A hurried glance passed between the C's.

'Your friend Mike must have seen this man.'

'I don't think…' Caitlin began.

'This is my sister. Please.'

Caitlin wanted to talk. Carmen pulled her t-shirt.

'Please, anything.' A hardness cut around Diego's mouth. 'Did Mike say what this man looked like?'

Caitlin did not want to endanger Mike or themselves.

'Please.' Stress overtook the anger. 'Please.'

Caitlin worried that if she said nothing, Diego might storm Mike's room, even with the officers there. 'He didn't get a good look at the assailant. He thought it was her husband.'

'What? But it wasn't. Felicia told me it wasn't. Did the guy look like Jesús, is that it? That's what this is all about, an imposter?'

'We have to go,' Caitlin told Diego. The C's rushed back to the corridor. Coffee didn't matter. 'I shouldn't have said anything. I thought he could somehow get to Mike if I didn't tell him something.'

'It's too late now,' Carmen warned.

'Thanks for the support.'

'I didn't mean it like that. You and I can't keep our mouths shut.'

Diego took the stairs. He wanted to get back to his sister and send his men out on the streets. He checked in with Pedro.

'Cops are looking for Jesús. His mug is all over TV.'

'Not Jesús, a dead ringer.'

'You sure?'

'Pedro, what the fuck? Are you at St. Francis yet?'

'Waiting for you, Diego.'

'Cops?'

'Haven't seen any yet.'

'Stay out of the way till I get there. They'll swarm the

place. The hospital staff reported her.' Diego began his calls on the way to St. Francis. If this imposter was still in Miami, he'd find him. Fed up with cabs, he'd take Pedro's car once he got to the hospital.

CHAPTER THIRTY-ONE

TO BRIGHTEN SPIRITS, Chef Ramon went all out with dinner in Margaret's suite. She had invited the gang. Dinner began with a tri-color vegetarian terrine with artichoke fritters stuffed with blue crab. Haddock in cream sauce was Margaret's favorite. The breads were mixed: nut-raisin grain, Austrian white, flax bread, and a baguette. Ramon's dessert was a raspberry mousse in a light cream chocolate base.

'Abby, you've been such a friend; don't feel you have to stay for dinner. I'll survive Jake. I have for 60 years.' Lila tried to be brave, but she wasn't convincing.

'I haven't seen Jake in a year. I'd like to chat for a while. And who could walk away from one of Ramon's dinners?'

Lila patted Abby's back. 'I'm glad. I'm quite sad really. I don't want Jake to reason me to death or to the point where I want to send him back home. I can be a terrible person, but I'm very pleased Sophie's not hosting to-night. I'm not up for her wailing wall of gilded framed photos of absent friends, animals and humans.'

'You ought to write a book on the OAWs!'

'Nobody would believe it! And at 88, I haven't the time.'

Margaret's dining room was sumptuous. The room sparkled with light and the glorious shades of early dusk, but the mood inside the room was sombre. The women felt guilty for suspending Sophie and worse for losing Carlos. Before Ramon began to pour the white Sauvignon, there was a persistent knock at the door. Ramon sighed and went to it.

James stepped too eagerly into the foyer and then too abruptly into the dining room. 'Ladies, I know what a terrible loss you have suffered. Carlos was my friend too.'

'Carlos detested James,' Lila whispered to Abby.

Abby smothered a laugh.

'I just want to say that Manager Hernandez has given me the honor of helping you ladies out whenever I can. I have the use of the van and I know a few restaurants you might enjoy. In fact, I can make tomorrow a dog track afternoon.'

'James, thank you for the offer, but it is a little premature,' Margaret said. 'We have plans to see Maria, Carlos's wife, tomorrow.'

'I just…'

'Thank you for stopping by, James.'

I wish the shithead were around for an hour to teach me his technique. Carlos wasn't even anglo! The old bags will come around; they need me. James left as quickly as he had come.

'Carlos had a way with him,' Lila said.

'He most assuredly did. He made it seem we were doing him a favor by going out with him,' Ethel added.

Muriel, the newly respected member, chuckled. 'I didn't even care when he overcharged me the odd time. He had a gallant air about him.'

The women looked from one to the other.

'Did you know that Carlos stole?'

'Of course we did, but he was just so sweet.'

Lila stood up. 'A toast to Carlos! He was quite remarkable – we were lucky!'

'To Carlos!'

In the far corner, the dogs Mischa and Israel were much too busy eating to worry about Carlos. Israel looked for Little Caesar but happily settled for a larger portion of food.

There was another knock at the door. Ramon grunted at the disturbance, but attended to it. Little Caesar was back! The vet carried him over to the dog corner and laid him atop his blue terrycloth blanket in a basket. Little Caesar sported a small, dazzlingly white cast. The dogs sniffed at the cast and went back to dinner.

A cheer went up. 'To Little Caesar!'

Ramon rolled his eyes. Lila caught him.

'Is there any news of Sophie?' Esther inquired.

'Not yet.'

Felicia was not sent to the ICU. Ponytail had broken a small bone in her wrist, and Dr. Roth set it with an elastic splint. The knife wound had caught Felicia on the ridge of her buttocks. No vital organs had been compromised, and the pain could be managed with medication. Dr. Roth saw Felicia off to a private room and then he called his wife.

'Sue, promise me on your life, you will never share any more of our secrets with Jennifer Gonzalez.' He explained. 'I could have lost my licence today. He even mentioned that I owed him the million. I'm not nearly out of this! A gift, my ass!'

'I never thought, Gabe…'

'We can recite *Godfather* dialogue and mimic the *Sopranos;* we knew better. The harm's done. It's the continuing fallout that worries me. What if he demands the million or another favor?'

'I'm sorry.'

'I shouldn't have taken the money. We have to worry now how he got it. What if something surfaces about that? We're implicated now.' Gabe trembled as he spoke.

Sue was crying.

'It's my fault too. Whatever you do, don't mention a word of this to anyone, ever.'

'I know that.'

'Postgraduates, and we're both stupid! I have to go

back and talk to him. See you tonight.' Gabe threw water on his face before he went out to speak to Diego.

🌴

'St. Francis!' Suarez closed his phone.

'What, Suarez?'

'Felicia's been taken to St. Francis.'

'We're on it! Do we arrest Diego for obstruction if he's still there?'

'What did he do? Got a call about his sister and went to her. The hospital reported the attack. He'd be out in an hour, Smyth.'

'If he had a chance to speak to her, he must know about the double.'

Suarez parked at the front of the hospital and kept his lights flashing. 'If Felicia tells Diego the perp even thought of raping her, he'll stop at nothing to get to him.'

'Damn, there he is! See, going up the steps?'

'Forget about him, Smyth. Let's get in to see Felicia. We'll go another round with Diego later.'

🌴

CHAPTER THIRTY-TWO

PONYTAIL DECIDED TO risk going back for his stuff later. He'd wait for darkness. At the moment, he wore a cap and shades. The back of the dilapidated hardware/key shop was located on NE 55th Street. For the first time since he'd put the plan into play, he felt like a mouse in a maze. He was right back where he'd started. The Taurus wasn't living up to its name and threatened to stall at almost every stop. When he got there, he couldn't find a space to park. Four blocks up ahead, he pulled in behind a dented, rusting white van.

Hiking back to the store, he bought four Mars bars, chips and bread. The sight of food reminded him he hadn't eaten since yesterday. He ripped the plastic off the bread bag and began wolfing hunks. *Damn! Forgot to get something to drink.* Beside Ruiz's place, he bought a Coke and chugged it down till he began to cough.

The shop was sinking into the cement and there were steel bars on every window. A two-inch thick chain hung loose from the bars on the back door. *For final lock-up!* Up till then, he'd walked lazily, trying not to arouse the attention of guys without work who walked the streets with brown bags, guys who looked at TV through grated store windows.

Going straight wasn't paying much to Ruiz. Pulling the door closed, Ponytail noticed how grimy the shop was. How could Ruiz make anything out of this junk pile? A 12-inch TV sat on top of a 20-year-old fridge. Ponytail could see from the doorway that it was on. 'Ruiz?' he called.

Ruiz got up from behind the dirty counter that had mounds of keys and rings, tools, empty soda tins, pens, a rusty spindle of shoelaces, rags and filthy notepads with curling pages. He was a small man with small eyes and a waxed moustache. He had more hair under his nose than on the top of his head. 'I can't help you, man.'

'What the hell are you talking about?'

'The cops were here today.'

'Why?'

'They found false ID for Jesús Alvarez inside a Mercedes.'

'Fuck!'

'They came right to me.'

'Did they mention a briefcase?'

'I don't give a shit about a case! No, they didn't bring that up. If you left it in the car, a civilian took it before cops got there. I can't help you, Ponytail. Your mug is everywhere! I'm not going back to the pen. Shit, not for you.'

'I have the money. You said you'd do the work.'

'That was before the cops showed up and your mug went public.'

'I could slice you right here.'

Ruiz brought a wrench up from under the counter. 'Wouldn't get you the IDs.'

'I'm desperate!'

'Yeah, so am I.'

'You'd rather die than go back to the farm?'

Ruiz tightened his fists around the wrench. 'Who says I'd die?'

Felicia was resting comfortably. The welt on her cheek was yellowing around the edges. Gabe asked her if she needed anything.

'Is Diego here?'

'I think he is. I'll speak to him first and send him in.'

'Thanks!'

Gabe walked warily back to Admitting in the ER where he found Diego in a heated conversation with badged officers. When Diego saw Gabe, he rushed over. Gabe explained: 'Your sister is doing well. She's out of danger. She has a small wrist fracture. The knife wound in her back did not compromise vital organs.'

Diego's face tightened with the mention of each injury. Smyth and Suarez stood a few feet behind Diego. Suarez read Gabe's name tag. 'Dr. Roth, Detectives Suarez and Smyth. Is she up for a few questions?'

'I don't want my sister bothered after all she's been through.'

Ignoring Diego, Suarez said, 'Doctor?'

Gabe had the steady hands of a surgeon, but both shook so pronouncedly that he shoved them into the pockets of his white coat. Diego's eyes bore in on Gabe.

Smyth picked up on the threat. 'Doctor, we're asking you as a courtesy. Mrs. Alvarez is not in immediate danger. Our questions are a matter of life and death for her missing husband.'

'Jesús is not my concern! My sister could have died!'

'She didn't. Doctor, unless you forbid us access, and you better have a good reason, please take us to Mrs. Alvarez.'

'I, uh…'

'Please, Doctor!'

'You're not seeing Felicia alone. I'm coming with you!'

'Diego, you stay put for a minute,' Suarez ordered. 'We have to speak to your sister alone.'

Gabe didn't miss Diego's expletive in *sotto voce*. He could feel the thud of a hammer on his hands.

Diego gave the cops a minute before he rushed into the room. 'Felicia! Thank God, baby, thank God!'

Felicia broke down. Diego hugged her. 'You're safe –

nothing more will happen to you. You were brave, Sis, fucking brave! *Los viejos* will be here shortly. *Estoy orgulloso de ti.*'

'You should not have worried Mamá and Papá. I was simply fortunate, Diego. There is no need for your pride.'

'Diego, we need to ask your sister a few questions. Go back outside.'

'You can wait.'

'No, we can't!' Suarez stepped up beside Felicia, in front of Diego, who refused to budge.

'Mrs. Alvarez…'

'Felicia.'

'Alright. Felicia, Detective Suarez and Smyth. Was your attacker someone who looked like your husband?' Suarez asked.

'When the man entered our suite, I thought he was Jesús. Then I knew he wasn't.'

'I already know it wasn't Jesús. This is a waste of time,' Diego scoffed.

'If you interrupt the interview again, Diego, you'll be escorted outside in cuffs,' Smyth informed him.

'Was anyone injured in the accident?' Felicia suddenly remembered the crash.

'Not seriously, I understand.'

'I had no other choice,' Felicia said.

'Would you recognize this man again?'

'Yes.'

'How did he get into your suite?'

'He had the combination. When I came in from the balcony, he was walking in the door.'

'Do you have any idea where Jesús is?'

'The man abducted him – I don't think Jesús is still alive. How could he allow either of us to live?'

'Did he have a partner?'

'He made a couple of calls, but I don't know if he was really talking to anyone.'

'Thank you. We will see you again. An officer will be posted outside your room.'

'I have men for that!' Diego said, stepping in front of Suarez.

'As I said, Felicia, an officer will be posted. We know that the transfer of your money did not go through. Good thinking on your part.'

'It was luck that Mr. Watts called.'

'And quick thinking.'

'Perhaps.'

'For your information, the money was being transferred to an instant bank account which the assailant could have collapsed and retransferred in a matter of hours, destroying the paper trail. That's the latest trend in identity theft.' Suarez then turned to Diego. 'May I see you outside?'

'I'd rather stay with Felicia.'

'Outside!'

Smyth stayed in the room. She had another question. 'We've seen the recording. It appeared he was about to sexually assault you, but didn't.'

'He feared my brother, I think.'

Out in the hall, Diego shuffled his feet like a kid, looking back into the room at his sister.

'Diego, listen up. You're not law enforcement. Hinder this search, and I'll charge you with obstruction. That's a felony with prison time.' Suarez opened his jacket to show Diego that he was taping what he'd just said. 'If you find this assailant and murder him, I'll charge you with first-degree and make it stick.'

'You can try.' Diego marched back into the room. Suarez followed him.

'Felicia, do you have any idea about where he was

taking you?' Smyth asked.

Felicia thought for a minute. 'In a way. At 79th Street, he said it was almost over.'

Diego noted this information. 'Now, you cops are finished. My sister needs rest.'

'For now. Thank you, Felicia.'

I'll get to him first – you won't ever find what's left of him.

Once the suits left, the cop on the door was not a problem. Diego got up and closed the door and went back to his sister. 'Felicia, can you tell me anything else about the guy?'

'When he opened his briefcase in the bank, he had a Mastercard and a Visa with his photo on them, but I think I saw Jesús's name under it.'

Diego kissed his sister. He was smiling.

♟

CHAPTER THIRTY-THREE

NEITHER RUIZ NOR Ponytail spoke or made a move. When the back door opened suddenly and a shaft of light sliced across the shop, Ruiz put the wrench on the counter. Ponytail turned away from the customer and feigned interest in second-hand locks hanging from the wall. 'Ruiz, my key fell into the old dryer. How much for a new one? I need a spare key.'

'Mrs. Hernandez, that's three keys in one month! Business for me, but you have to be more careful.'

'I can hear it clanging around in the dryer, but I can't reach it.'

'That'll be two-fifty.'

'What about two?'

'If you promise to be more careful.'

Mrs. Hernandez spilled coins on the counter and began to move pennies and nickels with her index and second finger. 'You're taking everything I have.'

'You have a shoebox full of coins. Be good!' After a few minutes he came back to the counter. 'Here's the key. Take care.'

'No deal for an old lady...' Her ankles were swollen, and her socks strained against them as she lumbered out the door. 'You need another light, Ruiz!'

Ponytail stepped quickly to the back and locked the door. He wanted to shave his head, but to collapse the account, he'd need to have ID for Jesús and not alter his appearance until he personally made the second transfer. He wouldn't make that same mistake with the other transfers. Ponytail knew there was no need to show his face for a money transfer, until the pickup. Small-time scammers kept a stash of seed money for a quick escape. Now even the stash was gone. The threat of discovery was ever present. Ponytail had been lucky to find the money on Carlos. He rapped his temples and walked back to the counter.

Ruiz picked up the wrench. 'Five grand now and I want you out of here while I work. Cops could be casing my joint.' Money had gotten his juices going.

'You're ripping me off!'

'You could say that.'

'Don't have that much with me.'

'Sure you do. You have one minute.'

He'd have less than two grand, but if he caught the flight... 'Throw in another American Express.'

'Nope – no time for that. Cops could walk in here any minute. I'm still a bottom feeder, but you've hit the big time, TV and all. You do someone to get all this attention? Twenty-nine seconds.'

'Fuck!' Ponytail began to count the bills.

'Go out by the front of the hardware shop. Don't come back. I'll leave the work at the tavern next door. Should take me two hours.' Ruiz lied. He had the negatives. 'Ask for Steve, big guy. I need another photo. Take off your jacket – lose the blade.'

On the street Ponytail felt itchy, as if there were sand ants crawling on his chest and back. There were too many people out. Any one of them could spot him. He turned around to see if anyone was on his tail. A beer was out – TVs in those dumps played from noon on. He got back into the Taurus. The sweating hadn't stopped though he felt a second wind, waiting for the IDs. He looked down at the watch, the Patek Philippe, the only trophy he had from the score. Ponytail followed the second hand past the dial, one, two, three... He could hear the seconds.

By now they'd found Felicia, but Ponytail felt he got her good enough in the back that she'd still be in surgery or too preoccupied with being alive that she wasn't thinking about the transfer. For now, he felt the money was safe.

The cops weren't his only worry. The mob was looking for him – they had eyes everywhere. Sneaking peeks out of either side of the car, he kept his hand on the knife and listened. A cop car passed a few feet from his window, catching him off guard. Warm urine began to soak his crotch. It had only been five minutes.

🌴

Carmen had gone for coffee and sandwiches.

Caitlin sat at the edge of Mike's bed. ''Forgive me for not believing you.'

'I still would have gone to check the Spyder if you had.'

Caitlin's heart began to race. 'Do you have a thing for Felicia?'

'She's beautiful.'

'Not what I asked you.'

Mike strained to kiss Caitlin's mouth.

'I love you, Halloran.' *You didn't answer the question.*

'Caitlin, by the time I'm able to go back to the Trump, I want your answer. One thing I've learned out of all this is that I need to know where I'm headed. If you don't want marriage, I have a decision to make. It's been two-and-a-half years. You lost Derek and then Chris, but life goes on. If you're afraid, it's time you climbed on top of your fear. Half an inch down, and I wouldn't be here talking to you. When I was caught in that riptide, at least I had a chance to fight for my life. When I was stabbed, I didn't see it coming. Direction and commitment are suddenly important to me. I know what I want – I hope you do. What I'm saying has nothing to do with my father. I want to know for me.'

'My time's up.' Her decision and the threat of Felicia were question marks, hooks that hung on her shoulders. The answers were in her head, but Caitlin chose not to see them or couldn't.

'Or it's just beginning.'

CHAPTER THIRTY-FOUR

'SMYTH, WE HAVE a list of ID forgers. That's where we start. The perp lost that work in the accident. He'll need to see his paper man again. You're the walking stats expert. How many are we looking at?'

'Off hand, I'd say sixty possibles. Reduce that number to the Rembrandts. I'd say ten or twelve.'

'We start there. Do you figure Diego knows that?'

'He's not stupid, Suarez – he knows about the double. He knows the importance of the paper man. The Cuban mob's a preferred client.'

'He just doesn't know the perp lost his IDs.'

'Doesn't matter. That's where he'll start. There's a reason we're generally a step behind the mob.'

🌴

Actually, Diego was about to prove their theory. He knew there were four top paper men. He also knew where to find them. At the moment, he was still at St. Francis because he'd asked a nurse to have Gabe Roth paged.

Gabe felt he was walking through quicksand as he made his way to the corridor, outside Felicia's room, out of earshot of the cop. 'Diego, Felicia's doing well. A few days here, then I feel we can send her home.'

'I'll take care of her, Gabe. Have no concern about that. You owe me.' The three words, an about-turn, were sharp and isolating.

'Excuse me?'

'You chose your licence over the million. In your place, I would have done the same. The problem is, you let me down. The hospital reported my sister being here. Worse than that, you let the suits in to see Felicia right after the surgery. You could have stalled them. Don't you feel that way, Gabe?'

'There was a question of obstruction. I'm a physician.'

'Don't panic. That's not what I want. I'm saying you could have told them she was still out. You know, given me more time with her.'

Gabe shook his head. Diego was right. Behind his permission to question his patient, Gabe had hoped the police would get rid of Diego. They hadn't.

'You and I have a new arrangement. You can start re-payment of the million, 25 grand a month.'

Gabe's Adam's apple stopped moving.

'I know big words. I won't charge you retroactive interest because you gave Felicia good care. However, if you fall behind, the interest, on top of the capital, is 30 percent.'

'I can't come up with that kind of money.' The tendons behind his knees began to burn.

'You have the million I gave you.'

'I borrowed that money.'

'I'm not a bank. Get your hands on 25 a month. You're a smart guy – you'll figure it out. A surgeon and all; you'll get it.'

'Why did you give me the money in the first place? It wasn't for friendship. I know that now.'

'I saw an opportunity. You realize that there was some effort in retrieving the full amount, expenses and pres-sure tactics. How old are you, Gabe?'

'Forty-eight.'

'You must still have money socked away.'

'I don't. I have two kids at university and a mother in a retirement home.'

'And the yacht and the two Beemers. You're a spender.'

'I'm just saying.'

'I understand you, Gabe. I have another suggestion. What about your house?'

Gabe's mouth opened.

'I want Felicia back on the Bay with us. If I take your house, you'll have enough money to buy a good property because of the sub-prime rate problems. I figure your house is worth three million. I'll give you one.'

'But?'

'You didn't expect me to give you full value? You didn't give me full value, did you, Gabe?'

'I'll find the money.'

'Knew you would, Doctor. Now, I have work to do.' Diego left Gabe standing there. When he could move, Gabe went back up to surgery, told the desk he was ill and left. On the way home, he called Sue. 'Where are you?'

'At Bal Harbour, at lunch with Barbara.'

'I need you at home.'

♟

Diego had stepped in as substitute boss of the Cuban-American mafia when his grandfather pleaded guilty to racketeering, conspiracy to commit murder and fraud. Ernesto Gonzalez had sired no sons, so succession thoughts had passed to the grandsons. (In keeping with the practice in Spanish-language cultures, Diego's legal last name was a compound of Gonzalez and his father's, but he always used 'Gonzalez' on its own to reinforce the dynastic connection.)

One of Diego's cousins was studying tax law; the other, Santo, had not proved to his grandfather that he was ready for investiture. Santo was Diego's first captain and there was no rivalry between the two. Santo was 25, seven years younger than Diego. Santo expected to be boss in a few years. Long before the trial, Ernesto

Gonzalez disbursed well over $500 million before the Feds moved in and grabbed the remaining 24 million. In prison, Ernesto Gonzalez wrote his autobiography, *The Voice of Power*. The book was six months on the *New York Times'* bestseller list.

Diego had used some of his share in his legitimate business to muscle-buy 51 percent of a large fastback luxury yacht charter company. He had just bought four additional luxury charter yachts at the Miami boat show. This kind of barefoot charter luxury fleet offered options to the wealthy who were qualified to be their own skippers and wanted the ultimate freedom to sail the Atlantic Ocean or Biscayne Bay. Bad money was laundered through his yacht business and real estate. Diego also had layered and collapsible accounts in Belize and Bahamian banks.

Diego's family business was the street gangs and their drug sales. He demanded loyalty from his five gangs and established their common interest as their bond. The Stingers, Hooks, Gamers, Tuners and Bad Guys were as colorful as the names they had chosen. Members ranged from Pensacola, to Tampa, to Miami, to the Keys. Diego did not permit them to adopt alliances with national gangs. Moving up to national gangs meant that law enforcement could more easily track their activities and make far more arrests. His soldiers were, by nature and conditioning, extremely violent. Inside each gang, Diego appointed a sergeant for two months at a time. With that move, he attempted to keep usurpers off balance.

Miami had long ago lost the 1981 pseudonym, 'Paradise Lost,' and had made one of the great resort-state comebacks. It remained, quietly, a center for the drug trade. Diego did not permit retribution to be carried out on the streets, as it once had when eight murders might have occurred in a single day. In the old days, the visible level of violence increased daily. Miami residents slept with guns under their pillows. In the comeback, violence went underground but it didn't disappear.

By the time Diego got to his office on the Bay, he'd sent photos of Jesús to gang cam-phones with a text message. The squirrel was not to be harmed but taken to storage #41 in North Miami, the kill room. *Squirrel* was the name Diego gave to targets. He didn't use names that might implicate him in the future. The room was equipped, but with nothing cops could use against them: a few chairs, cement blocks, wooden planks, hammers, nails and industrial rolls of plastic. Diego had dropped top dollar on the squirrel's head. The matter was urgent! Diego also sent out the list of paper men. 'Jack them up like Miami whores until they give it up.' Diego didn't enter the kill room; he had a lieutenant for such work. The sorting out that went on in the room could never be traced to Diego. This man was an exception. He wanted this man for himself. The man had laid hands on his sister. Diego was deeply wounded by this affront to his family and to his dignity.

🌴

Sue and Gabe arrived home within minutes of one another. Gabe poured them both double Scotches that they drained before they sat. Gabe walked around and told her about Diego. 'I can't come up with this money every month.' he shouted. 'He'll take our house if I'm late.'

'Can he just do that?'

'Sue, damn it all! Wake up. We cozied up to the Cuban mob!'

'Why is he coming after you? You helped his sister.'

'He wanted me to whisk her off to our home and care

for her here.'

'What?'

'Didn't want anything reported.'

'Was there any chance you could have done that?'

'Her photo was all over the hospital. By law, we had to report her presence. My licence was at stake.'

'Isn't there anyone we can call?'

'Like whom? I took the damn money, but you started things off.'

'I thought Jennifer was a friend.'

'Get rid of that notion.'

'Alright, Gabe. What about a second mortgage on the house?'

'We did that for our yacht.'

'Your yacht, you mean.'

Gabe threw his glass against the pale gold wall, which gouged it before the crystal splintered on the floor. His cheeks were stained with red blotches.

Frightened, Sue readily admitted her part. 'You're right, I started this mess. What about trying to sell the house secretly?'

'Diego would find out.'

'Sell the yacht, Gabe.'

'He's destroying our lives. I'll try. What about some of the art and jewellery?'

'We'll get less than half their worth, except for the art.'

'Don't you think I know that, Sue? I'd like to kill him.'

'You don't mean that.'

'If I could get away with it, I'd kill him.'

'Gabe, you're talking like a madman.'

'You know what, Sue? I don't give a good goddamn. We followed the rules, medical school, late nights, sacrificing, till, let me see, eleven years ago, all for what? Diego walks into people's lives and sucks them dry. The police haven't been able to arrest him. With all their advanced surveillance that we pay for, they haven't come close to him. I make one mistake. Diego never gave me a chance to react. He planned it that way. I shook hands with the devil and I'll end up paying for that with everything I own, including my health.'

'Why can't we borrow the money – you've paid the loan.'

'Diego doesn't care about the money. He wants our house, for a third of the price. And that's probably gone down because I refused his offer. He'll just take it. That's why I'd kill him, if I could...'

CHAPTER THIRTY-FIVE

SUAREZ AND SMYTH always made it a point to keep in touch with strong witnesses. That contact made things easier at trial, if there was one. Witnesses tended to have better memories when they felt they weren't just grist for the machine. 'Hello, Lila. This is Detective Suarez. I have some good news. Felicia Alvarez was wounded but she's safe now in a hospital.'

'That's awfully good news, Detective. What about the double?'

'We have some leads. The officer is still posted downstairs for you as a precaution. This man has no reason to go back to the Trump.'

'My son is arriving tonight.'

'All the better. I'll be in touch again.'

'Goodnight, Detective.'

'Felicia Alvarez is safe.' The OAW stopped talking and clapped.

'Lila, I'd like to see Jake. It's been a long time,' Abby said.

'Come on back to my place. Jake should be here any minute. He always says he'll be on a late flight and then he surprises me, or thinks he does. I've been on to him for years.'

'I don't think much gets by you, Lila.'

'More than I'll admit. Oh dear! Margaret, are you not feeling well?'

'Mischa and Israel have me tuckered out.'

'Alright girls! Time to call it a night. Is there anyone who'll take Mischa and Israel?'

Muriel volunteered. Margaret went right to bed. Mops hopped up beside her.

Abby and Lila were on their first herbal tea when Jake

announced his arrival. 'I'm down in the lobby. What's the code, Mother?'

Abby left soon after. Then mother and son were alone and Lila told Jake about the events that had transpired. 'Good God! I'm here now; you're safe.' Jake walked up and down the living room with both hands in his pockets. 'Mother, I've done some thinking on the plane.'

'I'm not surprised.'

'Over the years, I've wondered why you didn't move out to the West Coast with Aaron and me; we are your sons after all. Forget the fact that we worry about you. You're not a Floridian – you're a New Yorker. You know I want you to come and live out there. Don't just blame the fact that Aaron and I lead busy lives. You could have been a part of them, but you chose not to. I have to confess, I've been a little jealous of Carlos. This fellow stole from you and you were still fond of him.'

Lila had long expected this question and dreaded it.

'I'd like a chance to get to know you, and I don't think I do. In the law, I don't hear much honesty but I can handle it. I don't want to lose you before you know a little about me, either. I'm not such a tedious person.'

Lila smiled. 'No, you're not. When Rose Kennedy was asked what her greatest regret was, she didn't mention the assassinations of John or Robert, or the son lost in the war. She looked straight into the camera. Rose was close to my age then, Jake, but giving up her dancing at 12 was her greatest regret.'

Jake looked at his mother.

The silence between them was thick.

Lila smiled again, but it was an inner smile. 'When I heard Rose's answer, I have to admit I was surprised and thought her selfish. Then I realized she was lamenting a self she had put aside for most of her life. Families forget that mothers are people in their own right. In my life, first, it was pleasing my parents, then it was your father's career, and finally, it was caring for my sons and worrying about you through life. Here, I'm Lila, a person and somebody's friend. I think it's often hard for women to be people. You're not a kid anymore, but you're still my child. You might even invite me to live with you, but you want me settled, Jake, done, quiet, close to over. Maybe you don't see that, but it doesn't mean a good part of what I'm saying isn't true.'

Jake kept his emotions inside his heart, much like his mother. He took time digesting what Lila had said. No one ever accused attorneys of moving quickly. What he did next was something he hadn't done since he was a child. Jake got up and threw his arms around Lila. 'I'm not a kid, Mother, but I still learn every day. Stay here where you're happy – come home to us when *you* make that decision. Remember, I'm a person too – I miss your company. We don't have the luxury of many years ahead of us. A son can be a friend.'

'You've made me cry, Jake.' His arms were still around her, and Lila kissed him.

At the hospital, Carmen took out the watercolor to show Mike to get his mind off things. His mother hadn't arrived. 'I didn't see this!' Carmen complained. 'What I thought was a light grey line is actually a rip.'

Caitlin grabbed Carmen's arm and pulled her outside the room. 'You, or we, are not going back to Money Bags! I know how your mind works. Any excuse to get back there, and you're on an 'S' bus.'

'It's really torn. Look! I paid $70 for this. I don't want a damaged piece. If I can see the tear, other people will too.'

'I'll give you the money. A concierge has been

murdered, people are missing, and you're thinking of money that didn't belong to us in the first place. I have Mike's mother coming. If you decide to go back, you move out!'

Caitlin stormed back into the room, leaving Carmen bristling out in the hall, but not for long. She headed back to the Trump.

'Don't take everything out on Carmen.'

'Mike, that's not why I could wring her neck.'

'So tell me.'

'Remember that dangerous idiocy I told you about that Carmen and I were involved in down here three years ago? At the arts festival, we met Larry, a handyman who worked around the condo. Turns out, he's now co-owner of a bar called Money Bags.'

'Carmen thinks he ended up with the money?'

'Absolutely. I'm a university professor, starting a book on the ethos of today's youth. I can't revisit the past.'

'You should switch to mysteries. Talk to her. Carmen won't pursue this, not with what's happened.'

CHAPTER THIRTY-SIX

'JUST HAD A blowup with 'Pro-Ball'.' Lieutenant Ryder had gotten the nickname because he boasted to each recruit about his call-up to Philly and the weekend he blew his knee out. 'Pro-Ball doesn't want a cluster-fuck-up on this. He wants a clearance and he's pissed about the OT. The husband's still missing, he reminded me, the perp's in the wind, the mob's on the hunt, and all we have are witnesses. Oh yeah, our status as prospects for offices down the hall is dwindling. If we do fuck up, he says he has a place for us in Evidence Control.'

'Pro-Ball's a motivator, Suarez. Then again, he has to kick ass. Calls are coming in; guys on the desk are checking them out and will get to us as soon as they have a live one. I have the list of paper men. Let's meet our first man. Three of them are in the city. Did you think of telling Pro-Ball that we know who 'done' it?'

'He has no funny bone. The one positive is that there hasn't been a hurricane of press and media yet.'

'Finding Felicia will change that, Suarez.'

'Not if Diego takes her back to his compound. That'd help us.'

They drove their unmarked car with the cherry flashing, cursed the construction, parked in front of a hydrant and let the flashing light do its work. Their first suspect managed a paint shop. As Suarez questioned him, Smyth searched the place. These guys sometimes kept their camera and stuff at home. She studied his body language. *A no-go.*

'This perp's still doing his thing, just not this thing.'

'Suarez, take a look across the street.'

Three Tuners, young gangbangers, were taking in the scene. In their dark hoodies and designer sweats, six-inch gold crosses and work boots, they folded into the cement wall across the street. This search was a costly day for Diego. Gang members left their corners, sitters were on the move, money counters were out on the streets. A skeleton crew handed off the flake bags to the dopers they found. The crew carried coded pagers. It was a night, and perhaps a day, of empty brown bags of lost revenue.

'We have a chance of hitting the next forger before Diego's men.'

'They were probably already here.'

'Smyth, the perp's still standing.'

'True.'

🌴

Ponytail saw his reflection in the rusty mirror and it unnerved him. It was like seeing the bottom of his life. He sank back into the seat. He yanked his hair into unruly sideburns. The urine stain had left a yellow border around his crotch. What he needed was a dump and food. Once he made it home and began to pack the car, he couldn't take time for food or a shower. He had to blow more money. No choice. Pawning the watch in Miami was out of the question. He wasn't stupid. Cops and the mob would be all over the pawn shops.

The door creaked as he got out of the car. Wobbling just enough not to be picked up, he walked to a Shell station a couple of blocks up. Three more chocolate bars, two dogs, shrivelled on the rolling grill, stale buns, and two 16-ounce Cokes would hold him. He paid for his food and ate inside.

'Watch the mustard! I'm not cleaning up your mess.'

'No problem. I need a key to the bathroom.'

'Women only – Men's is blocked up. Don't take a bath in there. Slobs around here do that. I gotta pay for the paper towels.'

'I just blew 25 bucks. Give me the fuckin' key!'

'Over there, on the side of the door.'

It took a good push to get the bathroom door open. The room was filthy; stool floated in the toilet. 'Fuck!' At least it flushed. Ponytail put his grub and shirt on the tank and flopped down onto the toilet seat. Most of what he'd just eaten came out the other end. He felt dizzy and brought his head to his knees. *I have to get control of myself. Get cleaned up. Finish the food. Drink the Coke.* He wiped himself, ran the sink tap and leaned his head under it, letting the cold water clear his head. He tore open the paper container and grabbed what was left of the paper towels. He wet a handful and wiped his underarms and neck. He drank deeply from the tap.

In the bathroom, he finished the dogs, trying not to eat quickly. He wiped his teeth and tongue with paper and used what was left of the towels to dry off. He felt better. It was time to get back to the car and off the street.

🌴

Ruiz left by the front door with the IDs in a brown envelope. In the bar, he slipped Steve a twenty with the work. 'It's a pick-up.'

'Thought you retired!'

'A one-timer. No choice. Don't make the hand-over obvious, Steve. You know what I'm risking.'

'Hit me again.'

'You're hard.' Ruiz gave him another twenty.

'Business.' Steve pointed to the TV where Jesús was still a star. 'Tell me it ain't so, Ruiz.'

'You think I'm nuts?'

'To be determined.'

Ruiz hurried back to his store to destroy the

negatives.

🌴

Hot dogs and Cokes weren't the best things for a nervous stomach. Ponytail checked his watch. One hour and 35 minutes to go. Another part of the score moved further out of reach when Ponytail took off the watch and pocketed it. In the rear mirror, he saw two cops on bikes coming up on him. He reached for the key and started up the car, hoping this was their first swing-by. Bile rose in the back of his throat. The cops passed him.

There was no need to turn off the ignition. It hadn't caught. *Shit! I don't need this!* He wanted to start it up again, but he worried about the starter and sat back instead. He missed the bitch. Everybody who passed the car pinched his nerves. He began to scratch his head around the cap. When he pulled his hand away, he saw dirt under his nails. When he got home, he'd have to risk a shower. The air in the car stank of him. *What if Ruiz screwed me? I'll give him up.* He pulled the watch out. He still had an hour. *What if it was all for nothing? I have to think positive thoughts. Dad would never think I could get this close to the show.*

His father owned a Cuban joint on 11th Street and worked it with his brother. The food they slopped didn't bring in much. He wasn't going to be caught in that cage for the rest of his life, stinking of food and grease. When he was younger, Ponytail worked as a sales rep, but never made much. It was on that job that he picked up scamming. With that, he lived better than anyone in his family. So many Cuban families did well in Miami, but his father's place never took off. His brother knew that he was scamming. He didn't rat him out, but distanced himself. *Who the fuck needs him?*

Part of his perfect score was his plan to invite the

family out to the vineyard once he was settled on the coast. They could stay as long as they wanted. The Diaz family deserved a break, and he'd provide one. Ponytail looked around the car and forgot the dream. The murders began to gnaw at him. Big move; big steps; he felt he could almost hear them. He thought he'd accepted the price; thought Daisy had too. Forty-four minutes. Trying to keep an eye on the bar, there was no time to worry about someone finding Shirley. Right now Ponytail had to focus on everyone who came near him. The way he was sitting, it was difficult for him to see the door to Ruiz's shop. At first, he strained to eyeball anyone who went inside, but he was making himself too obvious.

He didn't see the two people who went into the shop.

CHAPTER THIRTY-SEVEN

'WHAT ARE YOU doing with the gun, Gabe? You're a doctor. Try to remember who you are. Please, put it away.'

'We need protection. At the range, I'm a fair marksman. The first payment's due. I want the gun with me.'

'Are you out of your mind?'

'I'm thinking quite clearly, actually.'

'You're not leaving this house tomorrow morning with a gun! We should call the police, or an attorney, somebody who can help us.'

'And tell them what, Sue? That we accepted a million dollars from Diego Gonzalez? I'm sure they'd be very willing to help us then.'

'I have a very good agent in mind. We should sell the house privately. We could leave quietly.'

'Are you nuts? You don't just disappear owing the mob money! No one hides from organized crime. All our lives, we waited for our own view of the Bay. Take a look out there. I'm not giving that up.'

'Gabe, your solution is a gun? Borrow the money. Pay him off. We've had too much to drink. Let's try to get some sleep.'

'Sleep? How many times do I have to tell you? I don't think he gives a pig's ass about the money. He wants our house.'

'Please come to bed. Maybe I can speak to his wife.'

'Speaking to her ruined our lives in the first place.'

'Speaking didn't ruin us! Taking the money did. You never even talked to me about it. You were in such a bloody rush to get it. Anyway, you're jumping ahead of yourself. If he wanted the house, why did he ask for 25 thousand a month? Why not ask for the house right off?

What if I went to my father for money?'

'Sue, we are not involving family.'

'I'm going to bed. There is no reasoning with you. By the way, pick up the glass on the floor.'

🌴

The OAW collected $10,000 for Maria, Carlos's wife. Muriel called down to the main desk to find out if the manager was still on duty. Normally Angel would be home with his family, but he felt it was his duty to keep the press and media out of the Trump, away from the owners. He stuck with a pat request. 'Whatever you need, please call Metro-Dade Police. This is an ongoing investigation. We cannot comment.'

When he was told he had a call, he reluctantly left his post at the front entrance. 'That's a very generous donation from all of you. Please extend my thanks. Yes, I will send security up for the check. I will also personally give the money to Carlos's wife Maria who will need it. No, I have heard nothing from her about any arrangements. Is there anything you need?'

'We're fine, thank you, Angel. This has been a terrible day.'

'Yes, Muriel, it has. Goodnight.'

🌴

'Do you have any idea when my mother said she'd be here?' Mike asked Caitlin. 'I'm feeling good enough that they'll probably send me home in a day or two.'

'You still have drains.'

'They'll be out tomorrow. Can I use your cell to call my mother?' Caitlin handed it to him. 'Mom! Yes, it's me. I'm alive. Where are you?'

'Still at Logan Airport.'

'Mom, you're wonderful to think of coming down.

I'm much better, out of surgery and probably back at the Trump tomorrow. Caitlin's here with me. We're fine.'

'You don't need me then?'

'Believe me,' he said wincing, 'if I were in real trouble, you're number one on my list.' Mike smiled over at Caitlin.

She knew he was helping her out.

'I'd like to come, Mike.'

'I'm a big boy, Ma.'

'You're stubborn.'

'Get that from you. I don't want you flying down and cabbing it through Miami alone.'

'Call me every day. I mean it.'

'Love you and I will.'

Caitlin breathed a sigh of relief. 'I like your mother, but she hovers at times.'

'I have an ulterior motive. I want you free to decide what it is you want.'

Caitlin felt air swell in her stomach. His mother's presence and concern might have given Caitlin a delay. Now she had to decide. She rubbed her eyes.

'I can wait till I get to the Trump.'

Caitlin closed the door and climbed up onto the bed with Mike.

🌴

Diego's bangers took great pains choosing their American names. Scar and Bags walked in Ruiz's back door. As soon as they got inside the shop, Ruiz knew who'd sent them and stiffened. They began with their familiar 'front and back.' Scar went to the counter; Bags walked back to the door and locked it.

'Guys, I got no real cash and I don't use. You want keys? I can give you a deal.' The hair on the back of his neck was wet.

'Looking around.'

'Go ahead, but I got no business today and I wanna close.'

Scar flashed his cell with Jesús's photo in Ruiz's face. 'You do work for this guy?' Scar had jumped the counter and landed on Ruiz's foot.

'Are you nuts?'

Scar pushed Ruiz into the keys hanging from the wall. Bags jumped the counter. He was opening the cash and taking the few bills. He began to pull out drawers.

'What do you guys want?'

'You know what we need, paper man.'

'I'm a two-timer. I'm outta that business. Think I'd be working this dump if I weren't?' Ruiz was praying Bags stayed out of the garbage. He'd cut up the negatives and buried them under the trash in the can beside the cash register.

'You haven't answered my question. Do you know this guy?' Scar rammed the cell into Ruiz's face. Before his vision blurred, he saw the wrench. He had no chance to get it. Bags picked it up. 'Ruiz, you scared like a bitch!'

'You see that, Bags?'

'Like a bitch.'

'Put your hands on the counter, bitch!'

Bags was slapping the wrench into his palm.

Scar shoved his hand into Ruiz's pockets. 'What do we have here?'

Bags slammed the wrench on Ruiz's hands. There was a heavy thud.

'You lied! There's like, what, four or five grand here. Didn't get that from keys.'

Blood spurted from deep cuts where the end of the wrench had caught his left hand. Ruiz didn't scream; that would encourage the beating.

'Where did you get the money?'

'A guy took my car.'

'For five grand? That's what it is. I just counted it,' Scar said, pocketing the cash.

Bags swung the wrench at Ruiz's back and he crumbled to the floor. Bags pulled him to his feet, lit a cigarette, took a couple of deep drags and put the butt out on Ruiz's neck. This time he screamed.

'Good, we have your attention.'

There were three light knocks on the back door. Bags hopped back over to the counter and opened the door to Slide. 'Stay on the look-out – page us if the cops show up,' he ordered. 'Time enough for you to give this guy up.'

Ruiz tried to figure out how to survive.

The photo of Jesús was back on TV, though there was no sound. All three were caught by surprise.

'See, Ruiz, this is one popular squirrel.'

'Tell us what you know, you live to work another day in this shithole. Don't, and we do you good.'

The level of violence coming from these tall, skinny boys was unnerving. The kids shared one passion – the American names they had chosen for themselves. Americans had everything, and that's what they wanted. Scar was 17; Bags, one month younger. Both Cubans were boyish in appearance, like kids next door. Their hair was clean and rich, their cheeks unblemished, their eyes clear. They were not smiling now, but when they did, they looked younger, even sweet. Nothing would change when they bludgeoned Ruiz to death or walked away. It was how things were.

Scar emptied the trash can. He got down on his knees and went through it.

'I did the work. The bastard said he'd slit my throat if I didn't.'

Scar's eyes lit up. This find might mean he'd get off

the corners, go inside, a promotion. 'Bags, get that chair.'
Scar dragged Ruiz to it and threw him onto it. 'Who's
the squirrel?'

'Not the TV guy – he just looks like him.'

'Who the fuck is he?'

'Ponytail – all I know is that.'

'What?' Scar shouted menacingly.

'Benito, I think, but I don't know, man. I know him as
Ponytail.'

'Number? Address? Anything?'

'A number.'

Scar grabbed the cell.

'Last name?'

'No.'

Bags swung the wrench at Ruiz's knee and there was
a pop of cracking bone.

'Bags, give the pussy a chance. You've done the work?'
Ruiz nodded.

'He pick it up?'

'I left it at the bar on the corner with Steve. He's the
bartender there.'

'When's the pick-up?' Scar was all business. He was
feeling the buzz of the man who'd snared a squirrel.

'Around now.' Ruiz locked eyes with Bags. He wanted
to see it coming. Most of his 37 years, life had hit at him
from behind.

Scar put his hand on Ruiz's head and knocked him
backwards off the chair. 'Let's get over there.'

🌴

Smyth and Suarez parked at the back of the shop.
While they didn't catch Scar and Bags hauling out of the
key shop, they did see them careening past their car and
into the bar. Without a word, Suarez went after them.
Smyth ran to Ruiz's and managed to pull Steve's name

and the location of the bar from the injured man. She called ahead to Suarez and gave him the name he'd need. Both car doors were left open.

🌴

Ponytail saw the bangers running wild-ass to the bar and the two others, leaning against the walls 40 feet from his Taurus. Sweat burst from his pores. Ponytail began to gag. His foot wouldn't move when he tried to put it on the gas pedal. In the mirror, he saw the flashing cherry near the back door of the shop. The next second, he was turning the ignition. It didn't catch. Ponytail looked wildly around the car. The doors were locked. He'd boxed himself inside. At the back of his brain, shame crept over his fright. *Why didn't I plan for set-backs?*

🌴

CHAPTER THIRTY-EIGHT

'WHERE'S STEVE?' SCAR called across the bar. He slapped both hands on the bar as though he were ready to pounce. The place was dark and reeked of cigarette butts and sweat.

'Yo? You see anyone else but me?' Steve kept wiping a glass with a dirty towel.

'Pickup from the key man. Anyone else ask you about it?'

'Nope. That'll be 20 bucks.'

'You shittin' me?'

Steve had seven tatts up and down both arms, could lift 200 pounds and knock most men out with his right jab. Bangers were different. They travelled in packs and fought the same way. Steve was 51 and he couldn't remember when fights turned mean and dirty. In his day, knock a guy down, you walked away, point made. These kids head-punched a victim to the ground and then erupted into a kicking frenzy. Steve had seen more than one kid back up several feet for a good running kick to the head. What they left behind was a bleeding mass of flesh that went to life support.

'How old are you?' Steve asked when he'd taken a better look at the kid.

'Old enough.'

Suarez burst into the bar running. His badge hung from a chain on his neck. 'Steve?'

'That's me, officer!' Steve said turning, wiping his hands on a wet towel.

Scar and Bags backed away quickly towards the old regulars and ran out the side door.

'That's detective to you.' Dammit! He'd have to wait to nail the young thugs. He needed the work on his perp.

'You're the man,' Steve gave Suarez that much.

The regulars had more important things to do, like drinking, to bother with the action. Cops in run-down Miami bars were common.

'Steve, give me the work from Ruiz.'

Suarez tore open the envelope. This was the perp. 'When was he supposed to get this?'

'Like I told the bangers, any minute. You guys probably scared him off.'

Scar and Bags knew Ruiz wouldn't give them up. Huddling brazenly outside the bar, the boys kept their eyes on the street. Scar's blood raced. There'd be no connect to a promotion if the squirrel got away. Close didn't cut it in gangs. He kicked the curb and pumped his fists.

In the distance, Ponytail heard the wail of an ambulance. Sharp pain raced up his shins. The two bangers outside the bar made his heart pump blood as if he'd just run ten blocks. Ponytail had no time to watch the rest of his plan break into pieces. He grabbed the wheel but his hands slipped. He tried the ignition again and it sputtered. He tried once more; the engine shook. He punched the wheel and swore. He worked the key a last time. Black smoke burst from the exhaust, but the Taurus started. He rolled down the window; he was suffocating. The car pulled away from the curb. Then it died. Ponytail took a deep drag of air and got out.

Scar took his cell out of a pocket that ran down well past his knee. He punched in the number Ruiz had given up.

Ponytail was sixty feet away when his cell rang.

Bags turned. 'Shit! Look!'

Ponytail ran.

Like locusts, they flew after him.

Ponytail raced across the street, in between cars that braked hard to avoid hitting him. He knocked two civilians down.

Bags and Scar shot across the street after Ponytail.

Smyth had come out to check on the ambulance when she caught the chase, joined it and alerted Suarez. 'I have the perp in my sights. The bangers are ahead of me. I got a good look at one of them.'

The race was on. Ponytail's lips were stretched across his teeth. Bags and Scar closed ranks and gained on him. Smyth's gym work paid off; Ponytail was still in her sights.

The one advantage Ponytail had was knowing the area. He whipped into a lane and nearly crashed into an idling car. A young woman was reaching into the trunk for groceries. In one motion, Ponytail dropped the trunk with one arm and knocked her down with the other. He threw himself onto the seat of the car and floored it. The door slammed shut when the car bounced over the first speed bump in the lane. For the moment, Diego lost his chance of slow-clubbing Ponytail to death.

CHAPTER THIRTY-NINE

'MIKE, I COULD sleep in that chair. You shouldn't be alone.'

'Oh no you don't! Get back to the condo and settle your differences with Carmen. I'm beat. I'll sleep the minute you leave.'

When her cab arrived at the front of the Trump, she too saw the press lingering around the front entrance. Ignoring a few questions thrown at her, Caitlin rushed inside and over to the elevator. There were no lights in Carmen's room. *Has she already left?* Caitlin flopped down on the nearest sofa and flicked off her sandals. One went up in a circle and came back down and hit her on the nose. *Great!* Changing into khaki shorts and a white golf shirt, she went to the beach, into a knot of late-night beach strollers. Weaving her way through them down to the ocean, she sat in the sand. Waves threatened to splash up into her face. The ocean was dark, shimmering silver with cresting waves in the distance. A warm breeze rushed the waves to shore. She loved the humid air that wrapped around her like a beach towel. If only life ran this simply.

'Hi!' Carmen had seen Caitlin head down to the ocean.

Caitlin turned around just as she was splashed by a bursting wave and seaweed that knocked her over. 'I called the condo. Thought you'd left.' Caitlin peeled the black seaweed from her cheeks and tossed it into the water.

Carmen sat down on the sand beside her.

'Or that you'd gone to Money Bags.'

'Wrong on both counts.'

Since neither friend knew where to begin, neither did

for a while. They watched the flow of the ocean.

Caitlin broke the uneasy silence. 'I'll ask this again, but as a favor. Please leave the bar alone. I can't go back there.' Caitlin put a wet hand on Carmen's shoulder. 'I did say I've been a shit, but I won't change my mind on this topic. I can't order you not to go, I know that.'

'No, you can't. I know you're scared about a lot of things, but you've brought some of them on yourself. Stop being afraid. I walk on eggshells around you. Losing a brother and a husband changes a person, but I'm still here and so is Mike.'

Caitlin was looking back at the ocean. She picked up a handful of sand and threw it in the water.

'Make up your mind about him. Give Mike a break.'

'You're right, but don't *you* get on me about that. Thank God his mother's not coming down. Promise me about Money Bags, Carm. Let's graduate from our stake-outs and sleuthing. Mike might have died.'

'I hear you.' But not all of it got through.

Caitlin pushed Carmen over on the sand. The tension between them loosened.

🌴

James was not about to concede he'd lost the old bags on the OAW floor. That afternoon, he'd taken a photo of Carlos from the file and approached the manager. 'Angel, I'd like to bring this home. I worked at a You Catch It – We Frame It shop before I came here. I can work with this photo and create a very tasteful memorial in the lobby. Carlos deserved better than he got.' James put on his best sad face.

'Fine, James, but show me what you have tomorrow. I want no large public display or something in poor taste. I don't wish to frighten our tenants further.'

'I agree. Perhaps we might invite his wife.'

Angel thought of the trip he'd save. 'I think that would be fitting.'

James worked with a gleeful smirk. *When the bags see how much I cared for their precious Carlos, they'll weaken and I'll step in!* Despite an ulterior motive, James produced a fine memorial.

🌴

In Lila's suite, the night wasn't easy. She was lost in thought about her conversation with Jake. He lay awake, reviewing the facts. He'd seen his mother's frail hand, and her slowness had grown since the last time he saw her. Jake was hurt, near galled, that his mother still chose friends over family. He was a good listener, but in the end he expected to prevail as he did in court. Today, he hadn't. He didn't want to leave his mother here, so far away. *It's not right.* Like James, he was not about to concede, not after this review of the facts. Tomorrow, he'd try again to convince his mother to leave Miami. He was a man who could work people with words. He'd use his arsenal. Acceptance was unacceptable!

🌴

CHAPTER FORTY

SUAREZ REALIZED IMMEDIATELY the stalled car belonged to the perp. *Stolen, most likely.* To be certain, he ran a quick check through DMV and came up with the owner's name, Gibbins, 69512 Harding Avenue. The address set off alarms. Suarez checked his notes. Felicia Alvarez had told him that on 79th Street, the perp had said they were almost there. Gibbins was on 69th. Suarez had long ago discounted coincidence, unless it was fabricated and it usually was. The perp must live in that area. Now he had a perimeter. Pro-Ball had given them another twenty-four hours with additional men and their over-time. Suarez called his officers and directed them to begin door-knocking in the vicinity from 79th Street to 60th. He called the CS techs for the car and yellow-taped it before he got back to Smyth.

'Suarez, he's got another car. The perp car-jacked a late-model white Focus.' Smyth gave Suarez the tag. 'I put out an APB. Got the registration from the vic. Two of Diego's bangers were so close that one of them threw a rock at the car that hit the back window. A car should be here any minute for me.'

'Cancel it – I'll pick you up. Crime techs just showed up. We have a perimeter.'

'Do you think he'll go back there?'

'Perps are creatures of habit.'

'I'm ready to crash. Two hours sleep is inhuman.'

'I'm on a two-day stubble. I'm not pretty, so suck it up. We'll load up on coffee.'

'My ulcer!'

'I'll get you milk. Should be there in minutes. Diego's bangers?'

'Still chasing the Focus.'

'On foot?'

'Yep! The lane has speed-bumps every 40 feet and a ton of cross-streets, not to mention a slew of kids and old people. Our perp has to keep his foot on the brakes, so the bangers must feel they still have an outside chance.'

On the third speed bump, Ponytail shot up off the seat of the car and struck his head on the roof. *Fuck!* Sweat poured down his arms and legs. He didn't dare leave the lane, which went on for almost 20 blocks, just to be snarled in Miami's slow-moving traffic. The bangers, at some distance, were still chasing him. A wave of nausea washed over Ponytail, then vomit sprayed the dash and his pant legs. He drove faster. He'd kill himself before Diego got to him. At that instant, the added thought of lying naked on some slab at the morgue drove him on.

He couldn't keep this car. Cops were already on its tail. He stank; his clothes were filthy and money was low. In this frenzy, Ponytail did not once think of the score – San Fran didn't enter his mind. Like a death, the air in it stopped pumping. All he could do was go back to his place for clothes, a shower and food. He'd take only what he could carry and beat the hell out of there and jack another car. He had no intention of staying more than an hour. *I should have grabbed the purse! Something else I missed.*

At the end of the lane, he was forced into the traffic. One street later, he ditched the car. *The least Daisy could have done was to leave me the car after she cleaned me out.* Running from the Focus would be a stupid move. Instead, Ponytail crossed the street, walked past two bus stops and stopped at the third and stood with four other people. An old woman was holding brown plastic grocery bags from Publix. 'Those bags look heavy. Do you need some help with them?' Ponytail watched a cruiser race by.

'I carry my own bags. Been doin' that for fifty-odd years. Don't intend to change now.'

'Good luck to you, ma'am.' *I could've used her place for food and a night's sleep.* He was in no position to draw attention. He heard the sirens before he saw the cars. *The cops'll be checking buses.* He walked away from the stop. *It'll take more than an hour to get home. I'll be visible all that time.* He spotted a cab and he hailed it. Twenty bucks might just save his skin. Thoughts of boosting the cabbie went nowhere. He'd need another car, but a cab wasn't worth the risk.

'Where to?'

'69th and Harding.' He slumped in the back seat. His eyelids were closing. It was an effort to keep them open.

'Make that 70th.'

'Got it.'

He regretted not taking a chance with the old lady. Food, a safe place, maybe even money, something to stake him until he got his bearings. When the meter hit $20, he stopped the cab. 'I'll walk from here.'

The cabbie didn't look at him. He'd been on autopilot for the past few hours. He was 13 hours into an 18-hour day.

Ponytail hurried down to Collins. There were more people to hide him as he walked the last few blocks. His stench followed him, and it hung in the heat, putrid. It curled his nostrils. He saw the cop car driving close to his curb. Running was out. In a rare stroke of quick thinking, he took off his cap, ran his hand across his forehead and fanned his face with the cap. The cop car passed. Ponytail ambled up a side street fanning his face and ran into the final lane that would take him home.

He thought of a home invasion, but if the victim got to a phone or locked the door before he got inside, he was in worse trouble. Cops would swarm the area. The fear that ate away at him had to be shunted aside for an hour. Regroup at home, then take off, jack a car and get out of town. That's what he had to do. The house was his hook because he had what he needed inside. There was another cell phone he could use.

Half a block away, he saw his place. Cops hadn't blanketed the area as far as he could see. Had they set up a sting in unmarked cars? As he closed in on the house, he took in the parked cars. Nothing. Sprinting the last half block, he unlocked the back door, rushed inside and bolted the door. Without a sideways glance, he ran upstairs, ripped of his clothes and showered, standing directly under the hot spray. He lathered, sprayed the soap off and jumped out. He towelled himself roughly and shaved. Next, he went for clothes he'd left behind. In the mirror, hollow eyes looked back at him. No time for a haircut.

Barefoot, he rushed back down stairs, carrying shoes. He didn't need socks. He found vodka and orange juice in the fridge. He drank from the bottle and chased the burn in his throat with the juice. If only he could sleep for a few hours! In the cupboard he found Apple Jacks. He ate them dry, by handfuls, and polished off the juice. At the front door, he frowned at his bags. Without a car, there was no chance he could take any of that stuff. He was standing near them when he saw a car pull up to Shirley's. Ponytail jumped back. A man and woman walked up to the back door and knocked. *The Taurus! Cops!* He watched them walk around the house, trying to peer inside the few windows.

'We go for a warrant, Suarez. We can't just break in. We have no suspicious activity that warrants a break-in. You have her stats?'

'She's 59.'

'She must work nights. Her car was probably jacked from there.'

Suarez used his cell to call her home number. There was no answer. He walked around the side of the house again over to the smallest window. Smyth knew his tricks. 'Don't break it.'

'Maybe she's in there.'

'I called Pro-Ball to get us a warrant. That'll take a few hours.'

'Stickler.'

'Of necessity, Suarez.'

Suarez saw Ponytail's house next door and went there and knocked.

🌴

Ponytail plastered himself against the wall by the door. He'd risked only one peek when he saw the cops at Shirley's. He spied the window across the room. The vertical blinds were open. If the cops came around to his place, they'd have a clear view of him and his stuff if he stayed where he was.

The rap on his door sounded like hammers against the side of his head. He crawled on his belly around the wall to the window. What if the cops got there as he was closing the shade? He scrambled the last few feet. At the base of the window, he listened. He got up on his knees and reached for the plastic handle, twisted slowly until the room went dark. He couldn't risk the noise of closing the window. *At least there's a screen.*

A knock at the back door loosened his kneecaps and he slid to the floor.

'Hello, is anyone home?'

'Let's try other neighbors. Somebody's got to be home.'

Ponytail heard that exchange because the cops were close to the open window when Smyth made the comment.

The freakin' neighbors know me! He slithered across the floor on his stomach to the kitchen, worked the secret panel and crawled into his hidden office. He hadn't touched the guns; they were still here. He slid the panel closed and discovered how little space he had when it was closed. *Fuck! I didn't bring water!* In a sense, he was packed away like Jesús. Gently, he pulled the chair in front of it back into place and locked the panel. He crouched behind it like a frog with one of the guns. The small office was as dark as a tomb.

CHAPTER FORTY-ONE

DETECTIVES KNOW A cop is only as good as his confidential informants. In Diego's world too, much of his success depended on CIs. It was his business to ferret out cokeheads or gamblers, cops on the take. Once they were his, he owned them. Corrupt cops provided alerts on crackdowns, inside information and a green light when drugs were packaged for street markets. Diego considered this back-and-forth simple business.

Once Scar and Bags got the tags of both cars, the Taurus and the Focus, and two possible names, 'Ponytail' and 'Benito,' Diego had his own cop run them through DMV. He didn't get to Shirley's until after Suarez and Smyth. When he did arrive in his Escalade with his entourage in tow, Suarez's presence did not permit him to get close to the house.

'Why doesn't he just break in? If we'd gotten here first, we'd be inside. What are they doing knocking on other doors? Get into the one that counts!' Diego turned to his muscle-man. 'Cops waste time and trip up. That's one of the reasons they only solve 40 percent of homicide cases. Learn from this. They didn't bring dogs. I won't make that mistake when we come back. Keep your eyes open. Let the cops do our work.'

Hench nodded in agreement.

🌴

Two homes down, a woman called through a locked door, 'What do you want?'

'Police, ma'am. We have a few questions.' Smyth set up her questions, knowing if she frightened the woman, she'd give them nothing.

'I've done nothing wrong!'

'Of course you haven't. I'm interested in your neighbor, Shirley Gibbins. She has a place a few doors down.'

'I don't like Shirley.'

'That's okay, ma'am. Have you seen her?'

'Haven't been out.'

'Please open the door, ma'am.'

She heard four locks turn. Mildred opened the door less than a foot.

'Thank you, ma'am. Does Shirley work?'

'Used to. She rents out and sweeps all day. Sweeps that dirt over at us. Never stops.'

'She lives with somebody?'

'No, she rents out the house beside hers. That one,' Mildred said, pointing to Ponytail's.

'I guess you don't have her extra key.'

'Wouldn't take it.'

'Do you know the people she rents to? We can't find them either.'

'A couple. Wife's a kid; husband's a looker. Fact, he looks as good as the guy all over the TV.'

'Does he look like the actual TV photo or is he just as handsome?'

'Spittin' image.'

Smyth waved Suarez over. Backup was there. Diego hadn't moved. He hadn't missed anything either.

Mildred wore the thickest coke-bottle glasses Smyth had ever seen. The old woman's eyes, the whites smeared red with burst veins, were huge, frightening. 'Ma'am, can you read my badge?' Smyth held it up for her.

'Nope.' Mildred disappeared and came back with a magnifying glass. 'Now, I can.'

'How do you know what the couple look like?' Smyth asked, with obvious consternation.

'I know what they look like because I watched them move in. I went down to tell them about Shirley's broom.

I can tell you something else.'

'You're terrific, ma'am.'

'You're telling me.' Mildred gave a loud harrumph.

'What is it?' Smyth wanted to know.

'No one has her key because she hides it behind her old mailbox. Thinks she fools me.'

Suarez ran back to Shirley's.

'We still need the warrant!' Smyth ran behind him.

'Fuck it, I'm going in. Probable cause.'

'We wait!'

'No, we don't. Gibbins doesn't work, her car's stolen and she rents to the perp. I'm in.'

🌴

When he heard no more noise, Ponytail felt for the flashlight that hung on the false panel. His finger pads felt along the panel until he found it. He held it against his body and flicked it on. When he spotted the half bottle of Zephyrhills water, he was relieved. With at least two Mars bars in the single drawer, he could wait them out. There was little room for him to get comfortable. He eased the chair away from him and he sat with his knees under his chin. The gun was on the floor beside him. He was sweating again.

🌴

'You blow the case, it's on you!' Smyth shouted after Suarez.

As soon as Suarez was inside the house, he followed the macaroni trail, careful not to step in any of it, from the table to the closet. *Sonova bitch!* He got down on a knee and reached into the closet, putting two fingers on Shirley's neck. Her lifeless eyes bulged. With his flashlight, he saw the broken veins. *The fucker choked the life out of her!* Suarez didn't call Smyth right off. In his mind, most DOAs had it coming, and he didn't feel much for them. The Shirleys on his cases, the wrong place, wrong time, little people, they counted for him. He smiled ruefully when he saw Shirley had ended up with her broom. He opened his phone. 'He got to her. Shirley won't be doing any more sweeping, poor bugger.'

'Guess we can work out the probable.' Smyth said, as she entered the house.

'Get out of the box, Smyth.'

'Who'd cover your ass? I'll make the calls. Body count at two.'

Suarez left the house and ran back to Ponytail's and spotted Diego. *Fuck!* 'Get back to your car and siddown! I'll cuff you before I let you blow my case away.' Suarez saw that Diego's face was blotchy red through the even tan. He called Pro-Ball. 'What about the warrant? Can't you text the damn thing?' He told him about Shirley.

'Hold on. I'll see where we are with that.'

Another wail of sirens told him that they'd have the manpower. What he wanted was to get into the second house.

'You there?' Pro-Ball asked.

'Where else would I be?'

'The warrant left almost fifteen minutes ago. Wait for it. I want a clearance.'

Suarez closed the cell and rammed it into his pocket.

'I'll go in!' Diego was back out of the Escalade. 'I don't need a warrant! She's my sister!'

'And she was lucky! Get back in the car or I'll have you run off!' Suarez was fuming when Smyth got to him. 'He could be in there, or maybe he's gotten out already.'

'Calm down! Some of those sirens are on the streets looking for him. How far could he get if he's not in there? Maybe he took himself out already.'

'School shooters and mailmen have the guts for that.

This perp has no balls; he's just ruthless.'

A car pulled into the lane and dust rose behind it. A young officer, waving a paper, ran towards them.

'That's it!' Suarez was back on the phone issuing instructions for the backup to surround the house and yellow-tape it. Both detectives ran for the side window. Suarez kicked in the screen and jumped inside. Smyth followed. 'Don't take any chances with this prick! Police! Come out with your hands in the air!'

Diego's furious glare never left the house. 'They'll miss something. They always do. I'll be back. We won't.'

🌴

Ponytail's left calf went into spasm when he heard footsteps and realized that the cops were inside his house. He felt for the gun and grabbed his leg with his free hand. The calf had gone as hard as a rock, and the spasm began to travel up his leg. He lit the light against his stomach and lowered himself to the floor, trying to stretch his leg. The pain was sharp and searing. Stifling a scream, he put down the gun and, using both hands, raked his fingers against his calf.

🌴

Suarez and Smyth rushed through the house with their guns drawn. 'Don't take any chances, Smyth. Shoot first; forget the questions.'

'What?'

'You heard me. I'm not risking our lives over this garbage. Look over there. He took the time to pack.'

'Or he never came back here when he didn't get the papers. We'll search first and get to his stuff later.'

When they found no one on the first floor they ran upstairs to the second. 'Police! Come out with your hands in the air!' Smyth took the bedroom; Suarez went to the bathroom. 'Shit!'

'What?' Smyth ran to him.

'The prick was just here. Look! The shower stall's still wet. Fuck!'

'What about the girlfriend? Could she still be around?'

Suarez looked at the sink. 'Only if she shaves. He was here! Check everything. He might still be here, hiding in a hole like a rat.' Suarez kicked the bed, and it slid across the floor to the far wall. He tore both closet doors open, and they slammed against the wall. Standing to the side of each of them, he rammed his gun arm into the hanging clothes. Smyth went to the second room and searched it. They went back down to the kitchen. 'Dammit, I smell the bastard. Look at the damn table; he ate here too! How much time do you think he had before we got here?'

'Twenty minutes, give or take.'

'Who is he, Houdini?'

⚲

Ponytail couldn't catch every word because he had grabbed his penis, like a 4-year-old, to keep from peeing his pants. He rocked back and forth a little. His bladder was bloated and painful. He'd let go of the gun. With his other arm he hugged himself and cried silently for his mother before he remembered that Jesús had done the same thing. He couldn't take the chance of trying to find the gun in the darkness with the cops so close. 'Shoot to kill!' He'd heard those words clearly.

⚲

Smyth leaned over the sink. 'See that?' She didn't wait for an answer before she ran out the back door to the garage. Suarez stayed in the kitchen and began to open the cupboards above and under the sink. Both detectives wore gloves. They'd get prints here.

Smyth used a rock nearby to break the lock on the garage door. With her flashlight, she located the switch and turned on the lights. Moving cautiously toward the back of the garage, she spotted the chair first and then the syringes. When she saw the freezer, Smyth had a bad feeling. Opening her phone, she called Suarez. 'Get in here!' She stood to the side of the freezer and flipped the top open. *Body count at three.*

'Smyth?'

'Down here! Think I've found Jesús. Take a look.'

Except for the fact that he was scrunched up like a roast, Jesús looked good through the plastic. The side of his face was pretty clear.

'I hate to do this, but Diego can give us a genuine ID. We're guessing. Better we know. This will just fuel his interference, but at least we're not chasing our tail anymore with Jesús. This was a neat plan. If the transfer had been made by phone, the way the perp planned it, he'd be in the wind now with the money.'

'He is, but without the money. Get Diego in here, Suarez. We need the ID.'

Diego got off the phone when he saw Suarez coming up to him. 'I haven't moved.'

'I think we found Jesús. We need an ID. Come with me; touch nothing!'

Diego hopped out and followed Suarez without another word. When he got to the freezer, he leaned over and took a long look. There was just a hint of fury in his eyes, anger that anyone would make a move against his family. 'That's him. Felicia is better off. He wasn't a good choice for her. She deserves better.'

'She took care of herself rather well, on a couple of levels.'

Smyth called it in. Suarez went back to examine Ponytail's bags at the front door. When he found the hard drive, he felt better. They'd have a name and the right face. 'We have to call it a night, Smyth. We both need sleep. Alert the men on both houses to call in anything suspicious. The techs are here for some time. We'll be back here early tomorrow. The perp can't have gotten far. He didn't have time. Doesn't compute that we have nothing on him. How can some street-level punk rip and run like this? Let's go to the lab with his stuff first before we call it a day. I want his name out there.'

Diego left the garage without being told to leave and got back on the phone. 'How far did you say the squirrel was ahead of you? Put Bags and Scar on this house, round the clock, till I say differently. They've seen the squirrel. The cops can't know they're around.' His first plan was to see Felicia with the news of Jesús and to take her home. Diego had good connections on the force. He'd work out a plan of his own for this crime scene. 'I want to get inside after the cops clear out. Without dogs, the cops are fouling up and leaving pieces for me.'

🐾

Ponytail listened to a ticking in his left ear. He let go of his penis and lay like a corpse.

🐾

CHAPTER FORTY-TWO

'I TOLD MAMÁ and Papá to go home,' Felicia said. 'They are so worried.'

Diego sat with Felicia. 'They have no need to be. I will take care of you. I was at the house of the man who abducted you. The police, the ones who were here, found the body of Jesús.'

Felicia turned her head into the pillow.

Diego sat on the side of the bed. 'The police remarked twice about your bravery and intelligence.'

'Jesús was not the man I fell in love with these past months, but he was not a bad man.' Felicia turned to Diego. There were tears in her eyes.

Diego knew she needed to talk.

'In the beginning, I was so happy. Jesús was enthralled with the money. Greed came to possess the man I knew.'

'I have someone calling his family. First, Felicia, I must take you home with me, back to the Bay. Our name will always be a target. My plan is to buy a home for you near us. That way, you will be safe. You could have died.' Diego held Felicia in his arms. *'Una mujer maravillosa! Espero poder ayudarte de alguna forma.'* Diego's vengeance was fierce, sworn with his private oath and determined. It did not seem likely now, but if the cops nailed the squirrel, Diego's hands reached into prisons. The squirrel would be skinned in his torture room at the storage unit or in prison. The end was simply a matter of place. Diego's eyes were dark with revenge.

I know how much I mean to you, Diego, but I know I like to take care of myself,' Felicia reminded her brother.

'You are stubborn, like me, but I will never take the chance of losing you a second time. For a while, until I purchase a house, you will stay with me and Jennifer. The house, you know, is large. You will have the privacy that I know you cherish.'

'There are no homes for sale on the Bay that I have seen.'

'I have one in mind and I have already put in an offer.'

'I will give your idea some thought.'

Annoyance crept around Diego's lower lip. This was no time to argue with Felicia.

♟

Inside the hidden office, Ponytail had a plan. For hours, he heard footsteps and voices he did not recognize, crime scene investigators. His body was one knifing ache. He hoped breathing slowly would help his circulation. After he heard the door close, he waited in sweaty agony before he quietly opened the panel into darkness, broken only marginally by a streetlamp. At first, he couldn't move. His body was stiff and brittle, like old wood. Frantically, he rubbed his arms and legs to get the blood moving. He crawled out grimacing, across the floor to the sink. Ponytail looked like an ancient caterpillar. A window near the sink kept him from trying to stand.

Easing his thumb behind the bottom cabinet, he used the other to ease it open. All the while, he kept his eyes on the window. He knew the cops were out there. He felt around the cupboard for the empty margarine tub, peeled off the lid, got to his knees and urinated into it. He held his penis against the base to smother the noise of the spray. He rose like a spider, still on his knees, and emptied the tub into the drain. In a bold move, he ran water into the tub and poured it down the drain to cover the odor of urine. He refilled the tub and crawled back with it to his hideout. He locked the panel, found his flashlight and the chocolate bars.

Carefully, he took off the wraps and hid them on a shelf. He put the tub above his head and the bars beside it. There was little to cause noise. He saw that he had more room to stretch out. If he could wait out another day, he felt he had a chance. Like the man who had killed Versace in South Beach, he intended to elude the Miami cops. All he needed was a day, two at most. With so little food, his stomach had shrunk and weight loss worked to his advantage. He wasn't hungry. Resting his head against his arm, holding the gun in the other hand, he fell asleep. Almost immediately, both eyes opened slightly as he slept. Ponytail looked quite dead. Only the rise and fall of his stomach contradicted that image.

🌴

Suarez and Smyth sat on stools at the lab, waiting for the tech to get what they needed from the hard drive. They didn't look much better than Ponytail. Smyth's eyes were red and dry. Her eyeliner fell off in specks that caught on her cheeks. Suarez was dousing his eyes with Visine every other hour. 'That stuff stings my eyes. I'll stick with dry,' Smyth said, as she watched Suarez.

'Coward.'

'I'm not. I'm ready to fall off this stool.'

'Guys! Got a name and a photo.' The tech was the usual geek and a master at going behind firewalls and breaking codes. He was in his twenties and had acne scarring below both cheekbones. He was oily and already losing his hair. Not a good combo. 'Benito Gomez. Ran him; he's 33. His name came up on large company scams, but he was never printed. Small-time, I'd guess. His family's here in Miami. Here's the rest.' He reached over and gave them what he had.

Suarez got to his feet and grabbed the information. 'I

can't believe a single digit, with no book, has almost pulled this off! Shit!' He snapped opened his phone and
called Brianna Melanson. He had her private number, a
deal he'd made with her when she held off on a story to
give him more time. Brianna was his exclusive contact
and he hers. A certain trust had built up between them.
He woke her.

'Do you know what time I go to bed?'

'The *Herald* never sleeps; figured you didn't either.'

'Shoot!'

Suarez did.

'Good you have this because the Trump story's been
dropped to one column on page six.'

'Somebody paid to keep this quiet,' Suarez shared.

'I know. My guess is the condo consortium of owners
for the Trump. The Donald doesn't own this one out-
right. It's just the name, I think. Serial murderer who did
his thing on their property is bad for business. Send what
you have. No Pulitzer for me, but recognition nonetheless.'

'I want his photo front page.'

'Get off the phone then, get the stuff to me and I'll do
my thing.'

'Done.' Suarez closed his cell and turned back to
Smyth.

'This perp really grinds me.'

'Get over yourself. Go home! That's where I'm going.
I can't stand my own grime.'

'Tell me about it!'

'You need more than a single shower. I was trying to
be nice. Men stink worse. Believe me.'

'You'd give them a run for their money tonight.'

🌱

The wooden table in the kitchen creaked. Ponytail

shot up and hit his head against the panel. He scrambled into his frog stance, held the gun pointed at the panel, shivering in the claustrophobic heat. He held it till it was too heavy for his hand. For the rest of the night, he didn't dare fall asleep. He waited for the next noise.

CHAPTER FORTY-THREE

EARLY THE NEXT morning, James was putting the finishing touches on the memorial for Carlos. The framed photo in a black background was hung closest to the OAW elevator. Beneath the photo was a small table, topped with the best Trump linen that James could find. He'd sprung for blue roses and a blue velvet memorial book of friends. Pens lay beside the book. Beneath the photo, James had written, 'One of Our Own.'

'That should work, James.'

James turned to the voice, startled that he'd been so quickly undone. 'Excuse me?'

Angel Hernandez gave James one of his rare smiles. 'The OAW will be duly impressed. If this attempt fails, I will have to think of someone else for the women. I want the ladies to continue to enjoy the good services we offer.'

'I'll do my best, sir.'

'I will call Mrs. Katz and tell her about the memorial and give you credit, of course.'

'Thank you.'

🌴

When her phone rang, it rattled Muriel. The dogs had worn her out. 'Yes.' Muriel's 'yes' was weak and tired.

'I'm coming home!'

'Sophie?'

'Who else? I'll have a wheelchair for a week or so. How are my little boys?'

Muriel felt the joy of early parole. 'They miss you terribly.'

'As it should be. Be sure to tell the *yentas* and Margaret! I'm hoping, with everything considered, my suspension will be lifted. I've been through quite the ordeal after all.'

'I'm very glad you're coming home.'

Lila had been up for quite a while when she took the manager's call. She and Jake were enjoying coffee and rye toast with marmalade. 'Yes, Angel, that's very kind of management. I will tell the women. No doubt we will be down to sign the book. Has anyone thought of inviting Maria? Oh, that was thoughtful. I'm glad she'll be present. Between ten and eleven; that'll be fine, James. Well, he is trying, I must admit.'

'Who was that?'

'The manager told me they've set up a small memorial to Carlos. You heard the time.'

'I'll go down with you, but first there are a few calls I have to make.'

'I was thinking it might be an opportunity to meet the gang.'

'I'd like that, Mother.'

Caitlin was looking at the work she hadn't begun on her new book when her phone rang.

'They're kicking me out! Once they'd pulled out the drains, they gave me my papers.'

'That's very quick. I'll pick you up.'

'Thanks for the offer, Caitlin, but you'll be snarled in the morning commute. I'd rather take a cab. That way, I'll leave here in 40 minutes and not have to wait for you to get here.'

'Are you sure? It's no problem.'

'Positive. This is the day you open the envelope and give me your answer.'

'I'll shower and fix myself up.'

'You heard my last comment?'

'Yup!'

'Have the shakes started?' Mike laughed.

'You must be feeling better – the tease is back.'

''Ain't no tease, pretty woman.'

In the shower, Caitlin stood under the hot spray. *Time to step up, I guess.*

When Carmen heard the shower, she hopped into her own.

🌴

Gabe hoped he'd get out of the house before Sue nabbed him. He thought he'd made it, but she was standing beside his car.

'Please don't leave here with that gun. Borrow the money. I'll give Jennifer the certified check. That might be the end of it. Or, we move.'

'We owe a million on the house. He gives me a million, means we have nothing. I'm tired. I don't want to fight. We'll discuss our options when I get home tonight. Don't breathe a word of this to your father.'

'Are you carrying the gun?'

'Sue, don't fight me on this. You won't win.'

'Remember, Gabe, you're the one bringing violence into this. You're putting your life at risk.' She left before he could say another word.

Gabe laid his briefcase carefully on the seat beside him. *That bastard's not taking my house!*

🌴

Earlier that morning, Lieutenant Ryder was leaning back against the wall in his wooden chair. When Suarez and Smyth walked in, his weight propelled him forward into his desk. Unlike his two detectives, he hadn't worked out since college football. Sitting behind a desk hadn't helped. His face was florid and wide. His neck didn't stop till it got to his chest. Pro-Ball was a good candidate for a stroke. His fleshy hands began to drum on his desk. 'You've seen this?' He tossed the *Herald* at Suarez.

'Melanson didn't print 'serial'? That was my influence.'

'Front page? You know the kind of pressure that puts on us?'

'The perp's popped three civilians, Pro-Ball. What else could she do? I don't own her. If there hadn't been some influence from the Trump, this would have been worse.'

'Why can't you tie a can to this perp's tail? You're my A-team. Where are we?'

'Minutes away from him. That's how close we were. Still can't figure how he jumped.'

'Someone will see his puss and we'll get calls,' Smyth threw into the mix.

'What about your CI, Smyth?'

'Nothing. Perp was a small-time scammer, worked inside, not on the streets. I have an idea.'

'Shoot.'

'Diego's on the hunt for the perp because of his sister. Why don't we put a tail on him? That way we have two separate nets. His men can reach into corners we don't know about.'

'*Metro-Dade enlists the assistance of the mob!* Lose that thought! If one of you decides to pursue that avenue on your own, that's a different matter.'

Smyth shot Suarez a knowing glance.

'You guys know the rules. What about his family? Think he'd go there?'

'I'm on that,' Smyth said.

'I'm back at the house. It's daylight. I'll see more.'

'Any breaks…'

'You're first to know, Pro-Ball.'

'Get out of here!'

🌴

When Gabe recognized the caller, he hesitated for a few rings, but then picked up. He was almost at the hospital. 'Yes?'

'Gabe, I thought things over and I've come up with a better offer. Look in your rear-view. I'm right behind you. Pull over. We can talk.'

'I just want to get to the hospital.'

'Please pull over. This will only take a few minutes.'

And Sue didn't think I needed the gun! Gabe guided his SUV to a curb. The tan Mercedes pulled in behind. The windows were tinted. When Diego got out from the back set, Gabe knew he wasn't alone. Both men wore light tan suits and shirts without ties. Gabe walked ahead of his car, so Diego would have to leave his man behind.

'Hold up there, Gabe. This isn't a race.' Diego took his time catching up to Gabe.

'I've discovered that you still owe a million on your house.'

'How...'

'I'm a business man too, Gabe. Anyway, I have a better offer. I'll raise my bid to two million. In return, you will render medical service to us when it might be required.'

'What?'

'Please allow me to finish. We do have a doctor on call, but not one of your caliber. The work would occur mostly at night, around your schedule, if we can.'

Gabe thought of his gun back in the car. 'Do you believe that I'm stupid?'

'Stupid? No! You're the man who failed to do what I asked and the man who owes me one million dollars. That's who you are, Gabe.'

'This money was a snare all along, wasn't it?'

'The more important question is why did you take the money? You knew who I was, Gabe. Do you think *I'm stupid*?'

Gabe headed for his car.

Diego moved up quickly behind him and whispered, 'Do not ever make the mistake of walking away from me again. Think about the offer. You have a day, Doctor.' This time, it was Diego who turned and left.

Gabe stood alone, staring after him. Sweat trickled down his legs. It wasn't just his house now. Diego had added his profession to the mix. Gabe looked up at the sky. He couldn't see a cloud. The sky was naked, he thought, just like him. It was still early, but already the heat felt like leaden weights on his shoulders. The area was unfamiliar. He stared blankly at a rectangular apartment, painted pink that had faded over the years. It had cement stairs on either end leading up to the second floor. A one-story bar and an adult video joint were beside it. Small lives, Gabe thought. He envied them. He couldn't muster a defence for himself or offer the money back. Time for such bullshit had passed. Diego's words rang in his brain. *Why did you take the money? You knew who I was.*

CHAPTER FORTY-FOUR

THE NEXT MORNING, when Suarez was back in the perp's house, he saw the tell-tale signs the techs had been there. Although he didn't need gloves because the work was done, he put them on anyway. He began in the kitchen, going through drawers, looking for stray notes people forgot they'd written, pads that left trace information that techs could draw out. For that matter, he could too, with a pencil. At the sink, he saw the tap was dripping and scratched his head. *Techs, I guess.* He caught an odor that hadn't been there last night. It was faint but stale and sharp.

Suarez left the kitchen and went into what served as the living room. The furniture was sparse. Made sense because no one had expected to be here long. The couch was cheap and soiled with what he figured was junk food or beer. Suarez got down on his knees and took a whiff. *That fuck was back here last night!* He took out his gun and began to search the house. *He might still be here!*

🕯

Ponytail recoiled at the sound of footsteps. He'd saved his water. The last thing he'd risk was peeing in the hideout. There was only one person in the house, he knew from the sounds. How he wished he'd brought soap suds with him to mask his sweat. Panic came out of his pores and it stank. When could he get out of this trap? He lay in a puddle of his own sweat. The footsteps were back and close. He stopped breathing. He thought of Cubans who had survived for days in the ocean hanging onto shards of wood. Another twenty-four hours, he could do that.

🌴

Suarez called out to the surveillance from inside the house. 'Any reports from last night's shift?'

'No. We would have been told.' The young officer came running inside.

'Shit! Smells like the perp was back in here. Any possibility of that?'

'Smells? I haven't been inside the house.'

'Yeah, dammit, it smells,' Suarez swore.

'I'm today's relief. I don't know what went on last night.'

'Krebs was on last night. He's a lazy uniform who probably liquored up and slept most of the night. Dammit! This case is high priority.' Suarez was shouting.

'Unless the windows were unlocked, nobody got in now or last night. Suarez, you have the night shift's number, right?'

Suarez had stopped listening. He'd remembered something and he ran to the side window in the living room. *Shit! It's still open.* He yanked the vertical and poked his head out to a cement walkway. *Here and gone! Dammit!*

🌴

Felicia Alvarez had managed to rise early, despite feeling uncomfortable with the bandaging and Diego's wife. The women got along, but preferred to have Diego around when they were together. Jennifer wasn't Cuban. At times, she was jealous of the love and attention Diego lavished on his sister. Unhealthy was how she'd thought of it. Felicia surprised Jennifer by coming down for breakfast and asking her a favor.

'Diego wouldn't want you going anywhere near the Trump. It wouldn't matter who you'd like to see.'

'Well, let's not tell him. I called the Trump earlier this morning and they gave me the number for Jackson Memorial. The man who tried to help me was released this morning. All I wish to do is thank him. He deserves that much. If you come with me, we won't be five minutes. I have no desire to go anywhere near the suite.'

'You're only out of the hospital yourself.'

'Please, I can't drive.'

'Well, as long as you tell Diego you forced me into this.'

Felicia smiled. 'I will tell Diego I take full responsibility. Let's go soon, before he calls to see how I am faring.' Jesús's death had freed Felicia. The familiar constrictions she felt in Jen for the short time she was in Diego's home compelled her need to escape them. She had saved herself from certain death. Empowerment swelled in her heart.

Jennifer snuck a call to Diego who cursed and said he'd join them. Jennifer envied Felicia's defiance of her brother, something Jennifer dared not attempt.

🌴

Smyth found the Gomez family on 28th Street in a blue pastel single home that she thought had been built perhaps a hundred years ago. The house had seen many coats of paint. She detected three on the sagging wooden railing as she walked up the stairs. On the balcony, two kitchen chairs served as the only outdoor furniture. The frosted glass slats of the front door were chipped but very clean. When Smyth knocked, Juanita Gomez answered and led Smyth without a word into the kitchen where her husband sat. The parents were obviously grief-stricken. To them, their son was lost already.

'Has Benito tried to contact you, sir?'

'I have only one son, and he is working opening the

restaurant.'

'This must be very difficult for you, but I'm certain you want the police to find your son before harm comes to him.'

'We have no news,' Juanita said, looking away from her husband's rebuke.

'It would help us to have more information about him.' Smyth smelled soap and soup. Everything in the small house seemed to have been washed a great number of times. It was pride this couple sought to preserve. In the old days, Pedro and Juanita would have been thought of as the 'salt of the earth.' In Smyth's mind, they still were.

Pedro's fists were clenched. Kitchen grease was under his nails. 'What is there to tell about Benito? His family was not good enough for him; honest work was not good enough for him. He calls himself Ponytail. What kind of name is that? He broke his mother's heart. Benito was her favorite son. Now, Juanita,' he looked hard at his wife. 'Your son, for I disown him, has brought shame and dishonor to our family for the rest of our lives. He is not welcome in this house. For the lives he took, he must be punished. Now I must go to work.' Pedro was in his middle 50's, but he walked stooped like a man of 70. When Juanita heard the glass in the front door shake, she began to cry, wiping her eyes with a dish towel.

'Has Benito contacted you, Juanita?'

She shook her head. 'He called me when he had money. Sometimes, when his father was at work, he came by and put $40 in the pocket of my apron and left. Benito had no time for us. He was also afraid of his father. If you catch my son, tell him I love him still and to pray for forgiveness. I know that Benito has cast his life away.'

Smyth handed Juanita her card. 'He may call you. Please let me know, any time of the day or night if he contacts you. He is in grave danger.'

Juanita took the card and slipped it into her apron pocket. With heavy-lidded eyes, she had a single question for Smyth. 'Should I return to you the $40 Benito gave me?'

'Hold onto it.' Smyth noticed as she left that the curtains in the house were drawn. Benito had closed down the lives of his family. At the curb, a TV van had pulled up.

'Guys, clear out. There's no story here. The family have nothing to say.' As Smyth pulled away, she saw that the van hadn't moved.

🌴

Sue Roth drove to her father's home in Pompano. In their entire marriage, she had never spoken to her father of money or asked for any, even in the early years when she and Gabe could have used it. That was Gabe's doing. Her father's three-bedroom condo was on the causeway, but the boat he'd owned had been sold, and the slip was empty. Sue and her 81-year-old father sat on the deck with iced tea while Sue told her father about Diego and Gabe.

'What you want from me is a million dollars in a certified check?' Deep creases worried the brow of Simon Grossman. He wore no socks in his white loafers and a blue vest over his pink golf shirt and a jacket over his shoulders. He rarely wore shorts. After his wife died, Simon got old overnight. Most days, he felt cold. Today, it was 89 degrees. Hearing this story made him colder.

'It's a great deal of money. I know that, Dad. Gabe would kill me if he knew I was here. I feel if I go to Jennifer Gonzalez and give her the money, the whole thing might go away. I'm so frightened for Gabe, Dad. What can I do? I can't just sit around, knowing he has a gun with him.'

'Why can't you go to the authorities? This is extortion, plain and simple.'

'Dad, I've explained it all to you. Gabe took the million from Diego. We can't implicate ourselves with the police.'

'I wish your mother were still here. She'd know what to do.'

'Couldn't you think of the money as my inheritance? I don't want to lose Gabe or the house. This whole affair is my fault. I should never have spoken with Jennifer.'

'Why do you have it in your head that seeing her a second time will solve anything? She may appear friendly, but she's a mobster's wife. Giving her the money is involving you personally in this extortion. How could you or Gabe have made such a blunder?'

Sue began to cry. 'Dad, I don't care about morality right now. As for the blunder, stupidity on both our parts. Now I want Gabe safe; I want to keep our house.'

'I didn't say I won't give you the money.' His voice was as thin as January air.

Sue got up and hugged her father.

'I haven't decided yet, but you can keep hugging. Hugging is still pretty safe. I don't feel I should act behind Gabe's back.'

'Dad, please don't tell Gabe about this.'

'I have to think things through. If only your mother…'

'But she's not. It's just us and I need your help.' When Sue put her hands on her father's shoulders, he looked away. When she saw a few inches of his legs, she herself tried to look away. They were scaly and dry, like thin sticks. After he lost her mother, her father gave up.

CHAPTER FORTY-FIVE

MURIEL PUT A good deal of effort into dressing the trio because today was *sayonara* to her three little charges. Little Caesar wore a miniature fedora; Israel, a white-studded miniature baseball cap, pulled to the side; and Mischa, a green sun visor and a small cotton vest. Little Caesar had learned quickly to manage quite well on three legs. All the dogs sported pastel leashes. Sophie loved her cell phone almost as much as her dogs and called Muriel every ten minutes to chart her progress.

'I'm just crossing the causeway on 163rd Street. I'll be home in minutes. Is the gang all there?'

'They're on their way, Sophie!'

'After my ordeal, I certainly hope so.'

It was Muriel's hope she wouldn't be alone outside waiting for Sophie. The others seemed more concerned with the memorial for Carlos.

🌴

Caitlin and Carmen waited anxiously for Mike's cab to arrive. 'I should have driven out to get him.'

'Would have cost him an hour. Oh my God! Look over there! Can you believe the get-up on those dogs?'

Because of her nerves, Caitlin burst out laughing. Carmen turned away from the dogs and stamped her foot to keep from bellowing a loud guffaw.

Caitlin took a long breath. 'Don't look at them. I don't want to be laughing when Mike's cab pulls in. Did you notice that there are no media vans?'

'What did you say?' Carmen had begun the laugh she had trouble controlling. 'I mean, just look at them!'

'Stop it!'

🕯

Lila and Jake came down with the other OAW members. 'Where's Margaret?' Lila wanted to know. 'I did call her.'

'She said she was very tired this morning and a little slow,' Ethel said.

Concern crept across Lila's face.

'Mother, give her a few minutes. She might have had a poor night.'

The elevator door opened. James was there to meet the women. With a whole new battle plan, he bowed politely and pointed to the memorial a few feet from the elevator. Angel Hernandez joined the group when he saw the women. 'Good morning, ladies! Carlos was a valued employee and, I know, a good friend to all of you. He will be greatly missed. His wife Maria will be here shortly. James prepared the memorial.'

'This is a fitting gesture, James,' Lila approved.

'I have a few words I'd like to say, but I think we should wait for Carlos's wife.' James was right on. He was sincere without being maudlin, proper without his pushy whine.

🕯

The canine trio began a raucous chorus before Muriel saw the Medi-car. Little Caesar jumped wildly, forgetting his cast. The din was ear-splitting. Sophie's fleshy, bouncing arm waving from the window wasn't prettier. 'Hello my loves! I missed you too.' The sun bore down, the humidity was high, but Sophie was the aging Cleopatra, arriving in her Egypt. Before her tears began, the women filed out to greet her.

'Hello everybody! I'm home!'

Lila whispered to Muriel, 'Should we tell her about

the memorial upstaging her return?'

Jake had heard. 'Mother, behave yourself.'

As the entourage wheeled into the lobby, Sophie saw the ring of people near their elevator. 'What have I missed?'

'You're just in time. James has set up a lovely re-membrance wall to Carlos.'

Sophie clapped. It was another opportunity for her to be the center of attention, all coiffed in her shiny new wheelchair with her adoring minions racing around her feet. 'Take me to Carlos!'

James hopped behind Sophie and wheeled her over. *Win one bag and you win them all!*

♣

'If I live to be that old and I ask you for a miniature anything, shoot me!' Caitlin told Carmen.

'You're just on edge. If you live to be that old, I say, "Get what you want." At that point, who cares? That's their charm. They don't give a damn what anyone thinks. What a great way to live!' Carmen was enjoying the women.

'I think this is Mike!' Caitlin hurried down the wind-ing entrance. She ran to the cab and didn't much note the Mercedes SUV behind it. Carmen stayed back. 'You're safe!'

Mike was pale. His tan was gone. He got out of the cab slowly, making certain he did not hit his bandaged arm against the door. Caitlin reached in for the few things he had with him. She put her arm around his good side and kissed him. 'I'm so relieved to see you. When I think of what might ...'

'It was like being hit in the chest with a bat.'

Carmen saw the women from the Mercedes SUV approaching. The valet had taken their vehicle. She stepped in and tapped Caitlin on the shoulder. 'Is that…'

Caitlin blanched. It was too late. Felicia had spotted Mike.

'Mike?'

Caitlin was still holding him when he turned around slowly.

'Felicia?' Mike's cheeks reddened. 'Let's go inside and sit down.'

The five of them walked to the first sofa inside the entrance. Mike sat awkwardly and Caitlin sat down beside him. 'This is Caitlin, and Carmen. You saw them on the beach that night.'

Felicia smiled. Disregarding the women, she bent down and kissed Mike. 'We were both very lucky. I came today to thank you for trying to help me. I worried often about you.' Remembering that she was not alone, she said, 'By the way, this is my sister-in-law, Jennifer.'

'Hi' was passed around.

'I had an idea that you might be in trouble. That was the reason I went to check for your car.'

'Have you heard about my husband, Mike?'

'No' came from Mike, Caitlin and Carmen.

'He did not survive.' Felicia did not elaborate.

A wave of silence wafted over the small group.

'How did you learn of…'

'It is much too long a story for now.'

'Felicia!' Diego's eyes flashed dark and anxious as he rushed into the Trump. 'You should not have left the house.' When he saw the women, he made an effort to control his obvious frustration.

Felicia ignored Diego's bluster. 'I would like you to meet and thank Mike who tried to help me as I was being abducted. He was stabbed and is as fortunate to survive as I am. He was very brave. Mike, Caitlin and Carmen, this is my brother Diego.'

Diego's features softened. He recalled the women very well from the hospital, especially the dark-haired one. He extended his hand to Mike. 'I am forever in your debt. In small repayment, would you all consider having dinner with us tonight? I will send a car.'

'I just got out of the hospital and I am tired. Perhaps another time,' Mike said.

'I understand. Here is my card. I will be in touch. Felicia, I think we should go.'

'Thank you for coming,' Mike said to her.

'Mike? I did not catch a last name,' Diego said.

'Halloran.' Mike caught Felicia's smile and returned it.

'Well, Mike Halloran, I will expect you for dinner soon.' With that, he escorted Felicia and his wife out of the Trump.

'What?' Mike asked.

Caitlin and Carmen were wide-eyed. 'He's some kind of criminal.'

'Come on!'

'He kept trying to get in to see you at the hospital. The police told us not to speak to him.'

'Guys, let's get up to the suite. I'm not up for this right now.'

🌴

James spotted Mike and made the connection. Sliding away from the women, he hurried over. 'Excuse me, the police asked us all if we knew you. You were the tenant injured when Felicia Alvarez was abducted, right? I think I remember you.'

'We're going up to our suite.'

'Didn't mean to intrude. I'm the concierge here. You might recall Carlos who worked with me? He's the guy who didn't make it. It was awful. That's a memorial to him over there. You were lucky, man! Good luck!'

'Carlos? I met him, Caitlin. The day I arrived, he told me to call on him for anything. Let's take a minute to see the memorial.'

'Are you up to it?'

'I'm good for a minute or two. I was luckier than I realized.'

The three of them walked over and stood behind the OAW group. Jake noted their presence, as did Lila. She knew who Mike was too. Turning to them she said, 'Welcome back. I'm very happy to see you out of danger. We heard about your bravery. I'm Lila Katz. Carlos was much more than a concierge. He was also a friend.'

'Mike Halloran, Caitlin Donovan and Carmen Di-Maggio. I met Carlos the day I arrived. I wasn't terribly brave, Mrs. Katz. I was just in the way.'

'I saw Felicia Alvarez a few minutes ago. I presume she's not coming back here.'

'I don't know about that, but I do know that she is with her brother.'

'Oh dear, I believe that must be Carlos's wife coming over with the manager.'

'Nice to meet you, Mrs. Katz.' The trio left.

As they drew nearer, Lila could see the familiar envelope with the $10,000 from the OAW women that Angel would present to Maria.

Sophie rarely missed anything. She asked to have her kiddies lifted to her knees when she spotted Maria. The barking stopped.

Maria Diaz was clutching her daughter Perdita. Tears glistened on her cheeks. Perdita had her head on Maria's shoulder. One was moved by the utter sadness of this young mother in such distress. Perdita's head shot up when Maria called out Carlos's name as she saw his photo. Her tiny finger pointed to the photo, '*Papi, Papi!*'

The women consoled Maria as best they could. Angel gave Maria the money. Maria wept more tears. James watched the teary show and felt he wasn't present. *He wasn't a bad guy – he wasn't a saint. I hope the old bags recognize that I'll serve them better.*

It was Sophie who had the best line after Maria left. 'I'm surprised Maria didn't comment on Little Caesar's fedora.'

Muriel shook her head and delayed a few hours telling Sophie her suspension was lifted. There was a limit.

'I'm very surprised that Margaret has not come down,' Lila said to Jake.

CHAPTER FORTY-SIX

'FELICIA, I WISH you had told me about your plans. This murderer is still on the loose. It's not safe for you to go anywhere without me. I am very busy looking for the man. Please, stay at the house for the time being.'

Felicia was angry that Jennifer had called Diego.

'Mike might have been killed on my behalf. It was something I felt I must do.'

'I understand that. You have feelings for this Mike?'

'That was not the reason I went, Diego. Caitlin is his partner.'

'Life has many curves and hills, Felicia. Nothing but death is certain. We will know more when they come for dinner. Jesús's body will be released in a few days. Considering the circumstances, his family is taking care of the arrangements. They will keep us informed, of course.'

Felicia was silent.

'I cannot be with you this afternoon. I have work to do.' Diego's world was complex. As the 'bank,' he controlled a great deal of laundered money, as well as straight money that he invested. He had no direct contact with the gangs. Removed three layers from street rips, he still maintained a source relationship with the daily business. This brutal attack on his sister's life had ratcheted up the raw gangster in him. His objective now was to get inside the house with his Rottweiler, Major. He had an idea.

Once he was alone on the road, he called one of his cops. 'So?'

'Diego, it's not my unit, I can't just bump a cop off shift and take his place. You've gotta understand.'

'You don't know any of these guys?'

'To see the odd time, but I don't work with them. It's Suarez and Smyth's crew.'

'What if you showed up at the house tonight and distracted the cop out back?'

'He'd smell something.'

'That's the plan. You have to go with it. Ride your bike and pretend an interest. The squirrel's a serial murderer. What cop wouldn't be hot for details? I plan to be there after nine when the cops get lazy.'

'I have a shift.'

'Call in sick.'

Damn.

♟

To keep himself awake, Ponytail had run his hand across his face and cheekbones. Over his chest, his ribs jutted out. *I could die in here.* He felt the dull thud of reality. He had to make a break from this house tonight, tomorrow at the latest. He had his knife and he could work the window with little noise. His water was gone, the bars as well. At first, before the cramps struck with a violent force, he felt chocolate was good. He didn't need to take a dump. That was well before his stomach knotted in pain so fierce, he covered his mouth with both hands to smother the scream. *How do the terrorists survive in Guantánamo?* He'd heard no footsteps this morning. The plastic bags were in drawers close by. He could wrap his shit, douse it with soap suds and bury the package deep behind the sink. Indecision lasted only till the next cramp. Then he pushed the panel open inch by inch, listening for any sound.

♟

That night, frustrated, Smyth and Suarez, had drunk a bottle of vodka, but they were back at their desks early the next morning, with ice-pick headaches, going through the calls. 'Most of this is useless, Smyth. Some jackass saw the perp in Daytona Beach when we know he was still here in the Mercedes. You'd think someone would have seen him. Nobody disappears.'

'The family's not hiding him. Stopped by the restaurant and spoke with his younger brother. Had the sense he might want to help his brother, but he's afraid of his father. I laid it out for the kid, what he'd be facing. Kid loves his parents.'

'Keep in touch with him, Smyth.'

'What if he got into a neighbor's house?'

'Let's get back down there, Suarez. You may have something.'

'First, I want to put the fear of God into the brother. A second scare will bolster yours. We get back to the house right after.'

Once they were inside the suite, Mike went out to the balcony and sat down gingerly. Carmen shot Caitlin a 'Should I leave you two alone?' look. Caitlin signalled her, 'Wait a minute.'

'Mike are you ready to talk?' She'd come up behind him and kissed him on the neck.

'Not at this very moment. I'm enjoying the ocean breeze. Down deep, I was pretty scared. First the riptide, then the knifing. I'm on my third chance. Lucky star, I hope. I'm buzzed, like it's not the same me.' He was also buzzed by Felicia.

Caitlin had pulled a chair closer to Mike and sat down.

Carmen remembered the last name of one of the detectives at the hospital and disappeared into her room. She called Metro-Dade Police. 'Good afternoon. I'm looking for Detective Suarez.'

'What is this concerning, please?'

'The Trump Condominium.'

'Hold on.'

Carmen hoped Mike and Caitlin would stay out on the balcony.

'Ma'am, Detective Suarez is not here at the moment. May I take a message for him and he will call you back? Perhaps I could be of assistance myself.'

'Well, I want…'

'Just a second, ma'am, I have him on a line.'

'Suarez.'

'Detective, my name is Carmen DiMaggio, and I met you at the Jackson Memorial Hospital with my friend Caitlin Donovan. It was her fiancé Mike Halloran who was injured.'

'Of course. How can I help?'

'Mike came home today from the hospital. We're back at the Trump. The woman who was abducted had someone drive her here to thank Mike for his help. Her brother Diego showed up and invited all three of us to his home for dinner. Mike declined because he's still recovering, but this Diego asked Mike's last name and was pretty determined to have us over. You told us not to talk to him at the hospital. The invitation has us concerned.'

'The brother and sister were at the Trump?'

'The woman arrived first with her sister-in-law. He came later.'

'My professional advice is not to accept any dinner invitation.'

'Is he some kind of criminal?'

'Do you have easy access to the internet?'

'At my fingertips.'

'Good, Google "Diego Gonzalez".'

'You can't tell me?'

'I haven't the time to give you the extensive information you'll find quickly for yourself.'

'Okay, I'll get online. Thank you!'

'Have they left?'

'In a hurry.'

'Any undue pressuring, get back to me.'

'I will.' Carmen booted up her laptop and went to
work. *Holy shit!* Carmen raced from her room with the
laptop.

Mike and Caitlin were snuggling, but silent. 'Excuse
me, you two. I have something you want to see.' She
handed the laptop to Caitlin. 'Mike, can you see this?'

'Not the way you're holding it; tilt the screen up.'

'Can you see now?'

'Wow! Scroll down.'

All three bunched together and read along with
Carmen.

'It would have been some dinner! All that money, and
I'd guess, guns and all. Imagine their home!'

'Carmen, you're incorrigible!'

'Cuban Mafia!' Caitlin exclaimed.

'I guess that's why Felicia was targeted. Mike, you
almost saved the sister of a mafia boss!'

'My risk quotient is done for a while.'

'He *is* charming. "I am forever in your debt." And he's
handsome to boot!' Carmen teased.

'Anyway, Mike, it'll be you who has to refuse. He has
your last name.'

'Let it go, Carm. Caitlin, any news from the office?'

'I have the messages written down, but the sum of
them is, they'll wait for you to call them, and you're on
paid sick leave.'

'Caitlin, would you get me the phone? I'll call my
mother.'

Carmen followed Caitlin into the living room, silently mouthing the words, *has he asked you yet?*

Caitlin shook her head and handed Mike the phone through the patio door. She closed it and left him alone to talk to his mother.

'Let me grab my laptop. I'll find more on Diego. Your life shouldn't be this hard.'

'I know that.'

Caitlin went back out with Mike. 'I'm here.'

'Hello, you!'

Mike turned to Caitlin. He winced, so Caitlin pulled her chair in front of him. 'I love you, Caitlin Donovan. You make me laugh and you drive me nuts. You're inside me; have been since the first night I saw you. You know the question.'

'Back at you. We've been together for over two years. I want to spend the rest of my life with you, but...' Caitlin didn't bother wiping away the tears that appeared on their own. If Mike left her, she'd begin the big wipe-down.

'But what?' Small words can sting like verbs.

'I like where we are. I don't want to be fighting over toilet paper or dirty laundry. I haven't got a single married friend who doesn't envy us. Everything about you still excites me. Why change what's working? We save the best of time for each other.'

While Caitlin was speaking, Mike listened with a half smile.

Caitlin memorized his every feature. She wanted to remember each one. She wanted to take his hand, but couldn't under the circumstances. Mike must feel deceived, led on and angry for the time he'd lost waiting on her. She thought of his parents' wishes. Caitlin had dropped a stone in a pool; the rippling effect was just beginning. She waited another few minutes for Mike to say good-bye, but the silence went on. Caitlin got up and kissed his cheek. 'I'm sorry.' She turned to leave.

Mike grabbed her hand. 'Stay for a minute. Don't be sorry for who you are. Sit down.'

Caitlin's nerves were shaking when she sat.

'When I picked you up at the airport, I scanned the crowd looking for you. I hoped you were doing the same.'

'I knew you'd be...'

'There?'

'Yes.'

Mike allowed Caitlin's single word to sink into her head.

Caitlin looked away from Mike. Her answer was small and selfish.

'That's the difference between you and me. I want you in my life. You don't need me in yours, except at the edges. When I was lying on the garage floor, trying to breathe and get to the door for help, I just wanted desperately to live. Now, I want more.'

Caitlin sat forward, caught in her own response. 'Are you saying we're done?' Her skin was prickly. At the moment she was about to lose Mike, Caitlin saw how she had controlled their relationship from the very first night. Grabbing her thighs, she drove her nails into them. She wanted to change her mind, but she couldn't lie to Mike, not now.

'I don't want to wait for my life to happen. I came to within a quarter of an inch of dying.'

'Are you leaving me?' Caitlin's whisper was frantic.

'I'm saying I might not be around when you finally make up your mind.'

'Is this about Felicia?' Caitlin asked.

'Felicia wasn't at the airport. This is about us.' He kept his thoughts of Felicia to himself.

'Do you still love me?' Caitlin bit into her pride.

'I don't know how to stop.'

'Do you want me to leave the condo?' Nothing felt steady to Caitlin. Visualizing herself from the outside, she didn't like the person she saw.

Mike looked steadily at her. 'No.'

'Then there's some hope. I guess I mean for me.'

'You can't count on me, Caitlin, not like before. We're both in a new phase of our lives.'

She got up and dropped her head on Mike's shoulders.

He felt her heart racing. He could hear his own.

CHAPTER FORTY-SEVEN

IN SURGERY THAT morning, for the first time in his career, Dr. Roth left the operating theatre and the closing to the resident. Supporting himself against the nearest wall, he tore off his mask. His skin was clammy and his breathing pronounced. *Panic! That's what it is.* He secluded himself inside his office and tried to make sense of what had happened to his life. He saw no exit wherever he looked. Borrowing the money to pay Diego back was out; losing his house paled beside the spectre of working for the mob. Quite suddenly, his career was secondary to prison. No one ran from the mob.

He left the hospital and drove home. When Sue wasn't there, he knew exactly where she'd gone. He'd been married to her for 24 years. They knew how each other thought. 'I told her not to go to Simon. She'll make matters worse!' He shouted these angry words, stomping through the house. He showered, poured himself a triple Scotch and waited for her by the pool. The burn in his throat warmed his belly. Gabe focused his anger on Sue. *If she had kept her mouth shut, none of this would have happened, none of it! I never gave the money a second thought. I was relieved to get it back. Forget what I did! It started with Sue. Now she's out there dragging Simon into this mess.* He'd taken the briefcase to the patio with him. Opening it, he took out the gun and held it, balancing its weight.

Gabe was right about Sue's visit, but he hadn't gone far enough. Simon had called the bank, and Sue had gone to pick up the certified check. She initiated the debacle; she'd settle it with Jennifer Gonzalez. Diego's car was in the driveway. Sue sat in her car across the street and waited. She'd wait all day, if need be, until he left and she could talk to Jennifer. Sue hated a/c and went without it, preferring the Bay breeze. It wasn't long before the car began to bake and the back of her head grew damp. Opening the windows hadn't worked. The air was a hot, damp heavy wave, and it was still spring. Surrendering, she blasted the a/c and watched the house.

A gut-wrenching cramp sent Ponytail rolling out onto the floor from his hideout. Pain shot up into his head. When he got to his knees, the room tilted. He held onto the panel until his equilibrium settled. Closing the panel, he crawled across the floor. Perspiration dripped from his forehead. He knew he was soiling himself. The acrid stench was overpowering. With every movement, stool escaped. When he was finally inside the bathroom, he didn't try to stop anything. Tears smeared his stubble. As quickly as he could, he peeled off his pants and rolled the mess into a bundle and wrapped it in his shirt. He grabbed a towel, wet it and wiped himself. He buried his mess behind towels in the cupboard, crawled into his bedroom and put on what he could find. Every bone and muscle ached with steely pain. Every movement was a struggle.

In the bathroom, he drank tap water, wiped his face and the sink, and threw the towel on top of the mess in the cupboard. He didn't know the face staring back at him. Maybe that was good. If he got out of the house, no one else would recognize him either. He crept back to his hole. And the "score"? Ponytail had more important things on his mind, like staying alive.

Could he survive another night there? Could he run? Were the cops waiting outside for him? He was breathing hard just crawling back into the hole. Should he try to eat more food from the kitchen? Could he risk another sortie in the house? He pulled the gun up beside him, slumped and tried to hold on.

🌴

Major was a fine attack dog. The only person he feared was Diego. He lived his life in one of the four garages, except for the nightly runs with his master. His voice box had been surgically excised. That way, when he was needed for any assignment, there was no barking. The mark's mouth was always taped. Things were quiet and neat. Diego waited for his cop to call. When he took Major into the squirrel's house, he'd pick up a scent, something he could work with.

As Diego waited, Scar made his pass around the squirrel's house. He was beginning to feel his talents were wasted here on patrol.

Diego heard from his cop. 'I'm booking off. Should be there in an hour.'

Diego closed his phone, took out the chip he'd just inserted. In his safe, he had phone chips he used for business and then destroyed to prevent a trace.

He inserted another chip and punched in a coded number.

'Yo.' Scar answered. Talk on phones was always kept to a minimum.

'Car?' That was all Diego said to him.

'Brang it.'

Diego took out that chip and got rid of it as well. After a quick change of clothes, he went to the garage for Major.

🌴

CHAPTER FORTY-EIGHT

THE OAW WOMEN filed back up to their floor, with Sophie and James leading the parade. Poor James had no inkling Sophie was not high on the pecking order, that it was Lila he had to win. With age comes a resignation to death. The shock of Carlos's demise began to melt like a hot knife through butter. Death had moved up to their floor long ago, and most of the women stopped being afraid of it. Sophie dismissed it. 'Carlos is not really gone. He's still here with us.'

Lila broke away from the group. She was uneasy. 'Jake, I'm going to check on Margaret.'

'If you need me, I'll be here.'

It wasn't like Margaret not to make a short appearance for Carlos. It wasn't like her at all. When Lila opened the door, she heard the reassuring voices of '*The Young and the Restless*,' a soap that Margaret had begun to watch when her knees kept her from her long walks on the beach. 'Margaret?' It was the TV in the bedroom that was playing. 'Oh dear, I hope I haven't wakened you.'

Margaret was fast asleep, her head turned toward the window, away from Lila. Mops was on the floor at the side of her bed. His head rested between his paws. He didn't move when Lila came into the room. Lila knew before she walked around the bed that she had lost her best friend. Margaret's eyes were slightly open. One arm lay over the cotton throw, the other was under it. Lila reached over and closed her eyes. 'Goodbye, old friend. You have your wish.' Lila sat beside her friend and used the phone on the bedside table to call Jake.

He came in and stood behind his mother, resting both hands on her shoulders.

'Margaret was a great walker and a better swimmer. She raised four children and she told me she broke their hearts when she moved here. She was from Canada. The winters got too cold for her. Walking and swimming were the only things that helped her arthritis. I'm not sad for her, Jake. Her fear was that she would end up in a nursing home because her mother had passed away in one of them. "I pray to St. Joseph for a soft landing." That's how she put it. Look, the throw isn't disturbed at all. She wasn't a simple woman, in any sense of the word, but she did believe she'd have some "touch" as she called it, with her husband Dennis and her daughter who died very young. God has smiled on you and gentled your passing, Margaret.'

'Are you alright, Mother?'

'I'm caught up in the beauty of Margaret's leaving.' A grief as wide as the ocean and as deep loomed above Lila. For the moment, it hovered there, stayed by deep waves of love. Lila had the depth of spirit to be happy for her friend. She would have time later to mourn her separate loss. 'Jake, the family numbers are in that drawer. Would you make those calls for me? I'd like to be alone with Margaret. The doctor can wait. We have no urgent need of him.'

Jake stood at the door, looking back at his mother, able to see beyond his need to have his life in order. He slipped back from future plans to the present, and this minute when pride for his mother suffused his own demands. If this was his mother's home, the place where she was the person she wanted to be, he wouldn't interfere.

Margaret had made her final arrangements simple and without the usual dour pageantry. Her son came down to take his mother's body back to Canada. Mops followed his new master. Next December, he'd see snow.

Margaret had had one wish: that the girls get together to tip a glass of Baileys Irish Cream as Lila read the note she had left for them.

Lila knew where to find the envelope and was surprised to discover one for her. She opened it on the balcony. *Well, old friend, if you're reading this letter, you know I'm on my way. We met in the twilight years of our lives. How rare it was to have found a soulmate in my eighth decade. My life has been long and rich. In the harmony and wonderful chaos of all those living years, you were the best friend I ever had. Margaret*

Lila folded the sheet and walked out onto the balcony. *It was strange, a Gentile and a Jew who had so much in common. We could sit together reading without interrupting one another when we found an interesting sentence. Finding one friend who knows you, complements you and challenges you occurs only once in a lifetime.* Margaret and Lila had found these golden moments together. Along the shore, she searched for Margaret. Often, she'd waved down at her and waited for a return salute. Today, the ocean was quiet, children shrieked; umbrellas blew in the breeze... Lila waved down to her friend one last time.

🌴

CHAPTER FORTY-NINE

SUE ROTH HAD never seen the Gonzalez property because it was hidden with a manicured eight-foot hedge, and security at the white wrought-iron gates. Talk among her friends was that Diego would have bought the property surrounding the Cape Florida Lighthouse and the lighthouse itself on the barrier island had he been allowed. Neighbors wished he'd bought elsewhere and left the Bay to decent law-abiding citizens.

Looking up at the gates, Sue knew that she had to put an end to the unjust stress that now threatened her marriage. When she saw Diego's black SUV Mercedes pull out onto the street, she picked up her cell and called Jennifer Gonzalez. 'Hi Jen, it's Sue. Do you have a few minutes for coffee?' Infusing her words with a forced casual air, Sue herself could still detect tension in her voice.

'Hi Sue! I have my sister-in-law with me. Could we do this tomorrow?'

'It's important, Jen. I wouldn't intrude otherwise. Look, I'll pick you up at home – have you back in half an hour.'

When Jennifer befriended Sue at Ocean Club months back, she was pleased Sue did not back away, the way the other members had. 'Alright, I'll be out front.' Jennifer knew what the issue was.

Sue counted off four minutes before pulling up to security and being waved up. Stress tightened the crow's feet and the lines around her mouth, yet she could not help but be amazed at the opulence of the estate, easily worth 25 million. The waterfront home was white stone, a rarity on the Bay. The windows themselves cost upwards of 10 thousand each. Her attention left the house and was drawn to two guesthouses. Why couldn't the sister live in one of them?

Jen was walking down to meet her.

'Hi! Hop in.' As they drove off the property, Sue parked on a side road. 'Look, forget the coffee. I just needed to talk to you. I know you want to get back.'

'I have a few minutes.'

Sue did not know of Diego's last proposition. 'This whole matter has erupted into something I hope neither of us intended. I should never have told you about Gabe's money loss. You meant well. No doubt Diego meant to help us too, but things have gotten out of hand. Diego wants our house at a fraction of the price. The fact is we still have a mortgage, and we don't want to move. In hindsight, Gabe shouldn't have taken the money. We know that.'

Jen hadn't made any comment.

'Gabe will throttle me, but I went to my father, and he gave me the money. My inheritance, we called it. I'd like you to take the certified check. I'll sign it over to you. Can we all go back to the way things were?'

'I don't know any of Diego's business. He's never brought that home.'

'But we're not business. We're friends, Jen.' Sue took out the check. 'Can't you fix this? Gabe is out of his mind. We both are.'

'I couldn't do anything behind Diego's back. You must see that. You're not any braver with Gabe.'

Sue smiled awkwardly. She didn't want to be put in the same pot as a mobster's wife. 'Jen, Diego wants to take our house for a million dollars when it's worth three!' Sue's voice rose. 'He helped his sister. She's doing well. He can have this money. Can't you intervene?'

'We don't need the money. I guess you can see that for yourself.' Jen was eyeing the check. It was clean money after all.

'By the looks of things, Jen, you don't need property either. Why can't the sister live here?'

'Diego wants her to have her own place. Felicia is everything to Diego.' Her voice was salty.

'So you know! I thought we were friends. Why does it have to be our house?'

'The million.'

Sue could not stop the angry tears. 'You're extorting us. It's not right.'

'Excuse me?'

'What else would you call it, Jen? I know people shy away from you because of Diego. I didn't.'

'Give me the check. I'll see what I can do.'

Sue held onto it.

'Fine, keep it!'

Sue signed the check and handed it over.

I can't believe it's this easy to take money from people. 'I promise you I'll try.'

'If you can't help me, will you return the check?'

'I told you I'll do my best. Take me back.'

'Jen, we're all flawed and we're not that different.'

'No, we're not.' The minute Jen disappeared behind the sky-blue front doors, Sue's stomach knotted. She wanted to run back after her, but it was too late. Her half-hatched plan slumped beside her. On the short drive home, she decided not to tell Gabe. If she'd just lost her inheritance, he didn't have to know. By the time she was unlocking her own front door, a nauseous surge sent bile up her throat and into her mouth.

'Your father has been calling for the last hour. Where have you been?'

Sue made a beeline for the bathroom. Gabe had been drinking. She smelled liquor on him as he ran after her. 'What the hell have you done? Your father told me he gave you a check for a million dollars! I told you not to involve him!'

Sue was beyond listening. Doubled over with her head in the toilet, she was trying not to choke up vomit.

Gabe stayed at the door to the bathroom and did nothing to help her.

Sue's hand flopped on the bathroom counter searching for a facecloth or towel. He pushed a towel at her hand. 'Thanks.' *What's he doing home?* Sue wet the end of the towel and cleaned her face. Then she got back up.

'What have you done, Sue?'

'Gabe, give me a minute. My head's dizzy.'

Gabe wasn't sympathetic. 'The only time you've been dizzy was with morning sickness. You've done something. I know it!'

'You're yelling!' Sue dropped back down to the toilet for another round.

When Sue slumped against the toilet, he went to her. 'I'm sorry I've been a jerk.' He picked her up and carried her to the bed. 'The last time I carried you, we were rushing to the hospital for Jeremy.'

Sue crumpled on the bed. Gabe sat down beside her. He reached over and grabbed a water bottle that Sue always kept on her night table. 'Try to drink this.'

'Not now. It wouldn't stay down.'

'If you went to Simon, that's your affair. Sue, are you listening to me?'

'Trying to.' Her face was ashen.

'Diego met me with a new offer. He'll give us two million, but I have to work for him as a mob doctor.'

Sue rolled into Gabe and hid her face.

'Maybe we should close the house and clear out. Start over with your million. I'm out of control and I'm afraid of Diego. They need doctors in Canada. I don't even know what I'm saying anymore. I love it here.'

'Gabe, I went to see Jen. I tried to put an end to this once and for all.'

'Sue, you didn't...'

She began to cry. 'I gave her the bloody money to help us. I didn't want to lose you. The minute I drove away, I knew I'd ruined things yet again. I wanted to go back, but it was too late.'

Gabe jumped from the bed and shouted, 'You just handed over another part of our lives. Are you bent on destroying us?' He slammed the bedroom door on his way out.

I've sunk us both deeper into this quagmire, so deep we can't dig ourselves out. Sue thought of Jen and the choices each woman had made.

CHAPTER FIFTY

DRESSED DOWN FOR the occasion, Diego wasn't alone in the SUV. Major was in his cage. Beside him was Hench, Diego's front man who trained attack dogs. Major couldn't talk, and Hench wasn't expected to open his mouth. The cost of breaking into the squirrel's house weighed on Diego. When he was a kid, like most Cubans, he watched *Scarface* more than a few times, but he wasn't blown away by the film. He was 14 when he saw it, but he knew then he didn't want to live his life on the street up to his knees in blood. 'You got a death wish – you go that way!' he'd tell his friends. He was going to be different.

One thing he shared with Ponytail was that he'd never been printed or mugged. He wanted a scent from the squirrel's house and he was certain he'd find something the cops had overlooked. He didn't trust them to do a thorough job. They were lazy and sloppy. He wasn't, and he had only this one case to work on. The first problem he saw was the surveillance cops on the house. He counted on his cop to take care of the one at the back of the house. Once he, Hench and Major were in the house, all he needed was ten minutes at most. As they drew closer, his heart pumped wildly.

He saw Scar's beat-up van and knew that Bags was around. He stopped the SUV half a block down, under a rotting Royal Palm. He carried his woollen hat and gloves. Hench took Major. They walked quickly up the lane to the house. Diego saw two men sitting in an unmarked car drinking beer. The duty cop was being distracted as he'd planned. Bags pointed out what window they should use. Three dark shadows noiselessly slipped into the side window, unnoticed. Hench held onto Major. The stench of feces curled their nostrils. Diego saw the dark stains on the floor. Major pulled frantically against his chain. He jumped wildly in the air.

Diego signalled for Hench to follow Major's lead. He followed.

🦩

Ponytail was half asleep when he was startled by the thudding. *What the fuck?* He heard no voices. He did hear a guttural groan. *What the fuck?* He brought the gun to his chest, balanced it with his left hand and steadied it in his right. Snot ran into his open mouth.

🦩

Diego moved soundlessly into the kitchen. He motioned for Hench to yank Major to the other side of the room, away from the window. With a flip of his fingers, he gave Hench, who was leaning backwards, straining to keep Major on the chain, the okay to free the dog. They both knew the direction Major was aiming for. Diego crept over. The Rottweiler stormed the panelled wall and struck it with all of his 150 pounds of muscle. He ran back and took another harder run at the wall.

🦩

Ponytail tried to hold his gun steady. His hands shook, slippery with sweat.

🦩

The panel splintered inward. A single shot burst from the splintering wood. Major crumpled to the floor as a trickle of blood began to ooze from his forehead. Hench eased himself along the wall, whirled around and landed a vicious, swinging kick to Ponytail's head. Diego pulled him out. 'Hench, get Scar in here. Bags stays on lookout. I want this prick in the van and stored. No further injuries from any of you. This is personal.' Diego karate-chopped Ponytail from behind.

🌴

Officer Morales, on patrol out front, came running without calling for back-up. Diego was standing near the broken panel. Hench rushed to the front door and unlocked it. He caught the cop with a ferocious chop to the jugular, and he collapsed like the panel. Hench locked the door. Scar slipped through the window, shocked to see his boss. 'What about the dog?' Diego asked.

'Leave him – he has no tags,' Hench answered.

'Grab some dog hair. Leave it on the window sill when you leave. Get the squirrel to storage. Pick up the gun. Scar, Bags stays outside to report on events once we leave.' With that, Diego climbed out the window and headed back to his SUV. He took off his cap and gloves as he walked. At home, he'd bundle everything he had worn and take it to a compactor he had on the property. He had a fondness for Major, something else the squirrel would answer for.

🌴

'Did you hear that? Shit! I have to get back.'

'Calm down. Backfire. That's all it is. Your partner's not calling you. You don't live around here. That damn noise is a way of life around here. Cheap cars backfire. Finish the beer, Officer Grover. You haven't missed anything.' It was tough keeping a cop he didn't know from his job. The hook was the money he'd earned to put his three kids through university. Of course, there was also his gambling debt. 'Shit, you want to go, go!'

'I don't want my balls chewed up on this!'

'Beat it!' Diego's cop drove off. *'I tried.'*

Officer Grover ran to the house and tried to see inside, shielding his eyes with his hand. He banged on the back door with the butt of his gun. 'Police!' He ran to the front door and hollered. At the side, he found the open window, pulled the curtain aside. He saw Ponytail lying on the floor. *Holy shit!* He grabbed his radio and began to climb in through the open window. Hench pulled him through the rest of the way. Grover saw nothing after that.

Scar climbed out the window and backed up his van. Hench made the deposit, and they drove to storage. 'Think I have a connect to a promo after this?' Scar asked.

'Get in the back with the squirrel.'

'This is my car! You get in the back!' Scar saw Hench clench a fist. He crawled into the back of the van with Ponytail, who was finally taking a trip, just not the one he'd planned.

🌴

Cops! Diego laughed. *The prick was there the whole time!* He began to plan for Ponytail. Another issue gnawed at him – witnesses. Hench had the loyalty of a dog. Diego knew first-hand that Hench would give up an arm, but he'd never cop to anything about his boss. Besides, he'd need Hench for the disposals. Scar was a different story. He was one of his best slingers, but he was also an ambitious braggart. Caught in a cop sting, he'd give it up, see Diego's bust as a business opportunity for himself. Bags was around as well. Diego was not in the business of making bodies for the cops. He'd never had to put down a Cuban. The squirrel would be his first. When he drove past his security on the Bay, he headed to the second guest house to clean up and change. The specter

of Scar and Bags dimmed the triumph of finding the man
he wanted.

CHAPTER FIFTY-ONE

SUAREZ AND SMYTH were both edgy because the perp was still in the wind. Time with the brother was a waste. Smyth had done the scare work the first time around. 'Quick clearance! Pro-Ball's pounding the walls by now! Let's get to the neighbors in the lane. I'll try Grover to see if he has anything.' Suarez cut the call when no one picked up and tried again. 'Hit the siren. There's no answer at the house!'

'That's where we should have been in the first place, but you had to re-check my work! It's not the first time, Suarez.' Smyth was far from finished. 'I'm sick of you calling our cases. Why is it that you're still ordering me around after four years? This mess is on you! Remember that.'

'Fuck me! I fouled up.' Suarez rode up a few sidewalks as he sped in and out of traffic. He drove into the lane off Collins for the last seven blocks. The car bounced off the speed bumps, and crunched hard back onto the lane and screeched to a halt at the back of the house. There was no surveillance. With their guns drawn, they ran to the back door and shouted, 'Police!' The door was locked. Suarez remembered the window.

They positioned themselves on either side of it, and shouted again, 'Police!' Smyth reached in, grabbed the blind and pulled it out. There was no sound from inside the house. Suarez took a quick peek. Officer Grover lay face down on the floor. He opened his phone and punched in the number. 'Officer down at .... Send back-up!' He raised his left hand to keep Smyth outside. He slid one leg over the window sill, and pulled himself inside. Dog hair stuck to his pants. He knelt by Officer Grover and placed two fingers across his neck. He shook his head at Smyth. Grover's neck was at an odd angle. Suarez figured it was broken.

Smyth followed him inside the room. She headed for the kitchen; Suarez walked upstairs. 'Police!' both shouted as they approached, using walls as protection. 'Suarez!'

He ran back down the stairs after her.

Smyth was already on her knees, trying for a pulse. 'He's still alive – get an ambulance!'

Suarez gave the dog a slight kick, keeping his gun trained on it, but the dog didn't move. He kept his eyes on the dog as he made the call.

Smyth was busy with mouth-to-mouth.

He saw the hideout. 'Fuck! I knew we missed something. We smelled the fucker for God's sake! He was here while we searched! We should have done more. I should have requested the K-9 sniffers! God dammit to hell! I was too preoccupied with Gonzalez to see what was needed here. The perp is gone. So is our fast track. What a royal fuck-up!'

Smyth looked up. 'For God's sake, shut up. Give me some credit for the foul-up. How the hell could we have known he was hiding in a wall? Work with what we have and stop the macho bullshit! Gonzalez has us off-stride.' She resumed mouth-to-mouth.

'How did the dog get into the house? Ha, the window of course. Where did it come from? This is no stray. Look at those muscles! Looks like a fight dog.' Using a pen, he searched around the neck for a tag. Careful not to step in any blood, he knelt down and parted some of the panel after he'd put on gloves. 'There's some kind of office in here. The whole place stinks of shit! He was two feet away from us. Now, he's in the wind again. No gun, no casing.'

They heard the sirens, getting louder as they snaked

to a stop around the house. The ambulance arrived in minutes. An on-call doctor went to the fallen officer. Smyth ordered round-the-clock surveillance on him. 'What are his chances?'

'The next 24 hours will tell us better.' Officer Morales was transported to St. Francis Hospital.

Lieutenant Ryder stormed into the house. 'What's the story? Thought I had my best on this.'

Smyth began. 'We were with the perp's brother when this went down.'

'So, you know nothing?'

'Sir, we know the perp hid right there after he jacked the car.'

'The fuck was here the whole time?'

'Yes. We did a thorough search. We...'

'Apparently not, Detective, apparently not. I have one dead officer, another near death, one dead dog from the looks of things, two healthy detectives and a perp who pissed on all of you!'

Suarez took over. 'Look, Lieutenant, yeah, that's what you have, but we've slept four hours in two days.' Suarez looked around. 'This perp is a killing machine or there was someone else here.'

'Is that the best you can do?'

'Diego Gonzalez swore he'd find the perp responsible for the attack on his sister.'

Ryder was losing control. 'Now you're telling me the perp hid out here, fooled my best, who paved the way for the mob to step in and snatch him up. You want to run with that?'

'I'm not sure of anything right now. Maybe the perp is another Rambo. The dead dog's not a stray. How could it wander into this house?'

'Do your detecting. This case will come down on all our heads if Crime comes up empty.' Pro-Ball left Suarez without another word.

Smyth had walked outside, angry. Bags sat on a rock in an empty field with a cell in his hand. Their eyes met. She'd seen this kid across the street from the hardware store. She walked towards him. Bags ran. She rushed back to the house. 'Suarez! I just saw Diego's banger!' She pointed Suarez in the direction Bags had run. Suarez tore down the lane after him.

Bags knew being eyeballed was a fatal mistake. He ran for his life. If Diego found out...

Suarez chased him until he became a speck in the distance. He ran till his shins burned. He ran till the speck disappeared from the lane, up a street that had a yellow house with rotting flowers. He doubled over, gasping and spitting. *Diego was here! If the cop survives, he must have seen him.* Suarez stumbled over to cement stairs for support and called Smyth. 'I'm down the lane. Pick me up. This kid can nail Gonzalez. We have to find him.'

CHAPTER FIFTY-TWO

CARMEN LAY ON her bed, waiting on Mike and Caitlin's news. She got up when she heard them back in the living room. 'Am I too old to be the maid of honor?' Carmen looked from one to the other, but they weren't giving it up. Both were somber. She didn't pursue an answer.

Mike broke the tension. 'Alright, where can we go as a threesome? Let's get out of here.'

Caitlin caught the glee in Carmen's eyes. 'No!' She didn't need more stress.

'Let me guess. One more visit to Money Bags.' Mike wanted to change the mood or escape it. Caitlin's rejection had pushed him aside and he'd felt the shove.

'Honestly, I just want to exchange this watercolor and, maybe, take one peek at Money Bags. We can't get into trouble if you're with us, Mike.'

'He's the walking wounded, Carm.'

'How safe is the Trump?'

Fight had gone out of Caitlin. 'We exchange the watercolor, peek in at Money Bags, but we don't instigate anything with Larry.'

'Sounds good, but we should go tonight. I forget when the festival closes.'

'Are there decent restaurants? I ate next to nothing at the hospital.'

'Good and upscale,' Carmen chimed.

Caitlin had a hard time standing.

'We're off then, but walk slowly. I don't want to jar the shoulder.'

🦅

Felicia learned that Jesús's remains had been released to the family, who had been solicitous from the beginning of the tragedy. They had not asked Felicia to be directly involved, because of her own ordeal. She assured Jesús's father that she was well enough to attend tomorrow's service with her family. The florist promised her a beautiful presentation. After the call, a sadness for her late husband enveloped Felicia's heart. Laying her head back, she began to recall the good moments in their lives together and the years he would never know. Memories of his clothes suddenly bounced around in her head. Felicia tried to count the colored cashmere polo sweaters Jesús owned. When she hit 15, she laughed through the tears. A shoe count would depress her and big-ticket items might make her erupt in anger. *Poor Jesús, at least you went to the Lord looking very handsome!* Another uninvited thought entered her mind and it stung her with guilt. *I wonder if I will see Mike Halloran again?* This idle revelry was broken when Diego walked into the sitting room. This beautiful room was generally bathed in sunshine, but Felicia had drawn the curtains.

'How's my little sister?'

'Diego, we are eleven months apart.'

'You remain my little sister. How are you feeling?'

'Much better, much stronger. The burial for Jesús is tomorrow at noon. Will you come with me?'

'Of course. I have something to tell you.'

Her shoulders slumped.

'You are not to worry. The man who assaulted you and killed Jesús will never hurt anyone again.'

'You found him?' Felicia whispered incredulously before she began to rock back and forth.

'No one but you, not even Jennifer, must ever know.'

Felicia nodded.

'Have you any words to say to him?'

Her hand went up to her cheek where Ponytail had struck her.

Diego's face hardened.

Felicia had begun to cry. 'I have nothing to say to him. He must answer for Jesús. I survived.'

Diego cradled his sister is his arms. 'He will answer for all of it.'

'Thank you, Diego.'

'You are my sister. Nothing bad will come to you ever again.' Felicia drifted away from him. Diego left her with her thoughts.

Jennifer poked her head into the room. 'I thought I heard you. Sue Roth paid me a visit today.'

Diego followed his wife out to the solarium, overlooking the infinity pool. 'Sue Roth…' His cell vibrated in his pocket. He gave Jennifer a quick kiss on her lips. 'I must take this; I'll be right back.'

In his study, he reached for another phone and inserted a new chip and called a number. 'Good. Make sure you have food and water, and clean things up. Both friends who helped prepare for the breakfast should join us. I may see about the preparations tonight, but breakfast tomorrow is at eight. I'll need another Major.' Diego said no more. He took out the chip, replaced the phone, went outside and dropped it into the compactor before he went back to Jennifer, who recounted her meeting with Sue Roth.

'She handed you a certified check for a million dollars? Civilians! To think they run the state! It's frightening.'

'Diego, Sue is the only friend I have, the only one who'll sit with me at the club. I understand about business, but it's hard when women walk away from me because they know who we are.'

'You'll have Felicia.'

'Sue got this money from her father. It's her inheritance.'

Diego had the squirrel, but what was between Gabe and him had become a personal affront. Diego respected women and he was feeling magnanimous. 'Return the check.'

'What about their house?'

'Never question me about my business!' Diego rose and left.

Diego confides more in Felicia than in me. I don't want her living so close. The two of them will freeze me out. Jennifer went for her cell and called Sue Roth.

'Hello?'

'It's Jen. I'd like to return your check. How about you meet me halfway?'

Sue wanted to beg for their home, but she feared she'd lose the money for good. 'Thank you for this, Jen. I'll leave now.'

'Good.'

Sue didn't bother telling Gabe, who'd locked himself in his office. Ten minutes later, she had her father's money in her hand. Sue said nothing but 'thanks,' and Jennifer couldn't offer her any other comfort. Sue had barely looked at Jennifer, fearing she'd uncover additional comparisons. She didn't dare to explore the pathology of her marriage to Gabe. It was Jennifer who watched her drive off and Jennifer who knew she'd lost her one friend.

At home, Sue knocked on Gabe's door. 'I have the money back!'

'What?' he shouted.

'Open the door, and I'll tell you. Here, look!'

Gabe took the check. 'This is something! Did his wife say anything about me?'

'No.'

'I'm still hung out to dry.' He raked his hand through his hair. Sue could see the white roots.

'Can't we still take off like you said? I have this money.'

'That was madman talk. Dammit, Sue! No one is going to run me off my own home! This isn't a movie! It's our lives. I have to work this out myself.'

Sue saw the gun on his white oak desk. 'Gabe, not like that. Please! People have lost their homes in hurricanes. They recover! What's happened to us is terrible. Let's not make it worse and lose everything. We still have each other, and our health.'

'Diego has it in for *me*. I see that when he talks to me. Yet the more he threatens, the more I resist. We stick in each other's craw. It's me he wants to destroy. You got the check back and that lets you off his hook.'

Gabe stared forlornly out the window. His yacht, 'Hands On,' was bobbing gently. 'When we bought the yacht, we knew not to purchase it from Diego's company. He offered us a deal, remember, but we wanted everything above board. How could I have been such a fool and taken the money? Yet I'm not the only physician to bungle a money deal. I could tell you horror stories about my colleagues. All it took was a momentary slip on my part. Have you ever taken a yellow light even though you know you can't make it? You didn't want to brake hard and you curse yourself for your recklessness. I'm caught on a red light. I'm still stuck there, and Diego knows that. I did this. It's my blunder, but that day Diego made sure he walked away quickly so I didn't have an opportunity to hand the check back. He played me but I was up for his game.'

Sue saw the flaws that crises expose. Gabe was beyond hearing her.

'As a kid, I was never in a single fight. Jocks fought and I wasn't one of them. Grew into my height only at seventeen. Before that, I was pushed into lockers at lunch and had my books punched out of my hands all through high school. Well, I'm not a kid anymore.' Gabe walked away from Sue. 'I save lives for God's sake. I won't hand over my savings to this hoodlum!'

Gabe thinks he can push back. He knew he'd take a beating if he fought back when he was a kid. Why doesn't he see he's risking our lives? We can't win.

In an instant, Gabe shifted the blame away from himself. 'I could kill Diego! I never dreamt I could say that about anyone. Please, leave me alone.'

CHAPTER FIFTY-THREE

CAITLIN TOOK A right on 68th Street from Harding Avenue and made another left on Collins heading back north till she found a place.

'The festival's still here! The booth is by the ocean.'

The threesome took a side road. 'It's the same woman who sold it to me. Wish me luck!'

Mike and Caitlin stood beside Carmen for support when they reached the booth.

'Hi! I hope you remember me.'

The woman smiled, but without recognition. 'That's my work you're holding. Is there a problem?'

Carmen handed the work over and pointed out the small tear.

The artist ran her rough fingers along the small tear and examined the back of the canvas. 'Could have happened in transport. Do you see anything else you like?'

'I love the one I chose.'

'Well,' the artist opened her box of colors, wet a couple of brushes and painted over the tear till it was invisible to the naked eye. 'How about I refund you half the price?'

'Sold a second time!'

Once they were back on Collins, Carmen walked towards Money Bags.

'Carm, we're looking for food, not trouble. There's a restaurant across the street. That's where we're going.' Caitlin may have lost Mike, but she wanted him safe.

🌴

When Ponytail woke up in darkness, he found himself tied to a chair and bare-chested. Was this an interrogation room? He remembered the dog and a loud blast. His chest ached, and his neck throbbed and felt thick. When he moved his head, he was nauseous. He tried not to move it. His eyes searched the darkness, but wherever he was, he knew the place was sealed. Something called out to him, a noise, breathing. He wasn't alone. He listened; it was there. He hadn't imagined it. The steady rhythmic flow of air, forced in and out.

When the thought struck, he coughed violently and vomited. The cops didn't have him. Felicia's brother had found him. *You can't hide.* He remembered her saying something like that. A numbness that comes from seeing the end shutting down crept though his body. He listened; the breathing hadn't stopped. He tried to turn his head, to wipe his mouth on his shoulder, but he became dizzy. With no way to wipe his mouth, he spat on the floor. Smooth and even, the breathing continued. Another thought cut as much as the first. Was he listening to himself?

🌴

Ramon had prepared an Irish stew for the women that evening. At an opportune time, James knocked on the door and was admitted. He bowed to the ladies. 'I have an idea or two for tomorrow, or the next day. How about a trip to Delray Beach and a special visit to the mystery bookshop, Murder on the Beach? Carlos told me that it's a favorite place. We can have lunch by the ocean. How does that sound? If that's not to your liking, I have found an art exhibit on Lincoln Road.'

'I'm not up for that just yet, James. I have my son with me.'

'I'll go for the mystery tour. It would be nice for the little boys to get out. It's a good thing to leave our troubles behind for a while. God knows they'll be here when we get back.'

Ethel, Muriel, and the rest were polled. James had his first outing and was prepared. He selected the best restaurant. If he had to work nights now, he fully intended to enjoy his afternoons. Figuring his take excited him. As he left the women, there was a swagger in his walk.

*

'Mother, I should fly back tonight.'

'Is there any possibility you could spend another day with me?'

'I'll make the calls.'

'Thank you, son. I'm at loose ends.'

'That's to be expected.'

*

Scar had his connect to a promotion, a call to the storage location. He'd heard of it, but only top soldiers knew of its location. He'd be somethin' before he was twenty. He called Bags to see if he'd been contacted, but he got no answer. *Who gives a shit about him? I got a call!*

Bags ignored his pager. If that cop reported seeing him at the hardware store… Stuck at a vacant worksite, he crouched behind a pylon and rubble with his radio. To his left, for more protection, lay an acacia tree uprooted and discarded with the rest of the pile. He'd know what he had to do if a search for him was on. Why had he broken his cover? Now he was a leak to Diego. Later, he'd go to his hideout for his take-off stash. So much had gone down that Bags had forgotten to get his half of the money they'd taken from the paper man. In a lane near his foster mother's house, he'd found he could lift what remained of a cement railing, a foot and a half of it anyway. Late one night, he'd dug out a good-sized hole and buried his stash before replacing the slab. Most bangers had such hideouts. Their lives could turn bad in a night.

Bags's 17 years could disappear. No one but Scar would ask where they'd gone.

What a fuck-up! An attorney and a bail bondsman worked for the bangers, but Bags knew this case was big and personal for the boss. The cops knew that too. No attorney or bondsman could help him. The boss couldn't have a witness against him still breathing. Sweat from the back of his hair dripped down his back. Bags was on his own.

CHAPTER FIFTY-FOUR

SMYTH AND SUAREZ were quiet in the car as each tried to make sense of their foul-up and the carnage at the house on 69th Street. Smyth broke the uneasy silence. 'Is my ID on that kid enough for a search warrant on Diego?'

'Unless we find him, it's not. Are you up for a sketch?'

'Of course.'

'We'll set that up. The kid *was* the lookout. They brought the dog. Bangers own and train attack dogs for protection. Diego's men took down the cops and hauled this Ponytail's ass out to some location for Diego. The way he feels about his sister, he himself was there. As we speak, I think Diego's laughing at us.'

'Suarez, is there any possibility the perp did all this?'

'Too much work for one man. It's Diego.'

'I'll drop you at the hospital, get back to the precinct and find the sketch cop.'

'Stay out of Pro-Ball's sights if you want to live.'

'My bet is that he'll be at the hospital.'

'Damn!'

'Right.'

🌴

Bags crept out from his hideout and found a pay phone, a dying breed. 'Scar?'

'Where the hell you been? I got a call! You probably did too. Early tomorrow – big day for us. You better check in.'

'How long we sling product, Scar?'

'Couple of years. Why you askin' that now?'

'A cop made me.'

'You're fucked, man. That jams you up.' Scar saw another opportunity for himself. 'You need a place?'

'Naw got my own.'

'We partners, you and me, Bags – you keep me hooked on this.'

'Wanna know how bad this is before I run.'

'Then keep me hooked.'

'Awright.' Bags felt a sudden spurt of hope. His mind raced with only one clear purpose. He had to get away from Diego.

Scar had something the boss needed to know. He didn't have Bags, but he knew all his stash holes. If need be, Scar could find him. This was big, and he was saving it till tomorrow.

🌴

When Smyth got back to the precinct, the mood was sombre. One cop was dead and another on the critical list. Jack Coleman was sitting at his desk reading the latest faxed reports. 'Jack, I need a sketch.'

'You the source?' he asked her.

'Yes, I am.'

'Sit.' Smyth had a cop's recall. The only snag was the face itself. She hadn't been close enough to it. The clothes, the jewellery, all that was letter perfect.

'Send this out to all media. The more exposure the better. You know the drill, and you have the latest news of the fax. "Wanted in connection with..."'

'Don't need help with that. Media's hungrier when it's one of our own. Not to worry.'

'Do you need me for anything else here?'

'Nope.'

Smyth set out for the hospital. There was no time to stand and give details to desk cops.

🌴

Before Diego reached the storage center, he had

changed cars three times and had his men driving behind to block off the routes to any possible police tails. His car was waved through by security at the shipyard and he drove past four lines of containers, known as "cans," before making a sharp right turn. To his left, the front flap of a can was open, and he drove the car into it and parked. He was escorted the rest of the way to another can that appeared to be a permanent fixture. It was attached to the wall behind it. Around the back, Diego found a steel side door, part of the renovation work on this particular unit. The door was unlocked, as he had expected it to be. He closed it gently, took out the flashlight he used when he was there and turned it on. He wore gloves and his wool hat. Halfway down, there was another door. He took a satisfying breath before he opened the door and stepped inside.

With a flick of a switch, two overhead lights exploded with pencil-sharp precision that bore down on Ponytail. Except for the thin beam of light coming from Diego, the rest of the small room remained in darkness. Hench had risen from his chair in the corner of the room to join Diego.

Ponytail lifted his head. Pain knifed up the back of his neck and throbbed in his ears. Since the night at the Trump, he'd lost nine pounds. Small hemorrhages reddened his eyes; heavy dark circles under them gave him a racoon look. Dried vomit had stuck to the side of his chin.

Diego was pleased his bangers had given him names for the squirrel. This visit was personal. A name added weight to the punitive damages Diego would inflict. 'Well, Benito, or is it Ponytail? I have looked forward to this meeting with great anticipation. Hench, get me a chair. Clean off his face and give him water. Filth disgusts me.'

Ponytail squinted into the darkness but could not make out the speaker behind the thin shaft of light. He knew without seeing who it was. He saw Hench when he threw a towel on his face and pushed his head back, rubbing off the vomit. He didn't scream with the pain, but he lost his wind and began to choke.

'Give him water.'

Ponytail gulped and choked down as much as he could.

'Wipe up! Then, leave us alone.'

Ponytail heard a door closing and felt nauseous again even though his stomach was empty.

'I admire men who take risks. How do you feel about that?'

Ponytail squinted again toward the light. Both eyelids were swollen almost shut.

'You disappoint me with your silence. You had a lot to say to my sister.'

Ponytail smothered a moan.

'You don't appear daring at all to me. I have nothing but contempt for men who fail. You'll soon feel how much. You laid hands on my sister.' Diego got up and walked to the back of Ponytail's chair. 'You hurt my sister!' He spat the last words into Ponytail's ear. Diego walked away quietly without touching him. He flicked off the light and left the room. His face bulged with anger. Hench had sat quietly, watching his boss. He knew his way around in the darkness.

Ponytail had bitten the inside of his cheek until it bled.

CHAPTER FIFTY-FIVE

BOTH HOMICIDE DETECTIVES sat at the foot of the bed in the ICU. Officer Juan Morales was on a ventilator, but his physician did expect the young cop to regain consciousness. His wife was by his side. When his cell vibrated, Suarez left the room to take the call.

'Brianna?'

'What do you have on Officer Morales?'

'Off the record?'

'First, is there anything I can use?'

'He's critical.'

'Recovery odds?'

'Not to sell your newspapers. Anything on Morales gets leaked, you lose a prime source and I lose the best cop-shop reporter.'

'You have to tell me?'

'The *Herald* gives up nothing on Morales, no location, no condition.'

'Not possible. We've already reported there were two officers on the scene. It's public knowledge one Officer Grover didn't make it. Can't leave Morales blowing in the wind.'

'Off the record, Brianna. He's high risk for another attack.'

'Nothing then?'

'Can't.'

'Off the record – he's alive.'

'When I have something, I'll get it to you.'

'Exclusive, remember, or I'll stop giving up my leads.'

'You have my word.'

'And mine.'

Suarez was not in the room when Officer Morales began to choke on the ventilator tube. He was shoved aside as medical help rushed into the room. 'Officer! Take a deep breath. I'll remove the tube from your throat. Don't shake your head, please. Take a deep breath, a deep one! That's better. Now, don't move.' With a hand on Officer Morales's forehead, the physician extubated with a clean, swift motion. The cop began to cough in earnest. 'Officer, put your head down, take deep breaths. You're fine. Dry throat is all. You'll feel better in a few minutes.' He looked back at one of the nurses. 'Get him some ice chips and take his pressure. Alright, Officer, try to relax; that's better. You're doing well. Whisper at first; don't put extra strain on your throat. Do you know where you are?'

In a hoarse voice, Officer Morales said, 'Hospital.'

'Good. I'll be back shortly. Take it easy.'

Smyth and Suarez allowed the officer's wife a minute before they walked to the side of the bed. This cop was the witness who could give them Gonzalez. 'Morales, Suarez and Smyth, Homicide.'

Morales nodded.

'You worked the surveillance.'

Morales nodded.

'Do you recall what happened before you were taken out?'

Morales's brow squinted in thought. 'A shot.'

'From inside the house?'

'Yeah.'

'Did you alert Officer Grover, or call for backup?'

Officer Morales blanched. He'd messed up. 'No time. I ran into the house.'

'The door was unlocked?'

'I didn't break it down.' His voice was hoarse and it cracked as he spoke.

Suarez paused before he asked the next question. 'This is very important, Morales, so take your time. Who or what did you see before you were clocked?'

The officer's face was white. He was using what energy he had to answer the questions. Clenching his eyes shut, he tried to recall the scene. 'I saw the dog.'

'Besides the dog?'

He squinted again, rubbing his forehead. His face was clammy. 'There was a black blur or figure near the cabinets. I'm not sure if that's when I went down.'

'You were barely inside the door when you were hit. By this blur, do you think?'

'Shit, I don't know.' Sweat began to bead on his forehead. 'I didn't reach the blur.'

'Alright. That's it for now. Try hard to get the room in view. It's very important you do. You have round-the-clock surveillance.'

Recognition and fear crept across Officer Morales's face. 'Grover? Did he see more than I did?'

'Officer Grover didn't make it.'

Morales closed his eyes.

'Please, detectives, my husband needs rest.'

'Take care of him, Mrs. Morales. We need him.'

As soon as they were outside the ICU, Smyth raised two fingers.

'My count as well; three with the perp. Diego got to him, either in person or had it done. For his sister, my bet is he was there.'

'The sketch of the banger will be on local channels tonight and in tomorrow's papers,' Smyth assured Suarez.

'If word leaks that Officer Morales is alive, his life's not worth jack shit.'

'When the kid's sketch hits the small screen, his life isn't either,' Smyth said.

'Smyth, work surveillance here – I trust you. I want Diego, but I need hard evidence. Knowing it's him isn't enough. We now have two key witnesses: Officer Morales and the kid too, if we get to him first.'

'Suarez, where will you be?'

'The goddamn paperwork. Pro-Ball's up my ass.'

🌴

Diego was swimming laps when he saw Hench's feet at poolside as he surfaced for air. Hench rarely set foot on property around the main mansion. Diego grabbed the side of the pool and, in a show of strength, he shot up out of the water. 'Talk.'

'The first cop survived.'

'Get to work!'

Diego shook the water off his arms. Another Rottweiler had taken Major's place in a side garage. That was covered at least. Diego tried to reassure himself he'd turned away from the door when the cop rushed through it. Had he moved quickly enough? He'd pulled the hat down to his brows. But damn, had he turned quickly enough? Diego stormed into the house without bothering with a towel. Sweat spread to the water on his body.

🌴

When Smyth saw Officer Morales sitting up in bed, an idea popped into her head. Opening her phone, she called Suarez. 'Morales is much better. I'd like to take him to a safehouse immediately, before Diego discovers where he is, and we're both vulnerable. Keep the location between ourselves. If you feel Pro-Ball has to know, you tell him, but not where. That's the only way we get a step up on Diego.'

'What about his wife? Can't leave her exposed.'

'They both go together. I'm half apartment-sitting. My neighbors are away for a month. I can stash them both there. My guess is we won't need more than a week, if that. If we find the kid, we have our connection. Morales is no longer our first witness.'

'I have to run this through Pro-Ball. Get Morales out of the hospital.'

Smyth wasted no time explaining the urgency of the situation. Officer Morales and his wife needed no persuasion. Smyth released the surveillance cops as they left. It amazed her how easily the threesome walked off the floor. Not a single nurse questioned them. The hospital would have to wait for her call advising them that Morales had released himself.

Smyth drove to 97th Avenue in Surfside. She'd checked her rear view mirror often. There was no tail. She parked in her spot around back. The apartment was a two-story building, painted pale green and white and called The Avenue. Smyth's apartment was the last one on the east side. She brought them to hers first. 'Here are the rules: you can't go outside the apartment; what you need, I'll get; don't contact your parents. I'll take care of that and get you food. Your job is remembering what you saw in that room. Treat the place with care. It belongs to a neighbor, and I sure as hell am not going to clean up after you. Understood?'

'What if I can't ID Diego? What if he wasn't there?'

'Our gut tells us he was. His sister was assaulted by the perp. Keep working on what you saw. You're here because by now Diego knows you're alive. He can't afford to take the chance you saw him. Got that?'

'Yes.' Officer Morales bit the knuckle on his left hand and looked nervously around the room. What chance did he have here if the mob wanted him found?

Smyth packed up what food she had, took them to number 48 and told them to be quiet so neighbors would not call the super to see who was in this apartment, and to keep the door locked. When she was alone, she made herself a peanut butter and jelly sandwich on four-day-old whole wheat and grabbed a soda.

Hospital staff wasn't pleased that a patient hadn't signed release forms.

🌴

James was buzzing around the lobby when they walked in. 'Hi guys, everything okay by you?'

'Fine, thanks,' Mike said. 'Feeling no pain after a few.'

'Great!'

As soon as they were inside the suite, Caitlin saw the red message light flashing. 'Mike, you want to see who called. Might be your mother.'

Carmen had gone to her room, singing "Margaritaville."

Mike picked up the phone and listened to the message: *Hello, Mike. This is Felicia Gonzalez. It was good to see you. You can reach me at …*

While they were out, nothing seemed changed between Mike and her. Now Caitlin felt she was back on the balcony, unsteady and scared.

'I'd like to take Felicia to lunch. It's something I want to do, Caitlin. Something we shared. Can you understand?'

'I don't think I have a choice, but I can try.'

'I'll call her tomorrow then.'

'Are you up for a walk on the beach with me? We can carry our shoes, just like tourists.'

'I can think of something better if you help me out.'

'You're on.' But Caitlin wasn't sure they were. For the first time, their love-making was tentative, almost unfamiliar.

🌴

CHAPTER FIFTY-SIX

AS THE HOURS passed, Ponytail was only vaguely aware of Hench sitting in a corner in the darkness. Dying wasn't part of this score, not his own at least. He figured he'd beat the odds. As a scammer, the most he'd ever looked at was a few years, and that hadn't happened. He could feel the bulge against his leg and remembered the watch. *Diego will punish me for this. Should have tossed it. Funny, I'm not thirsty or hungry. No spasms. Like I'm not here. Is that how you feel before you die, like you're somewhere else?*

Sweat leaked into his mouth. He tried to move his neck. It throbbed dully. Maybe he should try to sleep. *I can't waste the last hours of my life, but I can't get my mind around a thought.* He felt a warm moistness on his inner thigh. *Shit!* He began to swallow the sweat that pooled around his mouth. He ran his tongue over his upper lip and licked the snot that trickled from his nose. He began to worry about evaporating. He held his legs through the rope, felt the bones that were his, the tight skin over them. With his thumb, he touched the contours of each finger, the way one pets a dog before it's put down.

'What a beautiful baby!' Wasn't that what his mother had told him? His brother was short and stocky like his father, but he was beautiful. Neighbors had told her how lucky she was to have such a child. He would bring pride to the family... *If only I could go back... have a second chance. I'd be so different, Mamá. You'd see! I'd take care of you; I wouldn't run off. I'd work hard. You'd see, Mamá, you'd see...* Ponytail heard himself blubbering.

'Shut the fuck up!'

Ponytail tensed, and the pain in his neck burned so sharply, a flash of new tears burst into his eyes and stung them. He wasn't evaporating; he was still here. Diego was still coming.

♣

Diego hadn't slept either. He'd spent most of the night outside his second guesthouse. He was there when he heard that the cop had been taken out of the hospital. His contacts had no word of his whereabouts. He hated clutter, and now it was all around him. Cops had pulled him in before; he'd been out an hour later. This was different. Scar, Bags and Ponytail had to be attended to. Now there was this cop. He'd gotten his home address, but the wife had disappeared with her husband. If they had something hard, they would be talking to his attorney right now. Diego knew about Suarez and Smyth. Thorough, believers even, which was worse for him. They were working their evidence and they might find something.

The time he'd wanted to spend with Ponytail he'd have to cut short. Storage had to be cleared. Gabe Roth would have to wait. What an arrogant bastard he turned out to be! Returning the check to his wife hadn't worked for Jennifer, who'd come back downcast. 'She couldn't look at me.' *Look down your noses at us. I have a degree in business. Take a million from me and think you're better than we are? Hypocrites! You'll learn.*

Did he see me? Can he put me at the scene of a cop killing? Diego checked his watch. He'd meet with Ponytail in a few hours. He went into the guesthouse, showered, shaved and lay naked on one of the beds. Soon he pulled a sheet over himself and tried to sleep, but the scene in the kitchen played back in his head like a tape he couldn't scrub. *Did he see me?* Diego threw the pillow across the room. *Did he see me?* He kicked the sheet off.

♣

Scar was coming down. He tried to rehearse his lines to "the man." Drugged, none of them made much sense. He stared blankly at a dirty wall. Hours later, he was twitchy. He wanted the meeting over with; wasn't good with words. *Give me the extra points and I'll get back on the street. I'm a soldier.* When he remembered he had something for "the man," he felt better. He'd show the boss he was worthy. Bags should understand. Couldn't let a threat walk. Didn't happen. He looked at the clothes and felt better. He had something big; that made all the difference.

🌴

Bags was the only one of the four men who slept during the night. The only lesson he'd taken from his father was – if you can't solve the problem at night, save it till the morning. Though the day had been 90 degrees, the night had cooled down and it was windy. Bags woke after five and went looking for a newspaper stand. Too early. He went to the beach for a free shower. Although he was 17, he had nothing to shave. Today, he didn't mind the kid look. After six, he found a stand. Nothing of him he could see through the glass that hid some of the paper. He dropped 35 cents into the slot, reached in and grabbed four papers. Paper made good blankets. No chance he'd go back to his regular pod, the shed he called home. The color sketch of him was at the bottom on the left hand side of the *Herald*. Face wasn't perfect. What he wore was dead on.

He needed clothes real fast!

Scar was beeping him. Bags thought as fast as he could, though the first thing on his mind was clothes. As soon as word got around, he'd have a price on his head. The bangers reminded him of ants, crawling out of every crack. He ran through lanes and backyards. Up ahead, he saw clothes on a line. He ripped off everything he could and ran, chucked his own clothes and got into the others.

He had a thought. Took a chance on the street and phoned Scar from a booth that was surrounded by shattered glass. 'It's me.'

'You need a different place to crash. Go to my basement pod. No one'd find you there. Then you gotta run, but stay till tonight before you rabbit. I'll bring food and shit.'

'You sure?'

'Soldiers, right?'

'Yeah.'

Cops are looking to scrape me up. Wouldn't see tomorrow behind bars. Bags had some more thinking to do.

🌴

CHAPTER FIFTY-SEVEN

SCAR WAS DIRECTED to the general vicinity of the storage. Once he was waved through security, he parked and was driven the rest of the way. He figured the drive was a sign of his new status. When he knocked on the steel door, Hench opened it and steered him toward a chair a few feet from Ponytail. The spotlights had been turned on. Silence hung in the room.

Ponytail's eyes locked on Scar's, two reddened eyes reaching out to the only human he could see. Scar was spooked and shifted away from their entreaty. Diego appeared before Scar knew of his presence. The silence was eerie.

'Good morning, Ponytail!' Diego spoke softly. He walked up to Ponytail and stood over him like a canopy, or a priest about to administer the last rites. Diego bent closer to the man who would have murdered his sister, to be certain he was paying attention. He wore gloves. The blow struck without warning. Ponytail's head crashed against the back of the chair and flopped forward. 'That was for my sister.' Ponytail tried to open the eye that had already begun to bleed. 'Don't breathe on me!' Diego warned.

Ponytail slumped against the crush of his imminent death. Tears ran from both eyes; one track mixed with blood. 'Do it,' he pleaded, 'just do it.'

'Oh, I will, but you kept my sister waiting all night! You laid hands on my family!' Diego still whispered, adding a new dimension of terror.

Ponytail felt spittle on his cheek. 'Didn't touch...'

Diego struck next at both knees. Ponytail's back arched against the chair.

Scar balled his fists. He squirmed. *The boss should just*

kill the fuck!

'Whatever gave you the idea that you could come against our family?' Diego's voice was still eerily soft. 'Your arrogance and your ignorance amaze me. Do you want to apologize, beg for mercy, some silly thing like that?'

Ponytail felt needles in his flesh. One knee had collapsed when a bloodied shard of bone cut through the skin.

'No? I ran data on you. A two-bit scammer. You're not worth anybody's time. You don't count, yet you dare to come at my family?' Diego gave Hench a signal. A rope fell behind Ponytail. Hench walked behind the chair and looped it around Diego's neck and pulled hard.

'Any last words? No? I release you.' With a wave of Hench's hand, the rope, suspended from the ceiling, grew taut. In seconds, it pulled Ponytail and his chair a few feet off the floor. Ponytail's front teeth cracked, but he didn't scream before his neck snapped. Neither Diego nor Hench found the watch.

'You, help Hench.' Diego never oversaw disposals and moved toward the door.

Scar's throat was dry when he spoke. 'Boss, there's a problem.'

Hench had moved behind Scar with the pipe Diego had used. His motion aborted mid-shoulder.

Diego turned.

'Boss, at the house, Bags was eyeballed by the cops.' His right knee twitched.

'And?'

'He was made at the hardware joint too. He's on the front page of the paper today. Both places, Boss.' Scar took a step back. Bad news was never welcomed.

A knot at the nape of Diego's neck tightened. Anger worked behind his teeth. Scar took a step back. 'I know where he is.'

'Hench, call the others for this cleanup. Work with Scar. Fix things.'

Scar looked warily from Diego to Hench. Keep himself up front, that's what he had to do.

Diego stepped out into a mix of sun and cloud, but his world was bleak. Climbing into his SUV, he drove away quickly, punching the wheel with both palms. *A nobody, a goddamn nobody! Yet I now have three people who could do me.* When he heard the siren behind him ten minutes later, he pulled over to the curb and called his attorney before the street cop reached his side window. 'I may need you.' He began to suck his teeth and stopped.

'Say nothing.'

'I know the drill.' He rolled down his window.

'Licence and registration, please?'

'What's the problem, officer?'

'Licence and registration, please.'

Diego leaned across the passenger seat and reached into the glove compartment for the papers. He asked again as he handed them to the officer. 'Why did you pull me over?'

'This is a school zone. You exceeded the speed limit, sir. I'll be back in a minute.'

Diego spotted the gloves on the passenger seat. *Damn!* He whisked them to the floor. The cop in his rear view mirror was nodding his head. *At least I'm nowhere near the storage.*

'Sir, I'll have to write you up a citation.'

'So do it.'

The young cop with a bubble nose, heavy in the thighs and butt, wrote it up and handed Diego his copy. 'Have a good day, Mr. Gonzalez.'

Is there a tail on me? He tapped in his attorney's

number. 'I have a ticket for you to fix.'

'For?'

'Speeding in a school zone.'

'Ouch!'

'What?'

'Not so easy to fix.'

By the time he got home, Diego was in a stone rage. He'd picked up a copy of the paper, took a fast look and threw it on the floor. He had to believe Hench would take care of both problems. To loosen up, he did more laps before he went to the main house. Jen was moping, and Felicia was pensive, recalling her ordeal. The jealous resentment Sue felt towards her sister-in-law kept the women from connecting with one another. Sue wanted Felicia away from her brother. What bond they shared remained unspoken because Diego's attention and affection were lavished on his sister. 'Felicia, is there something wrong?'

'We have Jesús's service today.'

'I almost forgot.'

'I hope you can still come with me, Diego.'

'Of course, Jen and I will attend with you. But I must leave immediately after the service. We should take two cars.'

🌴

Mike, Caitlin and Carmen had finally all gotten into the ocean. Caitlin swam, Carmen rode the waves and Mike waded, trying not to wet the bandage and the incision. 'This is the life,' Carmen sighed as they lay on the hot sand later. 'Who'd ever want to get up and leave?'

'I don't know. People who don't want skin cancer maybe!' Caitlin added.

They did leave an hour later for lunch. 'Margaritas

tonight anyone?'

'I say South Beach, Carm.'

'We can figure that out after we've had another swim.'

The message light was flashing. 'I hope it's my mother,' Mike said.

It wasn't. It was Felicia accepting his luncheon invitation.

'Mike, please set up the lunch around here. What about the outdoor restaurant at the Bal Harbour Mall? It's safer.'

'I'll call her tonight.' He threw the phone onto the sofa. 'Maybe I shouldn't have…'

'But you did, so see it through.' Caitlin was still numb and everything felt tenuous.

🌴

CHAPTER FIFTY-EIGHT

SCAR KNEW HIS place and didn't speak in the black Lexus SUV on the ride to his pod. Once he'd given Hench the directions, he tried to assume the role of a "top points" man. That was the new position he felt was his. Working with Bags did not make them brothers. Slinging was a business. No one threatened Diego's territory. Blood was bad for business. But now, if Bags spilled to the cops, he'd implicate Scar as well.

He sat back in the soft leather, wishing Hench would use more a/c. When fifteen minutes had passed, he looked over at Hench, but the man ignored him and drove as though he were alone. Scar hadn't seen a gun, but that didn't mean Hench didn't have one. The guy was big, heavy and muscled, square as a brick. His thighs were the size of Scar's waist. He figured Hench was old, about forty. He had the focus of a Marine and the short hair. Scar began to squirm, spooked by the quiet he couldn't disturb.

'That it?'

'In the back of the building, my pod's in the basement.'

Most basements had rooms cluttered with discarded furniture, carpets, plywood, old phone books, broken tools and one workroom for the super where he stored his nose-curling cleansers. It was a good place for a second pod, with places to hide if one survived the stench and the roaches.

'He said he'd come?'

'I told him he was safe here.'

'Go and find him. I won't be far.'

Scar opened a ground-level door and went looking for Bags. 'It's okay, it's me. I have over two grand for you.

Bags. The paper man, remember?' Scar got down on his knees and began looking behind the stinking rolled carpets. 'It's safe, Bags. It's me.' *The little fuck didn't come!* He called and kept searching, but Bags was nowhere around. When he got up from his knees, he bumped into Hench.

'You said he'd be here.'

Scar rubbed behind his ear. 'I told him to come; figured he would.' Scar backed away from Hench. He had to take a leak.

'Beep him.'

Hench spoke to him like he was no-account scum. Scar beeped Bags. 'Is it safe to use my phone?'

'We'll get rid of the beeper and the phone after he calls. Tell him you wanna run with him, that it's not safe for both of you. You're freaked. Try that.' Hench walked back to his SUV; Scar followed. Then they waited.

🌴

James had gone out of his way for the Delray Beach outing. Lila allowed Muriel to convince her to make the trip. Jake had caught a flight back to San Diego that morning. Muriel sat with Lila and made a few comments, but she allowed Lila to stay in her own thoughts. To impress the women, James used the mike when they turned onto East Atlantic Avenue into Delray Beach. He drove to Downtown Delray, the eastern part of the city. The little bookstore was located on a side street, tucked away from the general traffic. The group filed into the store that stocked nothing but mysteries. Lila did not do much looking, but one book caught her eye because the setting was Sunny Isles, and the blurb on the back cover mentioned wonderful old places that no longer existed on Collins Avenue. She paid the owner for her copy of *The Sands Motel.*

After their excursion, Lila went to her room. The back blurb on her book mentioned all the changes occurring in North Miami Beach. How many years ago had she come to Miami? Too many years to recall their number. It must be 50! Lila remembered The Castaways and The Golden Strand and the yachts her husband rented for deep-sea fishing. They were so young back then. *How the years begin their flight slowly, then they gather together and soar through time!* Uncharacteristically, Lila lay down and fell asleep.

Sue tried to reach Gabe at the hospital, but he was in surgery. She searched the house for the gun when she discovered it was not in its safety box in Gabe's study. He was still carrying it although they had not heard from Diego. Maybe he was rethinking the extortion. When she remembered the money Gabe had taken, she poured herself a fourth cup of coffee. The phone rang. She dropped the cup and sent pieces of her favorite smooth, white Emile Henry scattering across the cream tiles, while her coffee stained the yellow grout.

The caller was Jen Gonzalez. Sue's stomach churned when she reached for the cordless. 'Hello Jen.'

'Sue, I did the right thing. I've felt miserable since I gave you back the check. You blew me off and that's not right.'

'I'm very grateful to have my father's money back. He might need some of it for medical expenses. Thank you.'

'That's it. Thank you? I went the extra mile for you because I'm your friend.'

'You have to understand how upset Gabe and I are.'

'Can't you separate what's going on with our husbands from us?'

'Could you, if my husband was threatening to

separate you from your home?'

'Our men have a lot in common, Sue. Don't delude yourself. Gabe took the money.'

'And we're paying double the price of his error.'

'Diego would call that interest.'

'We don't use the same words. I'm sorry, Jen, I have to go.' *How dare she equate us with them!*

CHAPTER FIFTY-NINE

ONLY FOUR PEOPLE knew where Ponytail was finally dumped. Diego, naturally, the security guard who was a second cousin, and two men who ran an independent cement trucking company. Their connection to the family was not discussed. It might have been an obligation or a lucrative money contract. When Diego, Hench and Scar left Ponytail hanging two feet from the ground, he dangled till the end of the work day. The security guard had a key. Inside the storage, he worked the rope. The body and the chair came back down to rest on the floor. The next procedure went quickly. Ponytail was untied, shoved into a black body bag and wheeled out to the guard's van. Soon Hench would work the cleanup.

The guard drove onto the company site on the outskirts of the city. Two trailer homes were housed closest to the road. Since the call had come in for work that day, a truck and a backhoe were on the property. Two luxuries the men allowed themselves were a tennis court and a basketball court based with cement. The guard could see the far end of the tennis court had already been cut open, and the backhoe was at work digging. Behind broken cement slabs from the court was a bag of quicklime. The guard backed his van up to the court. Ponytail was dragged from the van, the body bag was unzipped and quicklime dumped into it. The zipped bag was dropped into an eight-foot hole that was quickly filled by the backhoe. The men finished up with a smooth thick cement base.

The guard drove home. He'd spoken very little with the men. Anonymity was important to all three of them. Ponytail had disappeared. Once Hench got back to storage and hosed down the cotton fibres and seed hair, there'd be no trace for cops to find, even if they ever stumbled onto the whereabouts of the storage. Ponytail had ended his life as he'd lived it, on the edges and unknown.

🌴

The service for Jesús was not elaborate. Felicia's flower arrangement and the brass casket she had ordered were the most striking parts of the funeral. Jesús did not come from money. Once he married into it, he quickly shed his friends in an effort to move up into the world of the elite. In the year he'd been married to Felicia, he hadn't made much progress in that area because he'd used his time spending her money to make an impression. A brother spoke a few words at the end of the mass. Hymns were piped in during the service. Jesús's parents seemed shy to approach Diego, Felicia and Jennifer. Felicia had knelt with the family during the service uttering the usual comforting words: 'he had a good heart; we had some lovely times together; he is gone much too soon; I will miss him.'

Diego was eager to leave. He had urgent business. Felicia saw his impatience and confided to her in-laws that she still endured pain from the attack and needed rest. Minutes later, they left. As Jesús's father watched the Gonzalez family drive away, he turned to his wife. 'If Jesús had stayed with his own, he would be alive today.'

🌴

After leaving his pod, Scar took a quick look into the back of the SUV. The seat had been taken out. He saw a wrench and a hammer, lying on towels, and rolled carpet against a side wall. Hench had come prepared for Bags. As they waited, Scar tried not to squirm. Hench sat as quiet as a tombstone. A shot of nerves caught Scar in the mid-section, and he shifted on the leather seat. Hench reminded him of a zombie from *The Return of the Living Dead.*

Bags saw that Scar was beeping him again, but he didn't trust anyone. He was out on 58th Street because he was hungry. His face wasn't clear in the papers. On the street, in different clothes, scoping as he walked, he felt a measure of safety. His mind was clearer. Airports were out, buses as well. The cops and mob had set their traps in those places. Jacking a car was his best hope. After two Big Macs and a Coke, he felt better. He saw the phone booth on the other side of the street. What could a few minutes hurt? After scoping the area twice, he stepped into the booth, grabbed the receiver, dropped his coins into the slot, but kept one foot on the sidewalk.

When his cell vibrated in his hand, Hench gave Scar a stiff elbow that almost winded him. Scar jerked the cell to his ear. He opened the door of the SUV and hopped out. Hench didn't make a move to stop him. 'I'll do better alone.' *Shit! That hurt.*

'Howzit going? Where you at?'

'Safe. Didn't need your pod.'

'Listen, I didn't go this morning. Fuck the promo. They want you; figure they come after me soon 'nough.'

Bags didn't respond.

'Figure we run together; work somethin' in another city. I'm not jazzin'. You want to go it alone. Fuck! Do it.'

'You really solo, Scar, or you helpin' 'em come at me?'

'I gotta fly too, man.'

'You got a stash, Scar?'

''Course, plus the paper man's five. We pool it – we do better. Where you at?'

'Booth, 58th and Collins. Soldiers?'

'To the end, man. Thirty minutes; I be there.' Scar hopped back up into the SUV. 'Got it.'

'Where?'

Scar looked over at Hench. His eyes were half open, lazy. 'Booth, 58th and Collins.'

'Get in the back and hand me the pipe.'

Scar kept his eyes on Hench. He tried to reach the pipe by leaning back.

'Get in there!'

As soon as Scar climbed into the back of the SUV, Hench was on him. He wrestled the bar from Scar. With the full weight of his body on top of the kid, Hench held the pipe against Scar's neck till he knew he had broken his windpipe. There was no discernable noise inside the SUV. Hench grabbed the bar when he got back into the driver's seat and drove to 58th. *One down.*

CHAPTER SIXTY

SUAREZ SPENT HALF an hour with his lieutenant. 'This is the second time the perp has blown you both off like you were bleeping amateurs.'

'Pro-Ball, be reasonable, the first time he was in a car. We were on foot.'

'The second fuck-up shouldn't have happened. You should have been at the house. One with the brother; one at the house. Now, you want me to get a warrant for Gonzalez with jack shit!'

'Pro-Ball, same banger at both locales! Diego's boy! Either he himself was in the house or his men. My money's on him. It was his sister. You didn't see him at the hospital. This is family, Cuban family at that.'

'Where are you with Morales?'

'Smyth's with him. Dark shape at the kitchen counter is what we have. He fell a foot inside the door. No shape has that long a reach. There were two people in that room. I feel the perp shot the dog through the panel. The two men grabbed him up.'

'All gut. What about the banger?'

'Nothing yet.'

'Shit! For the time being, keep a tail on Gonzalez.'

'Done already.'

'These bangers are termites! Get back to Morales and push him. Something has to break. The perp?'

'Among the newly departed. That's what my gut tells me.'

'Get out of here.'

🌴

Smyth had gone back to her own place to use the washroom. 'Have you thought about what will happen

to us if you have to be a witness against the mob?'
Morales's wife asked. 'No badge is more important than
our lives,' she tried to tell him.

'What about relocation?'

'So you did see two people in the kitchen?'

'Just asking, Lindsay.'

'Leave our parents behind? Never see or talk to them
again. Who says *they'd* be safe? You can't do this.'

'Can't do what?' Smyth asked from the door. All she'd
caught was the last sentence.

Lindsay cringed.

Smyth wasn't fooled. 'You saw two people in that
room, didn't you, Morales? You carry a badge. Step up.'

'What about his obligation to his two-year-old?' his
wife cried.

'I saw the shape, like I told you. What else can I add?'

'Did you see the shape take aim at your head?'

'It happened so fast. I came through the door. I went
down.'

'Could the shape have struck you? It's a simple
question.'

'You want me to lie to nail Gonzalez.'

'I want the truth.'

🌴

Bags knew not to hide in a store. What if the back exit
was locked? He did not intend to be anywhere near the
booth. Traffic on Collins was one-way in this area. Foot
traffic could run at him from four directions. He crossed
a side street when he saw the cheap novelty store and
checked the back door. It was open and it led to a lane.
He broke his rule and stood looking at leather bands. He
couldn't hang around; he'd be kicked out. He checked
the clock in the store. He'd walk for ten minutes, and
come back inside and wait.

Hench loved speed, but he couldn't risk a citation with Scar's body in the back of the SUV. The kid didn't know him. That was an advantage. Once he parked, he'd walk and he'd find the kid. Hench didn't worry about much. What was the point? You lived or you died. It was simple to him. You breathed or you stopped breathing. When he got to 60th Street, he parked and climbed into the back. He had rolled one of the carpets over Scar. On Collins, he bought a *Herald* and walked the tourist walk, slow and curious. He had time. He was almost ten minutes early. He saw the booth up ahead. It was empty.

Bags was back in the store with a Dolphins' cap in his hand and his eyes on the street. He couldn't see the booth. He'd give Scar an extra five. After that, he was gone. A family came over to his rack and began trying on hats. Hench passed Bags as a little kid asked him, 'How much?'

'I don't work here. Let me see, nine bucks.'

Bags looked at the clock. Thirty minutes had elapsed. It was grace time. He went to the door and scoped the street. He wished he could leave the store with the family, but they were still shopping. He put the cap back and walked to the entrance. Both front doors were open and latched to their respective side walls. Bags stood next to one of them and looked toward the booth. Scar wasn't there.

Hench figured the kid was in some joint, so he headed back.

Most tourists were at the beach. Some were out shopping, but none as square and muscled as Hench. Bags had just stepped out when he picked up on the size of the man walking toward him. He slipped back into the store and ran for the back door, using both fists to burst through the door and out into the lane.

Hench didn't miss him. He ran for the lane between

two squat establishments, cursing. The kid was flying.
With his size, though he was remarkably agile, he stood
little chance of catching him. Then the "X" factor kicked
in. A side door of one of the other stores that lined the
block opened, and out came a rolling dolly with trash
cans. The kid tried to jump the mess, but went sprawling
instead with the garbage. Hench gained on him. Inside
his hand, he held a collapsible ice pick.

'What the hell is wrong with you?' the owner shouted. 'You're going to pick up this mess!'

Hench gained ground.

Bags scrambled to his feet. His knee had struck the
steel rim on the base of the dolly. The cut was deep. He
looked back only once. Then he ran. His knee buckled
once, but he dragged his leg up and kept running. His
nostrils flared as he ran. *Scar did me!* This time, he didn't
turn to see if the big man was gaining on him. He saw
the blood on his pants and he ran faster.

Hench watched him turn a corner. 'Fuck it all!' He
got on his phone and ran while he shouted into it. He
grabbed his knees, gasping and gulping air.

The store owner took in the chase for a second or two
before he went back inside and locked his door.

As it does often in Miami, the wind had picked up.
Loose paper and dust swirled in the lane around rusty
dumpsters. A dark cloud blew over the sun.

🌴

CHAPTER SIXTY-ONE

IT DIDN'T TAKE long for Diego to spot the tail behind his car. He drove within the speed limit. He saw that there was a message on the family phone as soon as he walked into the foyer. 'Jen, would you see who that is, please?' His nerves were frayed. His first impulse was to sequester himself at the guest house and wait on news of the morning's closures.

'The message is for Felicia.'

'Mike Halloran invited me to lunch with him at Bal Harbour. He was calling to confirm.'

'As well he should. Use our driver. I don't want you alone until I feel you are entirely safe. He can stay close by throughout the lunch.'

Felicia's smile was forced. She had tried to leave this barricade of protection with Jesús, to be free of its constraints. Now she was back in the thick of her brother's control. Mike Halloran posed no problem for her, but Diego's request must be followed. Felicia would never ask him about the man who had assaulted her. Her brother's business was his private domain.

As soon as he could, Diego left the main house and drove over to the guesthouse. From his safe, he took out a new phone from a different batch, inserted the chip and called Hench. Then he waited for him to find a public phone. Cops'd find no trace of this coded conversation. Ten minutes later, his cell rang.

'The tennis court's playable.'

'The promotion?'

'Secured.'

Diego felt a wave of assuring calm sweep over him. 'The tadpole?'

'Still swimming.'

'I need it for my collection.' Diego massaged his temples. 'Lucky number?'

'Haven't got it yet.'

'We need a clear sky.'

'Everybody could use a better day.'

Goddamn cop and Bags! As the compactor crushed the cell phone, Diego remembered that Gabe Roth had only a few days left in his house. His banker had the cashier's check for Gabe. That business was out of the question for now. Today belonged to the cop and Bags, but he'd see to it that Gabe broke. The ability to walk into a life and grab what you wanted, the ease of it all, fed Diego's sense of power.

Gabe had challenged that power. The investor who'd taken Gabe's money in the first place gave it up in one morning. He knew who Diego was! Gabe Roth who'd grabbed his money back thought he could defy him, first by not following his order with Felicia's care and now, by not giving up his house. Gabe had to be taught a lesson. Diego couldn't permit a civilian to question his authority. If he allowed a personal matter to get out of control... He'd made a mistake by allowing Felicia to move to Sunny Isles. He wanted her home, and Gabe Roth would make that happen.

Still, risks chewed at his stomach as he headed back to the guest house. *If the cop saw me, the badges would be pounding on my front door to embarrass me. The cop also knows what would happen to him if he gave me up. Bags knows that better than the cop. The problem is that together, they're a threat I can't get to personally.* Diego was close to the Bay, but it's calm eluded him. His heart raced, his palms were sweaty. For the first time in his life, Diego was scared. He began to suck his teeth in earnest, a habit from his father that he hated.

He spotted Gabe's yacht and saw that provisions were

being loaded onto it. *He's not going anywhere! I'll bleed that asshole dry. He'll learn who I am! I don't need to wait on anyone for Gabe Roth, I can do him myself!*

🌴

Gabe had told Sue to call her friend in real estate for a private sale. They had her inheritance. He looked at his watch. If things went as planned, they'd take off in 42 hours. He'd take a much-needed sabbatical with Sue and try to work things out together. Diego couldn't take the house without his signature on the deed. Gabe still had the gun with him. As long as he had the gun, he wouldn't sign anything. Not while he was alive. He had surgery in ten minutes; he hurried to prep for it. He'd told Sue not to answer the door or the phone if Gonzalez made an attempt to reach them. He was feeling stronger because Diego hadn't contacted him. He hoped he had other 'work' on his plate. In less than two days, they'd disappear. The gun was added insurance.

🌴

CHAPTER SIXTY-TWO

BAGS DROPPED DOWN the first lane he saw. *Scar did me! The jabber did me!* He hunched down beside an old garage, gasping and trying to come to terms with Scar's betrayal. His breaths bunched together, high color ran deep into his face. His arms and legs felt heavy and prickly. His right pant leg had stuck to his knee. He got down on all fours against the garage and began to roll up the pant slowly. He could tear the pants into shorts and use some of the material to bandage his knee. His mind was still ripping. *That fuck did me!*

'Are you alright, kid?'

Bags jerked around.

'Nothing to worry about.'

Bags relaxed. The guy was really old, hadn't shaved in days and smelled like old guys did.

'That's quite a cut. Stitches for sure.'

'Got no time for that.'

'Well, you gotta close the wound; you're losing too much blood. Look over there. You're leaving a trail.' The old man's face was washed-out. He had been tall once but now he was bent like a branch.

Bags tore one of his pant legs.

'Use that, you'll infect it for sure.'

'Got somethin' else to do?'

'Nope! But I got bandages. Get 'em for free, as a matter of fact.' The old man looked sadly down at the boy.

Bags kept on ripping his pants.

'I got scissors that'd do a better job. I got a basement room a couple doors down. Come or not, suit yourself.'

What registered with Bags was 'room.' *The old guy's stupid as a pigeon.* Bags struggled to his feet. His knee had tightened up on him, and he limped after the pigeon.

'Tell you right up – got prostate problems, social security's not in till next week. Food's low, got one beer left and no cigarettes. Nothing worth taking in my place. You can stay out here or come inside.'

'You got a chair?'

'Two.'

'Could use one.'

'Follow me.'

Bags's plan was simple. Let the old guy fix up his leg, overpower him, and use his room for a day or two. He was bone tired. If he got some sleep, he'd find a way out of Miami.

The bed inside the room was an Army cot. The fading rattan chairs had come apart on the seats. The table was a crate. There were two light bulbs. What clothes the guy owned were piled up in a corner. Bags flopped down on one of the chairs. The old guy came out of a bathroom that had no door. Bags was surprised the bandages were clean and still wrapped.

'Let me take a look.'

Bags brought his right leg up and laid it across his left leg.

'Like I said, stitches.'

'Can't go to no hospital.'

'Don't have to. I have tape and floss and one needle.'

'How come you got all this shit? You got nothin' else here.'

'Twenty years as an orderly at Mount Sinai and bad legs.'

'What?'

The old guy lifted his pant leg. His calf was bandaged and stained yellow and faintly red. 'I'm 76. The skin is splitting on both legs. So they give me the bandages; I steal the floss, best teeth cleaner. Got all my own. You're

not a beach bum. Your lips aren't cracked and bleeding.
No skin cancer either. Where did ya come from?'

'Streets.'

'You brave enough for me to stitch up that knee?'

'What?'

'Got a needle and floss, just as good. Don't do it, bad
infection.'

Bags looked at the wound. 'Pain don't mean nothin'
to me. Do it.'

'Gotta wash it first.' He went for his beer, his last.
'Here, take a good gulp.' He poured the rest of it on the
knee.

His knee burned like a hot brand, but Bags was
stuttering on something else. *Scar gave me up. The pigeon
gives me his last beer.* He wouldn't touch the old man.
'What'd they call you?'

'Martin. You?'

'Bags.'

'I like it. You gotta thread the floss; can't see that
good. Good. Look away. This will hurt like a bugger.'

Bags balled his fists and ground his teeth.

'Seven ought to do it.'

'Shit!'

'Three more.' Martin pinched the skin before he
pushed the needle through. 'Done. Just the bandaging
left.'

'Good job! Looks good. I got 10 bucks; you get us a
beer and somethin' to eat.'

'You sure?'

Martin took the $10. By the time he got back, Bags
was on a deep nod in his chair, his head on his arm. The
armrest was holding for the time being. Martin twisted
off a few caps and took a good pull on the first bottle,
even better on the second. Soon, he too fell off and
began to snore. For that night, both men were safe.

Pain from his knee throbbed in his sleep, but in his head, Bags was far away from Scar.

CHAPTER SIXTY-THREE

SCAR DIDN'T MERIT a cement trip. Hench thought of tossing his body in a canal, but opted for a quick drop on Washington Avenue in South Beach. The cops would attribute Scar's death to a drug deal gone bad. Hench knew the kid used and if there was an autopsy, it would reveal drugs in his system. The actual drop wasn't without a degree of danger for Hench. He had to be sure it was unseen and unreported. Before morning, he also had to get back to storage and cleanup. At least the squirrel was gone.

Hench parked on a quiet side street. He climbed into the back of the SUV and pulled Scar out from the carpet and propped him up in the front seat beside him. He drove slowly along Washington, but he saw too many people hanging on buildings or coming out of bars. Circling the street one too many times would draw suspicion. The first side street he saw without traffic lights, he turned down. It was deserted. He pulled to the curb on the other side of a cluster of newspaper machines. He opened the side door and shoved Scar onto the sidewalk. He drove away and didn't bother looking back. Tomorrow, he'd tackle the cleanup of his vehicle. On the way to storage, he checked in to see if there was anything on Bags. He got a negative. Failure wasn't something Hench took easily. He was surprised the cops hadn't picked him up. The kid had disappeared.

🕯

Martin was wakened by his own snoring, and he padded to the bathroom. The kid was still out. Martin took the top sheet off his cot and put it over the kid. He envied him that kind of sleep. *Too young for demons!*

Martin lay on his cot, cursed his prostate and tried to get back to sleep.

🌴

Earlier that evening, Caitlin, Carmen and Mike were in the suite working on their second large pizza from Papa John's. It was obvious Mike was feeling better. Caitlin saw that he was moving his shoulder a little.

'Do you mind taking me to the mall for some shopping when you have lunch with Felicia?' Caitlin asked.

'You'll be spying,' Mike laughed, 'but I don't mind.' He was enjoying the other side of things.

'I won't be spying. I want to go to Banana Republic and the Polo Shop.' Caitlin's cheeks were crimson. 'I want white shorts and sandals.'

'Whatever you say, Caitlin,' Mike chuckled.

'I'm serious.'

Mike and Carmen winked at one another.

🌴

The ladies were eating late. Ramon had prepared fresh snapper and avocado salad with an ultra light key lime pie for dessert. Lila and Muriel were the last to arrive. Little Caesar, Israel and Mischa were dressed for dinner in white linen vests and bow ties. Little Caesar was managing quite well with his cast and sat like the tiny emperor he was as Israel and Mischa did their best to chew off the cast. On the table, the candles were lit, the fine gold-plated china and crystal glistened in the twinkling light. The ladies had all dressed in long gowns for dinner. It was a ritual they enjoyed.

When James knocked at the door and arrived with pink roses, the ladies clapped as he walked around and put a rose on each dinner plate. 'I had a good time today. You have great stories, all of you. I learned a lot.' The ladies were flattered and pleased. Carlos appeared to have a worthy successor. Lila watched James closely and smiled. Even she had to admit that he was trying. James caught her eye and he made his best attempt to smile warmly. The only thing was, Lila wasn't taken in by James. *The difference between them is that Carlos never had to try. I miss Carlos.*

Lila missed Margaret. Around the dinner table, cheer was everywhere but in her heart. Lila waited until the coffee and pie before she stood and announced she had come to a decision. 'I'd like to take this opportunity to toast the ladies of the OAW, for our pluckiness and friendship!'

The coffee cups rose in salute.

'You've all been my family.'

The ladies nodded in full-hearted agreement.

'Most of you know I haven't the art of diplomacy.'

There were a few titters.

'I've decided that it is time for me to be close to my natural family. Losing Margaret has left a deep hole in my heart. I suppose the truth is that I was too fond of Carlos as well. I'm 88. It's time I get to know my own children all grown up. I've loved you and I wish you many years of health and good cheer.'

The ladies had gone quiet. To a woman, warm tears fell, creasing wrinkled cheeks. The loss of Lila was quite different from that of Margaret or Carlos. Neither of those friends had chosen to leave the women. Lila's decision tore at the core of the group. It was a crevasse that deepened because her departure would begin to force the women to question their own lives and choices.

'You can't leave!' Sophie blubbered. 'What will I do without you? Who'll guide me?'

When the little fellows saw Sophie's distress they began to cry in high-pitched barks.

'Sophie, you're very capable of taking care of yourself. Your little boys need you. Everybody here needs you too. This has been one of the very best times in my life. My leaving is a question of the heart. I know now that we still have lessons to learn at the end of the road. I love you all.' Lila got up from the table and left. No one touched the pie, no one drank the coffee.

When Lila got to her room, she called Jake. 'If you still want me, I'd like to come to San Diego.'

Jake hated to admit he missed his mother and still needed her. 'You haven't been out here for a few years. What I didn't tell you was that we've had an addition built to the house and it's waiting just for you. You'll have your privacy and us. Believe me, you won't be able to keep up with all the clubs we have.'

'When I get to San Diego, I'm looking forward to getting to know you.'

'I'm not such a dull egg.'

'I know that, Jake.'

'I love you.'

'I know that too.'

CHAPTER SIXTY-FOUR

CARMEN WAS UP bright and early, and already on the phone. She was smiling when she got off. If she worked it out right, she'd be through with her calls and at Bal Harbour by noon. *Sure, Caitlin wants to shop.* She *wants to keep an eye on Mike.* They were both still asleep, so she wrote Caitlin a note and taped it to their door.

🌴

Hench and Diego were down by the Bay, walking together along the water's edge. 'Everything but the last two items on the list has been bought and sent. I have the name of the cop. His parents have a place in Hialeah.'

'Don't do anything on that yet. The cop's a third of their case. Bags is the closer. The kid, testify for cops? I don't see that, but the cops could play Bags. Anything on him yet?'

'We've set up incentives on the street, but no feeds.'

'I have something else. See that yacht over there? Get a man in proper boat clothes on the dock. I want a heads-up if a couple attempts to board. I have to see them before they leave.'

'Need me?'

'Strictly private, a stone in my shoe. I heard on the radio about the body in South Beach.' Diego casually threw that into the conversation.

'Probably drug-related, as the cops like to say when they don't want to spend the city's money dogging leads.'

'I'll be up at the house. Dust the last two items.'

'Understood.'

The men parted. Diego walked back up to the main house. *Felicia will be happy on the Bay.* Diego did not expect to find much information in the *Herald*, but he was taken aback that there was no hard follow-up on this Ponytail. The man was a serial killer. The reporter, Brianna Melanson, who seemed to have the murder beat, was no doubt holding it back for the promised exclusive when the case was made. The other possibility was a payoff from big money to maintain a low profile. In his world, Diego liked the hunt. 'Wait and see' ground at his stomach. He had wrung out as much buzz as he wanted from this hunt. He wanted his catch!

The mansion was quiet. Jennifer had gone off to her golf lesson. Felicia was somewhere upstairs preparing for her lunch date. When she joined him in the reading room, he tried to shake off the roiling acid in his stomach. He rose to greet her. 'You are beautiful!'

'And you are my champion.'

'Has this Mike Halloran offered to come for you?'

'No.'

'Bad manners.'

'Remember what he did for me.'

'I do. I have the car ready. Try to forget Jesús and everything else and have a good time!'

'I will.'

🌴

Suarez was with Morales. Smyth listened to his attempt with the young cop who was obviously frightened. 'I'm not asking you for an ID. You're spooked; I get that. In theory, do you feel that the dark blur, as you call it, could have struck you? It's a simple goddamn question. Have the guts to give that up at least!'

Morales looked at his wife and back at Suarez. 'No,' he answered, slumping in his chair.

'Did you see anything behind the panel?'

'No. I saw the dog in front of it and the blur beside it.'

'That wasn't so damn hard, was it?'

'I can't ID Gonzalez.'

'Or won't.'

'Can't!' Morales shouted.

'Alright. Did you see a van or an SUV near the house?'

'I was in the lane, but there was a beat-up van, fuck, probably more than one. Are you still keeping us here?'

'We're not taking any chances. You're here till something breaks.'

🌴

Before eleven, Martin decided he better wake the kid. 'You alive there, Bags?'

Bags swung wildly before he remembered where he was. 'Don't come at me like that, man.' Bags sat up slowly. His hand went up to his neck. 'Shit! My fuckin' neck's bent.'

'No, it's not. Move it around a bit, not too fast. That's it.' Bags looked at the door. He didn't want to leave the protection of the room. 'Got no food, right?'

'Stale bread, cheap peanut butter and tap water and enough for another day-old loaf.'

'I give you another 10, get us some food and you let me stay till tonight. My knee's real sore.'

'This is a small place, but we could both use the food.' Martin grabbed a shirt from his pile on the floor, threw water on his face and left. Bags limped over to the cot and fell back into the sleepy flow of the beach.

🌴

Mike and Caitlin wanted to be at the Bal Harbour shops early. Caitlin had helped him dress. 'I don't want you to look too good, but it's a tough job when you have a face like yours.'

'You're jealous!'

'Maybe.' *Scared, you shithead!*

'Let's try to keep ourselves honest.'

'I'm to blame for this change, you mean.'

'Do you see another Caitlin Donovan in the room?'

'Got it.'

Construction tie-ups meant they arrived only in time for the lunch with Felicia. Caitlin took off for Banana Republic on the second level. Mike waited outside the restaurant. He saw Felicia walking towards him and detected a slight limp in her gait, courtesy of her injury. Mike didn't pay much attention to what she wore. The gentle sway of her body rocked him. They shook hands, and Mike held the chair for her. 'Good to see you.'

'And you. Would you order for us both?'

'Certainly.'

Carmen didn't often run, so she was winded when she found Caitlin in the store.

'What are you doing here, Carm?'

'You knew I'd find a way to get here. Let's get on the job we came to do.' With the sleuthing skills they'd acquired over the past few years, the C's walked nonchalantly down the hall that led to the restaurant.

'I'm glad you're here, but I don't want to do this. Even if I did, it wouldn't be easy. The place is open. We'll be easy to spot.'

'Not from my rental.'

'What?'

'I cruised the parking lot in my car, not an easy feat here. Over there, that's our surveillance. Caitlin, you haven't told me what happened between you and Mike, but I can guess. You can't commit and you rocked your relationship.'

'I can't talk about it.'

'I'd want to see what's happening at this lunch if I

were you. Mike can't see you from the car.'

'It's demeaning to spy on him.'

'We've demeaned ourselves before. Come on. We'll go out the front door and come up on the car from behind. It'll be our private shame.'

Caitlin followed Carmen as they dodged shoppers, snuck into the car and went to work spying.

'Their food's come,' Carmen noted.

'Forget the food. Watch the body language.'

Felicia put down her fork without touching her salad. 'Mike, I've wanted to ask you why you risked your life for me.' Her eyes were soft, dark and inviting.

'I thought you were in trouble.'

'But we did not know one another.'

'She's getting personal, Carm. Mike's leaning back. He's nervous.'

'Or aroused.'

'Carm, you're on my side. Nervous works better for me.'

'Fine. Wish we could hear them.'

Mike's cheeks were hot. 'You're a beautiful woman. I was the knight come to rescue you.'

'I will never forget that.'

Mike blushed.

Felicia smiled.

'Have you thought of what you will do now, Felicia?'

'My brother has plans for me, but I will address those later because he will not be pleased. And you?'

'I have work in Miami for the time being.'

'She's not letting up!' Caitlin's nerve endings tweaked.

'You were vulnerable the night we met on the beach.'

'I almost died that night.'

'A terrible shared experience for both of us.'

'Carm, let's get out of here. I don't feel right about this.'

'Alright.'

Mike reached out for Felicia's hand. It was soft and moist. 'I'm very happy you survived. From what I hear, you were very courageous.'

'And fortunate.'

The moment stilled, warm with the euphoria of a first touch. Lunch passed in that misty haze.

'Thank you for this invitation.'

Mike did not follow up with another. His only gesture was silence, a time-out because he felt there was nowhere for this to lead. He looked down at her hands but did not touch them.

The moment moved. Felicia felt she understood. Picking up her knife, she laid it beside the fork. 'I am a Gonzalez and all that accompanies the name.' Felicia smiled ruefully at Mike as she recognized a world that her family frightened, a world her family denied her. 'I should go.' She rose proudly and signalled to the man the C's hadn't seen. Mike paid the bill and watched her drive through the gates at the front of the mall.

He stood alone with a vague sense of defeat before he went looking for Caitlin. Inside, he felt a deep sadness for Felicia, and more. 'There you are! Carmen?' He found them at the Polo Shop.

'You know me, wouldn't miss a chance to come to Bal Harbour.'

Caitlin hugged Mike without the old confidence.

'Free margaritas anyone?' Carm asked.

'Why not! I could use a few drinks,' Mike admitted.

🌴

CHAPTER SIXTY-FIVE

GABE AND SUE went around the house in the daze of abrupt change. 'Judy has a buyer in mind and she'll hire professionals to pack our belongings and store them for up to six months.'

'I've taken stress leave from the hospital, so we'll have money coming in.'

'What changed your mind about all this?'

'Stress, us and the growing tension, life, and Diego naturally. I've felt like a duck on the Bay with Diego pointing a high-powered rifle at me. We're running; that's not admirable, but it's the best I could come up with. I see people die at the hospital, young and old. There's no great finale to dying. One day, it's over for you. Diego flagged me down on the street in my car. I thought that he could so easily have run me down. My death would have been listed as a hit-and-run. Poof! At least, we're taking action. I feel better about that.'

'What about the million dollars we still owe Diego? I worry about that, Gabe.'

'I hope I'll have your support with my plan. I've written Diego a letter and I'm hoping you'll lend me your father's check to go with it. I'll repay you the full amount when the house is sold. We'll have copies of the check and the letter as proof we have repaid our debt. I'll ask William to give it to Diego. We're still neighbors, after all.'

'What about holding on to the money till the house is sold, in case something goes wrong? We have no idea what Diego will do once he realizes we've left.'

'I don't know, Sue; I want this thing over and done.' Gabe walked from one room to the other, looking forlornly at the accumulation of a lifetime that he was forced to leave behind. 'I save lives. I just can't save my own. I can't get my mind around the fact we're sneaking off like thieves.' He sat down in the living room, knowing it was his last time. Sue joined him and they held hands.

'Gabe, we'll do better if we both accept our responsibility in this affair. I knew better; I secretly hoped Jen would tell Diego and he'd help. It wasn't a conscious thought, but it was there.'

'When Diego showed up with the money, I harbored reservations, but I felt I'd been duped out of the money in the first place. The money exchange happened so fast, I didn't think of consequences. Right now let's get moving with the packing. Sue, don't take much onto the yacht. We don't want to draw attention to ourselves.'

'No suitcase?'

'Not a one. Triple layer your clothes and pack a few knapsacks. That's it.'

'We're waiting till sundown?'

'That's the plan.'

'I'm nervous, Gabe. You're not taking the gun, I hope.'

'It's coming with us until I feel we're safe.'

'Please don't, Gabe.'

'Till we're safe.'

🌴

Diego had come up with a plan of his own. At that moment, he was sitting in the spacious salon of his yacht, 'Hot Property,' that was moored at his dock. Before he left the house, he checked in with his security at the gated entrance. The cops were still there. Without a 'copter, they had no way of knowing he'd left the house. With binoculars and four fingers of Cuban rum in a Christofle tumbler, Diego sat on a barstool inside his 92-

foot Hatteras. From the luxurious wraparound white leather barstool, near a tinted window, he had an excellent bead on Roth's yacht, a 57-foot Carver. *A common little fish!* He climbed the oak stairs to the flybridge and waved off his man on the dock. Didn't need him. All he had to do was wait for the couple. He knew they had planned a getaway. He'd also brought two new phones for news of Bags and the cop. What Diego wanted most was Bags. The other two mosquitoes were petty annoyances. As he brought the rum to his mouth, one of his phones vibrated on the bar. He picked it up.

'The cop is saying there were two people in the house. '

'IDs?'

'Just the number.'

'Did your source get everything? Could the cops be holding back?'

'He's reliable. Not sure on the second point.'

Diego hung up and took out the chip. He drained his glass.

🌴

CHAPTER SIXTY-SIX

BAGS WOKE UP while Martin was out buying food. *Scar did me!* The betrayal hurt more than his knee. Scar had hung him out. He couldn't go back for his clothes or other cash he'd hidden. Except for one, Scar knew all his pods. He got up slowly and yelped in pain. The place stank. *The room smells like shit!* He jerked around, balancing on one leg, as Martin came through the only door the room had.

'You finally up?'

'My knee's still got that yellow shit! What stinks in here?'

Martin put down the bagged food and went to take a look at it. 'Infection's still there.'

'Shit!'

'Siddown a minute.' Martin undid the bandages. 'Seen worse.'

'I gotta get out of here!'

'First off, the stench is you! So, shower. Let the hot water hit the knee. Don't use too much of it. I need this place, and the owner monitors what I use. Second thing, we need some real alcohol to wipe out the infection.'

'You got nothin'?'

'Got this room and myself.'

'I can't waste what I have.'

'Four bucks?'

Bags felt the trap moving into the room.

'I can get two small bottles at the liquor store, at a buck ninety-nine each. I won't drink any of it. We'll use both on the knee, unless you want to lose it.'

Bags reached into his pocket and pulled out a few bills. He handed Martin a five.

'Get in the shower. Do what I told you to do with the

hot water. I'll get the booze.'

Fuck! How am I going to walk? Bags grabbed the filmy bar of soap, stepped into the shower and felt the relief of hot water. He washed his sandy hair with the bar. He stood on one foot and raised the injured knee. The water felt good on it. There was only one towel and it was damp. He took it. Getting into the same clothes didn't bother Bags. He was clean, at least, but he'd made a mistake ripping off his pants at the knees. Long threads dangled on both legs, one side was shorter than the other. His work boots were the only remnants of his old clothes.

He'd have to jack more than one car; couldn't take the chance of being picked up. Bags wanted payback on the fuckers, Scar and his boss, Diego Gonzalez. That idea took root. They deserved the hit. For five years, he'd worked the corners, worked his way up, never jabbered on anyone, never dipped into the product or the money he took in. What had it gotten him? An "X" on his chest. What if he told the cops everything and ran? Sic the cops on "the man." He'd have a better chance of staying alive. He had 'the man' on murder. Bags was doing some hard planning when Martin got back.

'Lookin' better, Bags. Let's get at that knee.'

'You got a paper or somethin'?'

'To write on?'

'Like a newspaper, man.'

'Gave up on news long ago, but Millie buys them and hoards them.'

'Could you get me a *Herald* from yesterday?'

'I'll do the leg and then get the paper. That's it then, Bags. I'm not a gopher.'

'Last thing.'

'Better be.' Martin tore off the small seal and unscrewed the tops of both bottles. 'This will sting like a bitch, so take a deep breath.' Martin poured the alcohol slowly into the cut.

'Fucker! Shit!'

'Suck it up. Don't move your leg. Let it dry. I'll get the paper and pour on the other bottle when I get back.'

Bags could see bubbling white froth on the cut. Maybe this stuff was working. If he got the name of the cop, he'd work from there. *Pay phone? A meet? Shit, no!* It had to be a call that wouldn't be traced before he got away. Bags began to practice what he'd say. *Give up the main shit, keep it short.* For a second or two, he felt bad about jabbering, but he shook off the guilt. *Rat fuckers both of them!*

'Got the paper! Ready for dose two?'

Bags bit his tongue.

'Take another deep breath.'

Bags hardly winced. Martin wrapped it tightly. Bags was busy looking for a name under his photo. All he found was a general number. That would mean two phones. He pretended to read the last page, so Martin would not see what had caught his interest. 'You're right. Nothin' here worth reading. Where's the nearest pay phone?'

'Next block on Collins, why?'

'I gotta make a call.'

'Go make it. I'll have the food ready when you get back. Do your leg good to move it.'

'Phone? Left or right?'

'Left.' Bags limped down the lane. The knee hurt like a bugger. He'd memorized the number. He scoped the area. The door to the booth was broken, so he didn't have to worry about being closed in. He dialed the number.

'Metro-Dade Police.'

'Is there some reward for information on that kid in

the paper?'

'Must be. May I have your name please?'

'Who's the cop in charge? I wanna speak to him.'

'Detectives Suarez and Smyth.'

'You got a number for Suarez?'

'I can put you through.'

'Nah, I want to make the call.'

'Here it is. …..'

'You sure about the reward?'

'Detective Suarez will know for sure.'

'Awright.' Bags limped away quickly and hopped back up the lane. He wanted food in his stomach before he called Suarez.

Suarez listened to the information from the desk cop. 'It's a kid, a street snitch. They're reliable. Did you trace the call?'

'Surfside, payphone, the corner of…'

'Send a car. Might get lucky.'

Bags was surprised to find scrambled eggs and toast and beer.

'Always good with a hot spot.' They ate quickly.

'I gotta do something. Could I come back later before I leave?'

'Give me a chance to check the knee.'

Cloying street nerves were back in his stomach as soon as Bags limped down the lane. He had to find another phone. He knew enough not to use the same one. When he reached Collins, he tried to stay with small groups. It took almost five blocks before he found another phone. He could not articulate that he felt he was standing on a cliff – he could run, or jump into the chaos he was trying to evade. Payback pushed him to the pay phone. He knew injustice at 17, but he didn't think a corner punk he hung with would give him up.

Two cops on bikes rode past. Bags froze till he saw

they hadn't noticed him. When they passed the pay phone up ahead, he walked closer to it. As soon as the cop picked up, Bags would count to 60 in his head and cut the connection. A kid got to the phone before he reached it. Seconds later, two cops ran from some store and dragged him out. Bags walked slowly past, staring like a nosy prick. The kid was yelling, 'What the fuck?' Bags figured if he didn't gawk, the cops would sniff him out. When he looked back again, they were hauling the kid into a patrol car. Bags limped on.

Up ahead, he saw a gas station with a phone on the side of it. He headed there. From the wall, he had a clear view. No one could ambush him without him seeing the rush first. He rehearsed, grabbed the phone, dropped in too much money because he didn't have the right change, and dialed.

'Suarez, Homicide.' Suarez heard they'd picked up the kid. He was going down the stairs to join Smyth who was on the sidewalk to ID the kid as soon as he was driven to the precinct.

'Don't interrupt me. You're looking for me. I was at the house. Gonzalez and one of his men and a dog went into the house…'.

Suarez ran back upstairs to the squad room to put a trace on the call.

'The squirrel shot the dog – Diego and his man loaded him into a van and took off. Don't know about the cops. They never came back out. The squirrel's paid up.'

'We?' Suarez knew it was the kid. He tried to stay calm, to keep the kid talking, to get his location. Gonzalez on murder!

'Scar and me.'

'Scar? He have a long scar across his hand?'

'Left hand.'

'Your friend's dead, dumped on Washington Avenue.' Smyth had gone to the morgue to see if the stiff was their kid. 'I can't touch Gonzalez without you. We'll give you protection, probably immunity. Nothing will come down on you. You and I can meet.'

'Scar's dead?' The line was cut. Bags pumped his arms as he ran from the phone.

Suarez whirled around to see if they had a trace. 'Pay phone on 64th and Collins.'

'Anybody there?'

'They're with the other kid.'

'Cut him loose! Get them back over to 64th and Collins, fast! This goddamn case has been one mistake after another!'

Bags hopped hurriedly back along Collins. *Scar helped the fuckers, and they did him anyway! I'm the only witness.* He ran three blocks before he disappeared into a lane. His knee was bleeding again. His legs were heavy; the cement felt soft like sand. He'd dashed across three side streets before he realized he couldn't remember where the old guy lived. He hadn't looked up to see what street was closest to the old man. *Fuck! I'm dust! I'm gonna die.* Was that the lane? Was the old guy up there?

A U-Haul was parked deep in the lane, and guys were loading furniture onto it. Bags limped toward the truck. He fell against a garage and waited, gasping. When the guys went back into the house, he ran to the back of the truck, hopped up wincing and scurried inside. He crawled up to the front and squeezed behind a mattress that had been packed against a wall. He pushed his body against the side so he wouldn't leave an indent in the mattress that they'd detect. He heard voices.

'You're taking a lot of her shit.'

'The bitch deserves it. She threw me out. Anyway, she's too lazy to come to Atlanta after me.'

'Load up and I'll clear out of this dump.'

'I owe you for this, right?'

'You said 50.'

'You get it when we finish.'

Atlanta! It took a few nanoseconds for Bags to feel his life coming back to him and not dumped on some street like Scar's. *Atlanta! I could do that trip kneeling on my knee!* When he did smile, he felt tears rolling down the side of his face. He cried for quite a few miles before he fell asleep. *The old guy will wonder where I got to!*

🌴

A few hours later, Martin walked out into the lane, searching for Bags. *Guess he's not coming back.*

🌴

CHAPTER SIXTY-SEVEN

SUAREZ RUSHED INTO Pro-Ball's office. 'Lieutenant, I just had a call from our kid. He puts Gonzalez and one of his men in the murder house. Says they loaded Gomez onto a van and took care of him. They mowed down our uniforms in that house!'

'Do you have the kid?'

'He cut off. We have the location and uniforms at the scene. We traced the call.'

Pro-Ball began his furious pace. 'What the fuck do we actually have?'

'Morales puts it at two in the house. Kid corroborates that and puts Gonzalez as one of the men there. We don't have the kid yet.'

'Do we have DNA on Gonzalez?'

'Never formally arrested.'

'Motherfucker! Get to Crime; see what they have from the house. I'll call in a few favors and get the warrant. Should have it in an hour. Then you bring him in. Do it all! Bring in his muscle, Hench.' Pro-Ball knew the nicknames because they had a whole wall devoted to Diego's family. 'Rattle Diego's cage. Bring him coffee. He might fall for that trick to get his prints.'

'You're reaching.'

'Somebody has to. Try to bring him in before he lawyers up.'

'I'd like to know who he had on the force that got him to Gomez first.'

'He has more than one cop on his pad. Hard to believe he'd put himself there in the first place.'

'It was his sister, his blood. I can understand that, Pro-Ball.'

'Take Smyth with you. Do it big and flashy!

Embarrass the fuck. Long as he hasn't scraped the kid off the streets, he won't know we don't have him.'

'What about Morales and his wife?'

'Have Smyth drive them to a new safe house out of the city. We might find the kid before Gonzalez.'

'A snowball's chance in Miami.'

🕯

Hench was checking in with all the soldiers. Bags had vanished. He'd upped the purse on his head. Some of these kids would pimp their sisters out for cash, so he knew they were out there dragging the streets. He realized he'd moved too quickly on Scar. He'd wasted his best lead. Bags was a witness who could put them at a murder scene. Hench decided he'd run the streets all night before he'd report a failure to Diego.

🕯

Abby Wiseman was back at the Trump to see Lila who had just learned Margaret's sister Mary was coming to live in her sister's suite. The move gave Lila a moment's pause. The world here would go on without her. *No one can fill Margaret's place in my heart. The yentas will be happy to see a new face.* Lila was sitting on her wrap-around balcony when she buzzed Abby in. 'I'm out here, Abby. Have some lemonade and pull up a chair.'

The women soaked up the view in silence. 'The ocean's beautiful, isn't it?' Abby said. 'I never tire of it. There are so many different hues.'

'Strong and eternal; not like us.'

'Are you at peace with your decision?'

'The secret of the ocean's eternity is movement. I know I'm part of that ebb and flow and the challenge of it.'

'Life won't be the same here without you, Lila.'

'I hope not!'

CHAPTER SIXTY-EIGHT

GABE HAD LOCKED up the house and at that moment, he was eyeing Sue's knapsacks by the front door. 'Is there any way you can stuff everything into one bag?'

'I'll try.'

'Your realtor friend has the deed to the house?'

'Yes.'

'You should go down to the yacht first. I'll wait 15 or 20 minutes and join you. If you spot anything suspicious, call me. Soon as I get there and slip the dock lines, we'll take off.'

Sue had layered her clothes, and Gabe had done the same. Behind the front door, they kissed one another, something they hadn't done since their lives had run amuck. Sue shouldered her knapsack and hurried down to the yacht. There was no one around when she boarded it. She went immediately to the galley and put her bag on the granite counter. The climate control could wait till they were well out on the water. A smidgen of anger at Gabe tweaked her cheeks as she looked at the cherry-wood walls and floors. *For the number of times Gabe has actually used the yacht, it was such a waste of good money. He's always so busy.* Sue checked the provisions Gabe had gotten onto the yacht for their escape.

Diego put down his rum. He hesitated for a moment. Roth didn't matter, or his house. His effrontery did. Roth had to know who he was! Diego had been in the business long enough to recognize the end run – *you go first and I'll follow later*. He moved swiftly across the Persian carpet, down the hallway runner, off his yacht and across the grass to Roth's dock. When he reached the Carver, he heard Sue moving things around. Diego was in the galley before she was aware he'd come aboard.

He stood silently until Sue nervously looked back and found him, 10 feet behind her. She bolted upright and stifled a scream when she saw Diego had raised a finger to his lips.

All around, the sky was turning cloudy, grey and misty.

'Sit down, Sue. We'll wait for Gabe.'

'But…'

'I'd rather you'd not talk. Try to calm yourself. All I want is to settle things between us. There is no need for this anxiety.' While Diego was smiling, there was nothing warm in his dark piercing eyes.

A slap of nerves ran up Sue's neck. There was nothing she could do to alert Gabe. The back of her throat dried up. An internal alarm told her if she tried to warn Gabe, she'd die. Diego kept one hand in his pant pocket. Sue trained her eyes there. The seconds ticked by. Sue was counting them.

Through a porthole, Diego saw Gabe's approach. He waited with Sue until Gabe was bent at the dock lines. 'Come aboard, Captain.' Diego had pulled Sue up beside him. 'Don't think about running, Gabe. Come aboard and we'll talk.'

Gabe followed them dumbly into the salon. 'Please sit with Sue. She's been frightened. I have urgent business that requires my immediate attention. Let's focus our business on the house alone and the million-dollar price. We can close the deal today.' Diego walked around the salon and saw the provisions. 'Were you thinking of skipping out on me? That would greatly upset me, Gabe.'

Gabe was fingering the Smith and Wesson in his belt under his windbreaker. In surgery, it was important to think quickly. There was no time to mull over a situation. Diego was so cocky he turned his back on them for a few seconds. Gabe jumped to his feet, pulled out his gun and aimed it at Diego's chest. 'That's not the road you want to take, Gabe.'

Sue gasped and grabbed the back of Gabe's jacket. He pulled away from her. 'Do you think I was going to stand by while you plundered our lives?'

Gabe's hand was steady. Diego was surprised. 'Gabe, we're talking about material things here, not life and death. Put the gun away. You're out of your league. Have you ever heard of anyone pulling a weapon on a mob boss? Do you have any idea of the repercussions of such an act? You have children. The family has long arms. You'd die slowly and with great torture and...' His scalp grew hot.

'Get off my boat.' Gabe's face was hard as stone. 'I want you out of our lives. We'll forward the check to you to cover our blunder, but that's it.'

The hand on the gun was still steady.

Diego sat down. The muzzle followed him and trained itself on his heart. He shook his head. 'Put the gun away. You're not going to use it. You're too smart for that.' Diego took his hand from his pocket and whisked some imaginary dust from his pants. His hand was empty. 'Don't rouse my anger, Gabe, if you want to go on living. We're all adults here. Let's settle down. Walk back to your home with me and sign over the deed. Then it's over. Walk away.'

The edge of tension in the salon sharpened. No one interrupted the silence.

Finally, Sue broke it. 'Gabe, put down the gun! I don't care about the house. The house is not worth our lives.'

'Listen to her, Gabe.'

In his heart, Gabe knew he'd stepped beyond another line. If he handed the gun to Diego...

The hand with the gun wavered.

Diego stood up. 'Give me the gun, Gabe. I'll forget about all this. I know you don't intend to use it on me. I understand your anger. But calm down, and hand the gun to me.' Diego reached for the weapon, the way a cop disarms a perp he's talked down.

The hand steadied. The air coarsened.

Diego walked challengingly in front of Gabe. He put his hand over Gabe's. He pulled the gun from his hand slightly to the side. Instantly, there was a sharp report, like a firecracker. Diego took one step back. 'You stupid, stupid man…' He fell to his knees, grabbing his ribcage. Blood seeped through his fingers. He crumpled to the cherry wood floor.

'I didn't fire the gun!' Gabe screamed. 'Diego forced my finger when he pulled the gun from me! Call for help! For God's sake, call for help!'

It was far too late for catch-up.

'I'll do the best I can, Diego.' Gabe was weeping as he knelt beside him.

Diego looked up at him. His face was collapsing, crushing from the surprise of fatal damage.

🌴

The police routine of running an hour behind Diego Gonzalez continued. When the 9-1-1 call came in, Suarez and Smyth were driving onto the Gonzalez estate and hustled down to the yacht to find Gabe performing a tracheotomy on Diego. Both detectives stood in shock, staring down at the dying mob boss. Neither mentioned that they hadn't made their major bust. This was a high rent area, and paramedics arrived in record time. The on-call doctor assisted Gabe. Diego was receiving blood as Gabe worked feverishly on him. Sue was hysterical and taken to one of the two ambulances and given a mild sedative. Fifteen uniforms with patrol cars with flashing lights stood on the grass near the Carver. Pro-Ball appeared for the press. Diego Gonzalez was off their books! The lieutenant would find credit in there somewhere.

A half-hour later, Gabe was forced to call the time of death. A milky caul would soon begin to coat Diego's eyes. His body was lifted into a black body bag and driven off the Bay to the city morgue.

EPILOGUE

THE ROTHS REMAINED in protective custody until the crime techs' evidence supported Gabe's version of the events. Two days later, Diego's death was officially ruled accidental. Very soon after, the Roths boarded a flight to Vancouver, rented a place in Horseshoe Bay and applied for a name change. They took Sue's father with them. The couple grew timid and fearful that one day their lives would be snuffed out. Roth didn't practice medicine again.

Their home on Biscayne Bay sold for three-point seven million, well above market value. This was Miami and notoriety sells! A celebrity bought 'Hands On' for double its worth.

A year passed, and some of that fear faded. Gabe took up fishing. On occasion, when the fish weren't biting, he'd scan the area to be certain he was quite alone. Then he'd smile, remembering…

🌴

Murder beat reporter, Brianna Melanson, got the big scoop that took her story from the Metro section to front page news with a large photo. **Diego Gonzalez Dies Accidentally: A Twist of Fate**: *Reputed crime boss of the Cuban mafia Diego Gonzalez suffered a fatal gunshot wound at the hands of the surgeon who had treated his sister Felicia, assaulted almost one week ago. Two physicians worked in vain to keep Gonzalez alive. An hour after he was wounded, Gonzalez was pronounced dead at the scene. His death has been ruled accidental. The two men involved in the tragedy were neighbors, and the death occurred aboard the surgeon's yacht… Gonzalez was quoted when he took his grandfather's position in the family as saying, 'I fully intend to die an old man! Times have changed.' Unfortunately, he was not lucky* *or prophetic. Diego Gonzalez was thirty-two years old.*

🌴

The story heaved itself onto the entire front page of *el Nuevo Herald* that ran a four-page spread. After all, Diego Gonzalez was one of theirs, both loved and feared. The story didn't go to pasture for a week.

🌴

Late the night of the shooting Smyth and Suarez were beat and drove to a cop hole on Biscayne. 'Pro-Ball managed to squeeze some juice for himself out of this mess and mumbled our names in passing. Should keep our butts out of Evidence Control.' The job was still in her face. 'What a fuck-up!'

'On both sides. Gonzalez was the Florida drug king and big legit money. With all that jack, why the hell was he duking it out with a neighbor? Shit, capped by an everyday civilian with no crime stats. It's a laugher!'

'Testosterone, the male curse.' Smyth jumped on the last word.

🌴

Felicia's parents took her back home with them where the air was thick with grief and regret. Within a month, she left. Much to the happy surprise of the OAW, Felicia appeared back at the Trump. It was there she had survived the threat on her life. From there, she intended to meet its challenge head-on. Mike Halloran wasn't the reason for her return. Felicia looked to herself for strength.

Jennifer was left with the house. Felicia came only once to visit her. The women shared a common grief, but there was no emotional bond between them. Santo, Diego's cousin, took control of the money and Diego's yacht and gave the outsider what he felt she was due.

♟

Bags hopped and hitched from one truck to another. He ended up in Teaneck, a township in Bergen, New Jersey. He hadn't watched *The Sopranos* and didn't realize he'd traded the Cuban Mafia for the Italian mob. He had $83 when he jumped from a fruit truck. He stayed in a shelter for a while and began working in minimum wage joints.

Hench was demoted to a common button man after Diego's death when Santo stepped into power.

♟

Ponytail stayed under the tennis court, forgotten by everybody but his mother. In the end, Jesús was more fortunate than Ponytail. His family knew where he was and had the chance of a final farewell.

♟

The day Lila left the Trump, the women and the little canines, dressed to the nines, were all out in front, weepy, waving goodbye. A thought occurred to Lila. *So many young people lost their lives. Yet the old girls survived!* Wonderful things followed in Lila's long life. She loved San Diego and began to sketch again. Jake bought her a computer and taught his mother the basics. Lila was still a quick study.

James set the OAW women up in a computer lab they purchased at his request. He taught them to send emails and charged them. Sophie sent Lila four emails a day! It was a lifeline that kept the old gals connected and active.

♟

Only a New Orleans funeral rivals a mob send-off.

Diego's was a fitting tribute for the boss of the family and the devoted love of his only sister. There were sixteen flower cars. The church was a garden of flowers. Felicia and her parents followed the brass casket down the crowded aisle under a canopy of red roses.

The day before, Mike read the funeral announcement in the *Herald*. 'I have to go, Caitlin.' He handed her the paper. 'Come with me.'

The invitation hinted at the change in their relationship. Before *the question*, Mike would have assumed she'd go with him. This formality was a further distance between them, and Caitlin felt it keenly.

'Go? Go where?' Carmen called as she came into their suite towelling off her hair.

'Diego's funeral.'

'Mike, the entire Cuban mafia will be there,' Caitlin cautioned.

'I have to go.'

Carmen piped in, 'Another funeral on a vacation? We're still batting a thousand, Caitlin. You expect all the Cuban mafia, Mike?'

'You can bet on the whole organization. Diego was a boss.'

'I'm not about to miss out on any of this, Caitlin! We have to shop. Who brings black to Miami?'

🌴

At the funeral, the media circus stayed outside. Awed by the solemnity and the genuine grief of the many mourners, the trio huddled at the back of the church. Mike saw stoic resignation and a deep well of sorrow in Felicia's eyes. She acknowledged him in particular, and he her, as she walked by. Caitlin knew then that she had lost Mike. He'd move on. She stood very still on the edge, on the path she had chosen.

ACKNOWLEDGEMENTS

Gina Pingitore has been behind me for all six books. She's spoiled me with her continuing support, hours of her time, editing and line proofing, and attendance at each and every signing. I am deeply indebted to her.

No author is more grateful than I when friends offer to proof my work. Irene Pingitore has made such offers for the past two years. Thank you so much, Irene. Margaret Goldik, my dear friend, I am deeply in your debt.

Sandra Jarymowycz offered again this year to read the manuscript, and I was thrilled to have her help. Your time and expertise are very much appreciated.

It's wonderful to connect with a university friend, to renew that friendship and to be lucky enough to be the recipient of her generosity as a talented and tireless agent, using her legal skills to push me forward. Thank you, Marie Galanti.

Lucie Day and Shirley Shum have been wonderful and generous support at the launches and signings. Thank you very much for all your hard work. Thanks to Valerie Miller, Kathleen Panet, Debbie Hawker and Cynthia Iorio for joining us this year.

Bob Dillon kindly made the poster tags for our crew.

Amaury Socorro kindly helped me with the nuances of Cuban Spanish.

Mary, my little sister, has worked with passion and love getting my books out in Toronto with each and every one of them. Thanks, Mame.

Thanks to all my loyal readers and welcome to the new ones.

Special thanks to Leslie Gardner, my agent, who works assiduously for me in the big publishing world and keeps the faith.

To my publisher, David Price, I owe a huge debt of gratitude for his continuous support, his fine editing and his belief in my fictional world.

Finally, thank you to Sunny Isles, my escape from snow, my second home. What a beautiful and intriguing setting you have provided for two of my books!

Sheila Kindellan-Sheehan has published four novels, a memoir and numerous articles.

Her work has been featured in *The Globe and Mail* (Toronto), read on the CBC's *First Person Singular, Radio One* and *CBC Montreal,* as well as on radio station CJAD and television channels CTV and Global TV. It also appears in the anthology *Conscious Women, Conscious Lives* (White Knight Publications, 2004).

Her first book, *Sheila's Take* (Shoreline Press, 2003) was a critically acclaimed memoir featured twice on the Montreal *Gazette's* bestseller list. Of her four mystery novels, *The Sands Motel* (2004), *Cutting Corners* (2005), *An Easy Mark* (2006) and *The Wrong Move* (2007), two have been bestsellers.